Shooting in the Dark

Shooting in
the Dark

Carolyn Hougan

All the characters and events portrayed in this work are fictitious.

SHOOTING IN THE DARK

A Felony & Mayhem mystery

PRINTING HISTORY
First U.S. edition: 1984
First U.S. paperback edition: 1985
Felony & Mayhem edition: 2006

ISBN 978-1-933397-53-5

Manufactured in the United States of America

For the families Johnson and Hougan

The icon above says you're holding a copy of a book in the Felony & Mayhem "Espionage" category, which features spies and conspiracies from World War I to the present. If you enjoy this book, you may well like other "Espionage" titles from Felony & Mayhem Press, including:

The Cambridge Theorem, by Tony Cape
Disorderly Elements, by Bob Cook
Paper Chase, by Bob Cook
The Spy's Wife, by Reginald Hill
Who Guards a Prince, by Reginald Hill
The Romeo Flag, by Carolyn Hougan
A Gathering of Saints, by Christopher Hyde
The Labyrinth Makers, by Anthony Price

For more about these books, and other Felony & Mayhem titles, or to place an order, please visit our website at:

www.FelonyAndMayhem.com

or contact us at:

Felony and Mayhem Press
156 Waverly Place
New York, NY 10014

Shooting in the Dark

CHAPTER ONE

SHE WAS STANDING IN FRONT of the mirror in the bathroom, head tilted forward while she applied mascara. She had a dentist's appointment at nine, having planned to get it over with as early as possible to spare herself the usual crescendo of dread. She still held her head at an odd angle, eyelids at half-mast to keep the mascara from smearing, when Jeff came in. He stood behind her, wearing his white terrycloth robe, and said, "Claire, I've got to talk to you."

"What?" She smoothed blusher on her cheeks, wondering why she always dressed so carefully for appointments with dentists, doctors; why she always put on makeup. Some arcane defense against pain. She wondered if war paint...

"I've got to talk to you," Jeff said again, sending a little zip of warning through her. The phrase itself alarmed her—a bad-news phrase. A shuffle of possibilities: he's got cancer, I've got cancer, my mother/father has been killed, he's been fired. But when she turned from the mirror, his eyes skidded away from hers. He stood there with his hands bunched up in the pockets of his robe, staring at the floor, and said, "I'm leaving you."

First she felt a quiver of relief—No one's dead—and then she decided it was one of his jokes. He was always catching people with his deadpan delivery.

"I know, I know. First the teeth go; next thing you know, the skin begins to lose its youthful elasticity; the hair..."

She turned back to the mirror, opened her mouth into a circle and put on some lipstick, then pressed her lips together to smooth out the color.

"Claire!" He almost shouted it, and she stood there perfectly still, watching his reflection as he repeated in his helpless, excited voice, "I'm leaving you."

His lips were pressed together in a thin line, his eyes locked to hers in the mirror.

"I can't go to the dentist now," she said in a high, thin voice.

His words settled into meaning with a dull, hopeless thud in the exact center of her head. His eyes let go, and she found she was looking at herself. She looked exactly the same. She reached up with her index fingers and pressed up against the ridges of her cheekbones. The skin bunched up under her eyes; she looked as if she were pretending to be Chinese. Then she opened her eyes very wide and said, "My tooth hurts."

A sense of distortion set in, as if she were seeing things from a vantage point in the air, or she and Jeff were overlayered with movie footage, flickering. And the woman said with huge big-screen lips, "Is there someone else?"

And the man said, "Yes."

She shut her eyes. Very briefly, she felt sorry for him, wondering how long he'd been waiting for exactly the right moment, how many false starts he'd made, how long he'd been pretending everything was normal. His image burned in her head—his helpless eyes, his white robe. He looked so vulnerable, she had an absurd urge to comfort him.

But then plumes of white flared up in a sickening way behind her eyelids, and when she opened her eyes to look at him, she was a little surprised he didn't wither under her white glare. Irradiation. He touched her shoulder and she felt like grabbing him and knocking his head against the tiled wall.

"Get out."

She couldn't wait for him to be out of there. He seemed to be taking up every cubic inch of space, turning the air swampy and foul with deceit.

"I'm sorry. I—"

"Jeff, get *out* of here." She was pushing him toward the door with clumsy little nudges, and there was a ridiculous scuffle while they vied for territory. They knocked against the wicker shelf attached to the back of the door. A perfume bottle—a blue one, Je Reviens—fell to the floor and shattered, instantly filling the room with oppressive sweetness. He lurched back, to avoid the shattering glass, and she took advantage, pushing him out, slamming the door shut. She locked it.

"We've got to talk. I didn't mean to...I didn't mean for this to happen. I met her—"

"Jeff, *shut up*." She didn't want one bit of information.

"Are you all right?" he asked through the door. Asking absolution.

"Just get out of here. I can't stand for you to be here. Get *out*." Her voice got away from her.

She heard him walk away from the door and pull open a drawer. He's not even dressed for a quick exit, she thought, and was as mad about that as she was about anything. She turned on all the water faucets because she couldn't stand listening to him get dressed.

She began cleaning up the glass, picking up the larger pieces in a gingerly way, then taking wads of damp toilet paper and trying to get the tiny splinters off the floor. One stuck in her hand, and she extracted it with great precision. The room was now full of steam, and the perfume was beginning to make her sick. He must be gone by now, she thought. She turned off the water and cracked open the door. There he was, fully dressed, sitting on the bed. He gave a weird little shrug of his shoulders.

"It didn't seem right to just leave."

"What do you want to do, comfort me? I can't stand it that you're still here." She tried to push him off the bed, and when that was ineffectual, she hit him twice on the back as hard as she could. "Please, Jeff, get *out*. Just get *out*."

"I still love you. I don't want anything bad to happen." Tears actually glittered in his eyes. The tears enraged her.

"I don't want your moral torment," she said in a cold, reasonable voice.

"I called Eileen. She said she'd come over at lunch."

The presumption of this stunned her. Eileen was Claire's best friend, but..."You told *Eileen*; you told someone else before you even told me?" She started hitting him again. "Look, you said you were leaving me—isn't that how you put it? 'I'm leaving you.' So would you *leave*? I can't stand this."

"Claire."

She started for the door. "If you don't get the fuck out of here right now, I'm going to go out in the hall and start screaming as loud as I can." She opened the door.

He offered a defeated shrug but hesitated once more, at the threshold. She stepped aside, refusing to look at him. "I'll call you," he said.

The first thing she did after locking the door was take the phone off the hook.

She sat immobilized in the brown corduroy chair, thinking of nothing. The room seemed to be shrinking, while the furniture, the paintings, the objects she and Jeff had accumulated grew larger and more distinct. Everything had a crystalline quality: the coffee table, for instance, a miracle of defined edges, pure planes. She herself felt blurry and insubstantial, as if she might disintegrate slowly into the chair, leaving nothing but an oily stain.

The ghost voice of the telephone startled her: "…dial again. If you need assistance, dial the operator. This is a recording." Then it lapsed into an insistent bleating. She couldn't seem to move.

Her mind short-circuited and she kept thinking in clichés. Several times she thought, I'm not taking this well.

A small Waterford vase, now full of daisies, that she and Jeff had bought long ago in a moment of extravagance reproached her from the coffee table. She remembered buying it; she remembered with an almost frightening clarity how hard it had been to remove the price tag from the bottom, the gummy residue that persisted for years. She felt like throwing it into the fireplace; but that too seemed like something already seen in a movie. She could imagine the camera panning the shards of crystal, the scattered flowers, the spreading pool of water. Her feelings seemed plagiarized from an unpromising source.

She lurched out of the chair, swaying slightly. She wondered vaguely how long she'd been sitting there. Why not try the script where you go for a walk and have a few stiff drinks? she thought. A drunken stupor might be better than a catatonic stupor. Certainly worth a try.

Released from the room, she wanted to get outside, and waited for the elevator with toe-tapping impatience. She exchanged nods with the doorman and went out, watching gratefully as a cab pulled up seconds later. A woman with a vague resemblance to herself got out. Claire tilted into the back seat and pulled the door shut, watching the woman go into the apartment building. She had the uneasy feeling they were replacing each other.

"The Hilton," she decided out loud, in a voice that sounded squeezed out, like toothpaste. Certainly you could have an anonymous lunch and a few stiff drinks in the New York Hilton.

For once she was grateful for the foggy plastic shield that separated her from the driver. She didn't feel like talking; she wondered, in fact, if she *could* talk. If she said anything, it would be "Nice day." Then she thought again, I'm not taking this well, and recognized the clichéd thinking for what it was—stalling for time. A way to persuade herself that people did this sort of thing—husbands left their wives, out of the blue; it was normal.

A way to keep herself from doing something irrevocable like throwing herself out the door or screaming "I'm going to kill the fucker," or somehow going bananas in an awful, public way. The city slipped by outside, smooth as silk, and once again she imagined it from the air, the yellow lozenge of the taxi slipping from lane to lane as it sped uptown.

She'd never been in the Hilton before, but her instincts proved right. She felt securely anonymous among the businessmen with HELLO tags as she ordered a double martini on the rocks. She nodded gravely when the waiter asked if she wanted it with "a twist."

"What kind of convention is this, anyway?" she asked.

"Anesthesiologists," he confided.

"Perfect," she muttered. The waiter slid away.

When he brought her drink, she half-expected someone with a vague cinematic familiarity to approach and say, "Are you alone?" To which she would reply, "Not anymore," and the two of them would whirl away into a montage of nights on the town, walks in the park and misty sexual encounters. She couldn't shake this giddy sense of unreality.

She ordered a shrimp salad, to preserve decorum, and a second martini, to produce the gauzy alcoholic haze she pursued. Jeff's voice echoed in her head: "I'm leaving you." Everything was different. In one second, everything had changed. It was like finding a Russian tank, brutal and inscrutable, blocking the way up Fifth Avenue. All bets were off. Her heart started beating so hard she seemed to vibrate like a tuning fork. Ice chattered against the sides of the glass, and she set her drink down.

All right, said a voice in her head. All right all right. Anything could happen, everyone knew that; she'd always known that. Time is not a sanctuary. People got run over by cars, pushed under subways; planes crashed; there was no end of unexpected calamity. Her mother had a certain zest for grotesque stories, the ways someone's life could take a sudden U-turn. Claire was kept fully informed and constantly warned of possible dangers. Don't run with that pencil—you could fall and poke your eye out. Don't take candy, take rides; I knew a woman...But although she often worried about other people, she had never believed anything terrible would happen to her. That steady optimism was responsible for her easygoing nature, for the serenity Jeff admired. Oh, shit, *Jeff.*

Call a friend, commanded an anonymous interior voice that emanated from dozens of skimmed magazine articles. That's how these things are handled. Call a friend, talk it out, have a good cry.

But she didn't have any friends who were strictly hers; they were all *their* friends, even Eileen. Everyone had been drawn into the circle or abandoned. Just as the alone Claire had been abandoned eight years ago, and lived on only in a kind of shrine in her parents' house in Nyack, in photographic icons scattered on bureaus, standing in ranks on the piano. Even there, Jeff was represented, imprisoned with her behind glass in a perpetual marital hug.

If only she'd had some suspicion—couldn't Jeff have left clues, hints, *something*—so at least she could have enjoyed the seedy triumph of finding out? Probably he had, but she'd insisted on going along, stupidly being happy, until the guilt got to him; he couldn't stand the weight of his deception; he had to give it to her like a grenade.

How could she have been with him all the time, slept

next to him every night, and not have known there was "someone else"? There must have been some telltale hesitancy, some holding back—you'd think the knowledge would seep in by osmosis, through her pores, as she lay next to him night after night. And *who is this someone else?* She wanted to know; she didn't want to know; she pushed the question away. Her face burned like a radiant heater. She was tempted to hold the martini glass against her cheek, but she stopped herself.

The buzz of conversation around her seemed to be building in an ominous crescendo. She shut her eyes, and certain phrases carried above the roar with perfect clarity.

"...new intake valve allows a more accurate mix..."

"...almost fired the nurse anesthetist."

"...so I said to him, Look, Saul, you know and I know..."

Claire shook her head, deliberately, as if she had water in her ear; threw a twenty onto the table and fled.

She wobbled onto the street, feeling soothed by the fresh cool air. A brilliant day. Sharp points of light ricocheted off store windows; a red car gleamed at the curb. She headed down the street, trying to imagine the future.

What now? These marital fissions were common, after all, especially in New York. Everyone was well rehearsed. People would look the other way at the office while she wept into her coffee. Consoling arms would slide along her shoulders. The ranks of their friends would divide and form...teams. A tall black man, dressed entirely in leather, boogied past, holding a huge transistor radio to his ear. The music floated away with him, and then disappeared in the blare of a siren.

She had a brief vision of all their friends dressed in Knicks uniforms, loping onto a polished wood floor. "And at small forward, Eileen *Shep*arrrrrd." She leaned against the window of a boutique, and her eyes fastened on a mannequin wearing a white T-shirt and shocking pink walking shorts. The mannequin stared into the distance, shading her eyes with her hands.

Some friends would accomplish the precarious balancing act required to still be friends with both of them. "Should we invite Claire or Jeff to dinner?" People would deliver the pro forma "How *are* you?" with weighty concern. She might go to a shrink, a shrink to weave a little confusion, a little patch job over her...ego?

Heart.

This vision of the future had an alarming precision, a practiced, polished brightness. As if she had known all along, somehow. A subway rumbled somewhere beneath her, and she wished it were louder; much louder; loud enough to derail this ordinary day. She wanted these people hurrying around in such a regular way, she wanted these people diving for cover, screaming for mercy. She wanted...*parity*—such a stuffy word. She stumbled and walked on, numb.

Then would come the orchestrated banality: separation agreement, divorce papers, lawyers, judges, division of possessions. She'd been through all this, with Lally, with Nick and Edie. "I'll take the china; you take the T.V." She would call Jeff "my first husband." Did that mean there would be a second? "My ex-husband." "My ex-husband used to say." "My ex." Crossed out.

An interior voice sprang forward: *Jesus, you act like it's all over and done with. Maybe he'll see it's all a mistake, a terrible mistake, a momentary infatuation. Maybe he can't live without you—he's always said that.* "Never leave me,

Claire. Promise me. Promise me that." Reconciliation gleamed in her mind. He would come back, with that same earnest look on his face, a humble Jeff. "Just give me one chance, Claire." She could forgive him. She made a preliminary test of her ability to forgive him. She might, she might forgive him. But it would cost her something; it would cost them something. It would never be the same, never again.

She passed a shop with a fancy array of hairbrushes and toothbrushes in the window. Did he have a toothbrush at her house? At this other woman's house? Or didn't he need one, since he never stayed overnight? Maybe he used her toothbrush. Had he really gone to Washington two weeks ago? She looked around for a telephone booth. She would call the IRS, find out if there had really been a conference. She stumbled on. What an insane idea; she didn't need proof. He'd *told* her. She didn't want to know the details of his deception.

She stopped walking. He wouldn't come back. Jeff was decisive; Jeff was no dabbler. He committed himself, burned his bridges; she knew him. A slight breeze ruffled her long blond hair. What did she mean, she *knew* him? How could he do this after eight years, with no warning? How *long* had this been going on? Was it going on when they went skating and she sprained her ankle and he was—

Just then a man in a pin-striped suit bumped into her with enough force to knock her down.

"Are you all right?" He frowned with concern as he helped her up. The look lasted only the instant until she said, "I'm okay."

"Sorry." He sped off.

She realized she must be drunk, possibly very drunk. She felt steady, but the buildings seemed askew and people swam into view much too fast. The crowd surged around her as if she were a statue, a monument. She turned and saw the door to a travel agency. HORIZON TRAVEL SERVICE. She made her way to the door and stepped in, taking refuge in a display of glossy leaflets: cruise ships, mountains, bone-white beaches arrayed like dreams.

Of course, she realized. She would go *away*. Why do they say you can't run away? It's better than standing still in the middle of the sidewalk and letting people knock you down. It's one way to keep moving. It was so simple—she would *leave*. She laughed. It came out as a kind of muffled bark.

She studied the brochures for a while. Beaches were out. The pictures of bronzed people with their aggressive white teeth filled her with despair. The photographs showed them charging exuberantly out of the surf, surrounded by haloes of water droplets trapped in midair by the camera. They were obviously having the time of their lives. She lacked the energy even to imagine herself charging out of the surf. There were insets of smaller photographs, showing equally bronzed bodies, maybe the same ones, worn out from frolicking, stretched out on the beach sunning themselves. Moisture beaded their perfect oiled skin. No. The sun would beat her senseless. Indolence would do her in.

She needed to keep busy. She turned to Europe. Paris and Rome seemed full of hyperactive tourists, confirming sights memorized from postcards. London was out. She and Jeff had spent two well-planned weeks there, happily exploring. The thought of Jeff took her by surprise, like a trapdoor. Her body gave a nightmare jerk, as it did sometimes when she was falling asleep, wrenching her awake with a horrible spurt of panic.

She clutched a brochure that announced "Surprising

Amsterdam." Here were capable, sturdy-looking people bicycling past charming buildings. Old stone bridges arching over canals lined with houseboats. Serene art lovers gazing at Rembrandts, Vermeers, Van Goghs.

She sat on a swivel chair upholstered in orange burlap. The travel agent, wearing a neat blue suit and emanating a powerful floral scent, turned to greet her.

"May I help you?" she asked, revealing a perfect smile marred by a smear of lipstick on her front teeth. Claire wanted to tell her about the lipstick, but she felt people were seldom grateful for that kind of information. They preferred to discover such things in the privacy of a bathroom and then pretend that no one had noticed.

"I want to get a ticket to Amsterdam."

"Round trip?"

"One way. For tomorrow—no, the day after tomorrow."

The travel agent cocked one elegantly tweezed eyebrow. "It might be tricky right now. The flower season is in full swing. I'll see what I can do."

She swiveled around to her telephone and computer terminal with a brisk efficiency (shared by doctors' receptionists, stewardesses, nurses) that never failed to impress Claire.

"I can get you on a KLM flight that leaves Kennedy on April twenty-seventh at six P.M. All right?"

Claire nodded.

"In the meantime, you would be wise to reserve a hotel room." She offered a blue-and-white leaflet. Golden Tulip Hotels.

A few minutes later, it was all set up. The Golden Tulip Hotels were all booked up, but the agent managed to find Claire a room in something called the Dikker and

Thys Garden Hotel. "It's not in the old part of town, but they have a very good tourist office there—the VVV—and perhaps you can find something else after the first night." The room cost eighty dollars a night, which seemed a lot, but Claire was not going to scrimp; at least, not at first. She put the KLM ticket, the hotel voucher and her American Express card into her purse and zipped it shut.

She looked up and confided shyly, "You know, you have lipstick on your teeth."

"Oh! Thanks for telling me," said the travel agent in her grateful, chirpy voice. "And you have gin on your breath. Have a good trip."

Right, thought Claire, pushing out to the street. People don't want to know. No, they *do* want to know, but they hold it against you when you tell them.

In the back seat of the taxi, she flipped mindlessly through *The New York Times,* forgetting to read the words. A picture of Rosie Ruiz, suspected of fraud in the Boston Marathon, snagged her attention. Rosie continued to insist that she had run the whole race, but speculation was that she would be denounced. Would they make her give her laurel crown to Jacqueline Gareau, the runner-up? Would Jacqueline Gareau want a used laurel crown? Then there was Lillian Carter, shown presenting a painting to President Sadat of Egypt. The painting showed Sadat, Menachem Begin and Jimmy Carter standing together. Claire kept trying to read the story, but had trouble focusing. She sank back into the seat. How is it that we have a President named Jimmy? Menachem, Anwar and Helmut and Leonid…Muammar, Margaret, Indira and *Jimmy*. She tried the front page. And Tito. Wasn't Tito a nickname, a kind of slavic Jimmy? Tito was in a coma. She had to squint, even to read the smaller headlines; the stories themselves were out. She folded the newspaper together neatly and concentrated on extracting some money from her purse. Somehow, although she felt badly for Jacqueline Gareau, she couldn't help feeling sorry for Rosie Ruiz. Still, she knew she was a sucker for feeling that way.

CHAPTER TWO

IN WASHINGTON, ALAN DAWSON, Ambassador at Large for International Policy, had not yet found time to read his copy of *The New York Times*. Seated at his comfortable desk on the seventh floor of the Department of State building, he replaced in its file cover part of a long memorandum from the Bureau of African Affairs. It concerned Zimbabwe. He took a small notebook from his breast pocket and wrote a note to himself: *Call Davis. More on Mugabe.*

The Secretary was slated to make the rounds of Southern Africa in mid-May. Possibly the trip would be cancelled, in view of the so-called "crises" besetting the seventh floor, but his own analysis must be ready as scheduled. He shook his head at the thought of terming the Iranian situation, now more than five months old, a "crisis." But the press and even the Department of State were reluctant to exchange a punchy word like "crisis" for the more banal "situation."

He had finished reading the long section about Mugabe and felt little the better for it. Mugabe remained opaque, resisting prediction. He needed more. He didn't read for facts, but for patterns, pivotal events, anything that would give him some insight into the character of a man: in this case, the newly prominent world citizen Mr. Mugabe.

He glanced at his watch and began scanning the next section of the memorandum, "Strategic Minerals, Southern African Region." This was the point of intersection of East/West maneuvering, the Grail, the literal pot of gold at the end of Southern African strategy. Not *just* gold, of course. Chromite, manganese, copper, bauxite, vanadium, cobalt, uranium, platinum. Would this man Mugabe be smart enough to avoid being used as a Soviet fulcrum? He wondered just how high a priority the Soviets put on cornering the market in chromium and gold. No matter how distracted the Western powers were by Afghanistan and Iran, the Soviets would not be neglecting Africa. They were patient and persistent; most of all, perhaps, they knew what they wanted.

He opened the small notebook again and wrote: *Dept. of Interior, Chromium, USA? Technology Assessment, transition to less chromium-dependent processes. Time frame. Bur. of African Affairs: Mozambique status report. Angola. Zaïre. CIA Russian Desk: regional activities.* He replaced the report in the folder, and locked it into his desk.

He left the Department of State Building at precisely one forty and proceeded at a brisk walk up Twenty-first Street toward Pennsylvania Avenue. Every Tuesday, unless it rained, it was his habit to skip lunch and walk to the Dumbarton Oaks gardens, in Georgetown. In July and August, when Dumbarton Oaks was closed, he made do with just a walk.

He was a man who nourished his habits carefully, taking a great deal of pleasure from them. The older he got, the more acceptable his orderliness became. His secretary had given him a wink as he left his office today, saying, "Dumbarton Oaks?" While he used to be thought "weird," for instance, for routinely parking his car in the outermost reaches of parking lots, thus forcing himself to walk, he had now reached the more acceptable status of an "eccentric." Often, on his walk, he would be passed by a colleague, jogging; somehow, it was considered good form to go out at lunch and get drenched with sweat jogging, but still eccentric, at best, to walk any distance.

The Dumbarton Oaks outing pleased him because it had four functions. First of all, he was an avid gardener himself, his Cleveland Park home the horticultural star of the block, and he enjoyed the lovely grounds. Second, it was just far enough so that he had to walk very quickly indeed to make it to the gardens, look around and make it back within the hour and a half he allotted himself. He had no time to spare for exercise per se, nor much talent at sports (although he was a fan), so he walked whenever possible. He took the stairs instead of the elevator. These simple stratagems kept him quite fit.

Third, he skipped lunch on his Oaks day. One other day a week, usually Friday, he also skipped lunch, and walked to one of the Smithsonian museums. This, along with never putting butter on anything, kept his weight steady at 170.

As he walked, Dawson thought about Africa: It would take a very forceful presentation to persuade Vance to make some smart moves in Africa now, when they needed to be made. The increasingly defensive, whining posture of the government disturbed him. If Carter continued to insist on placing the United States in the innocent-bystander role, appalled and surprised by totally predictable events, he would do well to remember that innocent bystanders often appeared on casualty lists. South Africa, of course, might hold on for years. But was it too much to ask that these people look ten years ahead? He would recommend pouring some aid into the black republics in Africa. Why not cover your bets, loosen the stranglehold on exporting and processing that South Africa held, make the whole region more flexible? Carter's idea of placating the rest of Africa was Andy Young. Andy Young got taken out in such a simple back-door play...

He turned the corner and walked up Twenty-eighth Street, admiring a lilac in full flower beyond the stone retaining wall in front of a large brick house. A President Poincaré, he thought—too early for a Ludwig Spaeth. He had several lilacs in his yard, despite the fact that they fared poorly in the hot, swampy air of July and August, leaves turning white with mildew.

Dawson passed the playground on R Street and approached the brick wall with the gold lettering: DUMBARTON OAKS. Only then did he wrench his mind reluctantly from Africa to the fourth function of his stroll through the gardens: Sisyphus.

He frowned slightly, thinking of the code name. Even though he knew the man's real name, he was unable, after more than thirty-five years, to think of him as other than Sisyphus. One of the reasons he had resisted "graduating" from the OSS to the fledgling CIA was his distaste for the clandestine. He disliked the codes, the games, the mumbo-jumbo. He disliked the institutionalized schizophrenia of the field agents and detested the perverse mentality—official paranoia—encouraged by his own section of the wartime OSS, Counterintelligence.

He still had nightmares about Vercors, the Resistance stronghold where he had parachuted in as part of an OSS team in 1944. The form of the nightmare had changed, as the years went by, becoming almost stylized. Now it was something like a slide show, one horrific image following another in increasing tempo until there was such an avalanche of horror, he was jolted awake.

The Maquis leaders, under the impression that the Allies would provide them with heavy artillery and airborne assistance, had proudly proclaimed the Free Republic of Vercors. In the midst of their battle preparations, he and the rest of the OSS team had parachuted in. Their distasteful mission was to inform the Maquis that there would be no heavy artillery, no airborne assistance—light arms only—and that they should revise their strategy from the pitched battle they were planning back to guerrilla warfare. The advice was too late. A week later, on Bastille Day, the OSS supply drop provided hundreds of light arms, but even these were gathered at great expense amidst pinpoint German bombing and strafing. The Germans broke through Resistance lines on July 22 with an advance of SS troops, and on July 23 came the main German assault. With it came the grist for Dawson's nightmare.

For a long time, his conscious mind blotted out what he had seen—it was so far past the "normal" horrors of war that he couldn't quite believe it when he was awake. It was so grotesque as to seem almost trite, made-up, movie horror. But when he slept, he saw it all again—the women and children the Nazis hung from meat hooks; the horrible screams of the wounded, unable to move, from the inside of burning hospitals. It was something they never talked about, the surviving members of the team. Albright, who had escaped with him, was a historian—he returned to Cambridge after the war and wrote a book on the Resistance movement, with part of a chapter about Vercors. After he cautiously laid the blame not on the British but on the fact that the Resistance had too many masters, who could not agree on strategy (Vercors being the prime example), there was a brief recitation of the atrocities. Reading that was the closest Dawson ever came to "talking" about it.

But he dreamed, he still dreamed. Years ago the nightmare would leave him weak and shaking, stinking of fear, and he would get up, take a shower, spend hours calming himself down before he could risk sleep again. He seemed compelled to have the dream about once a week, and over the years his mind had learned to compress it into a shudder of horror—intense, but over quickly. Now when he woke up after his Vercors dream, he would look around the room, touch his wife's hair in a shy, ritualistic way and immediately go back to sleep.

Sisyphus was part of the nightmare, part of the coda at the end. Sisyphus and Canard.

Dawson had escaped the Vercors massacre with a Maquis unit, and shortly after V-E day resigned from the OSS to go to the State Department. In the midst of his last assignment, ferreting out Nazi intelligence agents still at large in Berlin, he had been summoned to the dingy little room where he had first met Sisyphus. The man's back was turned when Dawson entered the room, and he began, theatrically enough, saying, "My code name is Sisyphus because in fact the task is never-ending and very grueling." Then he turned and revealed his face. "We can ill afford to lose men of your caliber, Dawson. I think I can persuade you to stay on with us."

There was an extremely long pause, an interrogation tactic Dawson had employed so many times that he surprised himself by giving in and speaking first.

"I doubt it, sir."

Perhaps it was because Sisyphus had an extraordinary capacity for remaining still. He could sit or stand without moving a single muscle, inanimate as furniture. When he crossed to the closet and shrugged into his coat, Dawson felt he'd been released from suspended animation.

"I want to take you somewhere, and on the way, let me tell you something about Vercors."

They rode quite a way through the tattered streets of Berlin before he spoke again. The air in the car seemed charged with static electricity.

"Vercors was supposed to be the result of a bureaucratic wrangle between us and London, a tragic breakdown in communication." He let out a knife-edged laugh. "It really was something quite different—a classic intelligence operation. We never promised the Maquis airborne support and heavy artillery, you see; German intelligence did. And didn't you ever wonder how the Nazis knew, to the *hour,* when those supplies would be dropped on Bastille Day, and exactly where? First the Maquis got suckered into a battle, and then even what supplies we did send were gathered at a terrible price, and who ended up getting blamed?" He snorted. "We did. The Allies. I tell you, it was a beautiful piece of work."

They careened around a corner and Dawson had a brief glimpse of a bombed apartment building—just the outside wall torn away so that the rooms stood exposed, like a dollhouse.

"Last week an SS officer fingered the double agent. We picked him up in the middle of a party, celebrating 'our' victory." The car pulled up in front of a warehouse. Sisyphus gave a little laugh. "He'd just popped a new bottle of champagne." Instead of getting out of the car, Sisyphus pulled something out of his pocket and tossed it in the air a couple of times. "I saved the cork." At the time, Dawson had been astounded by this, but later he learned that it was typical for Sisyphus to produce odd bits of physical evidence.

"Anyway, I thought you'd like to meet him."

The room was small and intensely lit; guards sat at a table playing an inappropriately boisterous game of cards. Hunched over on a stool, fairly badly beaten and looking up at him with familiar sleepy eyes was one of the most popular Maquis leaders, a cheerful, fearless man they all called "Canard." Dawson remembered the man's odd ducklike walk.

Dawson saw a faint flicker of a smile at the corner of the man's mouth. He stood there paralyzed at the realization that the horrors of Vercors had been set into motion by this man, a man they'd considered brave but none too bright. An almost comic figure, a sort of mascot. How long he stood there Dawson wasn't sure, but it couldn't have been long because he realized he'd been holding his breath. When the air went out of him, he turned abruptly and left the room.

In the car on the way back, there was a prolonged silence. Dawson felt weak with shock but didn't want to show it. When he finally spoke, his voice was surprisingly clear and steady.

"I haven't changed my mind, sir."

Sisyphus negotiated a checkpoint and sighed. "I see." An accusation. "Well, there is an alternative. I'd like to be able to count on you…"

In the end, although he didn't agree to stay on with OSS/CIA, Dawson did agree to be "on tap," for "us," in an emergency. Sisyphus would be his only control. "If anything happens to me, the deal is erased. I won't pass you on." Dawson nodded, dully, exhausted.

In current Agency terms, he was a "stayback."

Dawson admired a stand of Mount Hood daffodils near the bamboo grove, and continued on toward their meeting place.

While he disliked the Agency's "games," he was unable to repress a twinge of pleasure whenever he received a summons. The latest one, meticulous as ever, had come in a letter from his Aunt Millie in Akron, Ohio, full of chatty news about her dog-breeding business. He really did have an aunt named Millie in Akron who bred and raised Shelties. *Uncle Albert says the azaleas at the Oaks must be spectacular.* The letter was not dated, but Sisyphus would certainly be here; Wednesday was their regular day. "Spectacular" had given him a jolt; something urgent—he'd seen that only once before. He descended some steps toward the patio where their meetings always began, passing under an arcade sweet with wisteria. The ancient wisteria vines were as thick as his arms.

He could see Sisyphus now, leaning forward from the stone bench, largely hidden by an arched trellis covered with the beautiful white wisteria known as "Ivory Tower." The bony head peered out, surrounded by long white racemes of blossoms, as if it were emerging from a cloud. A somewhat perverse vision—a wizened cherub. His face had not really changed in the years Dawson had known him, time merely refining features already set. He got up, leaning heavily on his cane.

"Alan. Good to see you. Gorgeous day, isn't it?" They shook hands and Sisyphus flashed his smile—oddly artificial, as if he'd learned it by observation. "Let's walk, shall we? The trouble with wisteria on a still day is that the perfume is too aggressive." They stopped to admire a planting of doronicium and white tulips.

"Very effective," said Sisyphus. "But then you have to

put up with that nasty foliage until August." He leaned on his cane. "Things are serious, as you probably guessed. The President has set into motion an absolutely disastrous rescue plan for the hostages in Teheran. He thinks he can pull off an Entebbe, but this plan is so full of tactical errors, it hasn't the remotest chance of succeeding. It's also full of cut-offs and exit points, as if he knows that. Or doesn't want it to succeed. Typical." He gave a braying little laugh. "It's so bad, in fact, that we don't need to sabotage it—it will sabotage itself."

"You don't want the hostages rescued."

Sisyphus looked directly at him and shrugged. His lips parted and he leaned forward slightly as if he were about to say something, but then he tilted backward and looked at the sky. A jet etched a straight white line across the pale blue.

"The Europeans will be mad as hell," Dawson said. "About the rescue."

Sisyphus took a few steps, then stopped again. He ran his hand through his shock of white hair. As always, Dawson had trouble looking him in the eye for long. While his hair had turned white, his eyebrows remained coal-black. His startling blue eyes had an intensity that seemed to transcend mere sight, like comic-book X-ray vision, and at the same time a sadness, a softness that warred with his bony harsh face. Dawson shifted his gaze and moved aside to let a young couple, arms twined about each other's waists, pass. "Mad as hell," he repeated.

It had taken months of cajoling and threatening to get the Europeans to agree to sanctions against Iran, and they had done so only yesterday, and with the tacit understanding that this would forestall any military intervention on the part of the United States. It was not just an understanding; it was more concrete than that, a—

"That's where you get your entrée, or where I hope you will. You're scheduled to go to a Circle Group Steering Committee meeting on Sunday, leaving here Saturday. A red-flag meeting, I believe."

Dawson shook his head. "Your intelligence, as always, is correct." He disliked the ooze of flattery he heard in his voice.

"We had better start walking back. I don't want to disrupt your schedule." They turned and looked toward the big house. Azaleas everywhere blazed with color. Sisyphus let his voice drop almost to a whisper. "Firelli is going to propose the assassination of the Shah."

"What?" His voice was too loud. A slight breeze ruffled the deep pink blossoms of an azalea they passed, and the color seemed to scintillate through his head with the powerful rush of a hallucination. Dawson felt disoriented and stumbled, almost causing Sisyphus too to lose his precarious balance. "Sorry."

"A bit shocking, yes, but not on the whole a bad idea, at least if you're basing it on the information Firelli has in hand. All of Firelli's intelligence is correct, by the way. The Shah *is* dying, and he has fallen under the influence of a mullah in Cairo, and he is considering a voluntary return to Teheran. A sort of martyr's gesture, you know, to heal 'Persia.' Look at that." He pointed his cane at a circular bed of fringed yellow tulips. "Tulip mosaic. They'd better rogue out that bunch."

While his mind staggered, Dawson's diplomat's voice didn't fail him. "I was explaining to my wife last week that fringed tulips are a genetic mutation achieved by irradiation, and now she's acquired a distaste for them. Hasn't cut a single one to bring inside."

Sisyphus chuckled and Dawson waited for him to continue. "Well, from the Circle Group point of view, the

Shah's trial would of course be a disaster—the whole array of multinationals would also be on trial. And suppose the Shah is bitter enough to reveal details of U.S. corporate and federal dealings with the Saudis, all those concessions he himself demanded? The military hardware, the aircraft, the advisers we kept back from the Saudis? Why, the Saudis could bring down the entire monetary system in a matter of weeks. They might not, but *is it worth the risk?* Incidentally, I have some further corroborating intelligence for you to take to the meeting—the Libyans and Palestinians have called off their assassination teams. By the way, I expect you'll be under some pressure to cancel your trip to the meeting. State will be in an uproar over the rescue attempt—whether it fails or not. Actually, it's certain to fail. Vance *will* resign this time and there will be chaos, but you must insist on going. It should be fairly easy to convince them; the Europeans will need to have their hands held."

They began to ascend some narrow stone steps. Sisyphus was having difficulty with the uneven surfaces. A few people bunched up impatiently behind them. When they reached the top and stepped onto a flagstone patio, the crowd surged around them. Creeping thyme grew between the flagstones and released a sweet fragrance as they walked. A young mother, with an infant attached to her chest in a kind of bag affair, spoke to her older child, a toddler.

"Don't pick anything. I *told* you. Just don't pick anything." The child's face contorted with rage and he began to scream, standing absolutely motionless.

Sisyphus pointed with his cane to an old wooden bench. "Let's sit down a moment. I'm afraid I'm getting feeble."

The wails of the child diminished as they made toward

the bench, and Alan could hear the mother yelling ineffectually, *"Jordy. Stop it! Jordy!* It's not *my* rule; it's *their* rule."

Sisyphus lowered himself delicately to the bench and
draped one of his arms over the back. Dawson could hear
his watch ticking.

"Here's what I want you to do: I want you to bug the
Circle Group meeting. In your room at the Amstel Hotel,
you'll find an attaché case which contains a tape recorder
and various microphones, quite sensitive. It has an ultra-
slow cassette, good for several hours. For some reason,
this is known in the trade as an 'attack kit.' " Sisyphus
laughed and shook his head. "Nomenclature has never
been a strong point in this business." He lifted his eyebrows and demonstrated his odd smile. "To activate it,
you merely turn the combination to three-three-three.
The next time you set it down, it will begin to record. Just
take it to the meeting and place it at your feet. You can put
papers in it, if you like. In fact, it comes all dummied up
with legal pads and so on. Opening it does not affect the
mechanism. Then I want you to arrange a meeting with
John Stenner, the reporter, and give him the tape. He's living in Amsterdam now. In fact, he's doing a book on
transnational groups—it's perfect cover. He protected you
when you leaked the Shafer/Milford stuff, and we feel he
will protect you again."

"Yes, I'm sure he will. But I don't quite understand—
this will at the very least embarrass some important men,
allies if I might presume. It might make them liable for
criminal conspiracy. And also, you presented an awfully
good case for Firelli's plan." Dawson shifted on the bench
and knocked his elbow painfully into one of the wooden
slats.

A long, tortured sigh escaped from Sisyphus' lips.
"It's complicated." There was a long pause, punctuated

only by taps of the cane. "The assassination must be stopped, at least for the time being." His voice sank to a whisper. "The gist of it is this: the Russians are planning an invasion of Iran, from Iraq, and they are banking on the support of Marxist factions within Iran and most specifically, within the Iranian armed forces. Not only don't we want the Shah to return and stand trial, it is important that he survive as long as possible, because hatred of the Shah, and the hope of someday 'bringing him to justice,' provides the only unity Iran has. Our feeling is that if the Shah were to be assassinated right now, by outside forces, Iran would lapse into *anarchy*. Khomeini would lose his tenuous grip and the Soviets would easily rally support for the Iraqi invasion.

"No. If anyone is to kill the Shah, it must not be now, and it must be Khomeini, because, sad to say, a strong Khomeini regime is our best defense against a Russian takeover. Once the Iraqi attack bogs down, as it will failing support from within Iran, then we will worry about the Shah. He will never stand trial—if need be, there are extremely competent people who can deal with him."

"Talk about the lesser of two evils," Dawson said.

The mother with the unhappy child was approaching, and Sisyphus waited while she passed. The boy had stopped screaming, but his breath came in shuddering gasps, and the infant had now begun to howl. The mother's mouth was set in a grim line. "I thought we'd have a good time," she muttered as she passed them. She took the little boy's hand and half-dragged him along. "Let's look at the flowers a minute and then I'll get you an ice cream," she said angrily. They disappeared around a curve in the path.

"As for Circle Group," Sisyphus resumed, "that is the other thing. It's really LeClerc...This will give me some leverage. He's important, Alan, critically important, even more important than the Iranian business. But you needn't worry about any exposure of Circle Group—no one's name will ever reach print. Stenner is just a cut-out, simply to protect you. His editor owes me a large favor and I am going to call it in."

Dawson frowned and twirled his wedding ring around on his finger.

"Look, Alan, I don't like to ask you to do this, but you know that we cannot count on any action from the Administration to stop the Soviet attack on Iran. They will just wring their hands some more; they won't do a thing. We can stop Firelli's plan at any point, and in a number of ways, but using you is by far the most elegant. Not only do we stop the Firelli threat, but I get a hook into LeClerc. Let me stress that LeClerc's information is absolutely crucial to national security."

"What will happen to Stenner? He won't be happy to have his scoop squashed. He'll pursue it; he's very persistent."

Sisyphus traced small circles in the pebbles at their feet with the tip of his cane. Then he dug in the tip with a grinding motion.

"I haven't quite decided what to do about Mr. Stenner. I may just let it happen the way it seems to be happening—let the paper close the story down and take the rap."

"It will make him bitter."

Sisyphus extracted his cane from the hole he had dug with it and began tapping it against his shoe to remove the dirt.

"I know. I don't want to create a Don Quixote—despite the ideal location. I may have to pull him in; explain, up to a point. You got to know him fairly well. What do you think?"

"He'd resent being used."

"On the other hand, secrets are power. The inside track is alluring. I could hand him a real scoop, after the Circle Group feint is over."

Dawson glanced at his watch.

"You have to be leaving—I know. The other possibility is simply removing the evidence. Reporters are incredibly casual about security—you'd scarcely believe it. Let's start toward the street. We can part company at the bamboo grove. Take my newspaper when we get up. I'm waiting, quite frankly, for a cable from my agent in Amsterdam, a capable man. He's become quite friendly with Stenner, and I want his advice. Incidentally, he's the only other one who knows the details of this operation—we're playing it tight. He's the one who will see that the attaché case is in your room, and also the one you will call if anything untoward happens. There are two phone numbers on the second page of the financial section. The one marked 'A' is the agent's. Identify yourself to him as 'Mount Hood.' He will identify himself as 'Scott.' 'B' is Stenner's number in Amsterdam. But I want you to call his ex-wife, or her parents—you're still friendly with the family?" Dawson nodded. "Good. It will be more natural—if Stenner ever checks up later—to get the number from them. Even if I pull him in, and inform him, he'll never know that you were—ah—running on the inside track too."

A large Army helicopter passed by overhead as they neared the bamboo grove. They both looked up. "Sloppy flight pattern," commented Dawson.

"Yes, and they'll hear about it, too. Residents of Georgetown are constitutionally protected from *undue* noise. Near the river it's barely possible to talk outside as it is." He whacked his cane against a stand of bamboo. "By the way, do you remember Le Canard?"

Dawson didn't reply.

"He died yesterday. I thought you'd like to know. I was going to have him killed, back in Berlin, but instead I turned him. Not so odd, really—he was always anti-Communist. He'd worked for me ever since; he was quite valuable." Sisyphus tipped his cane in farewell. "Never throw away anything you can use, no matter how rotten." He gestured vaguely at the earth. "Compost."

Dawson hurried out the gate and walked very rapidly back toward his office. He was going to be late.

CHAPTER THREE

"**O**PEN JUST A LITTLE WIDER, Claire. Thaaaaat's it." Dr. Cutler's face hovered inches above her own, tense with concentration as he repositioned his drill. It seemed impolite to stare intently at his pores or nostril hairs, as she was doing. By shifting her gaze to the left, she could see his young ponytailed assistant, busy with her suction tube. "Just a little wider, Claire. Goooood girl," said Dr. Cutler in exactly the same tone the vet used when doing something to her old dog Poppy. She remembered the day Poppy got run over by the man in the green car. He had jumped out, yelling over and over again, "He just ran right out in front of me, right out in front of me." And Poppy lay there, absolutely motionless. And then Poppy began to twitch...

"Rinse," said Dr. Cutler.

Claire spat blood and little bits of filling.

"Again."

For once it had been her father, not her mother, who

reacted first to the emergency. The screech of the green car's brakes and Poppy's shriek brought him flying out of his studio. He had been working and held a large flat paintbrush with a glob of yellow-ocher paint on it. He stabbed it in the air toward the man from the green car. "You shut up!" he yelled. "Just shut up." Then he pressed Claire to him so she couldn't look at Poppy anymore.

"Open," said Dr. Cutler. "Now close." He examined a small strip of what looked like carbon paper that he'd extracted from between her teeth. "Just a tad more off this corner."

Her new pink dress had ended up smeared with yellow ocher, and her mother had thrown it away. But no one did anything about the small dabs of paint that adhered to the dashboard and steering wheel of the car that transported Poppy to the killing mercy of the vet.

"I'll just polish this up a bit, so it will be nice and smooth. Open."

Those globs of paint stayed, growing dingy along with the car. The painting her father had been working on, a large canvas composed of patches of somber colors that seemed at war with other patches of uncompromising pastels, ended up entitled *Reveille,* and now hung in the Museum of Modern Art.

"I can't promise how long this will last," said Dr. Cutler as he undid the little paper bib from around her neck. "It really needs a crown. As soon as you get back from your trip, I'll expect to hear from you, young lady."

She winced as he escorted her to the door. His jovial, patronizing manner had never bothered her before, but today...

"And don't chew on that side for at least eight hours."

It was a bleak, overcast day, yet somehow the watery light produced a nasty glare. She squinted, looking for a cab, and ticked off *Dentist* from her mental list of things to do.

She had already done a lot. When she'd first gotten home from the travel agency and realized she had only two days to get ready, she'd gone into a panic, ransacking the desk to find her passport, tearing through the files for other papers she might need. It seemed critical, for some reason, to find her birth certificate, and when it didn't turn up in the folder marked IMPORTANT PAPERS—CLAIRE, she slipped into a desperate frenzy, taking out file after file. She threw one file against the wall, like a Frisbee, and paper exploded from it, then sifted down like giant snow. She sat down on the floor in the middle of the strewn papers and started to cry. Jeff would have known exactly where everything was, exactly what to do. The helpless feeling had subsided, and an alien, purposeful calm taken its place.

She had actually typed a list, titled THINGS TO DO, and moved through the tasks with a relentless efficiency.

First she called Fiona Wells, the editor she worked under at the Redbrook Press. Fiona shrieked. It was one of her mannerisms to shriek, even when confronted by the mildest surprise. The shriek was often followed, as it was in this case, by a wail.

"Whaaaaaat? But you can't just *leave*. What about the Slater book?"

"I really have to get out of here, Fee. I can't stand to stay."

"I know, I know." Then Fiona launched into an anecdote about some ex-lover who had left her. No matter what happened to you, it had already happened to Fiona in some more intense manner. Then she clicked into her pragmatic, editor mode. "I guess Irene can do the Slater book. Where are you going?"

"California," Claire lied, for no reason.

"How long will you be gone?"

"I don't know, Fiona. I just—"

"I'll give you a sabbatical. Come back with a tan, okay, kid? If I see Jeff, I'll spit in his eye."

Claire finally got a cab and now asked the driver to wait while she went into the post office and got some stamps. The stamps were for the little notes she'd written to her friends, odd, stuffy notes that all said the same thing: *Jeff has left me and I'm going away for a while. Love, Claire.* It seemed melodramatic just to disappear, but she couldn't bring herself to call them.

The postal clerk was a beautiful black woman, at least six feet tall. Her hair was in cornrows, each braid fastened with a cowrie shell. When she looked up, her hair jingled.

"Yes?"

Claire's mouth was numb with Novocaine. "Twenty fifteen-cent stamps, please."

She got back into the cab and stuffed them into her purse.

"Two-thirty Park Avenue."

The driver's name, she noticed, was Jesus.

At the bank, she discovered her birth certificate in the safety-deposit box. She removed that, along with some financial documents, her grandmother's engagement ring and their marriage license, and put them into another, personal safety-deposit box. She paid it up for two years. Some of the financial documents she put into her attaché case. She withdrew half the money in their savings account, about five thousand dollars, and converted it into traveler's checks. She took a peculiar pleasure in signing her name over and over again. Then she wrote a check for half the money in their joint checking account and set up a new account of her own. She left the bank with a leaflet listing all the overseas branches of Citibank. She was vaguely reassured to know that the Banco de Viscaya in Bilbao, Spain, was somehow linked up with her money.

Money, money. Jeff was good with money. One of the things she loved about him was his straight-arrow practicality, his earnest, Republican side. And while he professed to equally love her dreaminess, he was occasionally appalled. How could she blow all her money on lunch and have to walk home? How could she look at a painting so long that she'd be late to meet him and they would miss the beginning of a movie? He had got used to it, begun almost to brag about it. "Claire doesn't anticipate. Everything takes her by surprise." But he had been truly appalled by her carefree attitude toward money.

In their early years, living in a bombed-out set of rooms in Park Slope, he'd begun socking away bits of their meager salaries. She loved it—his prudence, his frugality. She would have lived on beans and rice for months had he required it. He began investing the money. Then he insisted she be "educated." He dragged her to investment seminars; he made her read *The Wall Street Journal*. He marked articles in *Forbes* and *Business Week* with neat red asterisks. She often felt when reading them that the world was demented. Here was a parallel, science-fiction universe of P/E ratios, massive power transfers; a secret galaxy of numbers that in fact ruled the world; caused wars, assassinations, the creation of sugar corn puffs. Jeff was so serious about it. Jeff was intent on laying bare for her the "real world," as he called it, the ravenous corporate heart of America.

Eventually, he forced on her half their accumulated assets—*her* "portfolio," which she was to manage with the help of Harold (Call me Hal) Burgess, their financial adviser.

She had walked directly from the bank to Hal Burgess' office. He was not happy with her plans.

"Jeff will be furious," he said. His heavy, mobile eyebrows met in a frown. "He's set this up so intelligently—some of these stocks have terrific long-term potential. And it would be stupid for you to take your money out of the funds, too."

"Jeff has nothing to say about this." Everything in Burgess' office, she noticed for the first time, had an almost oppressive solidity. The furniture was ponderous, crouching. The art was static—two Buffets with their heavy black lines, some clipper ships with their formally etched waves, imprisoned in black mats and heavy black frames. Even the plants—cactus, jade trees—suggested slow, dependable growth. It must be calculated, she thought. Hal Burgess himself looked solid, dependable, behind his large oak desk, flanked by his diplomas.

Now he shook his head. "And you want it all deposited in a checking account? *No* interest." He shook his head again. "How much did you get in traveler's checks?"

"Five grand."

"Think of the float you're losing. Just the goddamn *float.*"

The float. Jeff. Jeff was so different from her father, who often forgot to pay bills for months at a time, so that she and her mother had been forced to confront bill collectors, angry-looking men in cheap suits, who came pounding at the door. At first, they would be put off by her mother's powerful British disdain.

"Mr. Pemble is an *artist,* don't-you-know," she would say, as if that explained everything. The men would blink their eyes, as if her mother were an apparition. "I'm certain he will sort things out as *soon* as he can *possibly* spare the time." That would work once, but they would come back, and she and her mother would periodically hide in the attic. ("One of those wretched men is coming. Let's not be in.")

Once, their phone had been disconnected for six months because her father refused to pay the telephone company its requested deposit for reinstating service. He was passionate—"It's a monopoly. I regard it as a right, not a service. Besides, I paid the bill. I *always* pay the bill." She couldn't remember why he had ever relented, as he must have. The phone company never relents; that's what Jeff calls "the real world."

It was not that they were poor—her father had inherited money and the house, and was also an Associate Professor of Art at City College. He was just obstinately careless. Nor had his distaste for the practical really lessened now that his paintings were selling for great wads of money. But Jeff managed his money now.

She wondered what would happen to that particular arrangement. She remembered, with shame, pretending to be Anne Frank while hiding in the attic from the bill collectors.

"Claire?" Hal Burgess was looking at her with a fierce expression she guessed was meant to convey concern.

"Yes?"

"Are you all right?"

"Sound as a deutschmark, Hal. Look, I just want all the money in one place. I don't want to think about it. I know you're supposed to have your money working for you. But I just don't care—let's just say my money is taking a vacation."

"You wouldn't have to do a thing. I could do it all for you."

She relented to the extent of having ten thousand dollars in the checking account and the rest in whatever fund Hal Burgess would choose. It would be "perfectly liquid," he assured her.

Still, he was not pleased. He shook his head, shuffling through her papers. "I hate to use a cliché, but even if he's left you, aren't you sort of cutting off your nose to spite your face?"

"Probably."

"There's no reason for you not to *benefit* from the long-range planning here." He whacked his fist down on the stack of papers. "And have you thought of the *taxes?* Just on the Resorts stock, the capital gains…You'll still have to file a joint return this year. And Jeff is my client too."

"Jeff is the one who insisted I manage my own money. I'm managing it."

He shook his head some more, then threw up his hands in an abrupt "I give up" gesture. She didn't escape before he made a clumsy pass at her, which she handled badly, leaving his office with her face burning, humiliated.

"Lady?"

The cab was stopped in front of their apartment building. She felt guilty about taking so many cabs, but yesterday she'd tried the bus and got off after three blocks. She'd had the horrible feeling she was transparent, that her thoughts were audible. At least she could be grateful this hadn't happened during the transit strike. She overtipped the cabdriver and he flashed her a smile. A gold tooth winked from the corner of his mouth.

Jeff Jeff Jeff Jeff. She stepped into the elevator. Jeff had come out of the Midwest like a dream, a paragon, the capable man. She imagined him in the elevator with her: his short brown hair, his home-again smile enough to break her heart. Tears sprang into her eyes, but the elevator door wheezed open and she blinked them away. A man carrying a huge banana tree stepped in.

"It's going up," she said.

"Oh," he said from behind the leaves.

"Are you going up?"

"No. Yes. I'm just as glad to put this sucker down." He sort of wrestled it to the floor. "I'll go up. Then I'll go down."

"Do you want me to ride down with you and hold the door open while you get it out?"

"No. That's okay. I can manage. Say, do you want it? I'm just taking it down to throw it away."

The elevator arrived at her floor. She held the door open with her body. It thumped against her with its metallic pulse.

"Thanks anyway, I don't have room."

He sighed. "That's why I gotta get rid of it. But I couldn't bring myself to kill it, y'know?"

She nodded sympathetically. "Why don't you leave it in the elevator? That way, someone won't have to drag it in from the street."

"Say, that's a great idea. Yeah. Yeah. I'll put a little sign on it—'Free Plant.' "

"I've got to go."

"Hey! Thanks for the idea. I kind of like to think of it riding up and down. Hey, have a good day."

She leaned against the door of her apartment, feeling weak. Good day.

She went into the bedroom and lay down, confronted by the filing cabinet. It stood there like some monolithic deciduous tree, surrounded by its litter of white leaves.

She gripped the brass headboard, disoriented. She felt evanescent, as if she might dissolve into the air. What made her think she could—

A rap on the door, loud as a shot, made her jump up. The door was chained—another thing Jeff had taught her. He'd been shocked by her reckless habits—half the time she didn't even lock the door. ("People do get raped, Claire, all the time. Especially people who look like you." "It's not supposed to matter. Little old ladies get raped." "Is that meant to be a reason not to lock the door?")

She was afraid it was the banana-tree man.

She opened the door as far as the chain allowed and there was Jeff's face. She caught his earnest, determined look, a look so totally characteristic of him it brought tears to her eyes. She tried to shut the door, but he had his foot wedged in the opening. She hid behind it, so that he couldn't see her.

"Let me in, Claire," he said in a calm, deliberate voice. She almost did—how could she resist his confident determination?

"Come on, Claire." His voice was patient and tinged with ridicule, as if he were dealing with a sulking child.

"Fiona called me. She said you were leaving."

"That's right."

"Look, would you let me in? I feel ridiculous standing out here in the hall. I'm worried about you."

"Good."

"You know, I could have let myself into the apartment and waited for you to come back. I was trying...I was trying to be fair. Please let me in. I don't think it's the right thing to do—leave, I mean. Especially for someone like you."

Her heart was beating irregularly, in ferocious bursts. "So now I'm 'someone like you.' " She started to cry.

"Are you crying?"

"No! And if you don't get out of here, I'm calling the police."

"Don't be so fucking dramatic. I'm still your husband. What would you say?"

"I will! I will!" she shrilled. She ran from the door toward the telephone.

"I'm not leaving."

She did an abrupt about-face and marched up to the door, staring at him with her red eyes. She felt hard and impermeable, as if her skin had calcified.

"It would be one thing if you came back...if you, if you *wanted* to come back, or even if you really came back here to talk to me about something. But you're here to *manage* me." She saw him wince. "To see that I don't do something that will make you feel guilty. Well, you have no *right*. If I want to throw myself out the window, if I want to become a junkie, if I want to dye my hair fucking *green,* then *I will.*"

He made a defensive gesture, pushing the air in front of him. "I only—"

"I *know* why you came. But I don't want your fucking *advice.*"

He moved his foot quietly out of the way as she shut the door. They stood there, on opposite sides of the door, for a while, totally silent. Then she heard him walk away down the hall.

She was so angry, she packed her two suitcases with the choppy, abrupt gestures most people use only when there is someone to watch them. When she was finished, she turned on the shower with a violent twist and stood under the rushing water for a long time.

She didn't think at all, standing under the water. The water was an obliterating torrent. When she turned it off, she knew she had to hurry. If I'm going to get to the airport on time, she thought, I've got to beat the rush hour.

CHAPTER FOUR

LAWRENCE PRAGER, DIRECTOR OF PLANS at the CIA, was leaving his office a little early, trying to beat the rush hour. For two years now he'd been coaching his son Eric's soccer team, and he liked to get to the field ahead of the kids.

He had his hand on the doorknob, having already said good-bye to his secretary, Kathleen, when an urgent call came from Henry Fairfax, Executive Operations Officer, Counterintelligence section, familiarly known as the Counterintelligence EXOP. "Something on Headwind," Fairfax said, and Prager resignedly returned to his office. He was disappointed—coaching the soccer team was the one activity that really took his mind off his work.

"Headwind" was the code name for a surveillance operation Prager himself had ordered on the *former* Counterintelligence EXOP, Alexander "Sisyphus"

Carley. Carley had been forced to resign from the Agency in the wake of the Watergate scandal, when more than a thousand Agency employees were fired or retired. Many had gone into the private security field, and Sisyphus was no exception. He'd formed his own firm, Mountain Security. The thing that set Sisyphus aside was that he virtually took the Counterintelligence Division with him when he left. He followed a scorched-earth policy as far as files were concerned—removing or burning them. His entire senior staff and the majority of his junior staff resigned in sympathy. They were now employed at Mountain Security, and Prager suspected that most of the former Counterintelligence files were at Mountain as well.

Counterintelligence now was just a section of the Agency. But in Sisyphus' time (and a very long time it was, since Sisyphus had been the only Executive Operations Officer of Counterintelligence from the beginning of the Agency until his removal), Counterintelligence was rigidly separated from the rest of the Agency. Sisyphus' assets—his files, his officers, his agents, his operations— were not *known* to the rest of the Agency. Prager had recently ordered the surveillance on Sisyphus stepped up, because there was a whisper of evidence that Sisyphus was still running his agents; was still carrying on operations; was, in fact, running a kind of rogue CIA from Mountain Security.

Kathleen buzzed him on the intercom. Prager told her to send Henry Fairfax in.

"Hello, Henry. How are you?"

"Just fine, just fine, Larry."

"I was just going out to coach…" Prager began. "Damn, I've got to call Helen." He made a gesture toward the liquor cabinet. "Fix yourself a drink while I call."

Helen Prager was not pleased that she would be required to supervise the soccer practice.

"Look, Helen, just let them scrimmage. Except the goalies. The goalies should practice punching out high balls. Falls Church has a lot of strong kickers."

"You haven't forgotten we're to have dinner with the Rasmussens at eight?"

"No, I haven't forgotten. I'll be there. Listen, Helen, don't forget the whistle, for the scrimmage. It's hanging up in the garage next to the ball bag. If I can possibly get there, I will. Love you."

"So, how's the team doing, Larry?" Fairfax asked, adding some water to the generous shot of Scotch in his glass. Prager fixed himself a drink as well.

"So-so. Two and two. I just can't get them to pass. Except, of course, when they should be taking shots— then they pass like crazy. So?" He raised his glass. "Cheers, Henry. What's up?"

"Well, you know, I disagreed with you when you wanted me to step up surveillance. Maybe I half-swallowed the line I've been putting out on him all these years—you know, 'the legendary Alex "Sisyphus" Carley, now a senile, paranoid drunk.' But now...I think you were right." Fairfax extracted a folder from his briefcase and slid it across Prager's desk. "I don't know what the *hell* he's up to, but he's up to something."

Prager opened the folder and began to read.

Fairfax was a restless man; he lacked any gift for repose. His wife, Betty, called him "fidgety" and often cracked, "If you catch Henry standing still, check his eyes. He's probably asleep." Fairfax started to walk around the room. He stopped in front of a photograph of Prager's soccer team—Larry and a bunch of little boys in blue-and-white. Larry's T-shirt said COACH. He'd been a little bit pleased to hear they weren't doing so well, and now, as he stood there looking at their eager smiles, he reproached himself. He moved on, stopping in front of a framed print. He tried to puzzle out the signature, but it was illegible. He took off his glasses. He liked orderly paintings, not dark, chaotic messes like this. He peered at it from various angles, but could not discern any beauty in it. He took his handkerchief out of his pocket and began to clean his glasses. Eventually, he drifted over toward Prager's desk.

Prager finished reading the transcript and leafed back a few pages, pretending to reread a section. When the Agency hierarchy had changed following Watergate—when Don Crosby had taken over as Director, and he himself had been promoted to DOP, it had still taken nearly a year to get rid of Sisyphus. When the old man was finally forced out, Crosby had given a speech, vowing to "bring Counterintelligence back within the Agency." Fairfax had been appointed as the new chief of CI.

Henry Fairfax was a straightforward man, energetic, but not imaginative. Prager had pushed for his appointment. He looked at Fairfax standing in front of the window, and thought again how much he looked like Robert Mitchum. But a Robert Mitchum whose face had been put in a vise, the features squeezed together. Prager slid the transcript back into its folder.

"Nice work, Henry."

"Not really," Fairfax said, drifting toward Prager's desk. "His leg is really getting bad now—it takes him about five minutes to get in or out of a car, apparently. He's easy to tail and he doesn't really get out much. Still, we managed to miss the beginning of the meet. *And*"— Fairfax drained his glass and set it down—"as you are about to comment, it took a long time to get it to you."

"Yes," Prager said, careful to keep any hint of criticism from his voice. "I was going to ask about that."

"Took a while for the tech boys to clean off the tape. The wire had two little kids along, both of them screaming bloody murder. Good cover, but we couldn't hear a thing. They had to scrape that off, and even then, they had to amplify Carley's voice—it thins out, they tell me."

"Still," Prager said. "Good work." He rapped his knuckles on the folder. "What do you make of it?"

"Want to take a guess on who 'Alan' is?"

"I thought maybe Alan Kell—he's in Circle."

"Alan *Dawson*. Jesus *Christ*. Alan Dawson. Next thing we'll find out Jimmy Carter is one of Carley's sleepers."

"Alan Dawson," Prager said quietly. Alan Kell was a mid-level bureaucrat at State, a Circle Group member only because of his father's connections. Alan Dawson was a different matter.

"Why would he do it?" Fairfax demanded.

"I don't know, Henry," Prager said.

"Well," Fairfax said, "I checked with Mideast. They don't have any data that would indicate an imminent invasion from Iraq." That didn't really mean anything, Fairfax thought privately. Mideast had been dead wrong before. Look at Iran. "And as for the Shah, I think the protective measures on him should ward off any half-assed assassination attempt. But frankly, I just can't believe Circle would do this anyway. I mean they're not action-oriented, or they never have been. Suddenly, they think they're the PLO?" He threw up his hands.

Prager shook his head. "One thing is for certain—we can't allow Carley to get this kind of leverage on Circle. It wouldn't just be leverage on LeClerc; he could press any one of them. And we can't allow Circle to…" He frowned.

"I'm going to have to confer with the Director on this." Prager picked up the folder and tapped it.

"What do you suppose he wants from LeClerc?"

Prager gave an exaggerated shrug and smiled. He had his suspicions, but he did not confide them to Fairfax.

"Excellent work, Henry. You haven't made any progress at Mountain, I take it."

"Zero. I've never seen anything like the security there. State of the art, really. It's…" Fairfax was about to say it was light-years better than security at the Agency, but he stopped himself. "It's astounding."

"Keep trying," Prager said.

"It's even tougher now that they've moved into the new building. I hate to think that we probably paid for it." Fairfax emitted an odd sound—half moan, half laugh. "I mean not just the building, but the security system." Fairfax pressed his hands together as if he were praying.

Prager got up from his desk, holding the folder. "I'll let you know what tack we're taking with this, Henry. I'd better round up the Director in a hurry."

Fairfax recognized this as a dismissal. Disappointed that he was not to be included in the discussion with Director Crosby, he walked morosely toward the parking lot. He turned down the corridor that led to the front entrance, passing the framed photographs of the Directors. Twelve Directors, all of them smiling.

He passed the security check, walked over the compass rose set into the floor and proceeded to his car.

It was a different Counterintelligence now. Sisyphus had left him very little; he'd had to build the division up from scratch, or damn near scratch. At least, now it was not working at cross-purposes with the rest of the Agency, which Fairfax was convinced had been the case during the last decade of Sisyphus' tenure. The man had become paranoid, nearly certifiable according to some reports, obsessed with the notion that there were Soviet moles in high positions within the Agency. He saw a Russian behind every desk.

Fairfax drove out the gate and turned right on Dolley Madison Boulevard. The drive to his home in Vienna took him right by the new, sumptuous Mountain Security building. He didn't believe half the things he heard about Sisyphus—people seemed to enjoy embellishing the Sisyphus legend. As for the rumor that Sisyphus had siphoned off most of the funds from the Counterintelligence cache—he *was* inclined to believe that. Just looking at the new Mountain Security building tended to confirm his suspicions: where else would Sisyphus have come up with the money? Besides, the Senate testimony supported the notion. One thing Fairfax admired about Sisyphus was his conduct before the Senate Select Committee on Intelligence. He didn't lie in his testimony and he didn't "fail to recollect," as so many other Agency officials lamely did. He answered, but in such a way that he did not incriminate himself or the Agency. And when he would not answer, he sought refuge in the ballsy assertion that discussing certain matters would irrevocably compromise operations and agents. Fairfax fully intended to emulate Sisyphus if an investigating committee ever went after him.

It would be hard for him to claim he "couldn't recollect" something, since he had, and it was quite well known that he had, a photographic memory. It was a useful talent in intelligence work. It was not absolute, of course; sometimes, he couldn't remember what he was trying to recall. But that wouldn't be any problem with a committee. He *could* recall a nauseating number of times that committee members had said, "Let me refresh your memory."

He could recall absolutely Sisyphus' testimony about the Cache Division, pages 327-333 of the *Senate Select Committee on Government Operations with Respect to Intelligence Activities, Hearings and Final Report.* The Chairman, obviously primed, had set into Sisyphus.

CHAIRMAN: We would like to look into the so-called Cache Division.

CARLEY: That is what it is called, Mr. Chairman. That is not an alias.

CHAIRMAN: Would you care to explain what the Cache Division is, for the education of the members of the Committee unfamiliar with it.

CARLEY: I wouldn't *care* to explain anything to this Committee.

CHAIRMAN: Don't deliberately obstruct me over semantic niceties, Mr. Carley. Would you describe to this Committee the Cache Division of the Central Intelligence Agency and its function.

CARLEY: Certainly. The Central Intelligence Agency maintains a Cache Division, responsible for storing in every country in the world various items—gold, jewels, occasionally rare stamps and coins— items that do not leave "footprints." Items that are small and valuable in relation to their size, easily hidden, easily smuggled and impossible to trace. True to the designation "Cache," these items are often actually buried, in the ground. The cache is useful for crash operations, when funds are needed quickly and silently; when normal funding methods, for instance, through a proprietary, would either take too long or in some way compromise an operation.

CHAIRMAN: Thank you, Mr. Carley. Now, it is my understanding that there are in fact, or *were*, before your departure, two Cache Divisions at the CIA. Is that the case?

CARLEY: Yes.

CHAIRMAN: And one of the Cache Divisions was under your control? That is to say, Counterintelligence maintained a separate Cache Division?

CARLEY: That is true. Yes.

CHAIRMAN: Can you explain to the Committee why that was the case? It seems duplicatory.

CARLEY: Counterintelligence maintained a separate Russian desk, a separate Mideast desk, a separate Cache Division, a separate everything. Routine security measures, Mr. Chairman. The business of Counterintelligence, as anyone could deduce merely from the term, is not the same as the business of Intelligence.

CHAIRMAN: I am more interested here in the eventual fate of the Counterintelligence Cache Division.

CARLEY: It was, unwisely in my opinion, combined with the Agency Cache Division.

CHAIRMAN: How unwise could it have been, Mr. Carley, since the final accounting, which was, I remind you, conducted before you retired, showed that the Counterintelligence Cache had a value of less than two hundred thousand dollars?

CARLEY: I understand that the figure was in that financial neighborhood.

CHAIRMAN: Do you also understand that eight years ago, according to my records, there was a similar accounting, and that at that time the figure stood in excess of seven million dollars?

CARLEY: A much more exclusive neighborhood.

CHAIRMAN: What I am asking you, Mr. Carley, is what hap-

	pened to all that money.
CARLEY:	It was expended.
CHAIRMAN:	Mr. Carley, are you aware that there have been suggestions that you yourself have been systematically siphoning off the Counter-intelligence cache since the mid-nineteen sixties? How would you answer those allegations?
CARLEY:	I would say they are…"allegations."
CHAIRMAN:	You deny the allegations?
CARLEY:	Mr. Chairman, you have not put me in the position of needing to deny anything. Written records of Cache Division-funded operations are not kept. The funds were expended.

A pink Volkswagen van with a bumper sticker that read JEWS FOR JESUS nearly cut off Henry Fairfax as he tried to make the turn onto Orchard Drive. He had to loop around on Malcolm.

He was still irritated when he opened the front door and said, to no one in particular, "I'm home."

Claire called home from the KLM terminal at Kennedy.

"Claire, dear, how nice to hear your voice. What's up?" Forty years in the United States had done little to dim her mother's British accent, but odd idioms— "What's up?" "for sure," "No way, José"—now punctuated her mother's speech: souvenirs of Americanization.

"Well, Mother, I—"

"As a matter of fact, I was just going to ring you. Isn't that queer? I'd just put my hand on the telephone. Does

Jeff fancy goose, do you think? When you come for dinner on Tuesday, I thought—"

"Mother."

"I've invited Izzy Wentworth too. I *do* hope—"

"Mother."

She told her. The phrases stepped out, disciplined, like soldiers, to do their job. There were the predictable protestations of disbelief.

"I can't *believe* it. Not *Jeff*. I just can't believe it. I mean there's no way. Jeff is the last person on *earth…*"

Her mother, predictable again, begged her to come home. "Lick your wounds," as she put it. An alarming metaphor.

Odd as her parents were in some respects, they were traditional in their parent roles. And her room still waited, a Claire shrine. Full of the detritus of her adolescence, it had the ambiance of a museum. She had never understood it, why they left it like that. It was as if instead of growing up, going to college, getting married—the usual progression—she had disappeared. And they preserved her room out of some neurotic fear; to change it would mean they'd given up hope of her return.

Her flight was called, and she had to rush her goodbye. She felt she had robbed her mother of her maternal rights, the power to provide comfort.

"I wish you'd called before. You know, we might have helped." Forlorn.

"I'm sorry. I would have, but…" She promised to write.

Strapped into her seat in the KLM 747, she felt the wheels of the plane lift off the runway, herself lurch into the future. She watched gratefully as the streets of New York shrank into a grid. The plane nosed into clouds and New York disappeared. They punched through the clouds. Blue sky. This is it, she thought shakily. The fucking wild blue yonder. She fumbled out a cigarette.

"Pliss. May I?" said the gentleman in the aisle seat, offering his Bic lighter.

His name was Ram Krishnan; he was an importer on a buying trip. He had a smooth brown face, set off with squarish glasses tinted gray. He talked energetically about India, his importing business.

"The demand is growing all the time." He rubbed his gleeful hands together. "Have you ever been to India?"

"No, I haven't. Not yet."

He looked stricken. "But you must go. It is a wonderful place to travel."

The last time he had been there, he was just in time for Divali. This, he explained, was a festival that took place on the darkest night of the year, when all the dead souls are returning. So all India is blazing with light—oil lamps, candles, even electric lights—so that the dead souls can see their way back. He let out an exuberant giggle.

"We forget the energy crisis," he said, very much the modern man, "just for one night. Yes?" He clapped his hands together.

Mr. Krishnan talked while Claire drank two gins and tonic. He talked while they ate dinner. Dinner was peculiar; she couldn't seem to taste anything. It was like eating a photograph of the food. When the stewardess came to clear away the trays, she felt she couldn't listen to Mr. Krishnan any longer. He was so full of friendliness and goodwill, he was so vivacious, she felt dark and lifeless next to him. She excused herself and picked up her earphones.

"I think I'll just watch the movie for a while."

She felt a twinge of regret at his let-down look, but she was fighting an urge to burst into his monologue and tell him the story of her life. "I've just left my husband," she'd start. That wasn't even true: he'd left her. Distortions were already setting in.

The earphones pinched her ears, and voices kept fading in and out. The cowboys on the screen seemed incongruous galloping around in the jet. Despite its being "a new Western," the spunky leading lady was about to submit to the brutish seduction of the lead cowboy. Voices and gunshots buzzed in her ears. She couldn't pay attention. Her eyes strayed over to Mr. Krishnan. He was reading *Newsweek*.

A man walked up the aisle. The back of his head looked just like Jeff's. Tears burned unexpectedly in her eyes and she stifled a moan, pretending she was coughing. She pressed the call button for the stewardess and took off her earphones.

She turned to Mr. Krishnan. "Not a very good movie," she said.

"I thought not," said Mr. Krishnan. "As I recall, the review in *The New York Times* was not too favorable." He sighed as the stewardess turned off her call light and took Claire's order of a brandy.

"For you?" Claire offered.

"No." He smoothed out the air in front of him with his small hands. "It is not recommended that you drink too much on a transatlantic flight. The cabin air intensifies the hangover effect." She nodded, accepting his disapproval, but then he seesawed his hands in the air. "They may be wrong, of course," he said, giving her a dazzling smile.

She sipped brandy while he talked about Indira Gandhi, the U.S.-Russia-India triangle. She ordered a second brandy. He talked about festivals, food, his children, his plane connections, his "mee-graine" headaches. He glanced at his watch. Regretfully, he took off his glasses and folded them into a case, which he put into his brief-case. He took off his shoes and extracted from his brief-case a plastic bag containing some powder-blue stretch slippers printed with the words British Airways. He put those on and folded the plastic bag and its twist tie into a tiny square, which he placed in his breast pocket. "I must get some sleep, or tomorrow...you know, the jet lag..." His eyes looked large and defenseless. He lowered his seat and was asleep within two minutes.

She tried to do the same, but of course, she couldn't. She sat in the seat rigid, as if the tensile strength of her body could lock out thought. She was afraid that pain would take her by surprise; she'd start crying and never stop until she was sucked dry, a husk. She wanted to nudge Mr. Krishnan awake. She wanted the plane to crash. She thought of it breaking apart, the tearing metal-lic shriek as the wings twisted off from the fuselage, the plane somersaulting, exploding, a fireball diving into the sea. *Jeff would be sorry.* Her body gave a violent twitch.

Thinking like a two-year-old. She stepped over Mr. Krishnan and walked up the aisle to the lavatory. Just then the plane lurched, very slightly, and she caught her breath. She'd never quite given up the belief that her thoughts had actual power.

Everywhere people were slumped in the innocence of sleep; their soft, unguarded faces compounded her guilt. A few sat in their cones of light, reading. Getting on with their lives. She thought: I have to invent a new one.

She stayed in the cramped lavatory a long time, washing her face, combing her hair. She lifted up her hair and splashed some of KLM's free cologne on the back of her neck. She felt weak and hopeless, the emptiness shot through with threads of panic. She pushed against the door. There was an unexpected resistance, as if someone were pushing from the other side, or a ferocious wind were blowing against it. Am I doing something wrong here? she thought Her body seemed connected to her mind only by some loose and clumsy bond. To get it to respond to orders, you had to remind it, nudge it, give it a kick. Then she had the irrational fear that if she did get the door open, she'd step out into empty space and plunge down into the ocean like a stone. Finally, she realized she'd forgotten to undo the latch. She stumbled back to her seat. She read *The New York Times.* She hadn't looked at a newspaper since the day Jeff left. The front page was devoted to the abortive attempt to rescue the hostages in Teheran. Charred helicopters, dead Marines, failure.

Then she read the airline magazine, *Holland Herald,* from cover to cover. It was full of pictures of Queen Juliana, to abdicate April 30, and of the Queen-to-be Beatrix and her intensely healthy sons.

She read her guidebooks, planning her assault on the highlights of Amsterdam. And after Amsterdam? Then...maybe Vienna. Florence. Athens. She could keep on like this for a long time.

CHAPTER FIVE

ALAN DAWSON SAT IN HIS COMFORTABLE SEAT in the first-class section of the KLM 747. He was still dozing, despite the fact that his seat had been punched into the "upright position" of stewardess lingo. When the wheels touched down on the runway of Schiphol Airport—a thump of contact that set Claire, thirty yards away, to searching the seat pockets for things she might have missed in her previous scan—he scarcely moved. His eyelids fluttered slightly as he registered their arrival. Halfway between sleep and waking, he continued his reverie, part dream, part plan for the day ahead.

He was an energetic man, a man who hated to wait. But long ago, he had learned that waiting was a state of mind. If you are always occupied, there is no waiting. He didn't have time to wait. He didn't have time to hurry, as people were hurrying now, clogging the aisles long before the doors were even opened.

He was content to be among the last to leave the

plane, although it sometimes irritated people (his wife, Barbara, for instance) who were coming to meet him. A car would be meeting him here. Possibly it would be on the tarmac, a few steps from the plane, but such arrangements occasionally went astray, especially when one took a commercial flight. He was never surprised when arrangements broke down. He had often said something of the sort to his sons: I am never surprised, only disappointed. He was not oblivious to their barely suppressed smirks, the looks of disdain they flashed back and forth. They were unimpressed by his position, his power. They were openly scornful of the whole federal operation, seeing it as a monolith of corruption. "All politicians are crooks," his oldest son, Andy, now seventeen, had said on a number of occasions. Then with the magnanimity of youth, he would attempt to ally Dawson to his position. "You ought to know that, Dad, better than anyone."

That his sons should prefer this romantic view did not surprise him. The simplicity of blaming corruption, or evil in some form, was too much even for most adults to resist. It was certainly more comforting than his own bleak vision of a government being destroyed from within not by corrupt power brokers, but by cumbersome bureaucratic procedures. He viewed these as a kind of lethal dry rot behind the federal walls, undermining the very essence of government—its ability to make decisions and act on them. All that he saw now was a kind of senseless positional milling. He was reluctantly coming to share Sisyphus' view that regulatory procedures, choking the government, were forcing more and more action into the clandestine sphere. Of course, the intelligence services were not themselves immune, and they had suffered from an influx of regulation following Watergate.

He opened his eyes, sensing that the line was beginning to move. He glanced at his watch (already set ahead to Amsterdam time) and began to tie his shoes. He felt no superiority to the people edging forward, people who had now been standing in line for fifteen minutes or so. He envied them, a little, their eagerness, their restless anticipation. But for the past few years, he'd never been able to get enough sleep. Quite simply, his schedule could not be arranged to provide six hours of sleep. He saw fatigue as an enemy that must be outwitted—or more correctly, a trap that must be avoided, a kind of mental quicksand. He had seen more than one negotiation lost due to simple weariness. Fatigue sapped the will. Being a disciplined man, he had taught himself to rest, conserving energy whenever possible.

He put on his glasses, then rearranged his briefcase so that the new talking paper on Zimbabwe was ready to hand. Possibly he would be able to finish reading it in the car en route to the Amstel Hotel; probably the Africa trip would be shelved.

As Sisyphus had predicted, he'd left behind a State Department in chaos. Vance's resignation would be made public any minute, compounding the hysteria over the messy failed rescue attempt in Iran. Charred helicopter parts were strewn all over the front pages. He pressed his lips together and narrowed his eyes—his characteristic look of dismay.

The steward tapped his shoulder. "Mr. Dawson, your car is waiting."

As the Mercedes limousine nosed onto the P-3 toward Amsterdam, Dawson gazed without enthusiasm at the bruised sky and the dull rain-washed landscape. He allowed himself a sigh. Following his encounter with Sisyphus, he'd found himself in a black, lethargic mood. Some bitterness had surfaced; his normal cynicism had escalated into something closer to despair.

He was indifferent to the fervent guessing game he'd left behind: Who will be the next Secretary of State? It barely mattered, in his view, now that State had become an almost passive organism, responding to crises with all the forethought of an allergic child reacting to irritants. State no longer, in his opinion, formulated foreign policy.

Circle Group, and other like entities, did. At the last Steering Committee meeting, the subject had been their plan for the full Circle Group meeting in June. That would be the most substantial meeting in a very long time. For once, they had taken on a hard job, international currency reform, and the prospects for some genuine progress in June were good.

Perhaps, just this time, Sisyphus' intelligence was incorrect. It seemed scarcely credible that Firelli would stand before them and propose assassination.

The limousine braked sharply, and Dawson looked out the window. They were now in the immediate outskirts of Amsterdam, joining a thickening stream of traffic.

He had duly gone through the distasteful charade of calling John Stenner's in-laws—former in-laws, he supposed—to get a telephone number he had already memorized. A half-successful charade, at that. He'd been grateful at the time that he hadn't needed to take the deception straight to his friends Toby and Stella. Their daughter, Marlena, Stenner's ex-wife, had answered the phone. She seemed grateful for the chance to pass along a message. "I don't have his number, but I can give you his address. We prefer to communicate in writing, you know. Emphasize just how fine I am, won't you, Alan? Thriving, you might put it." She'd ended the conversation with a significant chuckle.

The hotel was surrounded by barricades, manned by policemen in white leather jackets. The driver spoke to one policeman. He and Dawson watched as the orange-

and-white pole slid aside, not without a good deal of shoving and guidance, into the slots of its metal stand.

"I would think it would be easier to move the whole barricade," Dawson said to the driver.

"I agree with you, sir, but of course it would never do to have our elite police manhandling barricades. Maybe they'll have it all mastered by the time the Prince arrives."

"The Prince?"

"Oh, you'll be in good company here, sir. Prince Charles, you know. Coming to watch our Beatrix get crowned."

"Are they expecting trouble?"

"Of course," the driver said cheerfully. "In Amsterdam, there's always trouble." He whistled as he came around and opened the door.

Amsterdam had been selected as the site for the meeting (which had hurriedly been scheduled less than a week ago) supposedly because so many Steering Committee members had commitments to attend Beatrix' investiture. Dawson suspected another reason: the security apparatus was already in place. Prince Charles might actually require less security preparation than Firelli, who never made a move without his bodyguards, his highly trained drivers, his retinue of protectors. Kidnapping was the popular mode of terrorism in Italy, just as it was in South America—ransoms were bankrolling the "revolution."

Dawson followed his suitcase as it proceeded from the driver to the doorman to the bellhop. It was an old leather suitcase with two parallel strips of bright yellow tape on each side, to make it more readily indentifiable at baggage claims. The bellhop cast it a disdainful glance as he waited for Dawson to collect his messages at the reception desk. Later, in Dawson's room, the boy stood at military attention as he accepted a few guilders.

"Enjoy your stay, *sir*."

A bowl of fruit and a half-bottle of champagne shared a small glass-topped table with a bouquet of orange freesias. Dawson glanced at the flowers as he went to the window to check for emergency exits. Having established the best route out in case of fire, he looked at the river. An old barge heaped with refuse floated slowly along. A man in a purple shirt stood on the side, peering at the water. Now and then he plucked out debris with a long pole.

Dawson looked for the attaché case and found it inside the wardrobe. Seeing it there, black and gleaming, caused an almost physical shudder of revulsion. He wasn't quite sure why. He thought about it as he poured a glass of champagne. Certainly, he had performed riskier assignments. Certainly, if there was a chance this would help keep Iran from the Soviet grasp, he was happy to do his part. Just as certainly, his conversation with Sisyphus had somehow pierced the tangled network of responsibilities that was his career and made it seem flimsy, a charade, a shadow play of distraction.

He checked his watch. About an hour and a half until the meeting. He rotated his head several times, trying to dispel the stiffness in his neck and shoulders. He could take a short nap and still have plenty of time to wash up, shave, change his shirt. He called Room Service and arranged for coffee to be sent up at eleven thirty, set the alarm button on his watch and lay down on the bed.

Claire was slowly edging forward in the passport-control line, listening in a dazed way to Mr. Krishnan's opinions of Jimmy Carter.

"I think he is good-hearted, but this is not enough."

A short woman, her wiry gray hair imprisoned in a hair net, sidled up on Claire's left. She had a pugnacious, forward-jutting face, like a bulldog's, and kept her eyes averted as she set down her plastic shopping bag. This was stuffed with *Archie* and *Veronica* comics and also held one tennis racquet. In her other hand she held a passport, bright orange. She must be Dutch, Claire thought. House of Orange.

"This man Zia, in Pakistan," said Mr. Krishnan earnestly—"he cannot be trusted; you know this." He set his briefcase down, to free his hands. He had energy to spare and used it to send his hands whistling through the air, shaping arabesques of emphasis. He spoke with great intensity, as if she were the personal confidante of Zbigniew Brzezinski.

"I'm sure you're right," she said. Her voice had the fervent quality Mr. Krishnan seemed to require.

The man directly in front of her wore hound's-tooth-checked pants, and she caught herself staring at the fabric until her eyes began to twitch. This man held a magazine curled in one hand, and it weaved in and out of sight as he stabbed it in the air to punctuate his conversation. When it came to rest on his hip, she managed to see the cover: a cowboy on a rearing horse and the words TERROR OF THE TERRITORIAL OUTLAWS.

The gray-haired woman moved on, easily outflanking a dozen people. She came to rest again next to a bald man wearing a safari jacket.

"It's not fair," Claire thought, and then realized she'd spoken out loud.

"Of course not," said Mr. Krishnan. "The man's a pompous fool, that's all."

As she got closer to the Dutch official, seated at a

high platform, she began to worry that something would go wrong. He would pluck her passport from her eager hand, scrutinize it and detect some irregularity: "This passport is a forgery; this passport has expired; this passport bears the code number reserved for those known to be unstable; please take this woman to the Inquiry Room." She knew this anxiety was ridiculous, but she couldn't dispel it. A momentary mental trick caused her to lean to the left—she expected to find the reassuring presence of Jeff's body. She stumbled sideways into thin air.

Mr. Krishnan caught her elbow. "Are you all right?"

"Yes."

"You're very tired. You must rest straightaway you get to your hotel."

"Yes. Yes, I will."

She stiffened her body against any more unconscious leaning and was bumped sharply from behind. She turned to see a Hasidic Jew, apple cheeks, a cherubic face. He beamed at her, and she attempted a return smile.

A square red memento in her passport: 28 Apr 1980 Schiphol. In. She and Mr. Krishnan said goodbye to each other at the motorized walkway in the regretful way of people unlikely to see each other again. He walked. All the people in a hurry were walking, easily outpacing those on the walkway, who hummed along at a leisurely rate. They were carried past a long row of posters. Peter Stuyvesant. Lee Cooper Jeans. Het Parool. Claire tripped when she stepped off.

At the baggage-claim area, she watched, mesmerized, as the suitcases emerged through a shield of blue plastic strips and thumped, one by one, onto the conveyor belt. A group of tall, blond young men, dressed in matching blue blazers, waited near her, talking in a language she didn't recognize. She was trying to figure out what sort of group they could be when they lunged toward the conveyor belt and came away with one suitcase and one bowling bag each.

"Are you *bowlers?*" asked a man nearby.

One of them nodded seriously. "Yes. We are the Finnish National Bowling Team."

She leaned against a concrete pillar outside, waiting for the KLM bus. She wanted the Number 2 bus, they'd informed her at the desk. It would take her to the Hilton, right next to the Dikker and Thys, they'd assured her.

She was amazed that there was a Finnish National Bowling Team. Who would have thought that the Finns bowled? Who would have thought that grown men in hound's-tooth pants would read *Terror of the Territorial Outlaws?* These tiny observations made her feel infinitely lonely. They were exactly the sort of things Jeff would find amusing—moments lit with a shared burst of recognition. Alone, she felt like a paid observer.

The sky was dull gray, cement. It was surprisingly cold, and she buttoned her trench coat at the top. The blue KLM bus arrived. She had some trouble on the steps of the bus, trying to get the little packet of guilders out of her purse while balancing her small suitcase. She half-turned to get Jeff to help her.

God, my mind is booby-trapped, she thought. She finally paid her fare and then shrank down into her seat. It's probably perfectly normal to have these mental lapses. Like people do when they have a leg amputated. They still feel like it's there, a ghost leg. A ghost Jeff. She shut her eyes.

Perfectly normal. One of her mother's phrases. "It's perfectly normal for you to be confused at your age, my dear. Everyone is." Normal was not ordinary enough for her mother. *Perfectly normal.* "It's perfectly normal for you to...have pimples, wish you were Theodore Roosevelt, wish you were dead." Case dismissed. Statistical normality. Claire had never figured out whether this had been intended to soothe her or her mother. *Perfectly normal for you to be* (here her own interior voice took over from her mother's) *out of your fucking mind.*

She opened her eyes. They were passing a long brick apartment building. Every window had white curtains, all different sorts, mostly different patterns of lace. Except one. Except one born iconoclast with bamboo shades. Rugged individualist flaunts convention on curtain front. "Er, Mr. N. When did you first think white curtains might not be for you?" "Actually, Tom, when I was two or three years old, I went on holiday to..."

She walked, lugging her suitcases, the half-block from the Amsterdam Hilton to the Dikker and Thys. She produced her room voucher and passport and was escorted with bored efficiency to her room. When the door closed, she felt weak with disappointment. Her room was a frighteningly accurate replica of a room in a second-rate Holiday Inn. The view from her large expanse of windows revealed a pebbly spread of gray roof that perfectly matched the sky. She lay numbly down on the bed, resting upon a thin pumpkin-colored spread. God, she might as well have gone to White Plains.

She woke up, several hours later, still wearing her coat, her purse wedged under her head. The room had not improved with time, and she decided to go out, look for another hotel, not be immobilized by...fate, or whatever.

She went into the bathroom to wash her face, and it confronted her from the mirror, disheveled, tired. A zipper-shaped imprint on her cheek. She would order some coffee, then take a bath. She made a mental list of exactly what to do. 1. Call for coffee. 2. Turn on bathwater. 3. Hang up trench coat in bathroom. Her head hummed with structure. These lists were barriers against chaos.

Now and then, during her bath, tears rolled down her cheeks, as if her eyes were an overflow mechanism. She barely noticed it. 18. Ask at the desk where to get a tram. 19. Get a map. 20. Have lunch.

CHAPTER SIX

WHEN DAWSON ENTERED the conference room, he felt a grinding rush of fear. The attaché case seemed stuck to his hand in the unpleasant way metal sticks to damp flesh in freezing weather.

There were a dozen men in the room, greeting each other. The sound produced by these greetings, and the shuffling of chairs as the men began to sit down around the oval conference table, was qualitatively different from the normal hubbub such activities would cause. Security at Circle Group meetings was always tight, but this odd atmosphere indicated a quantum leap.

Dawson nodded uneasily to Bruno Schellenberg, who looked as pale and unsettled as he himself felt. It *was* unsettling to be in an anechoic chamber, and amazingly enough, this conference room in the Amstel Hotel had become exactly that. Surely the Amstel Hotel did not maintain an anechoic chamber as part of its facilities. Dawson was astounded that Firelli had been able to arrange such an elaborate security precaution in such a short time.

The technique had been explained to Dawson the first time he had been in such a room—at CIA headquarters in Langley. A series of baffles were set up to protect a room from any external eavesdropping—to thwart even laser devices, which could read voice vibrations from the windowpanes and walls. But the baffles also had the effect of truncating all the sounds in the room. There were no echoes—every sound stopped dead; nothing carried. The room seemed stuffed with invisible cotton, and despite the fact that you could see and hear perfectly well, there was a sealed-off feeling, an acute sense of isolation.

The surge of fear Dawson felt on entering the room was propelled by this thought: If they've gone this far they might sweep the room, they might conduct a physical search. But no, he was one of them. As he sat down, he was once again composed. He set the attaché case at his feet. Its dull black gleam copied that of his shoes. He imagined the tiny gears clicking on, the tape slowly spooling, and felt the warm brush of relief that comes with commitment. He really had no choice—he could hardly excuse himself and return without the case. There was no point in worrying now.

Firelli stood up and called them to attention merely by saying "Gentlemen" twice. When he spoke, it was as if his voice were piped directly into Dawson's mind, without first having to go through the air and into his ear.

"First I must apologize for the havoc I have wreaked on your schedules." He offered a brilliant smile. We're all good smilers here, thought Dawson. World-class businessmen, like politicians and diplomats, need world-class smiles. "This is only the second red-flag meeting of the Steering Committee that has been called in nearly ten years." He paused. Now that his smile had faded, Dawson could see how haggard Firelli looked—the bruised skin under his eyes, the pinch of tension around his mouth.

Dawson remembered the previous red-flag meeting. It was during his first year on the Steering Committee—he'd been Ambassador to Poland at the time. The NATO computers had been funneling defense plans and codes directly into a Czech computer and, even worse, were in the process of being reprogrammed to override their instructions, when the penetration was discovered. Cooperation among the various NATO intelligence services had been, at that time, very poor. Moles in the British system and a leak-ridden French SDECE made for a ticklish problem. CIA and NATO intelligence had turned to Circle Group. And they had been successful—directly approaching the executives of the involved countries and getting them to sit on their defense-response systems for a few hair-raising days. They'd even been able to salvage a counterintelligence operation of their own out of the mess. The sidestepped Czech computer was left operative, feeding out false data that the Russians had every reason to believe was pure gold.

"This time too," Firelli continued, "some action will be required of us." He stopped and ran a hand through his silver hair. "No, it is not correct to say that. A decision will be required." He sighed. "Ten days ago, I was approached by an emissary from—what shall I call her—the exiled Shabbanou of Iran, Farah. She is a personal friend of mine. How she knew that I was this year's Steering Committee Chairman I do not know. It was in my capacity as such that I was approached. Of course I checked, and there is no possibility of the emissary's being a plant. He reported to me some alarming intelligence."

Several men, Dawson included, shifted in their chairs, as if bracing themselves.

"It concerns the Shah, of course. The source reports that he has become increasingly bitter, and in his bitterness and ill health he has fallen under the influence of a mullah who is very very close to persuading the King of Kings to become a true martyr in the Shiite sense—return to Teheran, confess his sins, denounce the 'West,' go on trial and unite the Persian state once again by the gesture of his death."

A ruffle of unease radiated out from Firelli: Exactly, thought Dawson, as if we are a pack of cards being shuffled. Karl-Heinz Schröder, the German banker, began to choke on a sip of water and got an irritated glare from Firelli as he stood up and attempted to gain control of himself. In the strange environment of the room, his coughing sounded curiously faked, as if he were a child imitating an adult's cough. He sat down, his face red and bleary, and emitted a few more staccato noises.

"But that's absurd," offered Atkins, of Petrexco. "Even if he were crazy enough to do that—and I don't doubt your source—I have it on my own that the man is definitely dying—he is not really *free* to do what he wants in Cairo. He's more or less under house arrest."

"You trust Cairo?" asked Liddell of the CIA. "The evidence suggests that would be foolish at this time."

Liddell's eyes widened perceptibly as Dawson offered Sisyphus' tidbit: "I think you must be right. I have it on good authority that the Libyans and Palestinians have called off their assassination teams. So Cairo must be making deals." Liddell clearly hadn't known.

After the lunch break, Dawson sat with his glasses off, massaging his eyelids. Discussion still sputtered around him, but he was no longer interested in what anyone had to say. Across-the-board reaction to the notion of the Shah's subjecting himself to any kind of trial had been horror. All of Sisyphus' points had been touched on. Banks and large corporations, all with a great deal to keep hidden, would necessarily also go on trial. For the banks, it would make things extremely touchy for their relationships with Arab depositors, current lifeline of the banking industry. The corporations would have problems with Third World countries in the region, not to mention putting at risk large numbers of personnel and equipment from half-completed projects. Nationalization had struck before—everyone remembered Libya. There was sufficient fragility to the banking system that just the loss of the Shah's own holdings would cause real havoc.

As the discussion wore on, the Shah lost his human aspect and was reduced to a kind of splinter, an irritant to the Mideast, a pivot of instability. Finally, Firelli had come out with it, bald-faced: the Steering Committee of Circle Group should arrange the assassination of the Shah.

Liddell, while he didn't object to the plan, complained that it would probably be blamed on the CIA, no matter how good the Agency's deniability. Several men rejoined that that might not be such a bad thing: restore the faith, as it were. Besides, the United States might well benefit the most. Its corporations were particularly entangled with the Shah. And it would be spared any further humiliating dealings with him. The cold shoulder of pragmatism, it was pointed out, looks like cowardice in a superpower. Unseemly. And of course, the hostages would become moot.

Dawson had argued as vociferously as he dared against the "barbaric" plan, invoking a morality that seemed almost quaint in the cold, practical room. It came down to cost benefit. All of them had certainly risked more for less. Were a few disease-ridden months of a man's life worth the terrible chaos his trial could cause? War in the Middle East? The cut-off of oil to the West? Suppose the Shah decided to reveal to the Saudis just why their deliveries of jet fighters and military hardware had been subject to those years of delay?

All Dawson got to support his side was Karl-Heinz Schröder's "I don't like it." And Schellenberg's frown, followed by "True enough, we set ourselves up here as managers of history. This we have always done, and always it has required distasteful decisions."

Dawson didn't agree with his own argument, so it was difficult to be persuasive. He, along with two others, made the puerile gesture of abstaining when the vote was taken. Otherwise, it was unanimous. The meeting was adjourned until the next day at nine, when they would take up the more practical aspects of planning and funding.

Dawson was buttonholed, as the meeting broke up, by Schellenberg and Van Dorn. LeClerc joined them in Van Dorn's suite.

"Klaus," Dawson said, accepting a bourbon, "you must have the best room in the house." He looked out at a magnificent view of the Hogensluis and the Magere Brug. Lit up for the night, the bridges had perfect, glimmering reflections in the calm water of the Amstel.

"I think Prince Charles does, actually." They laughed. He held up his glass. "Here's to being out of that nasty room."

"I'll drink to that," said Schellenberg "I felt half-dead in there."

Dawson spent the next half-hour in a halfhearted attempt to soothe their anger—or more correctly, their respective countries' anger—over the surprise rescue bid in Iran.

"Well, if what you say is true," mused LeClerc, "it's not just that the right hand doesn't know what the left hand is doing. They know, all right; they're just not attached to the same damn body."

"Fair enough. Of course, you fellows took a long-enough time to agree to those sanctions in the first place."

"Ummmmm."

"Nasty damn business."

"Carter's got a vicious streak, yes?"

"Petty. Behind-the-back like that. I mean with Vance."

"Now, if he were ruthless, that's one thing..."

The Europeans' low opinion of Jimmy Carter always surprised Dawson. They generally considered him the worst U.S. President ever to be elected.

"Who'll be the next Secretary of State?"

Dawson shrugged. "Richard Nixon, for all I know."

"I daresay most of Europe would approve."

"Seriously, I don't have any idea," Dawson said. "Could be anyone. Carter seems to prefer the 'new broom' approach to Cabinet appointments, so it probably won't be anyone from the ranks, anyone we expect."

There was a collective sigh. Van Dorn looked at his watch. "I've got to be off to a pre-investiture gala. Doesn't come up often, you know; we have to make the most of it. Our Dutch monarchs are extraordinary for their longevity." He ushered them to the door. "See you tomorrow, gentlemen," he said without enthusiasm.

While Alan Dawson tried unsuccessfully to reach John Stenner on the phone, Claire stood in a crowded

Number 12 tram, hurtling along Vijzelstraat toward Dam Square. She meant to be studying the map, supplied to her by the desk clerk, who had helpfully drawn a small asterisk in blue ball-point to mark the site of the hotel. Instead she stared at the small yellow tram ticket. DAGKAART. AMSTERDAM. She'd bought an all-day ticket. *Dag.* That must be day, and *kaart* must be ticket. *Am*sterdam. Here they said Amster*dam*. More like Ahmster*dam*. A childhood ditty rang irritatingly in her head, practicing this new pronunciation.

> *We all went down to Ahmsterdam*
> *We all went down to Ahmsterdam*
> *Ahmster, Ahmster*
> *Dam Dam Dam*
> *Ahmster Ahmster*
> *Dam Dam Dam*
> *You must not say that naughty word*

This ditty was tenacious and would not be dislodged even when she risked humming "The Star-Spangled Banner"—not out loud, of course.

A new voice intruded in her head—a woman's breathy, sexy sigh. "Jeffffffffff."

And the rockets' red glare…

"Oh, Jeffff, yes…"

An almost pornographic vision—Jeff making love to the woman with this voice. Their limbs were all tangled up; the woman's face was hidden. Jeff moved his head lovingly from one breast to the other. The woman's head was arched back; a glimpse of a long sinewy neck. "Oh, God, oh, God." The woman's head thrashed from side to side. They began to thud together with urgency.

> ...*say does tha-at star-span-gled bah-ah-ner-er yeh-et way-ave*

"Ahhhhhh, Jeff, Jefffffff," moaned the woman, her face still obscured by Jeff's head.

"*Rokin,*" said the electronically amplified voice from the front of the tram. Claire stumbled out. The tram ticket was crumpled in her sweaty palm to the size of a marble. She flattened it out.

She found the VVV, the tourist office, without much trouble, but it was incredibly crowded. She barely managed to wedge herself inside. She looked at the long lines—backpackers, leather-dressed punks with drastic haircuts, worried-looking elderly tourists edging forward in a kind of slow-motion stampede. She couldn't face it and contented herself with selecting some leaflets from an array on the counter. She walked down the Rokin, hopefully toward Dam Square. Dam Square was the center of all her guidebook maps, the canals arching around it in concentric semicircles.

She leaned against a stone lion and surveyed the chaos. The square appeared to be under construction. Barricades were strewn everywhere, blocking off some of the streets. Workmen labored behind one row, hammering together a viewing stand, unrolling sod directly onto the pavement, maneuvering large orange azaleas into stone tubs. The streets were unkempt; drifts of litter cluttered the curbs. Flocks of dingy pigeons loitered near an ice cream cart—IJS, it said; GELATI—flying a few halfhearted feet when the proprietor shooed them away.

The building behind all this she recognized as the Royal Palace, the National Palace. A triangular frieze seethed with unicorns, tritons, fish, faces. Jeff's face appeared momentarily in the middle of this swirling mass: blind marble eyes, a taunting grin. She shook her head and marched off toward one of the department stores flanking the palace, angry with herself.

Peek and Cloppenburg was a large department store in the process of being decorated with huge orange and red-white-and-blue banners. Some were already in place, fixed at the top with golden crowns and extending vertically to the first-floor balcony, where they were attached with huge golden Bs. She was thinking she might go in and look around when she spotted the Hotel Krasnapolsky and changed direction. She might as well check and see if she could get a room there. Most of the windows she passed held coronation displays—arrangements of orange flowers, photographs of Juliana and Beatrix. Sepia-toned baby Beatrixes and a youthful, skiing Juliana, poised on a slope. Banners saying ORANGE BOVEN, LEVE DE KONINGEN. Claire had figured out that *Leve de Koningen* meant "Long live the Queen," but *Orange Boven* remained a mystery. Something to do with the House of Orange. William the Conqueror? Or was that England? She passed Air France, where a man stood on a ladder attaching huge rosettes of red, white and blue carnations above the windows. She did not walk under the ladder.

She passed a souvenir shop full of blue-and-white Delftware, wooden shoes, a whole rack of coronation specials—buttons with Juliana's face, buttons with Beatrix' face, buttons with both their faces, orange T-shirts, orange-and-white ballpoint pens.

The Hotel Krasnapolsky (orange awnings) also seemed to be under construction, the approach to the door consisting of a plywood ramp. An unexpected shyness seized her at the desk. Jeff always did this sort of thing—asking in hotels, restaurants, antique shops, while she stood aside, mute, like an extra suitcase or a—

"Can I help you?" the desk clerk repeated.

"Do you, do you—I mean I'm looking for a room." He smiled regretfully and spread his hands wide. "So sorry. We are complete until May third."

One down, she thought, sitting outside in the center of the square, on one of the broad circular steps that surrounded a marble obelisk. She crossed out KRASNAPOLSKY on the yellow leaflet and took out a cigarette. A man in a dark brown suit lunged toward her to offer a light.

"Thank you."

"Are you on holiday?" he asked. British accent.

It struck her that "on holiday" was a much pleasanter phrase than "on vacation."

"Yes, I'm on vacation." More correct, in my case, she thought. Vacated.

"Would you—" the man began, and then they both turned their heads toward the palace. An incredible racket had started up, and a huge blue helicopter with two rotors loomed into sight, hovering just above the roof of the church next to the palace. The noise was incredible: the whole square seemed to pulse with it, like a gigantic heart. She wondered if it were for security reasons or could it be some kind of tourist trip. No. She couldn't imagine the people of Amsterdam regularly putting up with that. The noise seemed to penetrate to the very center of her head, a stimulus that immobilized her like a deer in the headlights of a car. She had the impulse to lie flat on the ground, as if the helicopter might begin strafing the crowd. Her hands were pressed against her ears; it seemed intolerable that the helicopter didn't go away. She got up and began to walk. The man who had lit her cigarette tugged at her sleeve. His grasp seemed somehow predatory; she broke away from him and began to run. She had trouble crossing the street; she couldn't seem to discern the traffic pattern. Two bicyclists had to swerve to avoid her, and a pale blue Mercedes slammed on its brakes. An angry-looking man blasted his horn at her. The blare of the horn had no impact—a frail whine lost in the deafening thud of the helicopter—but the driver's face was red, contorted, and she could see him slam his hand down repeatedly on the steering column. She made it across the street and began to run, stumbling on the uneven cobblestones.

CHAPTER SEVEN

JOHN STENNER HAD NO PROBLEM, from his vantage point in the helicopter, discerning traffic patterns. In fact, the whole range of activity in the square seemed purposeful, almost tidy from this aerial perspective. Cars and bicycles swam around curves in schools. Even the milling crowds had an orderly look from up here, migrating from corner to corner. A great circular swarm of people rotated around the nucleus of the National Monument like the electrons of a complicated atom.

That morning, Stenner had gone to Police Headquarters with his friend Frits Zonneveld to pick up his press credentials for the investiture on April 30. Somehow Frits, who worked for the Dutch daily *Het Parool,* had wangled them both seats on the helicopter, called in some favor from Okker, the security chief. The press card, a large laminated orange rectangle bearing the letters PRS and a surly Polaroid image of himself, now rested approximately over Stenner's heart, dangling from its metal chain.

A clutch of security men, including some out-of-town talent imported for the occasion, hunched over Okker now, obediently turning their eyes in the directions he indicated with his stabbing index finger. Some of the out-of-town talent—half of a four-man contingent of crowd-control specialists from the U.S. Park Service—had been hastily recalled to Washington when the hostage-rescue attempt failed so miserably. Even now, Stenner supposed, Iranian "students" were massing to confront the "Let's Nuke Khomeini" bunch on the Ellipse.

Okker was holding a large, crumpled aerial photograph of the square. Red crosses were liberally sprinkled across it, marking the specific rooftop locations where security men would be stationed. Peter Dils, one of the remaining Park Service men, saw the Post Office building as a possible staging area, but Okker was reluctant to draw off anyone from the buildings immediately surrounding the square—he stabbed the map, pointing in rapid succession to the Nieuwe Kerk, the palace, the Krasnapolsky, de Bijenkorf and Peek and Cloppenburg. Okker spoke to one of his aides, who went forward to have a word with the pilot. The helicopter lifted above the Nieuwe Kerk and hovered for a while over the Post Office building. The four black openwork spires took on a menacing aspect, as if even now assassins were holed up in them, living off their stocks of canned food.

Dils and Okker came to an agreement: that one of the six roving helicopters—small ones, not like this monster—scheduled for duty on April 30, plus a couple of strategically placed men (two more red crosses bloomed on the map) could handle the "Post Office threat." Someone pointed out that the chopper would have to retreat, at least briefly, during Juliana's abdication speech and Beatrix' investiture address, or else they would be inaudible. Okker made a note. One of the Dutch contingent asked if Moses en Aaron Straat would be blockaded, and that prompted Okker to extract another map, showing the plan, carefully worked out several weeks ago (but still subject to revision) to maximize pedestrian control. At the same time, the scenario provided plenty of "emergency exits" in case there was trouble. The last thing you wanted, Okker announced, was to create fatal culs-de-sac for panicked stampedes of good Dutch citizens. The helicopter began a slow turn around the perimeter of the square and they peered out the windows, studying the small streets feeding into the Dam with the fierce concentration of a pack of mentalists trying to force a vision of the future. Okker drew three tiny stick horses on the corner of St. Nicolaas Straat and the Nieuwen Dijk.

Earlier, back at headquarters, Stenner had briefly interviewed some of Okker's staff. They were busily coordinating the order-keeping forces—regular police, special mobile police, Red Cross volunteers and so on. The entire heart of Amsterdam would be closed to motorized traffic; tow trucks were massing in the Stadionplein to remove parked cars from all the major streets—a process that would begin tomorrow afternoon at four o'clock. Car-bomb specialists and an adviser brought in from Northern Ireland were standing by with disposal units.

It was not unlike the preparations for, say, Inauguration Day in Washington. In this case, however, Okker and his troops did not have the luxury of feeling that everything might go well.

Beatrix was not popular, but that would not cause the trouble. All week, Stenner had been hearing Beatrix anecdotes. Amsterdammers had celebrated her marriage to the German Claus von Amsberg in 1966 by covering the city with orange swastikas (Claus had been a member of

Hitler Youth), throwing smoke and stink bombs at the wedding procession and hurling dead chickens at the gilded nuptial coach. The police had, in return, clubbed hordes of innocent bystanders into submission—an overzealous performance that eventually cost the Burgomaster of Amsterdam and the Chief of Police their jobs. Okker was no doubt mindful of that. Since then, Beatrix had improved her position immeasurably by bearing four sons. The oldest, Willem-Alexander, was the first male heir to the Dutch throne since the nineteenth century.

The helicopter drifted slowly up the Rokin toward the Munt Tower. Okker pointed out the various routes the mobile police would use to converge on the square if they were needed. He drew a red circle around the intersection of the Rokin and Spui Straat. "They'll make a stand here, if necessary."

Stenner glanced at his watch. Three thirty. He was supposed to meet the *Life* photographer at five in the de l'Europe.

Frits stood up and tapped Okker on the shoulder. "Let's go have a look at Waterlooplein, shall we?"

Okker offered a weak smile. "Ah, yes, let's not forget Waterlooplein. The terrible thing," he continued, in a voice distorted by official sanctity, "gentlemen of the press, is that while these damn *kraakers* and punks and anarchists are having their spot of fun, people really do get hurt." Frits scribbled away in his notebook as the helicopter swung over the Munt Tower and followed the curve of the Amstel.

Stenner didn't bother. He already had more than enough information to write the piece for *Life;* they wanted only a thousand words. It just remained to see exactly how severe the "trouble" would be, what catch phrases Juliana and Beatrix might offer in their speeches, and so on. The photographs would do the rest. He was looking forward to doing the story—he hadn't done a bare-bones, who-shot-who piece in years. It would be a challenge, an exercise in discipline. So far, he had successfully held his investigative urges in check.

Waterlooplein, the former site of a popular market, had been razed to make way for the new Town Hall—a project stalled so many times, for so many reasons, it seemed doubtful now that it would ever really be built. As they hovered above the square, Stenner was reminded of some of the sections of Washington wiped out in the riots that followed the death of Martin Luther King. Like those desolate sections along 14th Street, Waterlooplein had been razed long enough ago that it no longer looked like a bomb site, but more like an archeological dig, an official ruin. The Town Hall project, and the building of the metro, which combined to cause the destruction of Waterlooplein, had been extremely unpopular with young Amsterdammers, and met with resistance each step of the way. A large tepee now stood in one corner of the battered square, and as they watched, a group of *Kraakers* emerged. Some of them whooped around in a circle—an Indian war dance. A couple of them pulled down their pants and stuck their bare buttocks up in the air. Another group took potshots at the helicopter with sticks.

Okker looked down in distaste. "Seen enough, Frits? I'll tell you, people are tired of this. Do they want to live where there *are* flats, these damn *kraakers?* Ach, man, no. They want to play their games." He waved to the pilot and said something in Dutch. "But we will show 'restraint.' " He grimaced. "Let *them* show a little restraint for a change."

Frits shifted in his seat. "They do have a point. I mean, all that money to redo the palace *could* be used for housing."

"They wouldn't live in it anyway. They've made their point, haven't they? Do they want to live in Bijlmermeer? No, no, now it's just an excuse. Let's go throw some rocks at the police, liven up the party. They haven't anything better to do."

If the traffic wasn't too bad, Stenner thought, he might be on time to meet the *Life* photographer.

When the roar of the helicopter subsided to a distant beating in the air, Claire slowed to a walk. She crossed a wide canal, passing a statue of a woman on horseback. STEM OBAS, it said, in clumsy, hand-painted letters, on a building across the canal. The STEM OBAS building seemed to be propped up with large wooden poles, and as she skirted them, walking in the street, a little Good Humor kind of bell jingled from behind her. She jumped back and almost collided with a bicycle.

The rider muttered something unintelligible and rode off again. Come on, she thought. Shit. If I walked around in this state in New York, I'd be dead by now. Even her most primitive instincts had deserted her. When something comes at you from behind, she reminded herself, you don't jump *backward,* Claire. To the *side.*

She passed a window that said SEX SHOP in large Art Deco letters. There was an array of books and devices in the window. In New York, it would be painted over—opaque blue, with some cartoon female for decoration—and say ADULT BOOKS. Here, the pornography was spread out in a careful fan...magazines on a coffee table. Vibrators stood in a circle like miniature missiles. Dildoes resembling sea anemones waited in ranks, lined up like flashlights, fuses, anything else you might want to buy. A family joined her in front of the store, window-shopping. There was a large, clumsy-looking device, prominently displayed, that seemed to be an electrified vagina.

She emerged one block later into the part of Amsterdam she recognized from her guidebooks. Graceful, tree-lined canals, old brick houses topped with different kinds of gables. The familiarity was reassuring, and her shoulders relaxed from their tense, defensive position.

She walked for a long while, looking in windows, admiring houseboats, looking at the sculptures on the old facades. She stopped at the crest of an old stone bridge and watched the ducks in the canal, trying to guess where one would surface after it disappeared under the water. She was thinking: No one knows where I am; no one expects me to be anywhere, do anything.

A glass-topped canal boat glided silently beneath her. She looked down at the tops of people's heads. She could imagine a large rock shattering through the glass and the people vainly trying to cover their heads with their arms. The boat drew slowly away. Masses of flowers decorated its stem, which was painted, in fancy script, with the name *Vincent van Gogh*.

She walked on. Soon, she supposed, her mind would make a map of these *grachts* and *straats*; she would know how to get from one place to another. She passed a house-boat where a calico cat sat in a patch of weak sunlight, cleaning itself. Right now, she had no idea where she was.

And she was tired. A clammy wave of exhaustion rippled through her legs. Walking was tricky here, the pavement uneven, the space for walking often so narrow two people could not walk side by side. Her calf muscles ached; she really had to sit down soon. She had passed several potential coffee places—Koffiehuis, Espressobar. But she couldn't decide which one to go into; Jeff made that kind of random decision. One seemed too small, one too crowded. There were no benches in Amsterdam; she'd seen no place to sit down since she'd left Dam Square. She was too tired to be indecisive. She pushed into an Espressobar.

A thin man with a mustache waved his arms at her, criss-crossing them.

"*Gesloten.*"

"What?"

"Sorry. We are closing." She stumbled out, feeling humiliated. She emerged from the small street onto a square. Cafés were ranked along the sides, and she went into the first one. It jutted out almost into the street, the front part glassed in. An outdoor café for a chilly climate. A waiter set down some small glasses of beer on the table next to hers and then turned to her with a kind of brief bow. He said something in Dutch.

"Coffee."

He said something else in Dutch. "Sorry, I don't speak Dutch."

He clapped a hand to his forehead. "But what a shame you are not Dutch." He flirted with her for a little while, talking about "Dutch blood," "a Dutch heart." She was used to being flirted with; she was good at being friendly without being too friendly. Although there had been mistakes, errors in judgment.

Once, after a harmless talk about the weather with a man on a bus, the man had followed her around for several days. He would wait outside her office, and when she came out, for lunch, or to go home, he would be there, with some corny token of affection—flowers, a box of candy.

"Please..."

"No, I really can't. I'm sorry."

She would be on a crowded bus and turn around and there he would be. She might be in a store, or a museum, and he would appear, suddenly, as if he'd materialized before her eyes. She didn't want to be rude; she tried to explain to him that she wasn't going to change her mind, there was no point in following her around.

"I'm persistent." He smiled.

What had seemed an ordinary, rather engaging smile now looked like a maniac's leer.

She stopped speaking to him; she even stopped looking at him. She began to eat lunch at her desk. After a while she grew frightened, and angry too. She didn't want to be anyone's obsession. As a child, she had been the kind of curly-haired, dimpled little girl that certain adults fawned over, and had developed a fear of going into stores—probably, according to her mother, because strangers asked cute questions like "Can we take you home with us?" or "How about this beautiful little girl— is she for sale?"

This man was turning her paranoid. Finally, he appeared one morning, holding a bouquet of daisies, when she was leaving the apartment with Jeff. The man didn't say anything, just stood there, smiling away. She pointed him out to Jeff, and Jeff approached him and said in a loud voice, "If you don't stop bothering my wife, I'll call the police."

The man bolted, colliding with the doorman, then running in a terrified rabbit kind of way up to the corner. He looked back at her, and gave her the saddest, betrayed look. When she and Jeff reached the corner, she saw the daisies scattered on the pavement. A woman in gray was gathering them up.

She had never seen him again.

But Jeff had been really irritated by the whole episode; irritated at her. He thought it was all her fault, somehow—he'd made that clear. She wondered what his new girlfriend looked like. She wondered…No. She would not wonder things like that.

The waiter returned with her coffee and set it down with a flourish. It came in a small blue-and-white cup, a chocolate mint perched on the saucer. The waiter pulled up a chair and sat across from her.

"Let me guess—you are Canadian."

"No, I am—"

He cut her off. "No. Let me guess. British?" She shook her head. "You are a dispossessed princess from the Malagasy Republic."

She laughed. "Just an American."

"Why *just*?"

"I don't know. There are so many of us, I guess." Some people at a nearby table gestured for him, but he took his time, talking. He urged her to come back, there would be parties in the cafés all week, he would like to see her again. She looked at her watch, almost automatically. It was one of the tricks she used to deflect people's attentions.

"My name is Klaes."

"Claire." He departed with a mock salute. Why should she be trying to get rid of people? *Jeff.* She wouldn't think about Jeff.

She thought instead, as she walked up a crowded street reserved for pedestrians, about their apartment. Her shell collection, gathering dust; the daisies drooping in the Waterford vase. Would Jeff have figured out by now that she had gone? Would he move back in? Would he move back in with *her*? Her jade tree, six years old now, raised by her from a dime-store midget, would need to be watered. Well, not really; not yet. She wondered if it would die without her; she thought how the fleshy leaves would shrivel and drop to the table.

She stopped in front of a men's clothing store and looked at a brown sweater. It would look good on Jeff; he would like it. She couldn't seem to stop thinking of him. Shit, there must have been something she should have done, or not done, or something, and this wouldn't have happened; he'd still love her. She stared at the brick wall next to the men's store. Painted graffiti: INFEXION. APRIL 30 DEMONSTRATIE. NO TRIX.

And she couldn't seem to do it, turn the love into hate; that alchemic transformation was beyond her. She stared into the window of an elegant women's boutique. The mannequins were all bald and wore sunglasses. What would he do with her clothes? Pack them all up in a box and give them to her mother, as if she were dead?

WHY DISCO? said the wall. WHORES ARE CHEAPER. A skull and crossbones. INFEXION. UP THE QUEEN'S KRAAK.

Perhaps she would never, never go back, and he would have to wait years and years for her to be officially declared an abandoner. Or whatever you got to be. She stopped in front of an antique store. ANTIEK. She would make him wait and wait; he would hate it. Even if she couldn't hate him, she could want him to suffer. She stood there twitching. She felt violent and deceptive, like a carnivorous plant.

She remembered her list; the list set her in motion. She must find a new hotel. She stopped at a sandwich shop—BROODJES, the sign said—and had two small roast-beef sandwiches on soft rolls. They tasted exceptionally good, but then she remembered she hadn't eaten all day. She must not forget to eat, brush her teeth, wash out her panty hose. These things were talismans against disaster.

CHAPTER EIGHT

The Hotel de l'Europe had the cozy elegance possible only for a hotel that has been around for a long time. The management had resisted cluttering up the place with old Dutch junk; even more to its credit, Stenner noted, there was no souvenir stand. He surveyed the tasteful charms of the reception area, the lobby, the bar. No one resembling Bill Phillips' self-description ("I'm big and bald. You can't miss me") was visible, so he returned to the reception desk.

"Ah, yes, Mr. Stenner. Indeed we do have a message for you. A Mr."—the concierge peered down at his desk—"Phillips just called moments ago from Schiphol."

Stenner flipped open the cream-colored envelope. *Plane delayed in Paris. Just got in. Could we meet at 7 in the bar? If not, leave a message. Phillips.*

Yes, he'd come back at seven; why not? The doorman held the heavy wood-and-glass door open and Stenner stepped outside, passing under the de l'Europe's red canopy. A misty rain was falling. Maybe *Life* would pop for dinner in the de l'Europe's supernaturally expensive Restaurant Excelsior. As he crossed toward the Singel, the carillon in the Munt Tower began to chime a tune to mark the half-hour. The flower shops along the canal were closing for the night. Shopkeepers lugged flats of seedlings back inside the protective plastic sheeting that jutted out into the street from the converted barges that were their shops. The Dutch were passionate about plants.

A couple of weeks ago, he'd reluctantly gone with a girl named Anneke to an "experimental" play at the Milky Way. He hated plays; he found the artificiality irritating, almost painful.

"I'm a moviegoer," he told Anneke. "I like to sit in the dark and I don't like to clap."

"Come on. Just for a change. You'll see." She'd talked him into it. He turned up the Huidenstraat.

In the play's last scene, the husband and wife, in the course of an argument, had dismembered a plant on the stage. Then they'd hurled various bits of the plant into the audience. One leafy vine had landed in Anneke's lap, and she'd jumped up and screamed, as if it were a snake. The audience gave out a collective gasp, and two well-dressed women got up to leave. The actor interrupted the scene to berate them: "Typical Dutch bourgeois mentality. You care more about a fucking plant than about the much truer emotions we are dealing with here."

The taller woman turned and glared at him. "You pompous ass. I, for one, find your play tedious, not shocking. And we are Canadian."

Stenner had enjoyed the actor's discomfort; and the weak rejoinder—"Typical Canadian bourgeois mentality, then"—addressed to a closing door, made him laugh out loud. Anneke had bristled with irritation at him for the rest of the night. She was ten years younger than he was, like most of the women he'd seen since he'd left Marlena. They all seemed at once more cynical and more naïve than he was; he didn't find the combination charming.

He crossed the Keizersgracht. The bridge was being repaired, and he glanced down at the barges full of metal reinforcing rods, sand, planks that were tethered to the canalside.

Maybe the hot water would be restored and he'd be able to take a shower. His flat—sublet from a violinist for the Concertgebouw who was on a sabbatical—was on the Prinsengracht, and as he turned the corner, he walked a little faster; if there was hot water, he didn't have that much time.

When he reached the second-floor landing, he heard the phone ringing and sprinted for his door. It stopped the moment he put his hand on the receiver.

"Hello. Hello."

Whoever they were, they'd given up. Damn. He went in to test the taps in the bathroom. Bad timing had plagued him lately. He wondered if it was possible to lose a step, like an aging wide receiver; lose a step on the world. Maybe a form of depression: getting out of sync with things—always getting to the stop as the tram pulled away, arriving at the newsstand as the guy in front of you was buying the last copy of the *Herald Tribune*. Ah, well, it was probably just Phillips. And he'd call back.

The hot water consoled him. He stood in the shower in a contorted position, to avoid scalding his calves with the fiery trickle that always leaked from the junction of the pipe to the wall. The phone began to ring again. He decided to ignore it and then changed his mind, wrapped a towel clumsily around his waist and ran into the living room, dripping and shivering as he picked up the phone.

"Hello."

Nothing.

"Oh, shit!" He threw the phone down and went over to flick on the electric heater.

Alan Dawson fished out the Dutch quarter-guilder from its metal slot, every bit as frustrated as John Stenner. He ducked out of the telephone's plastic globe—which would probably have proved ineffective against the rush-hour uproar of Centraal Station—and considered his options. If he was unable to reach Stenner by the next morning, before the meeting, he would have to call "Scott" and arrange the backup transfer. He had no idea how long tomorrow's meeting would take. Tomorrow evening he was supposed to be in The Hague, having dinner with Derek Winslow and Bruce Patterson at the Embassy. The dinner was not obligatory, really; the arrangements had been made largely to get him out of Amsterdam before it closed down for the investiture. A car was lined up to drive him from The Hague to Schiphol to catch the two-fifteen flight back to New York.

He would just have to hope he could reach Stenner tonight and arrange something for tomorrow afternoon. He glanced at his watch. Six fifteen. Perhaps he would go for a canal-boat ride. Why not? But he had the attaché case with him, hoping he'd be able to complete the transfer to Stenner. Also, he'd been somewhat reluctant to leave it in his hotel room: mere superstition perhaps, but still…

He looked around to see if there were any lockers nearby. Approaching him was a woman so extraordinary-looking that even his diplomat's manners deserted him, and he stared. She was a large woman, stocky, hair buzz-cut like a Marine's, wearing harlequin glasses studded with rhinestones. Her black wool coat was hacked off in jagged points at the hem. The collar consisted of the pelts of some kind of small animal, paws and heads still attached. These were draped over her shoulders like grotesque epaulets. Her legs were sheathed in green-and-black striped stockings, and on her feet were extreme high heels. The whole effect was not just ludicrous but some-how menacing.

To his discomfort, the woman stopped dead in front of him and took off her glasses, revealing eyes heavily rimmed in black.

"Take a good fucking look," she said. Strident Cockney accent. "Like what you see, do you?" She exe-cuted a little bump and grind. Then she stuck out her tongue and wiggled it, like a snake.

He recovered himself. "I beg your pardon," he said. "You're quite striking-looking."

She guffawed and then smiled at him in a hideous coquettish way.

She put her hand behind her head and posed, a trav-esty of a pinup girl. "Want to suck my pussy?" She spun on her heel and sashayed away.

The small knot of onlookers who had gathered to watch this curious confrontation offered him a nonver-bal display of sympathy—rueful little head shakes, shy smiles, disapproving clucks—and then dissolved into the general hubbub. Another wonderful by-product of Western civilization, he thought, as he walked toward a bank of lockers.

He shoved the attaché case into locker Number 123 and pocketed the key. He'd thought about taking the case back to the meeting in the morning, to tape the nuts and bolts of the plan, but decided against it. The conspiracy was documented; there was no reason to risk it. He sighed. He would enjoy having a couple of drinks and then gliding along the canals in one of the glass-topped boats, listening to a guide ramble on about this or that detail of Amsterdam architecture, history. He had begged off from several dinner invitations, claiming a previous engagement, and now he was profoundly glad.

He walked along a stretch of the Damrak gaudy with souvenir stands, cheap restaurants, pinball arcades. He felt suddenly tired, as if the attaché case had been a kind of battery, powering him along like a mechanical man, and without it...

He hated this business—the meeting, the deception, the various facets of his betrayal: betrayal of the men in Circle Group, betrayal of Stenner. He was unable to summon up the kernel of faith, the true believer's passion for his mission. He had always been able to do things he detested, because they were "important," because they "had to be done." This time, he would rather not be a factor in history; he would rather things went on, however they came out, without his intervention. Every step he took through the damp air, amidst the lengthening shadows, seemed to peel away another layer of energy. When he reached the canal-boat concession, he purchased a ticket mutely and sank down on one of the benches to wait, weary as an old man.

He would do it; he would see it through. But this would be his last chore for Sisyphus. He realized how much he disliked Sisyphus. It was as if for all these years he had looked at him only full face, and been mesmerized by his eyes, his will. Now he seemed to have stepped aside, and that change of angle revealed to him what the front facade had concealed all that time: an infestation, a pulp of evil.

When Sisyphus had been discharged from the Agency following Watergate, Dawson's concern for the Agency had been tempered by a sense of relief: the string attaching him to Sisyphus and the Agency would at last be broken; he would be freed from the need to do these occasional "favors."

Dawson had been surprised, therefore, to receive a summons, about a month following Sisyphus' official departure from CIA. They met in the cemetery in Rock Creek Park, near the famous Saint-Gaudens statue. Sisyphus had told him that his much-publicized departure from the Agency was a ruse— that he was now, under the cover of that dismissal, proceeding with investigations of Soviet penetration of the Agency; that he would be founding an ersatz "private" security firm to serve as a base for this investigation.

Dawson stared at his fingers and absently twirled his wedding ring. At the time, he had believed Sisyphus. Sisyphus was a terribly compelling advocate, and the story made a certain sense. If there *were* moles at the CIA, an in-house investigation would run the continual risk of exposure.

But lately, doubts had begun to surface. He couldn't think what had engendered the doubts, but...A sour smile occupied Dawson's mouth. Suppose he was doing "favors," "favors" he disliked doing, not for the Agency at all, but for a rogue agent, a demented private citizen with paranoid delusions?

He watched the canal-boat operator skillfully maneuver the boat up to the dock. Sisyphus had miscalculated when he'd told the story about Le Canard. Sisyphus had not been at the Vercors massacre; he hadn't seen what Dawson had seen; he hadn't dreamed...

No doubt rescuing Le Canard from prosecution or death and employing him as an agent was pragmatic. "Valuable," Sisyphus had said. But there was pragmatism and then there was a subterranean realm below the merely pragmatic; a mental sphere free of the turbulence of passion; cold, stifling, deadly.

Dawson felt for the locker key in his pocket and weighed it in his hand, watching the clouds scud low across the harbor.

"Would it be possible to see a room?" Claire asked. The lobby of the de l'Europe was perfect, but she didn't want to discover, later, that the rooms were replicas of American motel rooms.

"Certainly," the concierge said, and summoned a bellboy, who took the keys and escorted her to the elevator. "I'll show you the one I like better first," he said, and led her out of the elevator to Room 114. He held open the door, and she went into a pleasant room—pearl-gray walls, wainscoting, a wonderful small crystal chande-lier. "This one's just been redone, and even though it's smaller than the other one, it's really nicer." There was a sybaritic bathroom, tiled in pink. "And it has a better view."

He led her past a small, low marble table to some French doors. He drew the curtains aside and opened them, and she stepped out onto a balcony overlooking a canal. Across the way was a spire; two-thirds of the way up, there was a large clock face, the gold-filigreed hands pointing almost to seven. The arches above the clock were filled with bells, and above that the spire was topped off by an openwork ball and a cross.

"The Munt Tower," said the young man. "You know—how do you say it? The mint. It used to be where they struck the coins."

"It's a lovely room."

"Ah, there it goes." The bells in the tower began to chime. It seemed to her a good omen, as if they welcomed her. "The carillon plays each half-hour—not at night, of course. Do you care to see the other room?"

"No, I think this one is just right."

She went to the desk and happily arranged to take up residence in Room 114 the next day at noon. When that was settled, Claire started for the street and then hesitated so abruptly, in mid-stride, that she stumbled. *Now what?* asked a sharp voice from the upper left quadrant of her skull. Where are you going?

It was exhausting, being cut off from the matrix of habits, obligations, plans. It seemed so tiring to always be thinking of what to do next. What would she be doing in New York? She would be with Jeff, eating dinner, probably. Or clearing up. It was one of their unspoken routines. Whoever had cooked the meal sat in the tiny kitchen and talked to the other one, who washed up. Suddenly, she missed, with a terrible pang, her pottery jar with its bouquet of cooking utensils, the bright blue-and-orange label from the guava paste that was Scotch Taped to the cabinet where the glasses were kept.

A convivial bubble of conversation and laughter floated past this wall of reminiscence, and she turned to see the de l'Europe's bar and walked slowly toward it, like a somnambulist.

Of course, she replied to the voice. Now I will have a drink. Then I will have some dinner. Then I will return to the Dikker and Thys Garden Hotel and read until I fall asleep.

The barman leaned toward her and gave a questioning upward thrust of his head.

"Gin and tonic."

That upward, questioning nod was an almost exact replica of one of Jeff's mannerisms. Jeff would not appear in her head with anything close to the clarity of the kitchen utensils, the guava-paste label. She couldn't seem to remember what he looked like in person; all she could visualize was the way he looked in the photograph on her parents' piano, mouth in a beguiling grin, dimples framing his smile. She couldn't see him in any other way—just this sort of two-dimensional campaign photograph. During her long walk around, she had seen a photograph of Beatrix—several identical photographs, in fact—plastered against the temporary plywood wall protecting a construction site. Instead of lips, Beatrix had a zipper, and the zipper was pulled open to reveal fangs. She saw Jeff's piano photograph with this distorted mouth and then even that began to fade, as if the photograph were undergoing the reverse of the development process, shadows and details disappearing, his face reduced to two black holes for eyes, a smudge of nose, the crack of a mouth.

"You look so serious." The bartender set down her drink in front of her.

"Oh. Just thinking…"

He leaned across the bar and shook his head.

"You don't want to do too much of that."

"No?"

He began dipping beer glasses in the sink and shaking them out. "Dangerous. Highly addictive, you know. First you start out with a simple thought or two. Next thing you know, you're having *ideas*. I see it all the time, in my line of work."

"That risky, is it?"

"Oh, certainly." He began wiping out the glasses with a red-and-white linen cloth. Claire had an odd urge to help him; the way he methodically cleaned the glasses seemed so attractive, so satisfying. "I mean, there are good ideas, and bad ideas, so-called. But how often have you heard [and here his voice took on a terrible mournful tone] 'It seemed like such a *good* idea at the time'?"

There were some small tables set against the wall, and he looked over in that direction and then nodded. He whisked two tulip-shaped glasses onto the counter. "Dutch gin," he said, filling them right to the brim. "A bad idea"—he flipped up a hinged section of the bar and came around next to her—"if you're going to rewire a computer tomorrow..." He lifted the tray up, balancing it on his palm. "A good idea if you want to get totally smashed." He took off with the tray, and she looked at the bits of her face visible between the bottles at the back of the bar.

"Thinking again?" asked the bartender, as he ducked back beneath the bar.

"No, just staring dully into space." She smiled at him—a conscious effort. She could feel the skin stretch, her cheeks plump out.

"I'm sure you've been thinking. You definitely have a touch of the disease. That's what they call the chronic thinkers—you know, the really terminal cases—philosophers."

"I'll watch out for symptoms."

A man in a trench coat sat on the bar stool next to hers.

The bartender gave him the upward nod.

"A beer."

The man looked around and she followed his gaze, and saw that the bar was beginning to fill up. Then the man slid back the sleeve of his coat and looked at his watch. Gin buzzed in her head; she felt languid, almost relaxed. The bartender was filling orders, cheerfully, with stylish efficiency. He pulled a bottle of Boodles gin away from the mirrored wall and there was her face, perfectly framed. He put the bottle back and her face disappeared again. Gone with the gin, she thought.

It was such a solitary joke, it gave her a jolt of loss—for Jeff, for her friends, her left-behind life—so powerful, it was like a physical stab. It reminded her of the time she'd broken her ankle playing racquetball. She'd been warming up, hitting the ball lazily, waiting for Jeff to get there. She jumped up for a high ball and landed badly on her right ankle. It had seemed too humiliating to follow her first impulse and crawl off the court through the little door, and she'd tried to stand up, testing the ankle, putting a little weight on it. An unbelievable pain had shot up from the ankle to her head, and a momentary pulse of darkness blocked her vision. And she'd realized you didn't fool around with that kind of pain—it could knock you out.

And this was just like that; her sense of loss didn't bear testing. She stared at the bottles, reading labels. But she must have done something visible, because the man next to her touched her elbow: "Are you all right?"

"Yes." She smiled. "Just tired, I guess. I just got here this morning and I've been walking all day."

"Amsterdam is like that—always luring you down just one more street. It seems so compact, but somehow you end up walking miles." He touched his empty beer glass and nodded toward her glass. "Like another?"

She hesitated. "Sure. Okay."

He nodded to the bartender and made a circular gesture over their glasses. "So how is America these days?"

"Sort of hanging on."

He picked up his beer glass, held it like a microphone and spoke in a smooth, radio voice: "The mood is defeated, angry, the once mighty populace...Tell me, Miss..."

"Brooks."

The bartender served their drinks and he took a sip of his beer.

"John Stenner."

"Claire, Claire Brooks."

"So, what brings you to Amsterdam?"

"Just on vacation."

"Here to see the tulips?"

She was puzzled; she frowned. "Too-lips?" She repeated the syllables with all the comprehension of a New Guinean warrior being taught English by a missionary. "Too-lips?" she said again. It wouldn't jell into a word.

"Yeah, tulips. Flowers—you know. Holland is famous for them—exports millions of bulbs all over the world and all that."

Her laugh splashed out. "Tulips! No, actually, I've come to see the hyacinths." She shook her head, laughing some more.

"Hy-a-seent?" he repeated in a primitive accent, and they laughed together.

"Do you think it's entirely normal to lose fifty or so IQ points on the way across the Atlantic?"

Stenner nodded. "Once—Excuse me," he said, and gestured to a tall, bald man who had come into the bar and was looking around. The man ambled over, carrying a large Halliburton suitcase.

"John Stenner?"

"Bill Phillips." They shook hands.

"Terribly sorry I'm late—they actually sent my cameras"— he hefted the aluminum suitcase—"to Brussels;

no one could figure out why. Just give me five minutes to put this stuff in my room and I'll be right down."

When he'd gone, Claire looked at her watch. "I really should be going."

"Have you had dinner?"

"Well, no, but—"

"Have dinner with us. Or if Bill has already eaten, have dinner with me."

She smiled at him. "All right. I hate to eat alone."

CHAPTER NINE

MORE THAN TWO HOURS LATER, the three of them walked out of the Restaurant Excelsior. The man at the piano was playing a leisurely version of "My Blue Heaven."

"That was just about the most luxurious meal I've ever had," Claire said. "Thank you."

"The pleasure was *Life's,*" Stenner intoned, mock-serious.

"Good line, that. Of course," Phillips added, "we shall expect you to attempt to climb one of the lions in Dam Square on the big day, Claire. I'll take a photograph of the police dragging you down, your wonderful blond hair cascading against their brutal shoulders." They'd progressed to the bar. "Join me for a cognac?"

"Oh, I don't know. I think I might be getting drunk."

"Just a suspicion?" Stenner joked. "Or powerful enough to be called a hunch?"

"Oh, come on," Phillips urged, pulling out a chair for her. "Just one cognac and an espresso will see you right."

Stenner sprawled in a chair, looking totally relaxed. Like a rag doll, as if he had no muscles. Claire sat down, a bit stiffly in comparison, and admired his ease, an unguarded repose at odds with his taut, wary eyes. He looked directly at her momentarily, and she looked away. Her face felt warm, flushed with wine.

"Marvelous. I really *must* drink some more," Bill Phillips explained, "and I hate to drink alone. It's my new photographic technique…" He stopped and rubbed his hand over his bald head, repeatedly, as if he were polishing it. "The hangover technique, let's call it. My theory is that a hangover produces an altered state of consciousness—"

The waiter came and Phillips ordered a round of cognacs, coffees.

"Where was I?"

"Expounding on the hangover technique of photography."

"Oh, yes. I used to be in the 'cowboy' school, don't you know, forever lying down under horse jumps to get shots of blurry hooves hurtling straight over me—stuff like that. This is more suitable for my middle years. The worse the hangover, the more acute my sense of composition. I see lines of perspective, geometrical patterns…" His voice trailed off.

"Do you think it will work for journalism?" Stenner asked.

"Well, not for the sort of investigative stories you've made your name at, but for this sort of thing, certainly."

"And tourism?" asked Claire, as the waiter distributed the cognac and coffee.

"Absolutely. Tomorrow, go to the Rijksmuseum and see the Vermeers. You'll be able to see right through to the pure luminous Vermeer heart. And"—he puffed greedily on a cigar to get it started—"A couple of Vermeers will be better than a couple of Bloody Marys—set you right in no time."

Stenner slid his arm across the back of her chair. "Of course," he said to Phillips, "tonight must just be a warm-up for you; tomorrow night the really serious preparations will begin."

Claire tried to remember how to encourage gestures of affection. Physical affection. What do you do? Lean back against the arm? For years she'd been rebuffing this very sort of thing; she'd forgotten this silent language. She sat stiffly and took small, prim sips of her cognac.

"Well, yes, of course," Phillips agreed, swirling his cognac around. "I stay in training. I work up to it, like an athlete, hoping to peak on the big day. Like your joggers preparing for a marathon."

"*Our* joggers?"

"Well, you must have some national responsibility. Only Americans jog. You don't see that kind of thing here, do you? People in really quite unsuitable clothing hurtling past you." He downed his drink and laughed—a staccato laugh, like a repeating rifle.

"It's to fight time," Claire offered. "Americans don't like to get old; it's considered vulgar."

"'Fight' is the critical word there." Stenner offered around a pack of cigarettes. "Time as the enemy—we've always been a combative country."

"Not that you'd notice lately." Phillips stuck his hand up to call the waiter. "Really, Europeans may complain a great deal about America, but everyone feels Mr. Carter is letting the side down here. I mean, despite it all, we count on the U.S. to give the stiff-arm to the Russians every now and then. Boycotting the Olympics!" He snorted. "And what about those poor athletes—the marathoners, poor things. You know, I went to cover a marathon last year—the one in Boston—anyway, I got the most wonderful shots of faces, totally exhausted faces, attenuated with pain. Faces straight out of El Greco; unbelievable. Another round of these—that's a good man."

"Well, that's the Land of the Brave for you these days, everyone running around in sweat suits and eating alfalfa sprouts."

"We always knew you were barbarians. But surely you're joking. Alfalfa sprouts sound suitable only for livestock."

Stenner turned to Claire. "Am I right? You can hardly get a sandwich anymore without alfalfa sprouts cluttering it up."

"Absolutely true. Alfalfa sprouts everywhere. And then there are the yellow ribbons."

"The *yellow ribbons.*"

"Well, you see"—Claire leaned forward—"when the hostages were taken, a sort of grass-roots movement started, and..." She began to laugh and the laugh got away from her.

"What Claire is trying to describe is a vigorous national protest movement against the Iranian seizure of the hostages. A grass-roots movement, as she's pointed out. Everyone decided that the best way to let the Ayatollah know that we were *really* fed up with his hold-ing our people prisoner was to..." Stenner started to laugh but squeezed out the rest of the sentence. "...to ...to...well, to tie yellow ribbons around trees."

Claire tried to take a sip of cognac and choked, still laughing.

"But, but, but...why? And why *yellow* ribbons?"

"Well, there's a song," Claire started, breathlessly, but that got them laughing again.

"A song! I still don't see."

Stenner made an attempt to sing the song. *"Tie a yellow..."* but that set off new gusts of laughter. Finally, their hysteria subsided and Stenner tried to explain that there was a pop song called "Tie a Yellow Ribbon Round the Old Oak Tree"—the yellow ribbon, as he recalled, being some sort of sign from the wife to the returning prisoner that he was still welcome at home.

Phillips shook his head. "Extraordinary. Doesn't even really make sense. Absolutely extraordinary."

"Of course," Claire added, "the ribbons look pathetic now— some are in shreds, some are white from the sun..."

"It's worse than I thought," Phillips complained. "How can we adjust to this? America used to be the country you loved to hate. America was so good at things, so efficient—it was half envy, that hate, you know. A form of praise, really. Now what? I suppose it will have to be the Japanese?'

"Why not the Russians?"

"Well, they're just not *around* enough, not visible. You can hardly find a Russian in London unless you go round to the Aeroflot office. There are the Arabs, of course— plenty of Arabs to get you aggravated. But on the whole, yes, I think the Japanese are better candidates."

"They are efficient."

"I went to Burberry's the other day to get a new coat. Well, I was all right because I'm fairly large. But it was amazing, bloody amazing—half the racks were totally empty, all the smaller sizes completely gone. Like the place had been looted, or ravaged by locusts. Chaps who work there looked shell-shocked. I inquired—What's happened here, factory on strike or what? One chap just shakes his head, eyes all glazed over, and mutters, 'The *Japanese.*' Seems a party of tourists had just come in, bought *everything.* Manager of the store was quite upset— 'What am I to do if a customer comes in and asks to see what we've got in a thirty-six suit. We have no shipments due for a *fortnight.* Nothing, I'll have to say, absolutely *nothing.*' He was really in a stir." Phillips polished his head. "The Japanese won't be as much fun; quite an adjustment, really. Yellow bloody ribbons."

"Well, Americans are going through a transition, coming to terms with the idea that things aren't likely to keep getting better and better—financially, I mean. Fading-empire syndrome."

"Alfalfa sprouts. At least we had the miniskirt."

"That was post-fade."

"I guess you're right," Phillips said. He downed his cognac and licked his lips.

Claire leaned forward. "Do you think we'll be better liked as a second-rate power?"

"Oh, yes, but it's no good—a patronizing kind of affection, really. Such as one might feel for a faded beauty." An elegant woman in a red dress walked past, saying something peevishly in French to a fat, gray-haired man. The woman's hair was short and sleek. It reminded Claire of the fur of an aquatic animal—a seal, an otter.

"...manage to get my press credentials?"

"No, you'll have to pick them up yourself, tomorrow. They insisted on a Polaroid."

"At least my chances for a nice gray day on Sunday are good. Holland can provide one of those."

"The hangover technique too painful in bright sunshine?"

"There's that, but mostly, colors photograph better

when it's overcast. Sunshine washes out faces, and then you have all those shadows mucking up your elegant linear compositions."

Claire felt woozy; she clutched the edge of the table for stability. "I think I'd better go," she said, in a voice that reverberated ominously inside her head: *go...go...go.*

"I'll take you home." John Stenner held her coat.

Bill Phillips squeezed her hand. "...think when I've had a nicer time...tomorrow night...you."

Take your hand away, Claire commanded herself. Now smile, walk to the door. Her mind seemed a remote-control device, operating her body. She watched Phillips' face develop a pinched expression; Stenner seemed to be partially dragging her out the door.

"I'm not doing well," she said out loud. Stenner eased her past the doorman. "I think that last cognac..." Outside, the fresh air snapped and crackled. "Snap, crackle, pop," she said. They'd walked nearly a block before she fully realized it was rain.

He had his arm around her waist, half-supporting her. They stopped near a lamppost while he lit a cigarette. The reflections of light shimmering in the canal were dislodged by some unknown disturbance in the water. The way the lights swayed made her feel sick and she looked the other way. Faraway lightning made the sky flicker and tremble. She closed her eyes and heard the follow-up artillery of thunder.

"I'll be all right," she asserted. "Where can you find a cab? I'll take a cab home." The word "home"—thinking of that room in the Dikker and Thys as "home"—triggered a fit of laughter. She laughed so hard that tears oozed out of the corners of her eyes and dribbled down her cheeks, and that seemed to remind her that she should be crying. The rain came down harder, and for a minute or two, standing there crying, getting drenched, watching the streetlights star out like novas through her tears, she felt agreeably mad, released. Stenner was looking at her with a curiously bored expression. He raised his hand, and for a minute she thought he was going to slap her. She was afraid, not that he would slap her, but that she wouldn't feel it, and that would be the first step toward something irrevocable.

Instead he touched her very lightly on the shoulder—a touch that gave her a deep, unexpected sexual thrill. She felt a rush of desire so intense that she pressed herself against him and rubbed her mouth crudely against his.

He grabbed her tight, pinning her arms against her sides. For a moment she glared at him, furious, and was tempted, like a child having a tantrum, to go limp. But being immobilized seemed to make the frenzy go out of her, and she shut her eyes, embarrassed.

They walked. He opened a door and guided her up some stairs. She walked stiffly, as if she were a prisoner. He unlocked a door and they went into an apartment. The windows were open and gusts of air blew into the room.

"Shit." He closed the windows, then squeezed out some water from the hem of one curtain into a plant. "Shit," he repeated.

He left the room and came back to the doorway and tossed her a towel. She watched it tumble through the air, but her reactions were much too slow for her to even try catching it. She picked it up from the floor and rubbed at her hair. She could hear him in the kitchen, slamming drawers and cabinets—angry clattering. She wrapped the towel around her head like a turban and tried to think of what to say. She wished she had a card, like deaf-mutes on the subway: THIS WOMAN IS TEMPORARILY UNSTABLE DUE TO…

She heard the teakettle shrill.

She hugged her arms, as if trying to make herself smaller, but then stretched them out again, crossed her legs—composed. She closed her eyes; if she could just think about something, anything but Jeff or herself laughing and crying by the canal.

"Here's some coffee."

She jumped; her eyes flew open. He loomed up above her.

"I'm terribly sorry," she began in a high, stilted voice. "I know I'm behaving badly. I'll be all right, though. You won't be stuck with me forever. They say people won't help you in China, I think it's China, because then they are responsible, but you see..." She hated the way her voice sounded, as if she were a seventh-grader trying out for the part of the mother. "I mean, I'm only temporarily deranged. Drunk, you might put it."

"You're temporarily deranged," he said in a neutral voice.

She took a sip of the coffee. It burned her tongue. She perceived the pain in a distant way, as if it were happening to someone else. She felt obligated to explain. He flicked on the electric heater, and she watched three parallel lines grow orange.

"I..." she started. She didn't want to hear herself talking about Jeff.

He got up and put on a record. Bach cantatas. Past that flash of recognition, she couldn't hear the pattern of the music. She couldn't make out the melodies; it sounded like static.

"Oh, God," she said. She clutched her head in her arms. The gesture struck her as melodramatic. Borrowed.

"My husband left me," she heard herself say. "Out of the blue, after seven years."

"When was this?"

"Four days ago." She glanced at the calendar of her Seiko watch. A present from Jeff. "At least, I think it was four days ago. Is it a different day here?"

"No."

"So I left." An unpleasant laugh squirted out of her.

"Ummm."

"I should have stayed in New York, but it seemed so...I don't know. I didn't know I'd go wacko...God, I'm embarrassed. I'm sorry."

She looked at her arm. There were goosebumps on it. She looked at a rectangular patch of her skin, as if it were a medical illustration.

"You're shivering," he said. "I'll get you a blanket."

He gave her a blanket and she wrapped herself up in it. Then he got up to change the record. Jazz. This time she could hear the music. She concentrated on the slides of sound. When she closed her eyes, the notes produced patterned bursts of color, crystalline grids of color, like impossibly precise fireworks. The phone rang. The phone rang in double bursts, and each burst flushed blood-red in her head.

She heard him talking: "Alan Dawson! Hey, it's been a while...Sure, yeah, I'd love to see you...It's coming along—you know, slowly."

She heard a siren from outside, faint, far away.

She remembered one spring evening in Nyack, chasing a fire truck down two blocks from her house. The old house on the corner, the one the kids believed was haunted, was burning out of control. She hid in a dogwood tree to watch. The light on the top of the fire engine swooped around, flush upon flush of red. The petals of the dogwood pulsed, as if the earth were pumping blood.

She felt Stenner sit down next to her on the couch.

Maybe if she pretended to be asleep, he would just leave her there and she could stay all night in this cocoon. The idea had only a moment's plausibility. Her reticence made her sit up.

"I'm all right now. I'll go now."

"You know, that's about the tenth time you've said 'I'm all right.' "

"I'm practicing positive thinking."

"Is it worth it?"

"Oh, God." She stretched and looked at the ceiling. Tears came into her eyes. "I'm not all right. I'm a fucking basket case. I'm sorry."

"That's also about the twentieth time you've said you're sorry."

She lit a cigarette. "Well, I may not be all right. But I am sorry. It doesn't seem fair, I mean, to get hysterical like that. You're sort of an innocent bystander."

"I don't believe in innocent bystanders."

"I'm another innocent bystander. Standing by, and then Bam! Lightning strikes."

"I do believe in lightning."

"I was on my way to the *dentist* when he told me. Can you believe that?"

"Mmmm—that is low."

"How could I not know? I feel so stupid. It must have been going on for a long time."

He got up to change the record.

"Once Jeff and I were snorkeling. It was when we went to Cozumel. Jeff loved to go places; he loved to plan." She stopped. "I'm talking about him like he's dead. That's weird." She stubbed the cigarette out. "Anyway, we were playing this game, where one of us would throw a tin can back behind us and then we'd snorkel around and look for it. I was swimming around and I saw a place where the sand was kicked up. I dived down to get a closer look and then the sand itself lifted up, swooped its wings and shot away from me. A ray, you know—it was a stingray. But in the split second before I realized that, it was like the space between the spaces moved, like the universe was coming apart at the seams. It was like that. I mean, 'I'm going to the dentist.' 'Great, sweetheart. I'm leaving you for someone else.' "

"I'll tell you…" His voice trailed away.

"What?"

"I'm divorced," he said suddenly.

"Why? I mean, what happened? Never mind. I'm sorry."

"I don't know whether I left her or she left me. I never figured that out. It was all gone."

She felt as if she were going to cry again and turned her head away. He touched her shoulder, and she felt the same sharp sexual tug she'd felt on the street. She got up and went to the bathroom and splashed cold water on her face. When she came back, he was stretched out on the couch. It was still there, an almost teenage kind of lust. She started unbuttoning her blouse.

"Please," she said. "Please."

He touched her cheek and ran his hand back under her hair.

Her skin felt singed. He lifted up her hair, as if he were weighing it.

"Is this for revenge? A revenge fuck?"

She let herself down on top of him. "Exorcism," she said. When she came, she screamed.

CHAPTER TEN

HE WAS IN THE JUNGLE, waiting for the chopper to come and take them out. The guy next to him, Dietrich, had an Egyptian ankh symbol on the front of his helmet. Though he'd been with the guy for two weeks, Stenner had never asked him why. He wasn't curious about anything anymore. He didn't want to cover the war anymore; he was just waiting a decent amount of time, until he could go back. He didn't want to know any more stories.

Marlena appeared across the clearing, emerging from the jungle wearing a gaucho outfit. He wasn't surprised to see her there, but he did want to tell her that if she took one more step, she was likely to get her head blown off. She couldn't hear him, but he didn't need to worry; she was walking back and forth, not getting any closer. She dipped and posed, every now and then, like a runway model. He was listening for the chopper, and for a second he thought he heard it, but then some other sound kept getting in the way. He was irritated with the sound that was getting in the way; he wanted to hear the chopper when it first became audible, the very first beat of the rotors, the faintest whirr of salvation. The other sound was a phone ringing. "Jesus Christ," he complained to Dietrich. "Why doesn't someone answer the fucking phone?"

The ringing finally scratched through the fabric of the dream. He rose slowly to consciousness.

"Hello," he answered, before he'd really reached the surface.

"Did I wake you up?"

"No, no," he said in a voice that was too loud, as if he were compensating for a bad connection. "How are you, Alan?"

"I just wanted to make sure you'd be able to make it this afternoon. Last night, you sounded, ah, like you'd had a drink or two."

"Judging from my head, I think your count is low. But don't worry, I never miss appointments. Two thirty at—"

"Don't," Dawson barked. There was a pause. "That's the other reason I called. This may be unnecessary, but take a look over your shoulder when you come. I'm a great believer in caution, especially when it doesn't cost you anything."

"This is not a purely social occasion, then."

There was a pause. Stenner could hear the blare of a horn, traffic. Dawson was in a phone booth.

"Not entirely. Look, I've got a meeting now. I look forward to seeing you."

"Right," said Stenner, but Dawson had already hung up.

He carried the mug of Nescafé into the bedroom and set it down clumsily on the edge of an open book on his desk. It tilted and spilled over his hand. He sopped up the spilled coffee with yesterday's undershirt and laid the book, Gibbon's *Decline and Fall of the Roman Empire* (which he was reading as a form of discipline), on the windowsill. The coffee was soaking into page 217, where Constantine was successfully laying siege to Byzantium. Stenner stood there reading absently:

> He constructed artificial mounds of earth of an equal height with the ramparts of Byzantium. The lofty towers which were erected on that foundation galled the besieged with large stones and darts from the military engines, and the battering rams had shaken the walls in several places. If Licinius persisted much longer in the defence, he exposed himself to be involved in the ruin of the place. Before he was surrounded, he prudently removed his person and treasure to Chalcedon in Asia.

There was a soft rustle from the bed, and he turned to see Claire shift position. She threw her arm up over her head, like a swimmer. He carried his mug of coffee into the bathroom. He ought to shave.

Everything was reminding him of Marlena this morning. Marlena used to sleep like that, in that same posture, as if she were swimming through her dreams. And there was the dream. And even the passage from Gibbon reminded him of her. Like poor old Licinius, he'd removed himself prudently to Amsterdam, lest he become involved in the ruin of Marlena. Who seemed to show less aptitude for self-destruction without him as an audience.

He nicked a spot on his chin and stuck a little tuft of toilet paper on it. And Dawson. He'd first met Dawson through Marlena, or through her parents, anyway. He wondered—it wasn't like Dawson to be mysterious. Or paranoid.

He stood back from the mirror and took his ritual look at himself, an odd, almost sullen look, chin drawn back into his chest, eyes looking up solemnly. He believed he'd adopted this way of looking at himself as an adolescent—a sort of James Dean pose, which at the time had served to throw his acne-covered chin into shadow. Marlena had caught him at it: "Why do you stand like that? You don't look like that; you never have that expression." Then she'd started giggling. "You look like you're posing for a Marlboro ad." But he'd been doing it so long, he couldn't seem to break the habit.

In fact, he thought, as he began to dress, his habits tended to evolve into rituals, his rituals into compulsions: Nine bounces of the ball before taking the free-throw shot. Touching the doorknob in a particular way before leaving home. Wait for the phone to ring at least three times before answering—otherwise it might be bad news. In Vietnam, he'd developed some complicated ones.

Once, as he sat surreptitiously making circles with his index finger while he counted in a complicated sequence, the chopper he was in flew over some ground fire. The kid next to him was repeating "The Lord is my shepherd" so fast saliva poured out of his mouth. And Stenner had realized that what *he* was doing—this special way of putting his helmet on, touching his temples, this weird counting, this stuff with his fingers—was praying. He'd wondered at the time if everyone did it. Later, he'd learned that some of them were way past anything like that.

He ought to wake the girl up, get her out, get down to work. He was on the verge of needing some more money. If he could just finish up this section about

Retinger and the founding of the Bilderberg group—he wanted to close that chapter off with the first meeting at the Hotel de Bilderberg in Oosterbeck in 1954. Then he would go on to deal with the substantive changes the Bilderbergers had wrought on the world. After Bilderberg, his outline took him next to the Trilateral Commission, then the Club of Rome, and then possibly to the most powerful of all the transnationals, Circle Group. The more he learned about it, the more interested he became in transnational management of Western affairs—how successful these groups were in maintaining, for instance, the Atlantic alliance, particularly in the face of deteriorating U.S. status. He looked forward to talking to Dawson about that.

He went into the kitchen to make some more Nescafé. It was ironic, really. He'd agreed to do this book about the transnationals—take a leave of absence from the paper, do a book that wouldn't be too strenuous—mainly for Marlena's sake. They'd planned to live in London for a while, Amsterdam—most of the archival material was in Europe—lighten up, try to patch things back together. And he'd strolled right through the arrangements—got the paper to agree, got the book contract signed, sublet their place in Washington. They'd gone out to celebrate, the night the contract was signed, to Le Pavillon. When they got home, Marlena had cracked out another bottle of champagne—Perrier-Jouët, her favorite. She'd prettily set it out in an ice bucket, waiting to be poured into the two Lalique flutes, while he lit the fire. For once, the fire had leaped into roaring, crackling perfection, not requiring the usual fussing and poking he enjoyed. A flower arrangement, one of Marlena's spiky, asymmetrical jobs, decorated the coffee table. It was pure Marlena, one of her perfectly orchestrated moments. So why had he found himself hoping the champagne cork would break a window, a drunk wander to their door—something to snap Marlena's perfect progression. Nothing had happened. Marlena had clinked her glass against his, "To us." And he'd looked at her and realized he felt nothing, nothing at all. It was as if all the love there was had been there in the beginning and had been gradually withdrawn over the years, like a savings account, and the balance was now at zero.

He looked out the window, down to the street. A Heineken truck stopped in the middle of the street to deliver beer to the café on the corner. A powerful-looking man with gray hair, wearing a green plastic apron, hopped out and unloaded several kegs, bouncing them down onto the sidewalk. Seven or eight cars were now lined up behind the truck, trapped. The beer-man took his time, rolling the kegs into the café, stacking the empties neatly in the back of the truck. Then he disappeared inside, emerged with the manager, who leaned against the hood of the truck, signing the beer-man's paper.

Stenner had been caught in exactly this situation often enough to know that the drivers behind the truck were going berserk with impatience. The interesting thing was that no one honked his horn; it would have done no good, of course, but that would not have stopped the citizens of New York or Washington. The futility of a gesture did not—

"Oh, God."

He turned toward the bed, where Claire had disappeared, head and all, under the covers. He went over and knocked on the white bedspread.

"Anybody home?"

She moaned and then pulled the covers down so that only her eyes and the top of her head were visible. It gave her an odd, Arabian look, except that her eyes were blue.

Almost navy blue. For a moment, her eyes had such a vulnerable look, such an unprotected aspect, it made him feel he should offer her some sunglasses or something. As you'd offer your coat to a naked woman who'd just run out of a burning house.

She let the covers drop down, and her lips parted into a smile. There was something deeply sensual about that shy, vulnerable smile. He felt a sharp twist of desire.

Their lovemaking in the night had been surprisingly powerful—she made love with a scalding intensity that had quickly transformed his own why-not participation into something more compelling. They had been attuned, perfectly meshed. Most of the women he'd made love to lately—and even Marlena—were "technique" lovers. They would physically move his hand, reposition his fingers; they would give explicit directions. Orgasm was the sum of successful techniques. He didn't mind that, but making love to Claire was different. And at the end, when she came, she let out a strange scream, an odd, exultant sound, almost like—

"Good morning," she said.

He actually took two steps toward her before he stopped himself and turned away.

"I'll make you a cup of coffee," he said.

Come on, he told himself in the kitchen. You were drunk, that's all. Drunk. The last thing he needed was to get hung up on some woman right now. Some woman who'd just been ditched and was going to be all fucked up for a year or two.

When he came back in, she was dressed in her rumpled corduroy suit and zipping up a boot.

"Here you go," he said, and set down the coffee. When she looked up at him, her eyes had achieved some distance.

"I feel like a Xerox copy of myself."

He offered her a cigarette, lit it and then lit his own. They inhaled deeply. She smoked as much as he did, which was perversely comforting.

"I don't feel as clear as a Xerox," he said. "I feel *stunned*. I feel stunned like a quarterback who's just been sacked by some gigantic human being who barely knows how to speak." He let his face go slack. "Now I'm back in the huddle, my mind a complete blur, thirty seconds left on the game-clock. I call a draw play up the middle. It seems insane, an insane call, but the running back breaks it, thirty-five yards for a touchdown, we win!" He punched the air triumphantly and then sank back on the couch.

She wagged her head back and forth. "No, your tight end notices you can hardly walk and calls a time-out."

"No time-outs left."

"God is on your side, then. In your right mind you'd never call a draw play up the middle."

"I like to think God is not on the side of a gigantic human being who barely knows how to speak and moments before has just hurled me to the ground trying to permanently maim me."

"I don't think I believe in God. And if I do, I don't think God watches football games."

"I agree. Absolutely. God is into something obscure. Lacrosse, maybe."

"Why are we talking about God?"

"We're not. We're talking about hangovers."

"Oh, that's right. Stunned. Well, I don't feel stunned like that. I feel stunned like a bird that's just flown full tilt into a window." She let her face go slack. "I'm lying there on the ground. Some little kid comes along and thinks

I'm dead. He goes up to his closet and rummages around. He finds a little shoe box."

"I wouldn't go on if I were you."

"You're right. It's a little Buster Brown shoe box. Buster Brown and his dog. What was his dog's name?"

"Let's go out and get some real coffee."

"Tyke? I can't seem to remember his name—the dog, I mean. Anyway, the kid gets a soup spoon and starts digging a hole. The ground is hard; it's hard work. He makes a little cross out of Popsicle sticks."

"The tight end calls a time-out. I mean at the last possible second, the bird lets out a weak little peep and the kid is overjoyed."

She shook her hair back, out of her eyes. "No, no, no. This is *my* story. The kid is pissed off because now all his good work is in vain. He..." She stood up. "Oh, God, standing up is rough. Got any aspirin?"

"Wait a minute. Does the kid cream the bird or not?"

"I wish I had my toothbrush." She stumbled toward the bathroom but stopped at the doorway. "Do they have Bloody Marys in Amsterdam?"

"We could go to the Hilton."

"Let's do it. That's right next to my hotel. I mean the one I started out in. Today I'm moving to the de l'Europe. Oh, God, what time is it? I've got to get out of there by..." Before she finished the sentence, she checked her watch. "Hey, it's only nine o'clock."

"I'm still worrying about the bird."

"The kid doesn't cream the bird. The bird flies away in the nick of time. The bird—I mean, the kid grows up to be an undertaker. The bird...the bird saves the kid's life years later by pecking on his window one night when the kid's house is about to burn down."

"Why? He doesn't owe the kid anything."

"The bird's a saint. Later, he goes to a football game and is the little birdie that tells the concussed quarterback to call a draw play up the middle."

"Bravo!" he shouted, and applauded vigorously. She managed a little curtsy.

"I'll be right back."

In the cold, white room, she threw some water on her face and brushed her teeth with her finger. She tried to restore some order to her hair, exuberant with humidity. She borrowed his hairbrush. *You're handling this quite well,* a neutral, interior voice remarked.

The hangover was so intense, it was beyond pain. She felt giddy, numb, anesthetized. She bent over to pick up a barrette she'd dropped and her head gave a sickening lurch. She straightened up very carefully. She held the barrette in her teeth while she brushed her hair. Quick flashes from the night threatened to destroy her precarious composure. She tried to cut off the thoughts, but it wasn't working. Her head was filling up with embarrassing freeze-frames: carnal hysteria, teenage lust. She was clenching her teeth so hard, the muscles below her ears throbbed. She sat down on the toilet seat and reviewed the evening, gingerly, as if studying the memories through a microscope. She cringed; she felt like leaving through the bathroom window. On the other hand, What the hell, it's all over with now. Rite of passage, she thought, and sailed back into the living room.

After Bloody Marys in the Hilton bar, they walked over to her hotel. They stood under the baroque modern chandelier in the lobby.

"I think this chandelier is made of my personal kryptonite equivalent. As soon as I see it, I start fading..." She felt awkward, post-intimacy estrangement. This guy wouldn't want to see her again. This was goodbye. She glanced around the room as if scouting for fire exits, as if she didn't know where to put her eyes. But he surprised her.

"Look, want to meet me later? In the Rijksmuseum? Test out Phillips' Vermeer theory. I mean, the Bloody Mary helped, but this is a *serious* hangover."

She peered at him, trying to tell if this was a formality, a gesture she was meant to decline. He smiled—such a good-natured smile, she felt momentarily buoyant.

"Yes," she said. "Okay."

"Let's see." He looked at his watch. "About three thirty—I've got an appointment near the museum at two thirty. So I'll meet you in the Vermeer section."

"Three thirty," she repeated.

He leaned over and gave her a short, sweet kiss on the lips. She felt absurdly grateful.

She packed, checked out, and called a taxi, all in a daze. It wasn't until she sat down in the back seat of the cab that she realized once again how shitty she felt. A flurry of irritating thoughts buzzed her like a swarm of flies, thoughts so banal she was disappointed in herself for thinking them. Do I feel guilty? Am I ruining my life? Is it wise? Oh, shut up. She squeezed her eyes shut. She would do anything she had to do, use anything she could as a lever to pry Jeff out of her mind. Then she started worrying that she'd be too early, the de l'Europe room wouldn't be ready, she'd have to wait around in the lobby with this hangover...She turned her attention to this worry—a good, pointless worry that would be settled, one way or the other, in ten minutes.

CHAPTER ELEVEN

STENNER HELD THE SHEAF OF PAPERS loosely cradled in his hands and tapped them into a tidy stack. He put them into the drawer and slapped it shut, as if he couldn't wait to get them out of his sight. He couldn't seem to achieve any fluency today. Wads of crumpled paper lay on the floor around the overfull wastebasket. He picked them up and tried to stuff them in with his foot, but the contents of the wastebasket had achieved maximum density, and he watched resignedly as they slowly expanded and sprang over the sides.

The facts amassed from his research had achieved a parallel maximum density in his mind, a kind of mental gridlock. This had happened before, and he knew very well that the only way out was to slowly and patiently try to put them into some sort of order. Eventually, the false starts represented by the wadded-up paper would diminish and some kind of organizational method would reveal itself.

He looked out the window. A tree branch rocked up and down in the breeze, its tiny new leaves such an intense green they seemed almost iridescent. It was a sunny day, but the sky had a brittle look to it. It might shatter and drench them with rain. He shrugged on his coat and went down the stairs. Time to meet Dawson.

As he approached the tram stop, a weary-looking man wearing a leather jacket that was much too big spoke to him angrily.

"Sorry, I don't speak Dutch."

The man raised a string bag full of packages and hitched it over his shoulder. "No tram coming. A bomb threat or something on the line." He shook his head in irritation and trudged off. Stenner looked at his watch and decided not to waste time looking for a taxi. If he walked fast enough, he could make it on time.

He felt in his pocket for his cigarettes and found the postcard to Marlena. He ought to mail it. The card said yes, it was all right to sell the T.V., she could even keep all the money. Marlena had developed an uncharacteristic meticulous fairness since their divorce. He suspected it was meant to irritate him, but in fact it buoyed him up, allowed him to think he'd actually done her a favor by leaving, something he'd contended at the time. He didn't think that after five years she could go back and rely on her parents the way she had before. And that seemed to be the only way she could display her love, by relying on someone so totally, it seemed she was digging holes in herself so you'd have someplace to focus your attention.

He crossed the Leidsegracht. The few times *he'd* needed Marlena, she'd contrived to need him more, as if flaunting her weakness turned it into some kind of strength. And maybe it did. In the end, the very things they had found most attractive in each other—for him, her glittery rich-girl style; for her, his earnest dedication—were the things they found the most tedious. Inertia was the glue that held them together as long as it did. Too long. A neon bear glared at him from a café window. A neon star advertised Stella Artois.

He turned up Nieuwe Spiegel Straat; Marlena's wounded eyes floated in his head. The night before their celebration dinner, the night before he left her, they'd been out to eat at a Thai restaurant with a social-climbing lawyer who'd oozed flattery all night and also had been officious and boringly didactic about Thai food. Marlena led him on; she found it quite in order to be flattered.

"What an asshole," Stenner said, rooting through the mail. He hadn't been home yet that day.

"He'll do well," she defended him. "At least he shows a little interest in things apart from work."

Then she pulled out a little mirror and a leather pouch and began pulverizing cocaine with a razor, demonstrating a dexterity that appalled him because it revealed a great deal of recent practice. He tried to ignore her, but in the end, watching her concentrate—like a child, her tongue protruding just slightly between her lips—he rose to the bait once more.

"Marlena, don't. You'll be up all night."

She held one nostril shut and inhaled powerfully. "I thought we might go out again. Go dancing." Her eyes glittered. A demure little drop of white snot hung from the tip of her nose. She whirled around the room.

"I'm tired and I've got an appointment at eight-thirty."

"And it's important," she cooed. "Everything you do is so important."

"Jesus Christ, Marlena. We're going out *tomorrow* night. Big celebration. Remember?"

She tidied up another line of cocaine with her razor

blade. "I'll go out myself, then. Cookie and Hans will be at Numbers."

"Do what you want." He picked up some Senate testimony he was trying to get through and began to read.

"I think I'll walk," she threatened. "The fresh air will do me good."

The streets in their neighborhood were so far from being safe that his silence was a measure of his exasperation. She sailed across the frontier of his indifference with her chin stuck belligerently forward. The door slammed shut like a pistol shot.

The restaurant was so dimly lit, he was disoriented, and stood near the door waiting for his eyes to adjust. Waiters in white jackets moved around in the dark like moths.

There was Alan Dawson, at a table in the back, beckoning him.

"John." The firm politician's handshake accompanied by a smile which, though practiced, was still warm.

Stenner thought how odd it was that Carter and Nixon had never learned to smile. It always seemed as if their speechwriters wrote the smiles in: STOP. SMILE HERE. Carter's fat-lipped leer; Nixon's bared-teeth snarl.

Dawson's face had the celebrity aura, the glow of power. Media reverberation, Stenner supposed. Not a household face, but one that nudged you with its familiarity.

"Good to see you," Dawson said, and gestured for a waiter.

"How are you?" Stenner asked.

Dawson seesawed his hands in a so-so gesture. "But it's nice to be in Amsterdam ." The smile blinked on again.

The waiter, a Surinamese, came and took their order—coffee and a cognac for Dawson.

"You here for the festivities tomorrow?"

"No...a meeting. How's the book going?"

"Not as well as it might. It's not as easy as I thought it would be. This morning I got totally bogged down. So what's all this—"

Dawson seized the conversation like a hostage and started talking about Marlena. "Wasn't really surprised, of course, but still..." Stenner felt an unexpected hand tapping his knee. He looked up in surprise, and Dawson nodded his head down. Stenner parked his cigarette in the ashtray and put his hand under the table. A piece of paper wrapped around something solid was pressed into his hand. It was an awkward transaction—he almost dropped it, but managed to slip it into his pocket. All the time, Dawson talked on, now about European economic policy: Eurodollars, marks, zlotys, francs filled the air with camouflage.

"Planning to return to Washington anytime soon?"

"I don't know if I'm planning to return at all. I'm kind of enjoying being on the outskirts of power, not thinking that every word I write is going to make or break the Western World." He lit another cigarette. "An illusion, of course, but one that cost me a lot of sleep."

"Well, we miss you back there, John. One of the only members of the distinguished Washington press corps who didn't play tennis with Senators."

"That certainly irked Marlena."

"I'll bet, I'll bet." Dawson ran his finger around the rim of his coffee cup. He lifted his glass of cognac in the air and then drank it all in one swallow.

The pause extended painfully. Stenner's head was exploding with questions he felt he couldn't ask; Dawson obviously considered them under some sort of surveillance. And if that was true, then they shouldn't just stop talking, as if...

"Let me ask you something," he blurted out. "For the book. Off the record if you like."

"Fine." Dawson's eyes shone with something like relief.

"What do you really think of the trend toward these transnational entities? I can't seem to get my bearings—that's what was slowing me down this morning. I mean, the U.N. doesn't work, granted, so there seems to be some need. I don't know. On the one hand, I don't agree with the conspiracy theorists that Circle Group or Trilateral are a bunch of elitist masterminds plotting to control the world. On the other hand, a lot of agreements do go down bypassing the...congress, or parliament, or whatever the democratic framework is. I mean," he rattled on, "agreements on an executive level." He trailed off.

"Well, yes, it would be nice if the official channels—trade agreements, NATO, the U.N.—if they worked. But they are hopelessly bogged down in procedure...Do you know the water hyacinth?"

Stenner shook his head.

"A sweet little aquatic plant, introduced for its decorative aspects. Lily ponds, you know. Unfortunately, a rampant grower, absolutely without peer; it's succeeded so well that it threatens to totally clog up all the waterways in the South. Procedures are like that: first introduced to make things nicer, to simplify things, codify things; pretty soon they multiply and choke off whatever it was they were intended to simplify. You can see it in the foreign-policy arena quite clearly. The State Department is now such a fine network of procedure, almost no foreign policy can slip through. So, we have the NSC, formed in response to that. But the NSC is proliferating. Soon we will have some new, streamlined entity to replace it. So, I would say that there is a need for an informal forum to discuss matters of mutual interest to various countries, and any attempt to codify it—which would eliminate the potential abuses you talked about—would end up choking off its usefulness."

Despite Dawson's glib didactic speech and lazy grin, the tension at the table was palpable. He was tearing his napkin into bits, rolling the bits into tiny balls and dropping them into the ashtray.

Stenner sighed. "Ambivalence is hell."

"Do you really need to take a side? How about both sides?"

"It makes organizing the book so much easier if I take a side."

Dawson laughed. "Of course, I agree. It's exhausting to be fair."

Stenner attempted a grin and sat back. The charade was over; it was pointless to keep on. The point was in his pocket.

Dawson caught the waiter's eye and scribbled in the air, requesting the bill. "I've got to be getting back to the hotel. Time for me to be off to The Hague."

When the bill came, he took off his glasses to get a closer look, then gave the waiter his American Express card. "Oh, yes, before I forget—Marlena gave me a message to pass on. To tell you she was thriving."

Stenner laughed in a perfunctory way. "Ah, yes, Marlena. If you think it will cheer her up, you can tell her I'm just scraping by." He shook his head. "I really do hope she's doing well. In fact, I was counting on her to make a point of thriving, if only to spite me."

"Difficult girl."

"Yes."

Dawson signed the credit-card form and carefully tore off his blue copy. He folded it precisely and put it and his credit card into his wallet. "Shall we go?" He replaced the wallet in his inside coat pocket, then patted it, as if to make it secure. Their eyes met; the handshake lasted a shade too long. "Glad you could make it, John."

As they emerged from the restaurant, Stenner squinted in the intense sunlight. He was momentarily surprised, just as he always was when leaving a dark theater after a matinee. He paused, got his bearings; he and Dawson walked toward the crosswalk. The spires of the Rijksmuseum had the startling (for Amsterdam) clarity of an etching against the pale sky.

"I'm meeting someone at the museum."

"I'll walk along. Maybe I can get a cab at the rank there. Although I suppose I should walk."

The street was crowded and noisy. Stenner watched a large group of Japanese tourists emerge from a Key Tours bus. They too were headed for the museum, following a tall blond guide who seemed angry and made a series of violent gestures in the air. A Japanese man, half-running to keep up, nodded vigorously. His large head bobbed on the stalk of his neck like a marionette's.

The high-pitched chatter of the Japanese tourists set up a brittle counterpoint to the traffic's deeper roar. Despite their supposedly phlegmatic dispositions, Amsterdammers were demon drivers, aggressive as Italians. The only difference was that they didn't use their horns much. Dawson leaned toward Stenner and muttered, "Do be careful."

A barrel organ, pushed by a man in a blue work shirt, swung around the corner. It looked like a gigantic wedding cake on wheels. A blue Mercedes truck with a faulty muffler was speeding up, trying to make the light. It made a noise so loud, it seemed to reverberate inside Stenner's hungover head.

Two frilly shepherdesses stood on either side of the opening in the barrel organ, their gilded dresses outshining the dull brass gleam of the pipes within. Their painted eyes were cast down demurely, as if shocked by the gaudy pastel flowers, the baroque carved curlicues surrounding them.

Stenner guessed the barrel organ was headed across the street, to a strategic spot under a tree—a good place to work the museum crowds. It cut a swath through the Japanese tourists, who fell back into place in its wake snapping photographs. Dawson leaned toward him to say something over the din, and then there were two loud explosions. Dawson sprang abruptly back away from him, as if frightened by the noise.

Stenner thought the Mercedes truck had backfired. Then he saw that Dawson had fallen, knocking down a well-dressed woman in a fur jacket. Her legs were pinned under Dawson. The contents of her handbag spilled out on the pavement. He noted the scatter meticulously: coins, keys, an address book with a design of ferns embossed on the cover. A pair of sunglasses landed on the pavement, stems crossed, as if someone had placed them there. Two tampons rolled to rest against the sunglasses, followed by a one-guilder coin, which rolled on its edge until it hit a bump and then fell over.

Stenner kept expecting Dawson to get up, dust himself off, apologize. The woman was desperately trying to retrieve the tampons; she couldn't quite reach them. He leaned over to help Dawson up just as the woman freed herself and got shakily to her feet. A large patch of wet blood was smeared on her yellow skirt. She touched it, then held her hand away from her and stared at it. Still, his mind having made certain assumptions—truck backfire, a stumble—it wasn't until he rolled Dawson over and saw that half of his face was a bloody pulp that he fully realized the explosions had been shots. The woman shook her hand as if it were a rag, as if she were trying to shake it loose from her arm. She began to scream.

As he straightened up, it seemed all motion ceased; the moment expanded, suspended in time. All the noise had been sucked away except for the woman's screams howling in his head. Some people leaned toward them, trying to see; others were running away. His eyes seemed to catch them in mid-stride and freeze them, like a camera. He surveyed. There were several clumps of people, and he wondered dimly if others had been shot. The barrel organ's gaudy pastels caught his eye, and he saw a man near it staring at him. Pale blue, intense eyes, in a smooth, flat, almost Asiatic face. This man began to turn slowly away. Near the flat-faced man stood a young, black-haired man with a ruddy complexion. His eyes were darting about and came to rest on Stenner. Stenner picked out the blue metal wink of a gun gleaming at him from the cradle of this man's hand. Sound rushed back in, as if filling a vacuum, and he heard three more explosions, screams, the screech of brakes. He dived into a crowd of people, fell down, picked himself up and ran. Everybody ran.

A Heineken truck slammed on its brakes and skidded. People flooded onto the busy street. Two other cars screeched to a halt. One man rolled up onto the hood of a car. Flash of a child's face contorting into a wail. The child had bumped its head. Someone in back of him screamed. He joined a stampede of people going up the steps to the museum. They funneled past the guard in a chaotic mass.

Stenner didn't stop until he'd elbowed his way through the crowds queued up in the salesroom to buy postcards and reproductions, and into the men's room.

There, in that white-tiled room, his breath came in shuddering gasps. Each greedy breath made him feel more disoriented, as if the air were hallucinogenic. When he gripped the sink for support, the porcelain felt intensely cold. Cold rippled through his body. An old man turned from the urinal and buttoned up his pants. He stood at the sink next to Stenner, hawked, spat some phlegm and turned on the tap. Stenner watched the awful glob balance on the rim of the drain, wobble over and disappear. When the old man left, Stenner splashed some water on his face, doing it badly, getting quite a bit on his shirt. Then he let warm water run over his frozen hands. The warmth seeped into him like life itself. His knee felt wet, and he looked down and saw that he'd cut it when he fell. Blood seeped out through the brown tweed. As he watched, two drops fell to the floor. They stared up at him, from the white tile, like red eyes.

He seemed to know that the door was going to open before it did. At the slight rush of air, he tensed and held his breath. A redheaded man in a leather jacket and leather pants came in. He wore a gold earring shaped like a maple leaf in one ear.

"Anything wrong, man?"

Stenner managed a smile that took far too much energy.

"No."

"Something's going on out there. People screaming and crying, lots of police. Maybe someone slashed a painting." He looked at Stenner suspiciously, shrugged, pulled out a joint and lit it. He made an offering gesture to Stenner.

Stenner shook his head. He couldn't seem to stop staring at the man's hair, which sprouted from his scalp in exuberant tufts. Like clown's hair. Like fire. He got a paper towel wet and began dabbing at his knee.

Two older men came in, speaking German, and Stenner decided to leave. The door seemed to resist him; he felt he'd lost half his strength.

He went into the first uncrowded room he came to and stood waiting for the wooziness to subside. Just the adrenaline rush, he told himself, just fear. He stood there looking vacantly at the paintings. They seemed to shimmer in the air.

His mind ticked away.

If it hadn't been for Dawson's obvious unease, his concern about surveillance, if it hadn't been for that split-second glimpse of the gun barrel, those cold blue eyes focused on him, he would have thought...A guilty thought stabbed him. What if Dawson wasn't dead? He should have checked.

Suddenly he remembered the thing Dawson had passed him under the table. He felt frantically in his jacket pocket and pulled it out. The paper unfolded to reveal a short, stubby key, the kind from a coin-operated locker. On the paper was printed, in tidy black letters, CENTRAAL STATION.

Dawson was leaking him something, for his own reasons, and...and had it gotten him killed? Stenner couldn't quite believe that. He began to wonder if he hadn't been mistaken, that split-second glimpse of the gun barrel an invention of his mind. No. There was something else, something his mind had registered, but that he couldn't now remember. Something just beyond his reach; some bit of information that had signaled his own specific danger and sent him scrambling away from

Dawson. That had made him not just run, but run and hide. He stared at the painting in front of him, a Flemish still-life. A feast spread out on a table, a centuries-old wedge of cheese still oozing moisture from a cut, oysters luminous with clarity.

He tried to reach, to retrieve the nagging bit of information. He closed his eyes. The oysters shone persistently on his eyelids, like the afterimage of a flashbulb. He couldn't remember it, whatever it was.

He thought he heard the whoop of a siren. He could imagine the scene outside—the police, the curious crowds, the photographers, the implacable paraphernalia of disaster. No. He couldn't possibly hear a siren in here. He should go out and give his information, he should—

A voice detonated his nerves: "John? John?"

He whirled to see Claire. Of course—he'd forgotten. Her voice chirped away, fading in and out of his flabby concentration like a weak radio signal.

"...though...the Vermeers...couldn't blame you... wondered...all right? Are you all right?"

When she touched his arm, everything snapped into focus.

"A cop," he said out loud. One of the men near the barrel organ—not the smooth-faced man but the other one, the one with the black hair and the gun—was a cop, a Dutch cop. He'd interviewed him, the day before: one of Okker's men. He'd interviewed him at the station, about the security preparations. Van Heyden? Van der Heyden. Yes.

He steered Claire into a corner.

"I don't know what you mean," she was saying. "What do you mean, a cop?"

"How long have you been here?"

"About an hour."

"Then you wouldn't…Listen. Something just happened. I…" He hesitated. "There was an incident outside while I was on my way here. A man was shot on the street. Several people may have been shot. The man I was with was shot."

Her eyes widened. She looked at him warily, as if she didn't believe him.

"I—are you all right?"

They were obscuring a painting, and an irritated man asked them to move out of the way.

Stenner led her toward the museum's entrance. "I was a witness to the shooting," he said. His voice sounded unconvincing, even to himself. "I don't know what to do," he rattled on. "I'll have to go and deal with…" His voice trailed away as they passed into the cavernous central salesroom. The vaulted ceiling seemed to fly away from him. He felt the agoraphobe's lurch, the fear of space itself.

The room was jammed with humanity. A crackle of excitement shot through the normal hubbub like static electricity. Stenner saw the group of Japanese tourists—a tidy clump in the corner surrounding the taller figures of the blond guide and two uniformed policemen. Near the racks of posters a young woman was sobbing, being comforted by a man in a beret. People were jammed up around the sales desks; querulous, worried voices combined to produce a nervous whining undercurrent. One British man right next to Claire asked no one in particular, "What in bloody hell is going on?"

Stenner was angling over toward the Japanese tourists, a vague intention of speaking to one of the cops there forming in his head, when he spotted Van der Heyden near a water fountain, conferring with three museum guards. He seemed to be establishing his authority, brandishing some piece of identification, sweeping his hands over his shabby clothing as if to dismiss it. Just then he looked up, and his eyes caught on Stenner's. A jolt of recognition transformed his expression into something predatory. He started toward them, jostling through the crowd, leaving a wake of angry irritation behind him.

Stenner began to drag Claire with him down the stairs. She said "Hey!" in a surprised voice, but he just pulled harder on her arm. "Wait a minute," he heard her say in an alarmed voice. "Wait a minute! What's going on?" Claire's voice was irritating him—what was she yapping about? He dragged her along to the bottom of the stairs. When they reached the door, a museum guard said something in Dutch, but Stenner kept on going, through the door, down the outside stairs. He turned to go through the passageway that ran underneath the museum. Posters interspersed with graffiti lined the arched brick walls, flashing by like a speeded-up slide show. A huge skull and crossbones in orange Day-Glo stared at him from the overhang just before they emerged from the tunnel. A cartoon balloon looping out from the skull's evil teeth said FEVER. INFEXION.

Once he saw the black-and-white cabs lined up in the semicircular drive, be realized that that was where he'd been heading. He shoved Claire into the back seat, then followed her in.

"Centraal Station," he managed. They were both gasping for breath.

The cabdriver seemed to be moving in slow motion. Stenner watched him insert a bookmark into a copy of *The Man Without Qualities,* place the book carefully on the seat next to him, adjust his cap and roll his head back toward them. Any second, Stenner expected to see Van der Heyden pounding on the window.

"Centraal Station," he said again.

"I heard you the first time," said the driver, his ruddy face betraying no irritation. He turned the key and swung the car out into the traffic.

In his peripheral vision, Stenner saw Claire edging uneasily away from him until she had pressed herself up against the left-hand door. When he turned to look at her, he saw such an uneasy, fixed look of shock on her face, it made him lose his composure, like a wader stepping off a hidden underwater ledge and finding he can't touch bottom. His head lolled against the back of the seat, his neck boneless.

Claire felt like screaming, but she didn't scream. She took shallow, silent breaths and concentrated on remaining as still as possible. She watched Stenner warily, carefully. A voice in her head shrilled, *He's crazy. He's crazy. He's crazy.* He turned slightly toward her, and she averted her eyes. They fastened on his knee.

His knee was bleeding.

The blood, the sight of the blood, stirred her from her defensive paralysis. The sight of the blood made her want to do something, say something. "Hey, you hurt your knee," she heard herself say, inanely.

She dug in her purse and found a packet of Kleenex. She pressed a wad of tissues up against his knee. *Shot,* he had said in the museum. *Man got shot.* Her head throbbed dully. She watched intently, morbidly, as the blood soaked into the Kleenex. When it was sodden, she couldn't figure out what to do with it, and she held it pinched between her finger and thumb like a flower. Finally, she stuffed it into the ashtray attached to the back of the front seat.

Stenner sat up too quickly, like someone who had nodded off in a lecture. He leaned over the seat back toward the driver. "Look, can you drop her off at the Hotel de l'Europe and then take me to the station?"

Claire exhaled gratefully. She seemed to have been holding her breath.

"Yes, of course," said the driver laconically. "But perhaps I should tell you first that we are being followed. A tan Opel. It's an unmarked police car," he added. "All the tan Opels in Amsterdam are unmarked police cars. They must have got a special price."

Spiky points of blond hair stuck out from underneath the driver's cap.

"Can you lose him?" Stenner asked abruptly.

The driver shrugged. "Tell me why I want to," he said evenly.

Silence.

"Yes," Claire said in a breathy voice. "What's going on? Why does he want to?"

CHAPTER TWELVE

CLAIRE SAT DIRECTLY BEHIND THE DRIVER and stared at the back of his neck. She rubbed a spot at the base of her own neck where her hangover had localized, a bright knob of pain. When she kneaded it, almost pleasurable surges radiated up the side of her head. She waited for Stenner to say something, and it seemed like a long time until he did. He spoke rapidly, and his voice kept getting louder and softer without warning.

"The guy who got shot—he was one of my sources. I mean back home. State Department. Did I tell you someone got shot? Shit!" Stenner slapped the vinyl upholstery and then rubbed his hand over his forehead. "All right. This guy was here in Amsterdam and he called me—wanting a meeting. So we met at a restaurant near the museum. And during the meeting, he passed me something under the table—a key. When we went out to the street, we were waiting for the light to change; I thought it was a truck that backfired. You know, I thought he just stumbled, but then I saw he was *shot*…in the head.

"*Okay*. And then I saw these two guys near a barrel organ. And one of them was a cop, a plainclothes cop. He had a gun. I don't know what I thought. I thought he was going to fucking *shoot* me."

Claire stared at her fingertips where Stenner's blood had soaked into the whorls of her skin.

"*Look*," Stenner said in a very loud voice. "I know it sounds crazy." He rummaged through his pockets. "Here's the *key*; here's the fucking key he gave me." He extended his open palm. The key lay there, exposed, and then he closed his fist over it. "Are they still back there?"

The driver shot a glance in the rearview mirror.

"Oh, yes. He's just staying well back, keeping a steady distance."

Claire started to turn and look out the back window, but she couldn't seem to move. She stared at her fingertips. The blood was dry now, separating into tiny flakes. She looked up. Some large drops of rain splotched the windshield. The driver looked back toward Stenner, to scrutinize him one more time.

"I believe you, but I don't really know why I should help you," the driver said evenly. "Maybe the police just want to question you as a witness. Probably you are imagining things." He shrugged. "Then again, I don't see why not. I don't want to help *them*." He jerked his head backward. "Amsterdammers don't like police; maybe it goes back to the Nazis, the Occupation—I don't know. I especially am not a fan of police. They cracked my rib once in a demo. For nothing, too, for no reason…just that they have a club and I have a rib, you know? Okay," he said decisively. "We give it a try."

"Thank you," Stenner said. "I—"

"Mind you, it's not easy to lose a car here. No curves. Too flat." He made a circular gesture, and Claire looked out the window. They were no longer in the dense part of the city, and she was surprised to see that they were on a highway. The road stretched away from them like a lesson in perspective, coming to a point on the horizon. "By the way, my name is Maarten," the driver said. "Two A's, in case you ever want to send me a thank-you note."

Stenner laughed shakily. "John Stenner, and this is Claire Brooks."

Claire nodded and rubbed her fingertips together. The tiny flakes of blood dusted off into her lap. Hemoglobin. She remembered doing tests in biology class—pricking her finger with a lance, watching the drop of blood plump up, then sucking it into a pipette, waiting a minute or so and snapping the pipette in half to see if the strands of hemoglobin had formed. She put her index finger into her mouth.

Maarten chuckled. "We introduce ourselves as if we just met strolling through the Vondelpark."

Claire remembered that her blood had clotted exceptionally quickly. The biology teacher had pronounced her lucky, "a good healer."

"You're quiet," Stenner said. "Are you all right?"

She nodded too vigorously and gave him what she hoped was a reassuring grin. Unexpected tears pricked at the inner corners of her eyes, and she turned her head away.

"What's the matter? Are you scared?" She shook her head. "What are you thinking about?"

"Blood," she heard herself say. She turned to look at him. "Hemoglobin. I'm a quick healer. Are you? I mean it's your blood."

"Hemoglobin," he repeated, with a puzzled, slightly

disgusted look. And looking at his face, she realized she sounded crazy, that it wasn't wise to divulge every thought delivered by a momentary snap of the synapses. There were conversational rules to obey. It was possible to side-step questions like "What are you thinking?" It was possible to lie.

Stenner started to say something, but the cab suddenly accelerated, and they both sat forward on the seat to look out the front window. They were well outside the city now—there was an occasional house, with a cluster of trees near it. Apart from these houses, flat fields stretched out on both sides of the road. They rapidly approached the rear of a large red-and-white truck.

"If I can just get by this lorry here," Maarten said in a surprisingly loud voice. The car accelerated in a burst and then jerked to the left, hurtling past the truck. They were heading straight for a brown VW.

"Oh, God!" Claire screamed, and her eyes slammed shut. *This is it,* she thought, in a calm, final voice. She grabbed Stenner, waiting for impact. She felt the car lurch farther to the left; there was a pebbly rush of gravel under the wheels. The blare of a horn screamed past, and then the car jumped back onto the pavement and careened off to the right. She and Stenner were jammed up against the door. The brakes shrieked, and her eyes flew open just as they passed a large gray windmill. It looked unreal, a giant's toy. Stenner sat up, but she stayed crumpled against the door, looking out the window. The whole landscape had an unreal, tidy look; it reminded her of a model-train layout.

"One of our picturesque windmills," Maarten said. "Worth a visit, the guidebooks say. Better appreciated at a reduced rate of speed, but..." He blasted his horn, and Claire watched a group of bicyclists flare off to the side of the road. One tall man wearing a bright orange windbreaker raised his fist at them. She could see him clearly for an instant—his hooded brown eyes and his mouth, bracketed by full, muttonchop sideburns, open, angry, yelling.

"I think you lost them," Stenner said, checking out the back window.

"No," Maarten said. "Once they get past the lorry, they will see we didn't go straight on. They'll be back along this way; but it's all right—we'll be gone."

They passed two red-roofed farmhouses, and then he turned the car abruptly up a gravel drive that ran alongside a row of poplar trees. The feather-shaped trees bent and twisted in the wind, their tiny leaves turning inside out in rushes of silver.

They pulled up behind a large house and Maarten jumped out of the cab, yelling at them to get out. They waited on the gravel drive while he backed a battered Deux Chevaux out of an old shed. He drove the cab inside and then emerged and pushed the doors shut. He fastened them together by turning an ancient piece of wood that pivoted on a nail.

Claire was noticing that everything had taken on a miraculous clarity. Each piece of gravel was distinct as a jewel, each blade of grass an uncompromising spear of green, Maarten's gestures so precise as to seem choreographed. Fear cures hangovers, Claire thought. Adrenaline. Adrenaline cures hangovers. Adrenaline, hemoglobin, the silent machinations of bodies.

Stenner took her by the arm and tugged her toward the door.

"Whew," he said, country-boy style. "That was some driving."

"Come in," Maarten said, holding the door open. "Let's have a beer."

"Do you live here?"

Maarten shook his head. "No, not me. Some friends of mine. A bunch of clowns, really."

"Who's that?" called a voice from another room.

"Maarten!"

"Got any cigarettes?"

"Yes!"

Maarten gestured for them to sit down at the dining-room table. It was covered with a slightly dusty Oriental rug. Lying on top of it were three puppets, face down. They looked as if they'd been murdered. Claire was afraid to pick them up, afraid she would find tiny, puppet-sized pools of blood under them. But she did. She picked them up and turned them over. They were beautifully made and recognizable to her as Beatrix, Juliana and Prince Bernhard.

"What gorgeous puppets," she said.

"Francesca—it's her place, really. She makes them."

Stenner picked up the Bernhard puppet and put it on his hand.

"Ah, Prince Bernhard. I'm writing about you. I'd like to ask you a few questions." He made the Bernhard puppet cover its eyes with its hands.

"A story?" Maarten asked. "About Bernhard? I didn't think there was anything left to tell."

"I'm writing about transnational groups. You know— Bilderberg, Circle Group, Trilateral."

"Ah, I see," Maarten began. "I wonder—"

"*Cigarette!*" cried a desperate voice. A short man, dressed in an orange leotard and tights, bounced into the room.

"Claire, John, this is Tucker."

Tucker bowed, stood back, did a backflip and bowed again.

"Pleasure." He took a cigarette from Maarten, lit it and blew out a long stream of smoke, then walked over to the table, put the cigarette in an ashtray and picked up three oranges from a chipped Delft bowl. He started to juggle.

"I've got to be off to meet Francesca. A little street theater,"—he wiggled his eyebrows—"on the eve of the great event."

"Look, are you taking the Deux Chevaux? If not, I'd like to borrow it."

"No, no," Tucker said. He caught the oranges and returned them to the bowl. "Can't park downtown after four, you know; they're towing all the cars out. It's not raining, is it?"

"Not really. A few drops."

"I'll hitch. Can I have Bernhard?" he asked Stenner. He put the three puppets into a rucksack. "Gotta go. Gotta go. Nice meeting you folks—drop in sometime. Catch you later, Maarten. Can I have another cigarette?" He tucked it behind his ear and pirouetted to the door.

"You weren't kidding," Stenner said, "about the clowns."

"This is what remains of the cultural revolution," Maarten said, going through a swinging door painted electric blue with hundreds of tiny stars glued to it—the kind of stars teachers stuck to your papers in grade school. "Tucker, Francesca, lots of others like them," his voice continued. He reemerged. "This isn't very cold." He handed them each a bottle of Grolz beer. "Anyway, they are some of the by-products of the sixties. The rest seem to be making plant holders out of macramé."

"And they can afford a house like this doing puppet shows?"

"Oh, no, they couldn't get a closet with what they

make off puppet shows. That's Francesca's family—Dad's someone big with Unilever. What I can't get over is that Francesca has lived with Tucker for ten years. Can you imagine that?"

"Is he always like that?"

"Yes, always. He has incredible energy—claims he's hyperactive. He expends it all sort of bouncing around. Francesca, however, is quite a good artist—a talent she persists in fiddling away making puppets. There's a lot of this sort of thing in Amsterdam—left over, you know, from the grand old days. Counterculture as a cottage industry."

"In the States, it was like that for a while and then everyone went to law school." Stenner grimaced, then laughed. "I think I prefer puppets."

"Law school—did they really? Even puppets aren't as tedious as law. Look, let me get you a plaster for your knee. You're bleeding all over Francesca's seventeenth-century floor. Not that anyone would notice."

Stenner was anxious to get to Centraal Station to see what Dawson had left in the locker, but Maarten persuaded him that it would be safer to wait. They sat around for what Claire guessed was a couple of hours, discussing the abdication and investiture, the hostages, the squatters, the best places to get rijsttafel, the Moluccans. Finally, they rattled back toward Amsterdam in the old Deux Chevaux.

"Why does it look so funny?" she asked. "I mean the outside—it looks sort of *furry*."

Maarten spoke in a near-shout, to overcome the noise of the engine.

"Tucker's work, of course. He borrowed it once for an ecology demo, but he wanted to disguise it. It looked too metallic or something. So he put some sort of glue all over it and then covered it with autumn leaves. It did look really wonderful for a day or two; but then, of course, the leaves began to shred, it rained…"

They were passing through the outskirts of Amsterdam, high-rise suburbs. Stenner was shaking his head. "I don't believe this," he said in a high, manic voice. "I don't fucking believe it."

Claire looked out the window, watching the buildings slide by. She felt exhilarated in a lethargic way, like a child on a long trip.

"I was shot at once," she said in a sleepy voice.

Stenner thumped his foot on the floor. "Really?"

She sat up straight. "Well, not really shot at. I was just in the way. It was in New York; there was an armed robbery. You get used to seeing these things in the movies, and when you're in the middle of one you forget to be scared. I stood there like an idiot, like a spectator."

"I did that too, *exactly,*" Stenner said, "when I first got to Vietnam. Bullets were zipping by and I wanted to *watch.* Some guy tackled me and brought me down and I was pissed off, struggling to get up. I didn't do it twice, though."

"Me too," Claire said—"that's what happened to me. I mean Jeff tried to get me down and finally he knocked me down, hard. I was dazed for a minute. I was lying there on the concrete, and some lady was saying [She mimicked a thick New York accent], 'Put something in her mouth; she'll swallow her tongue.' And Jeff was saying, 'Stand back, give her some room.' I thought I'd been shot. I wasn't sure. Then Jeff started asking concussion questions in this weird anchorman voice—you know: 'What is your *middle* name?' 'Now I'm going to hold up some fingers. Tell me how many you see.' After a while the police came over and apologized. 'Hot pursuit,' they said."

"Sounds like a porno movie."

"I've never been shot at," Maarten said. "Clubbed and gassed, yes; shot at, never."

They all laughed.

They were stopped at a light.

"Do you like driving a cab?" Stenner asked.

"Think I'm cut out for better things, hey? Well..." He turned around and grinned—a wide, loopy smile. "In fact I do like it. It's the only job I've ever had that I like very much. It's necessary. It has no point—I like that about it. Also, no future—I am not going to rise through the ranks of taxi drivers to become some taxi-driver king, you know? That keeps me from living in my dreams—a problem of mine. At one point, I was an ambitious anarchist—can you imagine this creature?"

"But you seemed to think your friend Francesca was wasting her time making puppets."

"That is a different thing. Francesca is ambitious and I am not."

"Were you a *provo?*"

"Yes, I was one of those. It got to seem more boring than anything else after a while—inventing a point, inventing the future, trying to shock, to manipulate. It all seemed like cheap thrills." He negotiated a curve and pulled up to the curb. "Here we are, Centraal Station at last." He tore a small piece of paper from *The Man Without Qualities* and wrote his number on it. "I'd like to find out how all this comes out. Ring me up some time."

"I don't know how to thank you," Stenner said. "For what it's worth, if I can ever do something for you..." He shrugged and started to open the door. There was no handle.

"You have to reach outside to open it."

"Jesus, I must owe you a small fortune. I almost forgot."

Maarten wouldn't let Stenner give him much money—"Just enough to pay the petrol."

Stenner argued with him, but he wouldn't change his mind. "I set my rates, hey? I don't try to make money. Only the government does that."

"They might have seen your license number."

"I already thought of that. I took the lovely couple to Haarlem, dropped them off at the Frans Hals Museum." He shrugged. "That's all I know."

"Take care."

"You too."

They stood on the curb. Claire felt abandoned, awkward. They stood there and watched the Deux Chevaux merge into the traffic and disappear.

Stenner turned around without looking at her, and Claire trailed him into the station like a child following a parent. Like a very small child, she wanted to take his hand, to be led; she wanted the comfort of touching him, contact. Instead, she tucked her hands into the pockets of her trench coat and followed him. He stopped, and she watched him look around. He stood on the balls of his feet, somehow predatory. The noise of the station rose around them, an industrious, purposeful hum. He strode toward a bank of lockers and opened one. When he turned around, he was carrying an attaché case. He headed for the door.

She had trouble walking as fast as he did. Her heels clicked furiously against the floor. They pushed through to the outside and joined a huddle of people waiting for a tram. A chilly wind tugged at the curbside litter and dislodged a paper cup. Claire watched it cartwheel down the street until a tall man stepped on it.

"You ought to go back to your hotel now; I forgot to ask Maarten to drop you off."

"But I want to see…"

Stenner tried to think of the right words to get rid of her. When she looked up at him, her eyes were exhausted. The train arrived, and the crowd nudged them toward the door. He lacked the energy to resist them, to resist her. They funneled into the doorway and he bought her a ticket. There was no place to sit. The tram started up, and she lurched into him.

"I'm sorry," she said automatically.

Stenner maneuvered toward the rear door, and she followed. He was resisting the impulse to open the attaché case right there in the tram. There was a man in a brown corduroy coat standing directly in front of him, and Stenner stared at the man's neck, as if he needed to commit it to memory; each pore, each wrinkle, the way the collar nudged the flesh into a ridge, the whorls of silky black hair. Superimposed on the topography of the man's neck his mind kept flashing him Alan Dawson's fall—the moment Dawson leaped back into the air, the arc of his fall, the way he landed on the woman in the fur coat—just that much, over and over again. He couldn't stop seeing it—it was like the crucial footage of a disputed game-winning touchdown that the announcers kept replaying from every possible angle. Someone nearby was humming "When the Saints Come Marching In." How could he *ever* have thought Dawson had stumbled?

"I'm sorry," Claire said, at the exact moment the tram came to a halt with a dull screech. "I'll get off here. I'll go back to the hotel."

"No, never mind. This is my stop." The man in the brown corduroy coat stepped aside to let them through. Stenner was surprised to see that he was an Oriental.

The light was fading, and streetlights flickered on as they walked. They passed a café built to look like an enormous wine barrel turned on its side. A chalkboard listed the specials. A stack of bicycles leaned up against the wall, their saddles covered with plastic bags against the drizzle. The bicycles obstructed the sidewalk, and Stenner took Claire's hand as they walked for a short way on the street. She held his hand tightly, but when he looked over at her, she seemed unaware of him, self-absorbed. As they passed under the tree in front of his building, a gust of wind loosened some raindrops caught in the leaves, and he looked up toward the windows of his flat. Claire let go of his hand and wiped at her hair.

He opened the door and had gone up about five steps when he stopped suddenly. Claire was ahead of him, and he lunged for her, grabbed her arm roughly and pulled her back out the door. He heard the door open upstairs and feet on the stairs. They were back outside, and he dragged Claire across the street toward the cars, angle-parked against the canal.

"Down." They crawled between two cars and wedged themselves in front of one car that didn't have its bumper firmly up against the iron railing.

"What's the matter? What's happening?"

"Someone was in there, in my place. I saw the light on, I saw them from outside, but it didn't register until we started up the stairs."

And then an odd thing happened. The window of the car next to them, an Orange Volvo station wagon…shattered…silently, spontaneously, of its own accord. It sounded as loud as an avalanche.

They heard some shouts and screams and then the sound of someone running.

"Silencer," Stenner said. But Claire thought he'd said "Silence," and she pressed her lips together. Then she heard the sharp metallic bark of metal striking metal and she realized he meant a gun. A gun with a silencer.

Stenner jerked into motion at the sound. He clambered over the short metal railing, motioning for her to do the same. They hung from it by their arms—Stenner by only one arm because he still held the attaché case. The wall of the canal sloped out toward the water, and they were able to use their feet to remain in a kind of crouch. The surface was slippery with algae, and Claire lost her footing. Her knees and chin banged up against the wall. She was too frightened to make a sound.

"All right?" Stenner whispered.

She nodded. Her feet scrambled for purchase against the slimy wall.

"Can you swim?"

She nodded again. She could feel blood ooze from her chin. He jerked his head to the right. "We'll swim around to the back of the houseboat." He let go. The moment she saw him start to slide down the wall, she let go too. The momentum carried her underwater, and when she came up, she couldn't see him. The water was cold enough to take her breath away, and she took several short reflex gasps that didn't quite supply enough oxygen. Adrenaline flushed her chest like a spreading burn. She spotted Stenner a few feet away, his white disembodied head bobbing in the water. She dog-paddled after him, still gulping air, and followed him under the bow line of the houseboat. Strands of algae hung from the rope and flopped against her face as she swam under.

Just as they reached the stern, a canal boat slid around the bend. The guide's voice carried eerily over the water: "The Prince's Canal—de Prinsengracht." They swam toward the houseboat's ladder. A small dinghy rocked gently in the waves created by the canal boat. Stenner grabbed the side of the dinghy with one hand and threw the attaché case over the side. Claire could hear him panting with the effort. Then he tugged the dinghy over to the ladder and got into it. When Claire reached the ladder, when she got into the dinghy, when she had stopped moving, a nauseating wave of fear flowed over her. She felt like a body surfer rolled over by an unexpectedly powerful wave. But the fear did not produce a sharp, alert state; it deadened her. It was thick, glutinous, surrounding her and pressing against her eyes, her nose, her mouth; the fear sat on her chest like slime.

When she had a coherent thought, it was that the dinghy was moving. She heard herself breathing—long, torturous gasps. She sensed that this lethargy was dangerous, like the fuzzy feeling victims are reported to get before freezing to death. Maybe this is how people die of shock, she thought. Not from a sudden slam, an explosive short-circuit of nerves. They dissolve into their fear, like sugar into coffee, and then their substance is gone.

She heard the rhythmic dip of the oars in the water. They passed under a footbridge. She sat up.

Stenner looked over his shoulder and corrected the heading of the dinghy. He was aiming for a space between two houseboats where two tires, painted white, hung down as fenders. They stared at him balefully, two huge eyes.

Claire rubbed at her chin with the clumsy, disconnected gestures of a marionette.

"Are you all right?" he asked in a flat, emotionless tone.

Her head wobbled. He guessed it was a nod.

Thoughts and questions slid through his mind. How did they know where I live? Who the fuck were *they?*

What did they want? The attaché case? What's in the attaché case? How did they know about it? He rowed backward to keep the dinghy from crashing into the canalside. They thumped softly into one of the tires, and he tied up the boat. Were they being followed? He stood up, and the boat rocked; he lost his balance and fell into the water. He heard Claire scream.

A small crowd of onlookers had accumulated at the side of the canal. Stenner levered himself back into the boat, and they both climbed—up onto the tires and over the iron railing. The knot of people loosened and backed up.

"What a night," Stenner said to no one in particular. "Is there a taxi stand near here?"

A short man with gray hair, restraining a small barking dog, pushed through the knot of onlookers.

"Spritzi! Shhh! What are you?" he demanded. "Canadians? Britons? Americans?"

"Americans."

"So. Shhh, Spritzi!" The man shook his head. "You will surely catch a chill walking about like that," he said in the exasperated tone of a disapproving parent. "The taxi drivers will not take you if you are so wet—I can tell you this." He wagged his finger at them. "They have got very fussy now." Claire's teeth began to chatter. She pressed her hand against her mouth. "Look at you, look at you," the man said sadly. "You are going to get pneumonia. Spritzi! Sit! Well, all right," he went on angrily. "I don't know why it is me, always me, who is helping people." He cast an accusing glance at the thinning crowd of onlookers. "Come on, then—my flat is directly across here. I guess I can warm you up a little."

When Stenner and Claire didn't immediately move, he said, "Well, come on, then." They trailed him across the street. He pointed to a crumpled metal post on the corner. "Just last week, a car crashed into this. Who do you think calls the ambulance? Willem Hofmans, that's who." He stabbed his chest with his thumb and sighed.

When they were at his door, he asked them to remove their shoes. He went away and returned with some heavy gray blankets that smelled of mothballs, and two flowery towels. "So. Come in and sit down. I will prepare some hot chocolate."

Claire and Stenner sat close together on a Danish Modern sofa in a room so crowded with plants it resembled a jungle.

"Quite a green thumb."

"We are depending a lot..." Claire began. Her voice evaporated.

"On the kindness of strangers. I know. It's a bad sign." He arched his head back and looked up. An enormous fern hung directly over his head. He shifted over, closer to Claire. "Can I come back to the de l'Europe with you?"

"Of course."

Their host trudged into the room with a tray bearing three steaming cups of hot chocolate. He handed each of them one of the white porcelain mugs and took a seat across from them in a bentwood rocker. Claire and Stenner chorused their thank-yous.

"Once you have warmed up a little, I will find you a taxi."

"You're very kind," Claire said. "John was saying what a green thumb you have." She gave her head an admiring shake.

"I'm Willem Hofmans," the man said, beaming a smile.

They introduced themselves, warming their hands on the mugs and sipping the luxurious cocoa.

CHAPTER THIRTEEN

SERGEANT VAN DER HEYDEN was also sipping hot chocolate, but instead of the rich steaming liquid in porcelain mugs that Claire and Stenner were enjoying, his was thin and watery and tasted of the Styrofoam cup it came in. He was waiting for Commissaris de Groot to look up from his work and acknowledge his presence. He shifted from foot to foot for a while, then reprimanded himself. Relax, he ordered. Bodily displays of nervousness are not suitable for the successful man. He forced himself to stand still.

The commissaris closed a folder and set about filling his pipe. Van der Heyden stood there like a light pole. Although he was a handsome man, his black hair stylishly cut, his appearance was marred by a perpetually eager look in his eyes that made him seem childish. De Groot sighed. He couldn't bring himself to like Van der Heyden. Almost no one liked Van der Heyden. He was too earnest, too well-meaning, too *good*. He had no bad habits. He neither smoked nor drank. He had once confided that he did a hundred sit-ups and a hundred push-ups each morning. Now he had given up caffeine. The man was a walking reproach. The commissaris lit his pipe and sucked on it greedily, spewing out sweet-smelling clouds of poisonous smoke. His call to Okker came through.

Okker was understandably agitated. As chief of security for the next day's investiture, he had a thousand things on his mind, and it was not surprising that he had been confused by De Groot's message. De Groot puffed on his pipe and let Okker rage on for a while. He could hear him slamming his fist down on the desk for emphasis.

"Hans? Hans, you got the message wrong. I didn't *pull* the surveillance. I just switched it."

He endured another blast from Okker.

"Because while they were keeping an eye on your supposed Red Army terrorists, they witnessed a homicide."

Van der Heyden and Reisbergen had been temporarily detached from Homicide to help out the security forces and had been assigned to carry out surveillance on two young Japanese suspected by Interpol of being Red Army members.

"I *know* it's not *convenient,* Hans," De Groot said.

Van der Heyden was paying close attention to the commissaris' style. Obviously, Okker was steaming at the other end of the phone, but the commissaris was cool and smooth.

"The two men I have replaced them with are not 'dildoes,' as you put it, Hans. They are perfectly capable of following your Japanese."

Van der Heyden allowed himself an inward smile. If his replacement was considered a "dildo," then *he* was obviously *not* considered one.

"Look, Hans," the commissaris said, his voice sliding from the cool to the icy. "You're not the only one in the world with problems. This wasn't just any old so-and-so who got himself shot down on the street in broad daylight—he was a United States State Department official."

Okker must have calmed down at last, because the commissaris was obviously accepting an apology. "No, it's all right, Hans. I understand you're under a great deal of pressure."

Van der Heyden surreptitiously dug out a tiny sliver of dirt from under his fingernail.

"Reisbergen has briefed them. Apparently the group has now left the Rijksmuseum and is touring the red-light district. The entire group—according to Reisbergen, they go everywhere together, like a school of fish."

Van der Heyden buffed his fingernails against his corduroy pants.

"Good luck to you tomorrow, Hans."

The commissaris set about relighting his pipe. The trouble with pipes—he had given up cigarettes five years back after a bout of pneumonia—was that they went out if you didn't keep puffing on them.

"Would you sit down, Sergeant?" he said to Van der Heyden. Van der Heyden marched over to a chair. He seemed to be in uniform even when in plain clothes. De Groot thought he barely restrained himself from saluting. He wondered, not for the first time, why Van der Heyden hadn't gone in for a military career. Police work was not really suitable for someone who believed in the perfectibility of mankind.

Detective Johan Reisbergen, a short, muscular man with a full mustache, erupted into the room. He immediately strode over toward Van der Heyden. He had a simian look to him, his long arms held out from his body like parentheses. The men called the pair Beauty and the Beast.

"You complete asshole, there you are. Jesus Christ on a cross, where do they come up with shitheads like you? Are you out of your fucking mind? First firing into the air like that? And then where did you fucking *go*?"

"I was in pursuit," Van der Heyden said demurely.

"In pursuit of *what*? Your dick?"

"In pursuit of the assailant, of course."

The commissaris knocked his ashes into the ashtray and intervened.

"Gentlemen," he said. "Before we come to blows here, I would like to hear your versions of the event, beginning with you, Reisbergen." Not only were they physically as different as night and day, but their personalities were antithetical as well. They made a surprisingly good team.

"All right, all right," Reisbergen said in an irritated tone. "The Lone Ranger and I were across the street from the Rijksmuseum. We had the targets well in sight. They were about to cross the street—they were just waiting for the light to change. We were standing next to a barrel organ. The Japanese were clicking away like mad with their cameras. And then, *bang*"—Reisbergen punched his fist into the air—"there was an explosion. *Bang,* another explosion. The guy that got shot was right next to the Jappies—I *saw* him get it. Head shot. Large-caliber bullet, I'd say. Well, from the angle of the fall, I know the shot has come from the direction of where I'm standing. Then everyone starts moving in—toward where the guy got shot. You know what jerks people are. So I turn around to look behind me. And a guy near the barrel organ—I just get a glimpse of gun metal going into this guy's pocket. He's a strange-looking dude, flat-faced, like, kind of Oriental-looking except he's got blue eyes. And he's starting to melt away, stroll off. Then I hear some more shots and I think, What the hell is going on? and I look away from the guy with the gun for a minute. And I see this fucking idiot"—he jerked his head toward Van der Heyden—"is firing shots into the air. But it's still not too late. I yell, 'Come on!' to Junior here. And then, 'Halt! Police!' Of course, the flat-faced guy stops strolling and starts turning on the juice, you know, and he damn well knows I can't shoot him in the middle of all these people. I'm not worried. I know Mr. Athlete is here with me, radioing in for help and hot on my heels. But me, I'm running out of steam fast. So we get to a place where I think we can pincer him in, and I look around for Mr. Athlete and he's not even in fucking sight. I chase on for a bit, but poof!"—he snapped his fingers—"the guy gets away." Reisbergen paced around in a tiny circle. "I still can't believe it. I can't fucking believe it. Here's a murderer—a goddamned *assassin*—and he shoots down some guy in *broad daylight* and he has the bad luck to do it while he's standing *right next to* a couple of cops and he *still. fucking. gets. away.*" Reisbergen was trembling. The commissaris stood up.

"Johan," he said, putting his hand on Reisbergen's shoulder. He half-expected Reisbergen to be hot to the touch. "Calm down." The commissaris was very fond of Reisbergen, but he was always startled by the detective's capacity for rage. The commissaris himself was incapable of being that angry. He got mad in a totally different way—a disappointed, cold, cynical way. On the other hand, Reisbergen was not a vengeful man; his anger was released and spent. The commissaris envied him that—he himself was capable of holding a grudge for decades.

"It wasn't that way at all, sir," Van der Heyden said in a sort of pompous whine. "The way I saw it, or should I say, heard it, the shot sounded as if it came from right next to the victim."

"A silencer!" Reisbergen shouted. "Is your head full of mud? You know a silenced bullet makes no sound unless and until it breaks the sound barrier. You know what a silencer is, super-sport?"

"Johan," the commissaris reprimanded.

"As I was saying," Van der Heyden continued, "there was a shot, and I thought it came from close range. There was a man right next to the victim, and as I approached, he started to make his move. So, I fired into the air."

"You caused a fucking stampede! And how is this man supposed to know you're the Lone Ranger?" Reisbergen shouted. "You're not even wearing your mask." His arm shot out and clipped the commissaris in the shoulder.

"Johan," the commissaris said, with more volume. "I would like to hear the sergeant's account."

"I pursued the suspect into the Rijksmuseum, lost sight of him for, oh, I estimate five minutes or so and then found him again. He rushed out the door when he saw me—I mean *sprinted*—and got into a taxicab. Fortunately, our car was parked right there and I was able to pursue the taxicab."

"He's got the keys to the car; he's got the radio," Reisbergen mumbled.

Van der Heyden glared at him momentarily. "I radioed for help and tailed the car. But when we got out on the highway, toward Haarlem, well...I was keeping the getaway car in view, waiting for the backup, when he shook me. He used extremely professional tactics, you may be sure, sir. Obviously a professional driver. Of course, I got the license number of the taxicab. It was probably stolen, but it is somewhere to start."

"Let me ask you one thing, Sergeant," the commissaris said, filling up his pipe. "You did pull your gun? I mean when you first heard the shot?"

Van der Heyden never answered questions quickly. He pondered and then said, "Yes, I did, sir."

"And then you fired shots into the air?"

"Well, yes..."

"Well, then, isn't it possible that the 'suspect' thought you were in fact the assailant?"

"If I were the assailant, I wouldn't fire into the air, would I? Besides, how do you explain the getaway car's tactics? I was driving an unmarked car, after all. And I was keeping back a way."

"Half of Amsterdam knows those are police cars."

"Half of Amsterdam doesn't drive in such a way that my mother would have died on the spot of fright. The driver pulled up behind a lorry and then, despite the fact that there was traffic coming from the opposite direction, pulled out to pass. He went all the way over to the opposite shoulder and then cut back in front of the lorry. There was a side road there, and that's where he turned off. It must have been a planned route, sir. By the time I was able to get past the lorry and reverse direction and get back to that road, the taxi had vanished. None of the backup, which had finally arrived in the area, spotted it either."

"Hmmmm," said the commissaris.

"What's more, sir," Van der Heyden continued, *"I recognized the man. I recognized the suspect."*

The commissaris exhaled.

Van der Heyden bounced on his heels. "That is, I don't know his *name.* But I saw him at security headquarters yesterday. He was with that reporter from *Het Parool.* He had press identification around his neck." Van der Heyden paused for effect. The commissaris watched the pale blue swirls of smoke dissolve. "Needless to say, the thought of a possible *murderer* with press accreditation running about tomorrow— well, it sets my teeth on edge, to say the least."

"All right, Sergeant," the commissaris said in a weary voice. "You go down to security headquarters and check the press files. Also run the taxi's license plate through and question the driver."

"Sir," said Van der Heyden, and strode efficiently from the room.

Reisbergen was looking out the window. On the windowsill were what looked like three damaged pieces of Lucite mounted on wooden stands. Actually, they were slabs of bulletproof glass. The caliber sizes of the bullets that had inflicted the damage were engraved on brass plates. Only the .45 slug had done much. Stress lines from the glass radiated out from the point of impact. Reisbergen put his thumb into the large hole gouged out by the bullet.

"I couldn't live with him if he were right," Reisbergen said. "Fortunately or unfortunately, he *isn't* right."

"*Un*fortunately, I suppose you are correct. But would you recognize the other man, the one you chased?"

"Absolutely—he was unusual-looking, as I said. An odd face, Slavic probably, with Oriental-shaped eyes. But the eyes were blue—pale blue, like smoke. And what about the victim? Any more information there?"

The commissaris shook his head in a worried way. "He was staying at the Amstel Hotel, our Mr. Dawson, attending a Circle Group meeting."

Reisbergen frowned. "Circle Group? Isn't that one of those—well, a Bilderberger kind of outfit?"

"More so," the commissaris said. "Bilderberger to the tenth. You could blow up a Circle Group meeting and wait for the Western World to come screeching to a halt. They are finished with their meeting now, and most of them have already left Amsterdam. I'll have a go at a couple of them, but I don't think I'll get very far. They say it was just a routine planning session. And *you* are going to the files to look for this flat-faced man."

Reisbergen grimaced and got up to leave. "What a way to spend the night."

"At least we have an eyewitness, hey?" The commissaris stood up and put on his raincoat. "I'm going home for a bit, to see how Willi is doing. Call me there if you turn up anything."

"How is she?" asked Reisbergen as they lingered by the door.

Reisbergen was one of the few who continued to ask about De Groot's wife, Willi. Most people preferred to give him searching glances when they thought he didn't see them. Willi had cancer. Her body had suffered through an intense onslaught by chemical and radiological agents. The cancer had been unimpressed, but Willi's body had shrunk and lost hair. She was frail as a leaf, and De Groot occasionally had dreams now in which Willi evaporated right in front of his eyes. Only her smile was left in these dreams—exactly like the Cheshire cat. Willi would attack him when she thought he was being oversolicitous: "For God's sake, Hendrik, get your hand off my arm. I'm not going to die right here on the street."

"She has her good days and her bad days. That's the jargon you use when someone is dying—I am finally catching on. You should come and see her, Johan; she will cheer you up about it." De Groot ran his finger down the glass in the door. "She is unbelievably devoid of self-pity."

"I will come and see her, then, if she is feeling like it. After tomorrow."

"After you check the files, go over and see Hoppe and get him to sketch this fellow, hmmm?"

"Right."

Commissaris Hendrik de Groot did not go directly to his home. He stopped off at a café and drank two genevers. He thought about the dead man. The dead man had been fifty-nine, exactly Willi's age. He thought he would prefer being blasted from the face of the earth to slowly disappearing from it, like Willi. Perhaps he was wrong—perhaps he would be brave, as Willi was, and relish the knowledge of his coming end, or rather, relish the special quality that knowledge lent to the time left.

He had been drinking too much. He had been doing everything too much—smoking his pipe too much, working too much, eating too much. He had become a man of excess. A veneer of excess had been constructed between himself and the fact of Willi's approaching death.

He pushed out the door into the starless night. A light drizzle misted over him. The streets seemed oddly spacious, deserted. Then he saw a tow truck removing a car and he realized what was different: there were no cars. The center of the city was being cleared of vehicles for the investiture tomorrow.

Mercury-vapor lamps turned the sky a sickly orange. For a moment, the deserted streets and the orange-tinged air combined to produce an eerie, post-nuclear feeling. It sent a shiver up his spine. He thought: Tomorrow will be bad.

He walked along, depressed. He was worried about death, the finality, the loneliness he faced. He felt, as a child might, that he was being abandoned. Willi, on the other hand, was worried about decorum.

"If I start shitting all over the place like a baby, that's it," she said one night. "I'm off to the hospital then, you must promise me." The thought of Willi, his strong, capable Willi, declining into some barbaric second infancy had startled him at the time. And then the thought of her worrying about being *embarrassed*—that was even sadder. Willi had joked him out of it, as usual. "Don't pull that long face, Henk. God knows, you might depress me. Besides, I'm not that decrepit yet."

He stopped at the flower stand to buy Willi some flowers. All sorts of flowers were orange. Flowers that even the mad floral genetic engineers of Holland had never considered breeding to be a color so flashy (and these were fellows who had managed to produce tulip blooms as big as men's heads) were now dyed orange. He located a single bouquet of white daisies, paid for it and walked on. The prevalence of orange had a redeeming aspect. Because of the investiture tomorrow, the press boys would be far too preoccupied to devote the attention they might to the death of Alan Dawson and its investigation. This would make things much simpler—fewer lunatics offering false leads, fewer publicity-mad volunteers for the role of assassin.

Still, he would need to know a lot more about Alan Dawson before he could discern a motive. Such a flashy killing! Why?

He arrived at his front door.

CHAPTER FOURTEEN

CLAIRE AND STENNER, STILL WRAPPED in Willem Hofmans' blankets, which they had promised to return, pushed through the door of the de l'Europe. Claire was too cold to feel embarrassed. There was a polite stir of interest as they entered the hotel's genteel lobby. The clusters of people seemed merely to rotate slightly in place. A brief look of alarm crossed the concierge's face, which then resumed an encouraging, helpful look.

"One Fourteen," Claire said.

"Ah. Of course. Mrs. Brooks." He turned to get her key, but did not immediately relinquish it. "But what has happened to you?"

"I fell into the canal," Claire said, repeating the fabricated story Stenner had offered Willem Hofmans. It had seemed extreme to mention bullets in Hofmans' ferny living room. And it seemed unwise to bring up bullets in this genteel lobby. Bullets or dead men or crazy stories. She didn't want to get into that at all.

"Fell into the canal?" the concierge repeated. He cast a bewildered glance at Stenner.

"And I can't swim, so my friend rescued me." She looked over at Stenner, hunched in his gray blanket. They might have been members of some bizarre religious sect...an irregular baptism. Stenner managed to look bored. She clutched her blanket tighter, feeling like a refugee. "But he lost his key."

"Lost his key," repeated the concierge.

"The key to his apartment. And so we are going to try to get warmed up. You see, we were getting into a boat..." She broke off. There was no need to embellish, but she couldn't seem to stop. "And I caught my heel and..." Her voice trailed off. "I'm sorry," she said, stupidly.

"How terrible for you; *I* am so sorry." He clucked and handed her the key. "I will send up some brandy and coffee. And...er...if the gentleman would care to have his clothes laundered, it will require only an hour or two. Are you sure you don't want the doctor? Are you all right?"

"She fell into the canal," Claire heard someone whisper.

"I'm very cold," Claire said weakly.

"Of course. You have hurt your face?"

Claire's hand flew to her chin, as if she wanted to hide it. "Just a scrape." She smiled her just-a-scrape smile and they headed for the elevator. The clusters of people rotated once more.

Claire was about to run the bathwater when the brandy and coffee arrived. The waiter was a Surinamese with bad skin. She fished for money in her soggy purse, but he shook his head. "Compliment of the house," he said in a high, musical voice.

"But for you." She offered damp coins. "Thank you." She had always felt it was bad luck not to tip generously. It was also bad luck not to give money to beggars or street musicians. In Jeff's view, she was a sucker. Once, back in their poor days, she'd given a wino a five-dollar bill. They'd had a big fight about it. She had confessed: unless she gave beggars money, she imagined their afflictions would be transferred to her, to Jeff, to someone she loved. "That's not even charity," Jeff had raged. "That's just giving in to irrational fears." She told him it was a form of insurance. He declared her the most irrational person he'd ever met—she ought to see a shrink. "It's cheaper than going to a shrink," she countered. She recalled, peevishly, that he had dropped the subject.

Stenner was sitting on the bed peering inside the attaché case. He lifted up a soggy yellow legal pad. He lifted out a flat section of leather. Underneath, she could see a tape recorder.

"Oho," he said. "Mm-hmm." He started fiddling with the buttons.

"I'm going to take a bath," she said. He didn't seem to hear her.

She took her brandy and coffee into the pink bathroom. She felt safe there; it radiated warmth and comfort. A womb.

She turned on the water. She felt like being alone, just herself and the comfort of the water. She felt like locking the door. She thought about it while she tried to open a complimentary foil packet of bath gel. Her fingers were cold and clumsy; she couldn't get it open. She opened it with her teeth and got a horrible soapy taste in her mouth. Stenner said, "Shit!" from the other room. No, it would be ridiculous to lock the door.

She took off her boots and laid them on top of the radiator. Her mother's admonishing voice nagged her: That will make them crack; you'll ruin them; leather can't take heat. She couldn't imagine the boots would ever dry without heat. She struggled with her wet clothes, having trouble with fastenings. She concentrated on buttons and zippers. Finally, the clothes were all off, lying in a sodden pile in the corner. She looked in the mirror: a goatee of scraped skin, puffy lips. She made a face at herself. She heard Stenner moving and jumped into the tub. Her frozen hands and feet burned in the hot water. He cracked open the door.

"Can I come in?"

"Mm-hmm."

He sat on the toilet seat wrapped in his gray blanket, sipping his brandy.

"Are you all right?"

"I may never get out of this bath."

"The tape recorder doesn't work." He rubbed his palms up and down over his eyes. "Too wet, I guess. It's just a cassette, but I called all the people I know who have a tape recorder and no one's home." He jerked his hands into the air. "No one's home."

The room pulsed with pink warmth. Claire concentrated on feeling warm.

"There's a robe on the door," she said. "You should take off your wet clothes." He looked at her as if he hadn't understood what she said. "You look like a dissipated monk." He put his brandy on the lid of the toilet tank and stood up. He started peeling off his clothes.

"What a day. What a fucking day." He threw his clothes angrily in the direction of hers.

"Someone will be home later; you'll find a tape recorder. Take it easy." She didn't sound convincing as a consoler. She hadn't consoled anyone in years. He was down to his underpants, the shape of his buttocks revealed by the wet cloth. A twitch of modesty sent her underwater. She swirled her hair around. She lathered it without looking at him.

"What are we going to do?" he said, almost to himself. "I mean what am *I* going to do? Jesus Christ."

"We're going to order some food from Room Service. We deserve at least a feast. And champagne; we'll definitely need some champagne."

"Seriously," he started.

"Seriously," she mimicked. "I'm too hungry to think. *Way* too hungry to plan." She rubbed conditioner into her hair. "And what can you do until you find a tape recorder?"

He smacked his fist into his palm. "It's so frustrating. I still have no idea what's going on."

"Get the menu." She rinsed out the conditioner.

He returned with the menu. "Let's see. There is the Dover sole with sorrel. The *terrine de canard,* lamb roasted with thyme, *quenelles.* And of course, the *entrecôte au poivre,* the *tournedos, saumon en croute.*"

"Do they allow eating in the bathtub?"

"Absolutely not."

"Too decadent?"

"Too soggy. Also, too selfish. I'm still freezing."

"Your turn is coming. Let me see the menu."

He held it in front of her.

"Something simple—nothing too baroque. I think the *saumon fumé,* green salad, the *entrecôte au poivre*—rare; and let's see—just the strawberries, I think."

"I want things steaming. I'm going to go with the mussels to start."

"That's because you haven't had your bath yet."

"And lamb with roasted potatoes. And Black Forest cake."

"Hearty. What about champagne?"

He flipped open the wine list. "Let's see what's...reasonably reasonable. They've got a Piper, they've got a Mumm's..."

"Moët et Chandon." The water was cooling down, and she wanted him to be out of the room before she got out of the bathtub. The bubbles made tiny cracking noises as they collapsed into themselves.

"I'll go and order."

"Get them to come and get the clothes, too."

She jumped out of the bathtub and started toweling off. She couldn't decide whether this modesty was a normal state for her or a reaction to her excesses of the previous night. She wrapped a towel around her hair, trying to remember the distant, pre-Jeff past. She remembered being relieved, after their marriage—being released from a lot of sexual fencing, a lot of sizing up, a lot of exploratory action.

Stenner stepped through the door, and an involuntary "Oh!" escaped her.

"Our clothes," he said apologetically, and gathered up the soggy pile.

Her legs were riveted together. She clutched the towel over her breasts. He went out. God, now was she going to find out she was a prude?

She emerged from the bathroom secure in her towel, bent on nonchalance. Stenner was sitting on the bed in the terrycloth robe, dialing the phone. She waited until he was in the shower to get dressed, feeling foolish.

The waiter arrived, the same helpful Surinamese. She declined his offer to stay and serve the meal. He pushed the serving cart—crowded with plates in metal domes—toward the little round table by the window. He set out plates, napkins, cutlery, champagne flutes. His gestures were deft, precise, studied. He relocated the small bouquet of flowers about an inch from its original position and stood back, as if to admire his work. Stenner got his wallet from the dresser and pried a bill loose from the damp wad.

"Here you go."

"Oh, yes, thank you," Claire said. Her voice went on, nervous, automatic. "Here *we* go." She searched for appetizers. "I'm hungry."

A fog of steam escaped when she lifted a cover. "Your mussels, sir. Steaming. This will warm you up." She wished she would shut up. "Now if you'll open the champagne, I'll find my salmon."

He wrestled with the champagne cork.

"Ummm. Here it is. I found it." She whisked it to the table. "Looks great. Delicate pink flesh dotted with jade-green capers and tiny bits of translucent onion."

A soft explosion announced his success with the champagne. He poured. "Do you write menus?"

"I write jacket blurbs sometimes." She sat down. "William Smith's *Chrysanthemum* expands a powerful theme only hinted at in *Hollyhock,* and he tells it in a merciless prose that is at once compelling and strangely…*fragrant.*"

He laughed, as he was required to do.

"One thing we really have to do is dry out this money. We're leaving a trail of soggy tips."

"Soggy tips," Claire said in a brittle voice. "The author of the strongly praised *Wet Cash* finds the full range of his gifts in…"

Stenner lifted his glass toward her and she met it with hers. The delicate chink of crystal against crystal.

The sound seemed to hover in the air and expand. Claire's head reverberated.

"To—" Stenner began.

"Dry money," Claire said with an abrupt laugh. She gulped champagne. Stenner raised one eyebrow and emitted a grudging laugh. Claire's hand was shaking; her cheeks burned. She was having trouble getting the salmon on the fork. Small motor control—small motor control was poor and deteriorating rapidly. Stenner poured some more champagne and she took another gulp, leaning over close to the table so she wouldn't have to lift the glass too high. Everything required too much energy or too much control. She could never keep it up. She sank back in the chair and took a deep breath.

"The champagne is going to my head," she said, "as they say."

"It's been a tough day."

"Did you ever think about who 'they' are? It seems to me my parents were always referring to 'they,' or 'people.' I used to think of them as a kind of Greek chorus, only since one of my father's things was that he always listened to this black radio station, I imagined them as blacks. Blacks in glittery clothes, you know, doing the backup vocals. The Supremes. The Vandellas. If I wanted to wear my old clothes, my mother would say, 'People will think we're poor. They'll think I'm a bad mother.' And I'd imagine these three beautiful black ladies: 'They're *poor,* doo-wa, she's a *bad* mother.'"

"No, you've got it all wrong. To me, 'they' were like that minister and his wife—you know, the guy with the pitchfork; you know, that painting?"

"*American Gothic!*" She said it too loud. She said it like a quiz-show contestant.

"Yeah. *American Gothic.* Very severe. Strict."

"Ummm," Claire said, concentrating on her salmon. It seemed to her she had to keep talking, that every gap in the conversation was threatening, that she was walking on air, that only this verbal wire was keeping her up. "My Greek chorus isn't like that. Not strict. Just neutral."

It seemed that if she blinked her eyes, she might be back in her apartment in New York, sitting there with Jeff in *his* terrycloth robe. She was here in Amsterdam in a hotel room drinking champagne with a stranger. She couldn't remember what she was like. She was living on air, living on reflexes. She cut up her salmon carefully. I do like salmon, she thought. I remember that.

"So do I," Stenner said.

"Did I say that out loud?"

"What?"

"I like salmon?"

"Yes."

"I'm a basket case again. It seems to come and go. I can't seem to remember what I'm like—I mean when I'm alone."

"Thanks a lot." He faked a hurt voice. "The invisible man."

"No—I mean, I'm sorry. I mean when I'm not with Jeff."

"I know; I know what you mean. And just what you needed was to parachute into this little contretemps of mine. A few bullets, a high-speed jaunt with police pursuit...Just what the doctor ordered." He put a mussel into his mouth. She watched his face go through some odd contortions. Finally, he extended his tongue. He touched the tip of his finger to it and displayed a small gray pearl. "Jesus. A perilous pearl. I came within an inch—I mean, if

I'd bitten down just a *teensy* bit harder, I could have kissed a bicuspid goodbye." He sipped champagne.

"Pearls are not good to eat," Claire began in a didactic voice. "That is one of the first lessons a bivalve fancier must learn." Stenner started to choke on his champagne and stood up while he attempted to gain control. "High-risk dining," Claire said, and thumped him on the back. He sat down again.

"Don't," he wheezed. "Don't say anything funny."

"I'm sorry."

"It would be just like me to survive getting shot at, survive the fucking cab ride, only to drown in a glass of champagne. Oh, I forgot—we also avoided drowning in the canal. See, I'm a brave man: I'm going for another mussel."

"We're going to need some more champagne. I'm planning ahead."

"I'll get on it after I finish these mussels." Stenner was rummaging in the shells. "All gone," he said. "As I was saying, somewhere back there...at least, I think I was saying—you *deserve* to be a basket case. You think it's entirely *normal* to have a day like today? You're worried about personality quirks?"

She whisked away the plates.

"I know what you're feeling," Stenner went on. "Like an observer. Right? After Marlena and I split up...Ah, thank you." She'd delivered the entrées. "I went through this narcissistic period, observing myself, like Marlena was some link to direct experience. And away from her I was, I don't know, *divorced*. I wasn't just divorced from Marlena—I mean, actually, I wasn't divorced from her yet. But I was divorced from all my habits, all my routines. Nothing seemed normal." He shrugged. "The feeling goes away."

"I guess." Now she felt tired. The buzz phrases of best-sellerdom circulated vaguely through her head, the self-help litany. Emotional trauma. Marriage. Crisis. Number one. The champagne arrived, and they gave the waiter some more damp money.

She ate some of her meat. "I think you were right about my Greek chorus."

"What?"

"I don't think they're the sinuous black ladies going doo-wa, doo-wa. I think it's the guy with the pitchfork after all. Every time I feel halfway good, he lays one of those tines up against me. Not enough to hurt. Just to remind me: Hey! Remember, you're supposed to be miserable." She poured some more champagne. "I'm drinking too much, though. Maybe that'll do it. That's a bad sign, right?"

"The guy with the pitchfork is very, very hard to satisfy."

"He is?"

"He gets up at five-thirty every morning, for one thing. He does a hundred sit-ups and then his Bible study. He eats oatmeal and stewed prunes for breakfast."

"Every day?"

"On Sunday he has scrapple and whole-wheat bread with apple butter."

Claire started to giggle. "He wears long underwear in the winter," she managed. "He calls it his union suit."

Stenner shook his head. "Long johns."

"He darns his socks."

"You don't quite have it, Claire, but you're close. His *wife* darns his socks. That's *women's* work."

"She uses something called a darning egg. I've read about them."

"She churns butter."

"No," Claire said, sadly. She sighed. "These are Jeff's parents, practically. She uses margarine. She calls it oleo." She closed her eyes.

"Laying his pitchfork on you?"

She nodded.

"Forget it! They've just won an all-expenses-paid trip to Disney World! They're wearing the hats with the little ears. They're riding around in teacups. They *can't* be strict."

"I'll be right back."

She sat down on the toilet seat and cried. Jeff's parents lived in Iowa on a farm. They had a glider on the front porch. They had miles of corn. When the corn was high and you stood in the fields, with the tassels rustling in the breeze, the hum of insects rose around you like a delirious cloud. It was intoxicating, the fertility of it. Jeff's parents called each other "Mom" and "Dad." They called Jeff "Son." They called Claire "our sweet Claire," "our beauty." She would never see them again. She would never see Jeff's mother shelling peas into her apron— never, never again. And if she did, they would be distant. They would give her a polite glass of lemonade. If she went to visit them, she would be like blight, bad weather, something to be got through. She would have no place there. They would be formal, fixed. They would be implacable as the corn. In a way, it was what she liked best about them.

She dabbed at her eyes and went back. "I'm sorry," she said. "I'm going to be like this, I guess."

Stenner reached over and touched her arm. "Eat your salad," Stenner said. "Here I am lusting after my Black Forest cake and you haven't even started your salad."

"Where are my manners?" Claire said in a fussy voice.

❄ ❄ ❄

Lawrence Prager, lunching in McClean, Virginia, was not having such a sumptuous meal. He had waited until Len Adair, his luncheon companion, had committed himself to *escargots* and *boeuf bourguignonne* before asking the waiter if the kitchen could manage anything as humble as a peanut butter-and-jelly sandwich. Prager performed an apologetic grimace; he mentioned his stomach. The waiter regretted; the kitchen could manage a grilled cheese sandwich on white bread. Adair studied the wine list nervously.

"Some wine, Larry?" he asked doubtfully.

"No, no, you go ahead," Prager said expansively. He ordered himself a glass of milk. Adair almost whispered his wine order.

This was supposed to be a fence-mending lunch. Still, they started out talking about Teheran, about the Vance resignation; they tiptoed into the real subject. Adair had had his toes stepped on by the Office of Security. Jim Hallihan, of the OS, had been all over Adair's section, questioning, probing. Now he had questioned Adair's deputy, Linkovski. Adair was hurt and belligerent. Prager wanted to dislodge him from his offensive stance, and he was using a tactic. Prager had a tactic for everything. This was the spartan-lunch tactic. It seemed to put men at a terrible disadvantage—to eat well while someone else was not eating well. The waiter delivered Adair's plate of *escargots,* spitting-hot and fragrant with garlic.

"Where does OS get off?" Adair asked. "To question Linkovski without even informing me?"

"It's nothing personal, Len. You understand that."

"It *felt* personal. It felt like a kick in the balls."

Prager donated a little speech about Procedure while Adair ate his snails. He'd suffered the same sort of thing himself years before. He'd been as surprised as Adair when he'd heard about *this* investigation. It was a spot check, perhaps; mere quality control. Even though their procedures were there for Our Own Good, even though they were *routine,* you couldn't help bristling; it was human nature.

Prager's glass of milk stood in front of him on the table. It proclaimed him a man without guile. In fact, he was responsible for the investigation. He wanted Adair out.

But he didn't want Adair to know he was out until he was right at the exit point, with no options. Adair was no fool, and it was also necessary to avoid hard feelings while he was still in place. Prager aimed at totally invisible maneuvering, so that when Adair realized he had to leave the Agency, there would be a certain inevitable feeling about it, a certain relief. In the meantime, it wouldn't do for Adair to look too closely at the Linkovski business. There was a path there that could lead back to Lawrence Prager. A byzantine path, to be sure. But until he was able to obscure the footprints even more, Adair had to be soothed.

The main courses arrived. Prager's lonely grilled cheese sandwich accused Adair of gluttony.

"Well, I'll tell you something, Len, and this is just between you and me." This was another tactic, the secret tactic. Considering their field, it was not widely used.

"Of course," Adair said, between forkfuls of beef.

"This is just a rumor, of course, so take it as you will." Prager leaned forward. "Hallihan may be on his way out. Word is he has a drinking problem. OS won't put up with that, you know—they're all Boy Scouts." This was an outright lie, a slander on Hallihan. Prager was satisfied with the effect. Adair looked thoughtful.

"That puts a different light on it," Adair said.

Prager nodded—a meaningful nod. He was good at meaningful nods, meaningful looks. He was really very, very good at tactics. He paid for the lunch.

When Prager got back to his office, there was an urgent message to call Rob Davenport, the Head of Station in Amsterdam.

Davenport told him that Alan Dawson had been shot dead in Amsterdam by the contract man.

"What?"

"Look, I know, I know. Our man exceeded instructions."

"Exceeded instructions. Jesus Christ! It was a simple lift. All right," Prager said, his voice thin with amazed disgust. "All right. What happened?"

"You didn't give me much time," Davenport said. "And I had this guy, the perfect guy."

"I guess he wasn't absolutely perfect. Not letter-perfect."

"You wanted deniability. Remember? *Complete deniability.* That's what you said."

"Look," Prager said in an entirely reasonable voice. "Tell me what happened so we can decide what to do. Let's not fence: you don't defend; I won't accuse." He heard the tension gone from Davenport's voice. They were on an informative level now, back to business.

"I had this guy—I thought he was ideal for the job. I had him by the balls, too. It wasn't just pay-and-play, you know? Anyway, he couldn't get into the Amstel. The security was too good. I mean, apart from Circle, god-damned Prince Charles is staying there now. So he dogged Dawson, and he never got a good chance. I believe him there. And I had briefed him about when Dawson was going to leave. There was less than an hour before Dawson was leaving for The Hague. At The Hague, he was going to be at the Embassy, out of reach. And I don't know, maybe it's *because* we had the guy by the balls. He felt he had to do something. He felt he had to *perform*."

"So, he took him out," Prager said in a neutral voice.

"That's what happened. It gets worse, Larry."

"He didn't have the tape."

"The Amsterdam police didn't find any tape on him. No attack kit. Nothing. Nothing at the hotel, either."

"What about the reporter? The cut-out?"

Davenport paused. "Stenner?" When he spoke again, he sounded exhausted. "The cards just didn't fall our way today. We had him. Two men inside, one outside. The outside man went to take a piss. Missed the approach, I guess. I don't know how Stenner figured it out. We still don't know how he got away. Awfully quick, awfully *alert*—I mean, for an amateur."

"They lost him," Prager said grimly. "They'll have to find him."

"We're watching his place. We're doing everything possible."

"And when they find him, and it had better be soon..." Prager's voice was building in a way he didn't like. He took a breath. "All right. First of all, this is prior-ity, Rob. I don't care what else you have on your plate. I don't care how deniable this contract man is—we can't afford to have him walking around. And I want that tape, if it *exists,* found. Either get it, or destroy it."

"Wait a minute. If it *exists?* You said there was a tape."

"We have to assume that."

"Dawson was meeting with Stenner. That's the word from the contract man. He was walking with Stenner. The guy tried to get Stenner too, but he missed."

"We have to assume Stenner has the tape. If you can get it, fine. If you can't, then Stenner will have to be dealt with. But not *first*. Let's not make the same mistake twice. First you make absolutely sure he doesn't have it. This could still be a plus operation if we can get the tape. Otherwise, we're just chasing our mistakes."

"What about Stenner? I just want to be clear here, you understand? If we get the tape, what do we do with him?"

"Nothing," Prager said. "Think about it. Without the tape and without Dawson, what does he have? From the Dawson – Sisyphus conversation, I don't think Stenner knows what he's doing. He's working blind. Without the tape, he's got nothing. Daydreams. Conspiracy theories. Nothing but air. Nothing."

"Identification. He could put agents in jeopardy."

"Up to you. Nothing noisy, though. No more fire-works."

Davenport sighed wearily. The wires faithfully trans-mitted his fatigue. Prager thought suddenly: It's night there.

"It's going to be a mess here tomorrow," Davenport said.

"What do you mean? What kind of mess?"

"The Queen is abdicating. There will be ceremonies: the abdication, the investiture. Then demonstrations. We're expecting riots. The squatters...the *kraakers,* they call them here. That's what they riot about here—hous-ing. Nukes and housing."

"I'd forgotten," Prager said, "about the Queen. Still, it might work for us. It will play down the Dawson thing. That might help."

"Still," Davenport said morosely, "it's going to be a mess."

"Everything's totally fucked up," Stenner complained, hanging up the phone. Scott wasn't in. Frits wasn't in. John Macy, George Feaver, Will Genthner weren't in. Anneke had a cassette recorder. She wasn't in. Maybe they were all at the same large party.

Claire said, "What?" and turned off the hair dryer.

Sometime during dinner, one of them had decided it would be a good idea to try dehumidifying the tape recorder with a hair dryer. One had been summoned from Room Service, along with two cognacs.

Of course, it hadn't worked. Once that was clear, they felt stupid and giddy. After a laughing fit, Stenner had redoubled his efforts on the phone and Claire had decided to dry out their money and her traveler's checks with the hair dryer.

"It's going to be a mess here tomorrow," Stenner said. "Riots. Crowds. Festive chaos."

Claire held up her booklet of traveler's checks. They looked rumpled and dirty. Each one seemed to have quadrupled in thickness.

"If I were a merchant, I'd definitely think twice about one of these." She cocked her head. *Merchant.* That may be the first time I've ever said 'merchant' aloud. Merchant. Merchant. Merchant."

"Merchant of Venice."

"Maybe. Maybe *Merchant of Venice.*"

There was a knock at the door—the valet returning their clothes.

"Great," Stenner said.

The valet stared at the bed where Claire sat Indian-style, surrounded by two arcs (one his, one hers) of dried money.

"Here you go," Stenner said. He gave the valet some coins.

Claire looked up at that moment and caught the man's amazed look. "We're just drying our money," she explained. Stenner closed the door.

Claire pushed the money into two stacks. She was laughing but in complete silence, as if she lacked the energy to produce sound. "I wonder what he thought."

"Bank robbers."

"Desperadoes. He'd be right, there. You're desperate for a tape recorder. I'm desperate for..." She frowned slightly.

Stenner noticed she had a fleck of strawberry at the corner of her mouth. He had an impulse to lick it off.

"Sleep," she said finally. "I'm desperate for sleep."

The fleck of strawberry winked at him from the corner of her mouth. He reached with his index finger to wipe it off. She shied away from him.

"You have a piece of strawberry on your mouth." He pointed to his own mouth to indicate its location.

"Oh." Abashed. A smile that did not succeed. She found the piece of strawberry, examined it and licked it off her finger. Her finger stayed in her mouth; she forgot to take it out again.

He thought there was no way they could get into bed together right now and he could keep himself from making love to her.

"I'm going to take a shower now," he said, making the gesture.

"But," she started to say. Her finger came out of her mouth slowly. "But you already took a shower. Didn't you?"

"I want to think. Besides, I forgot to wash my hair."

"Oh," she said. "Okay." She sounded as if she were already asleep.

He stood under the water considering his reluctance.

There had been episodes during the evening when Claire seemed out of focus. She spoke too quickly, she waited a little too long before replying, she made too many jokes, she laughed too much. There were lapses when she didn't seem to hear him at all.

It was a recognizable state. In Vietnam, the officers called it combat fatigue. The men called it flaked-out, spaced-out, burnt-out, out to lunch, out of it. *Out* was the operative word.

Claire was in that out state, vulnerable, at risk. He didn't want to make it worse.

In Vietnam, being "out" was a more-or-less permanent state of being. Not that there was so much combat. There were bursts of activity interspersed with intolerable periods of waiting. A canopy of grief lay over the whole country like a deadly fog. The only relief from the grief was in rage, and that rage produced its bitter crop of atrocities.

Still, the ones who were capable of rage were not the worst of them. There were men he had met who were beyond rage, beyond being scared, beyond any kind of feeling. He had avoided them. Everyone avoided them. They gazed out of eyes blank with a devastating serenity. He thought of them as the living dead, because they reminded him of the zombies in the George Romero film, munching on arms and legs with the mindless enjoyment of kids eating Popsicles.

He lathered his hair. Violence always reminded him of other violence: there was an absolute similarity to all of it—the electrifying quickness, the visceral churn of fear.

When he came out of the shower, Claire was asleep. The tape lay on the bedside table, mute, blank. Its secrets, its magnetic coding would yield to the most widely available key, a simple cassette recorder. Yet it might as well be a message in hieroglyphics, Mayan knots, whatever.

He called the desk to request a 6 A.M. wake-up call. *Everyone* would be up at 6 A.M. He dialed Richard Scott's number and was cheered to get a busy signal. He glanced down at Claire and she stirred slightly, as if she could feel him looking at her. Her lips made tiny, barely perceptible sucking motions. He felt a mild ache, a yearning, a stir of desire, and retreated. He lay down on the edge of the bed with his back to her and closed his eyes.

Images of the day's events assaulted him. The blood on the woman's bright yellow skirt, the man juggling oranges at the farmhouse; Alan Dawson's backward leap; the policeman's expression of recognition in the Rijksmuseum; the spill from the woman's handbag, the tampons rolling on the pavement; the pearl displayed on the end of his finger; Claire in the bathtub covered with bubbles; the back window of the Volvo exploding; the fleck of strawberry at the corner of Claire's mouth; the white-painted tires suspended from the canalside; the arc of Alan Dawson's fall; the man in the museum men's room with the gold maple-leaf earring; the white-painted tires like eyes, the drops of his blood on the white porcelain in the men's room like eyes—like two eyes; Claire's face when her hair was wet, the tilt of her jaw, her perfect, translucent ears; Alan Dawson's face, Alan Dawson's ruined face. He tried to think of nothing. He tried to think of nothing but a gray square, to meditate, but Alan Dawson's ruined face kept squirming back into his mind. Alan Dawson's remaining eye, with its look of deep surprise. He sat up abruptly and opened his eyes. He got out of bed and dialed Scott's number again. It was still busy.

Claire turned over and gave a soft moan. He resumed his position, back to her, at the edge of the bed. He explained his desire to himself: it was a wartime reflex, a kind of hormonal response to danger. Danger excited the body, stirred it up. Physical danger seemed to heighten sexual awareness. That much had been all too obvious in Vietnam. He had noticed it also in Marlena—fights excited her, aroused her. He wondered if it wasn't an entirely natural phenomenon. He thought he remembered reading that people wanted to fuck in the middle of earthquakes. Nature encouraging one last chance at procreation. Or the body got so keyed up that once danger was past, it naturally sought release. The raping after battles. Masochists might just be people with such low sexual drive they could be aroused only by danger, by pain.

He lay separated from her by a foot of cloth.

Even as he sought distance in this analysis, his body edged closer to hers. He could detect her body heat. He could hear her breathe.

In the end, a foot of cloth, the fence of analysis, his chivalric intentions were nothing at all compared with the intentions of his body.

In the end, when the distance had shrunk to inches, when he turned over, when his body finally touched hers, when his cock rubbed against her—the moment of contact took him in a lurch past any way of being able to stop. She said, "Jeff, Jeff," in a sleepy voice, and even though he

heard her, he didn't pause for a second, and when he was
inside her, there was no question of stopping; he thought
he could never stop, he loved it, he submerged in the
rhythm of it, they would fuck all night.

Even when she said, "Jeff, Jeff," Claire was lying, side-
stepping. She knew it wasn't Jeff. It was an attempt to
transfer responsibility. A shoddy attempt at absolution.

But Stenner went into her so easily because she was
not really asleep, and she was moist. The wetness itself
seemed a betrayal. She was as bad as Jeff. She could give
in and give in and give in.

She was giving in; she was sinking fast. She tried not
to pay attention. She tried to draw away in the most halfhearted gesture. She sought the remove of irony; she
made a joke in her mind. "Really, I'd love to, but I have to
wash my hair." She wasn't saying a word; she was making
sounds. She tried to concentrate on not coming. But her
body was paying attention, paying direct attention. It was
starting to happen. If she could just not come, if she could
just concentrate and not come, it would be all right. She
said no. She said it out loud. But her body kept on, kept
on. Her body was saying yes. Her hips were positioning
themselves for maximum pleasure. Her mouth was saying
no, no, no, even as it was kissing, biting, tasting his skin,
and even as she slid over the edge into the sweet electric
blur of orgasm, she heard herself whispering no, no, no.

Stenner didn't come, though—not for a long, long
time. Instead of her desire diminishing, the longer it went
on, the greater her passion, until her consciousness of
what was happening began to dissolve into one long blur
of sensation. It went on and on; she was flayed; she was

nothing but nerve endings. She would remember getting up at one point to drink water. She felt that every drop of moisture was gone from her body. She drank four glasses of water in rapid succession. When she went back to the bed, she lay on it like a medical specimen. Some not-quite-swallowed water drooled from her mouth. Stenner reached down and touched her cheek with one finger, and her whole body throbbed and twitched like a frog's leg succumbing to galvanic action. In the end, there was one long tremor of pleasure that struck her with such force, she wasn't entirely sure she hadn't suffered a convulsion. Her body felt dead, exhausted beyond any possible response. She did not so much fall asleep as collapse into it.

CHAPTER FIFTEEN

CLAIRE WAS DREAMING. She was on a sailboat; they were running before the wind, propelled by a powerful breeze through water so blue it seemed artificial. The Genoa jib, striped red and white, luffed momentarily; when the boat's course was corrected, it bellied out steadily against the wind's thrust. Jeff was at the tiller; Claire and Jeff's brother, Richard, were playing with the baby. Claire held the baby up in the air and tickled its tummy with her nose. The baby chuckled. The baby's eyes sparkled like the sea.

Richard was asking what they were planning to do when the baby was older. They weren't going to live in Manhattan, were they? Would they move to the suburbs?

Claire joked, "No, we're moving to the Midwest when the baby's three or so. We want to avoid that Manhattan pallor. We want her to grow up with that healthy, corn-fed look. We want her to grow up to be a Cornhusker, or whatever. Weren't you and Jeff Cornhuskers?"

"Boilermakers, Claire. Purdue."

Claire clapped her hand to her forehead. "Never. Certainly not. Baby wants to be a Cornhusker, right, baby?" The baby gurgled. "A Razorback; possibly a Sooner." She tickled the baby under the chin and the baby spurted laughter. "She wants to wear one of those T-shirts that say 'Go, Hogs.' "

There was a strange beeping noise, clearly audible over the hiss of the water. Richard looked at her, puzzled, but then Jeff stood up and gestured for Richard to take over the tiller. Jeff had a beeping device hooked to the waistband of his swimming trunks, and as he approached her the noise got louder and louder. She couldn't understand why he didn't turn it off.

All at once, she woke up enough to realize it was the telephone. She opened her eyes, able to make out only the contours of the furniture in the thin light. It took a while to find the phone.

"Yes?"

"Good morning. You requested a call to wake you."

"Thank you."

The dream faded slowly, reluctantly. The baby. They'd never had a baby; they kept putting it off. Was the dream telling her she should have had a baby? She stumbled toward the bathroom. A baby, a baby, you can't use a baby for glue.

Still, now that she was awake, she longed for the world of the dream. It wasn't Jeff she missed; it wasn't being with Jeff. She missed the baby. She began to brush her teeth. How was it possible she could miss something that had never existed more than something that did? Maybe it was the vanished possibility. The possible baby was a ghost now. A ghost of the past now, when it had always been a ghost of the future.

She looked in the mirror and immediately regretted it. God, she looked awful. She looked as if she'd been beaten up. Red, puffy eyes. The place where she'd scraped her chin on the canal had resolved into several stripes of hard, clotted blood. Her hair stood out from her head in a wild tangle, stiff with sweat. And she smelled. Through the minty overlay of toothpaste, she smelled of stale sex, stale sweat, stale tobacco. She smelled of depravity. She smelled of guilt. She smelled of excess.

How could she, how could she? The first night she'd been drunk, tired, crazy. But last night...she wasn't.

It seemed to her that by the very excess, by the ferocity of her passion, she had relinquished her right to being the wronged one. The right to be wronged! Jesus, what drivel. The right to be wronged.

She refused to think about it. She didn't want to consider meanings; she didn't want to probe significance; she didn't want to discover anything about herself, anything at all.

She went out to wake up Stenner. It must have been Stenner who'd wanted to wake up. She didn't want to be awake at all. She wasn't sure how to do it, how to wake him. She rubbed his shoulder and said, "John." He mumbled something and vibrated slightly, as if her hand were a fly he wanted to shake off.

Just that brief touch, touching his shoulder, was enough to transmit to her body a liquid erotic thrill. She wanted to climb under the covers and wake him up with her body, with her mouth. She wanted to disappear again under the onslaught of sensation.

She couldn't understand what was happening to her.

She couldn't understand this state of continued arousal. She wasn't like that. She had to be in the mood, or she had to be lured into the mood, coaxed.

She backed away. "Time to get up," she said, far too softly.

He didn't even stir.

She marched toward the phone. She would lure normality back into the morning. There was a right way to do anything, a pattern for anything. She ordered two coffees, two croissants, two orange juices and a *Herald Tribune.*

She would take a bath. And if the arrival of breakfast, the knock at the door—if that didn't wake him first, she would wake him then. She would take refuge in cutting up square pats of butter to smear onto croissants. She would rely on pouring coffee, on dipping her knife into tiny dishes of marmalade, on reading the paper. She would do the crossword puzzle and struggle with obscure definitions.

She sank into the bath gratefully, paying attention to the way the water felt against her skin.

When he dialed Richard Scott's number, Stenner got a busy signal. He thought he must have dialed it wrong. It was only seven o'clock, and Scott was a notoriously late sleeper. He wouldn't be on the phone at the crack of dawn. He dialed again. Busy. Scott must have come home last night with a girl and left his phone off the hook. He called Frits Zonneveld. Frits was in a hurry, just on his way out the door.

"It'll just take a minute. Do you have a cassette recorder I can borrow? It's important."

"Can it wait? I'm late already. I'm supposed to be at the office five minutes ago, coordinating our, uh, team. And I can't even drive. I have to take the tram."

"I *really* need it. I really need it now, and I can't... Look, what if I pay for a cab?"

"Okay. Okay," Frits said with resigned impatience. "I'm on my way."

"Wait! I'm not at home. I'm at the Hotel de l'Europe. Or do you want me to come to your office? I can do that."

"No, no, it's going to be a zoo. Meet me outside. Outside the de l'Europe. With money for the taxi. Money and intense gratitude. This better not be a new Bruce Springsteen tape. Shit, I'm leaving. I'm already gone."

"You found someone," Claire noted.

"Yeah." Stenner pulled on his clothes.

Claire was sitting on the bed with her head wrapped up in a towel, doing the crossword. "Satellite of Uranus," she said. "Five letters. Starts with A."

"Astronomy is not my—Wait! Is that today's paper?"

"Yes. I had it...I had them—"

"Let me see the front page. Did you read the front page?"

"No, I—"

He grabbed the paper and folded it over to reveal the front page. It was sickening, somehow; it gave him a lurch—seeing it there in black-and-white. U.S. State Department Official Slain in Amsterdam. He scanned the story and went downstairs to wait for Frits.

Richard Scott was not, as Stenner had imagined, sleeping in post-coital bliss with his phone off the hook. In fact, he had been up all night, attempting to locate Stenner. He was calling to make the latest of several progress reports to Sisyphus. Scott felt shattered when Sisyphus called with the news that Alan Dawson had been murdered. He was Dawson's contact man, and he felt responsible. It was embarrassing, too, that he should have learned the news from Sisyphus and not the other way around. He was right here in Amsterdam, where it had happened; it seemed askew somehow that the news should have detoured across the Atlantic to Virginia and then back again.

He and Sisyphus had quickly established that Dawson must have met with Stenner. Otherwise, Dawson would have called Scott, his fallback. Dawson had been shot only an hour shy of his scheduled departure for The Hague—he wouldn't have postponed calling his fallback that long. Scott had also been able to find out from a source at the police property room that no tape or attaché case had been found on Dawson. Nor had the police search of his room at the Amstel produced anything. Scott had spent most of the evening searching fruitlessly for Stenner.

Sisyphus came on the line at last. "Yes, Richard. What do you have?"

"I went by his flat again, about an hour ago," Scott said. "The spooks that were there earlier are still there."

"The Agency boys, you mean. The probable Agency boys."

"Yes. But also, now the Amsterdam cops have the place staked out too. We're practically bumping into each other out there."

"Hmmmm," Sisyphus said. One of his long pauses followed. Scott lit another cigarette despite the fact that his chest ached from smoking too much.

"It's too long now," Sisyphus said. "Something must have put him off going there. I want you to concentrate on his friends. We'll try that angle."

"*I'm* just about his best friend here. Of course, if he's

been trying to get me, I've been out on the Prinsengracht almost all night."

"Well, if you do find him, yes...if you find him, I believe it would be best to get him—and the tape, of course—out of there. Out of the country. Arnoldsen will handle it for you. I'll put Arnoldsen ready. Düsseldorf would be best for me; Copenhagen would do."

"How much can I tell him?"

"You will have to expose yourself, of course. And my role. There's no way around that. I've been thinking. I've been studying Mr. Stenner." There was another long pause. Scott had learned not to fill these pauses. "I suspect the best thing would be to tell him everything. Certainly, you'll have to tell him he was being used as a cut-out to protect Dawson. He won't like that. People generally resent finding out they're pawns, when all along they considered themselves at least, oh, bishops. Or in Mr. Stenner's case, perhaps a knight is the more appropriate piece. Unless I am reading him wrong, I think the best way of smothering that very natural resentment is to overwhelm him with information—do you see?"

"You mean Yes, we used you, but *in a good cause.*"

"Well," Sisyphus said, and paused again. "Not precisely. What is disheartening about being a pawn is not that one is being used, exactly, but that one is being used without one's knowledge. I believe if we overwhelm Mr. Stenner with knowledge, he won't mind so much. He will be knighted again, if you will." The musing tone evaporated instantly from Sisyphus' voice. "All very nice, theorizing about people's feelings, but useless unless you find Mr. Stenner and find him fast. Before they do. In the meantime, also find out how the Amsterdam police have connected Stenner to Dawson."

"I'm on my way," Scott said.

"A few more matters, Richard. I'll be brief. First of all, let's set up some call times. It's about seven A.M. there. I want you to call me every two hours, regardless of your progress. If Stenner *has* got the tape, he will likely call Abe Zweifel. I may be able to learn Stenner's location from him. I'll call Zweifel the minute I finish talking to you."

"So I call at nine, eleven, one and so on."

"Yes. One last thing. If, after endowing Mr. Stenner with all the knowledge that you have, he is unwilling to give you the tape, you must be prepared to get it by any means necessary."

Scott inhaled. "I see." He was afraid he did.

"I don't mean by that that anything should happen to Mr. Stenner. He's not going to die for it, not willingly. He's too hard for that. I'm sure you'll find a way."

"I still can't figure out how they knew about Dawson. I've gone over everything I did in my mind—"

Sisyphus cut him off. "I suspect the leak came from my end." Sisyphus sighed—a deeply weary sound. The bantering tone left his voice. "It's an important matter, but it will have to wait. You find Stenner: that *can't* wait."

"Nine o'clock," Scott said.

Sisyphus hung up, as usual, without any form of farewell.

A file lay on Sisyphus' desk. The tab, hand-printed in block letters, read STENNER, JOHN R. He did not immediately open it, thinking, instead, about how the Dawson operation had been blown. He had noticed, about a month ago, that surveillance on him had intensified. A heartening sign, he had thought at the time, because it told him someone was nervous. Still, it was just possible his conversation with Dawson at Dumbarton Oaks had been the source of the leak.

He could not entirely discount the possibility that Scott had been the source—even, possibly, a willing one. It would be necessary to set up a dummy operation, after this one washed down—a feedback loop, a trap for Scott. Tedious, of course, but necessary. He opened Stenner's file.

There were a *curriculum vitae* and photograph, standard to all his files, and a few handwritten notations having to do with Stenner's personal life, a string of addresses and telephone numbers and then a thick pile of Xeroxed news stories and magazine articles with Stenner's by-line. He began leafing through them.

CIA RIFT WIDENS

CROSBY NAMED NEW CIA DIRECTOR

CIA PURGE CONTINUES

COUNTERINTELLIGENCE ERA ENDS – *Carley Retires*

THREE DEFECTORS – A BYZANTINE PUZZLE

Sisyphus paused to read the last article, a magazine piece. The handwritten flag read *Analysis, June/1978.*

The graphic showed a garden with several beds of flowers, labeled CIA, FBI, NATO, DIA, NSA. Below the ground, three moles burrowed busily through a labyrinth of tunnels. Above the ground stood a gardener, a caricature of himself. He had one hand tied behind his back and was shown ineffectually stabbing at the tunnels with a child-sized shovel. Looming behind the gardening shed was a gigantic shadowy mole, one eye eerily bright as he aimed a raised shotgun at the gardener. Sisyphus began to read.

THREE DEFECTORS –
A BYZANTINE PUZZLE
By John Stenner

Is the CIA penetrated by Soviet agents?

In 1961, KGB Major Anatol Zverkov defected to the West. What he had to say shook the foundation of Western intelligence, exposing Soviet penetration of the French, British and Swedish intelligence services. While operatives in other countries were exposed with Zverkov's help, the CIA achieved no such successes at home. This alarmed Zverkov, and increasingly paranoid about his own safety, he left the U.S. for Europe in 1963.

Sisyphus frowned his distaste at the word "paranoid." Zverkov had had ample reason to fear for his life. Toward the end, he had subsisted on sealed, bottled water and eggs boiled in his presence so that he could discern any tampering with the shells—any signs of injected toxins. That story was well known, and might well have indicated paranoia, if one did not know what had prompted Zverkov to adopt such an extreme diet. One night, one of Zverkov's "baby-sitters" had committed the fatal *faux pas* of a final tasting from the bowl of onion soup set out for Zverkov, and had promptly died—botulism toxin.

CIA Director James Keller and Chief of Counterintelligence Alexander "Sisyphus" Carley defended Zverkov's analysis and understood his fears.

When Yuri Golyadkin, a second KGB defector, arrived in 1964, Carley and Keller were suspicious of his *bona fides.* Zverkov had predicted that *false* defectors would arrive. Certainly, the KGB would mount a "disinformation" campaign aimed at discrediting him.

Golyadkin asserted that there were no moles; the CIA was not penetrated. He was subjected to a prolonged and hostile interrogation in an attempt to break him down and learn the truth.

Before that process was completed, the FBI announced that it had netted a defector as well, codenamed "Caviar." "Caviar" was different from Zverkov or Golyadkin, however, because he was a *defector-in-place.* In other words, he remained an employee of the KGB, ostensibly, while he toiled in truth for America.

Ostensibly.

Caviar's information corroborated that of Golyadkin—that there were no moles at the CIA. FBI Director J. Edgar Hoover believed Caviar. The CIA did not. Some of Caviar's stories were exact repetitions of Golyadkin's stories, and were, more to the point, repetitions of *proven* lies. But Hoover believed Caviar so completely that when the CIA *insisted* Caviar be treated with extreme caution, Hoover severed all liaison with the CIA.

At CIA, Keller and Crosby were distraught. The FBI was dancing to the tune of a Soviet agent, they felt, and they couldn't even hear the balalaika.

Now we begin to paddle through the muddy waters of speculation. It seems that this is what happened:

Keller and Carley found the situation—being cut off from the FBI when the FBI was in thrall to a Soviet agent—intolerable. They *at least* needed to know what Caviar was up to, and what he was telling the FBI. In order to normalize their relationship with the FBI, they had to *pretend* to accept Caviar as a *bona fide* defector.

To make their about-face convincing, Keller decided that it would be necessary to officially whitewash their own false defector, Golyadkin. Carley aide Wally Jurgen was ordered to conduct a new "investigation" of Golyadkin. The "Jurgen Report" officially exonerated Golyadkin, and he was pensioned off. He had no role at the CIA, however, and was not trusted. Hoover was happy. The CIA had finally recognized what a jewel he had in Caviar. Liaison between the two agencies resumed.

Alexander Carley quietly continued his investigations and accumulated evidence against CIA officers he considered possible moles. Before his work was complete, the Watergate scandal and subsequent House and Senate investigations rocked the CIA. Keller resigned as Director and was replaced by Richard Crosby. Crosby proceeded to fire more than a thousand employees, an unprecedented purge. Alexander "Sisyphus" Carley was one of those forced into retirement.

Sisyphus paused in his reading. It astonished him that Stenner had been able to piece together this scenario so well. It was especially impressive that he'd been able to puzzle out the meaning of the Jurgen Report. He remembered Stenner's repeated requests for interviews. He had not helped Stenner at all, in the end granting him only a two-minute telephone conversation.

After Watergate, interesting things happened to the three defectors.

CIA files on Yuri Golyadkin contained a "definitive" report exonerating him: the Jurgen Report. On the basis of this deliberate whitewash, Golyadkin was wholeheartedly embraced by the new Crosby-led CIA. Golyadkin became (and remains) a highly paid consultant and lecturer on Soviet intelligence affairs.

"Caviar" had boasted to his handlers at the FBI and the CIA that he would be promoted to Chief of Counterintelligence for the KGB in the United States. Instead, he was reposted to the consular staff in Chad.

And Anatoly Zverkov, the original defector, the one who raised the awful possibility that our intelligence service was riddled with Soviet double agents?

Anatoly Zverkov had been living, since 1963, in the town of Senlis, outside Paris, under an assumed name and under the joint protective surveillance of SDECE (French intelligence) and the CIA. On December 15, 1975, exactly one day following Alexander Carley's departure from the CIA, Zverkov was murdered. The peculiar brutality of the murder attracted some worldwide press attention. Zverkov's tongue and genitals had been cut off and placed in his mouth; his lips had been sewn shut with dental floss. His wife, Ilona, and two young children, Irina, 7, and Aleksandr, 3, were found hanged in the living room.

So. Is the CIA penetrated?

Reached at his offices at Mountain Security, Alexander Carley declined to comment on that question, but said, "It is instructive to observe certain foreign-policy reversals—I refer to Iran and Afghanistan—and note how they were generated by faulty intelligence."

And Antatoly Zverkov? Was Carley of the opinion that Zverkov's grisly murder would have a chilling effect on would-be defectors?

"What do you think?" Carley asked in reply. Then he hung up.

Sisyphus closed the file, impressed anew. Stenner had managed an analysis that was right on the money—working basically from shreds. Perhaps it would have been better to have approached Stenner directly. He might well have played. Then Stenner would be working with his eyes open now, instead of walking blind.

Sisyphus rarely allowed himself the barren luxury of hindsight. He reprimanded himself.

There were still two factors working in his favor. There was an excellent chance Scott would locate Stenner before any other pursuers did. Scott had the classic advantage of intelligence—simple knowledge, that is, of Stenner's haunts, friends, habits. The other chance was that Stenner would telephone his editor, Abe Zweifel.

He glanced at his watch. Two forty-five. He had talked with Zweifel earlier that evening, just after the news about Dawson came in. He had arranged a sterile line to receive Zweifel's call, if and when Zweifel heard from Stenner.

He leaned over toward the telephone and dialed Zweifel's number. He wanted Zweifel on his tiptoes. He wanted Zweifel to call the very second he had any information about Stenner. And he needed to tell Zweifel to find out where Stenner was, his physical location.

"Hello. Could I speak to Abe?…No, Mrs. Zweifel, not bad news. Urgent." Sisyphus waited through murmured voices and vague thumps. He and Zweifel did not like each other. There was a certain sour pleasure to be derived from calling him in the middle of the night for a good reason.

Zweifel fumbled with the phone and came on the line. "Zweifel here. Who the hell is this?"

"Alexander Carley. Look, Abe, have you heard from John Stenner?"

"Jesus Christ. It's three in the morning."

"I know. Have you heard anything?"

"No. No, I haven't *heard* anything."

"We can't locate him. When he calls, I want you to find out where he is. Get his phone number. I need his *location,* and I need it the *instant* he calls. He is in danger, in considerable danger." Sisyphus hung up.

CHAPTER SIXTEEEN

CLAIRE WORKED STUBBORNLY on the crossword puzzle. Could 59 Across—"Triangular"—actually be DELTOIDER? It fitted, but was it a word? Would they use a word like "deltoider"? It fitted with FERN. "River entering the Fulda" could be anything. She was working in pen, and hesitated. She decided to go with DELTOIDER. "Monogram of Prufrock's creator" would be TSE. "Lascivious" would be LEWD.

Lewd.

Memories of the night before floated into her mind. She put down the paper and started to tidy up the room. *Going to hell in a handbasket,* remarked an interior voice. She couldn't remember anyone she knew using that phrase. She probed her memory. Irene occasionally used old-fashioned phrases—a somewhat irritating affectation. Irene would say things like "Gee whizzikers, what a fucking nightmare." But then Claire remembered. It wasn't Irene at all.

It was Jeff's grandmother. Grandma Beebe was a wonderful old lady with a face completely stitched together with fine wrinkles. Claire loved the bumpy ridges of Grandma Beebe's face. Grandma Beebe had flinty blue eyes and a sardonic sense of humor. She watched soap operas with lascivious glee. And that was when she'd said that. Claire remembered her getting up with surprising agility and flicking off the TV set as the characters from *All My Children* faded behind the credits. "Going to hell in a handbasket," she'd said, and laughed wickedly.

Claire went back to the crossword. EXTOL. That would fit for "Praise highly." It suddenly seemed vital to her that she finish the puzzle. It would be bad luck to leave gaps, to—

Stenner burst through the door holding a tape recorder over his head like a trophy. "Now we'll see what's going *on* here. Okay, okay." He plugged it in and inserted the cassette, staring intently as he rewound. "Okay," he said. "Here we go."

When the tape started playing, the voices sounded like Donald Duck on helium—high cartoon voices, accelerated past the point of comprehensibility. Stenner jabbed the machine off.

"Shit!" he yelled, and began to laugh in an exhausted way. "Shit, I should have known."

He did an imitation of the tape, his arms gesturing wildly as if he were making a speech, high gibberish coming from his mouth. Then he hunched over with his hand supporting his head and said, "Oh, God." He began to laugh almost silently, his whole body shaking, only wheezing sounds coming out.

He stood up straight again. "And now, ladies and gentlemen, the secret of the universe." He repeated the high gibberish.

"It's a different kind of tape, right?"

Stenner squeaked through his laughter. "A different kind of tape, yeah." He laughed again, making a staccato rattling sound like a loose lid on a boiling pot. "Oh, shit. I'm sorry."

"Maybe the other one is dried out now," Claire said. "Maybe it's just the batteries that are wet. Did we even check the batteries? Does it have batteries?"

"Okayyy. It's just when those voices came on." He shook with laughter again. "Oh, Goddddd. Okay, okayyyy. You're right; we'll check the original machine. Frits's machine won't play these ultra-long-playing tapes. I've got one that does, but..."

He found the battery compartment and removed four nine-volt batteries. He dried them off on his towel and then dried the contact points on the machine. "This is probably futile, but what the hell. Maybe God will decide we need a break." He looked up at the ceiling. "That's right. We're requesting divine intervention here."

When he inserted the cassette and got ready to push the play button, Claire found she was holding her breath.

"Here we go," Stenner said, and pressed down with a flourish. They both saw the tape begin to move. When a voice spoke, it was so incredibly loud, Claire clapped her hands over her ears and squeezed her eyes shut. Stenner must have turned it off, because the sound stopped.

"First we get chipmunks, then we get *deaf*." He rewound and adjusted the volume.

There was some idle conversation—people saying hello, chairs scraping, that sort of thing—for a few minutes. Then one voice said, "Gentlemen," and the hubbub subsided. "Gentlemen," said the voice again. "First I must apologize for the havoc I have wreaked on your schedules. This is only the second red-flag meeting of the

Steering Committee that has been called in nearly ten years."

"Dawson bugged the Circle meeting," Stenner said softly.

It was a long tape. Claire got up every now and then, as she did now, to stretch her legs. Stenner maintained absolute concentration, staring at the tape as it crept past the heads, as if he were mesmerized, as if the tape itself might provide some visible evidence he couldn't afford to miss. Occasionally, he wound it back to replay a section. The tape was difficult to listen to. People often spoke at the same time, canceling each other out.

"He is dying anyway," someone said.

"That's right. There's no question about that."

"Just a matter of time."

"Speaking of time," said a voice Claire recognized as belonging to the man who had opened the meeting, "we're quite short of it. It seems to me we are tiptoeing toward a conclusion which our discussion has already implied. We... we cannot afford to let the Shah go on trial. We cannot afford to have him telling the Saudis—well, we have been through all this. The damage he could inflict is incalculable. If he were in his right mind, the Shah would be the first to see the logic that will prevail here. He could bring most of our banks and companies to their knees, and that would bring our countries to their knees. No, gentlemen, we cannot have this because a man is dying, because he is having second thoughts, because he is bitter. He is a huge problem, and what we are edging toward in our discussion is that he will have to be eliminated."

"Assassinated," said a voice with an American accent.

"Yes," said the leader's voice. "Assassinated. We must arrange his assassination. There we have it. In all this discussion, we have not produced an alternative. Because there *is* no alternative."

People began talking all at once. The discussion went on for a while. One man spoke out against the idea.

"That's Dawson," Stenner said.

In the end, a vote was taken. Only three abstentions blurred a unanimous decision.

"Most of us have obligations this evening, so we will adjourn until tomorrow morning at nine, when we will discuss the more practical matters of funding and, let's say, personnel."

The tape wore on for a while with some sporadic discussion, largely blotted out by the sounds of chairs scraping; and then abruptly, although the tape spooled on, the recording came to an end.

Stenner stood up slowly, stiff from sitting in the same position for so long. He rubbed absently at the back of his neck and looked out the window at the Munt Tower. The minute hand on the tower clock lurched forward. Eleven o'clock. The bells jerked into action, chiming out a slow, dirge-like tune he didn't recognize. He looked down at the canal directly below. The water was light brown, opaque, and the surface gave off a nasty, oily glare. He wished for a moment that he'd lost his grip on the attaché case last night, that it had disappeared in that brown water. He sank back into the chair. Just standing seemed to exhaust him.

The tape represented an electrifying story, a story he would have groveled for ten years ago, and the truth was...he didn't want it.

He had spent his whole career as an investigative reporter going after the abusers of power. And he was good at it. He was even great at it. He was relentless, he had wonderful sources, he poured a dazzling amount of energy into his investigations. If he'd had even a glimmer, a few years back, that a group like Circle (the cutline would read INTERNATIONAL CABAL OF BANKERS, STATESMEN AND CORPORATE LEADERS) had sanctioned an assassination, he would have been off like a shot, investigating every possible access point to the story.

"Shit," he said.

"What's the matter?" Claire asked.

He threw himself down on the bed. "Here's a story that five, six years ago I would have—well, I wouldn't have killed for it. I would have *maimed* for it. And now it's just fallen into my lap, and the truth is, I kind of wish I'd dropped that attaché case in the canal last night."

"Well," Claire said. "People change. Or is that what bothers you—that you changed?"

"I don't know. I'm just trying to figure out why I lost interest, or when I lost interest. You wouldn't believe how I used to be—so gung-ho. It sounds corny, but I thought I was in the service of The *Truth*. I thought—can you believe this?—I really thought the pen was mightier than the sword. I would lay the wicked *low*. I was *vicious*."

Claire stood by the phone. "Want some coffee? I'm going to get some for me."

"Sure. Yes, some coffee. At the very least I need some coffee. Do they have anything stronger? Oxygen? Adrenalin? Cocaine, maybe? Vitamin B injections?"

He *had* been vicious. Back in his earliest, most predatory days, he'd ruined men, ruined careers, ruined organizations with no qualms. He went after corruption with the grim determination and the same righteous anger as...Eliot Ness...the Lone Ranger. He started laughing.

Claire lay down next to him on the bed. "What's so funny?"

He put his arms behind his neck and stared at the ceiling.

"I was thinking I used to be like the Lone Ranger. I mean I was *intent*. Maybe I didn't really lose interest; maybe I just lost ambition."

"That's not always such a bad thing."

Stenner propped himself up on one elbow. "Maybe I began to change when my sources started calling *me*. That didn't seem right, you know? I mean, I used to call people thirty times a day if I had to—I'd tell their secretaries, 'Look, either I'm going to call you every twenty minutes for the next year, or you'd better persuade your boss to talk to me.' Or I'd trail them to lunch and start firing questions at them while they attempted to eat their vichyssoise. When they started calling *me,* that was weird. It happened after Watergate. *Exposés* were the big thing. Whistle blowing was the sport of the hour. My sources were chatty; all of a sudden they were exhibitionists. I'll bet I got a dozen phone calls a week offering stories, offering information. At the time, it seemed to me that nobody wanted to *keep* a secret. Everyone wanted to do a piece, do a book."

"I see what happened, maybe," Claire said. "Instead of being a critic of the power network, you turned into part of it."

Stenner laughed. "You're probably right. I think half the phone calls I got back then—what they really wanted was the name of my literary agent."

"Being a natural renegade, you resented this sudden chumminess."

"Are you fond of natural renegades?"

"I guess so. I seem to be. So you—"

"What I did was go to Vietnam. Maybe that's where it started. Ordinary human corruption didn't seem so bad in Vietnam."

There was a rap on the door. Claire rolled out of bed to answer it. It was Room Service with their coffee.

Stenner got out of bed and looked out the window. That probably was where it had started—Vietnam. A little embezzlement, a little black-market action—that sort of thing was almost *endearing* in Vietnam. Everything else seemed so much worse. Maybe when you start forgiving the little things, you begin to forgive the larger ones. Everyone in Vietnam seemed in over his head. When you ran across some guy with enough energy left to run a scam, it was almost reassuring. Over their heads—the generals, the countries, everyone. The world. His own efforts seemed puerile and eventually worse. He had left when he began to feel parasitic, the war his host.

Certainly when he'd left the paper for this year's leave of absence to do the transnationals book, he'd hoped the year would expand indefinitely. If he could make enough money writing this sort of book and freelancing articles, he would never go back to the daily grind. He'd been weakened, somehow; he lacked the energy.

He turned away from the window. Claire was looking at him. The tape recorder seemed malevolent, accusing. And the tape was his responsibility. Dawson was dead because of it, almost certainly. *Dead.*

"I don't know what to do. I don't know whether to go to the police, the Embassy, call my editor back home, what."

"Your *editor?*"

"That's what Dawson expected. That's why he gave me the tape. It was a professional relationship, not a friendship. It was a business transaction, source to reporter. Not that he expected to get blown away over it."

He looked out the window. People were swarming on the streets in the normally deadly intersection of the

Muntplein. He realized for the first time why the scene presented such a nineteenth-century look. There were no cars.

"It doesn't add up. Even if Circle somehow realized Dawson was bugging the meeting, how did they know who I was? How did they know where my flat was? They didn't have time. And why did that cop fix on me? The whole thing stinks. It's some kind of setup. *Goddammit.*"

"I don't know," Claire said softly.

"This wasn't the kind of thing Dawson would do. He was no crusader. He was the ultimate pragmatist." His voice trailed off, and he shrugged. "I'll call Zweifel, I guess—for advice if nothing else. Maybe he knows someone at the Embassy, *something.*"

As it turned out, the hotel de l'Europe's antiquated telephone system did not allow for direct international dialing. And the lines were all booked up for the next two hours. "There are many journalists staying in the house," the desk clerk said. "The investiture," he added.

Stenner booked a call for one o'clock, as a fallback. It should be possible to get a call through from the Central Post Office. They met the waiter with their coffee in the hall. They went back to the room with him, paid him and had a few sips of coffee. Just as they were about to leave again, Stenner turned back. He removed the cassette from the tape recorder and closed the attaché case. He put the case under the bed. "That thing looks a little too James Bond, you know." He tossed the cassette up in the air and caught it. "I'd really like to hide this, but"—he glanced around the room—"hotel rooms don't provide many good hiding places."

"They probably have a safe downstairs."

"I don't think I want to get into that." He was walking around the room, opening drawers, shaking his head in dissatisfaction. He picked up her small blue suitcase and shook it. "What's in here?"

"Dirty clothes."

"Do you mind?" She shook her head. He opened the suitcase and hid the tape in a pair of dirty socks. He gave her a wry smile. "This wouldn't fool an intelligent three-year-old, but..." He threw up his hands. "I'll think of something later."

They were both surprised at how warm it was outside. Claire took off her blazer and carried it slung over her shoulder.

"If we time it just right," Stenner said, "we'll just be able to catch the abdication speech." They were walking down the Rokin toward Dam Square. They passed the black statue of the woman on horseback.

"I think that's the only statue of a *woman* on horseback I've ever seen," Claire said. "Who is it?"

"Wilhelmina. Juliana's mother."

The crowds were getting thicker. They passed a series of stalls set up along the Rokin, selling herring, French-fries in paper cups, inexpensive jewelry pinned to boards covered with black velveteen. A little girl wearing a paper crown stopped them and said something in Dutch. She was holding a piece of cardboard covered with rows of tiny orange bows stuck on with straight pins.

"For the new Queen?" she asked in English. Stenner shrugged and bought two of them and put them into his pocket. Claire wondered if he gave money to beggars.

"Sees-ka-bob-sees-ka-bob-sees-ka-*bob*," shouted a dark man with elaborate sideburns. Claire couldn't believe how fast he said it, and she paused, just to hear him say it again.

"Sees-ka-bob-sees-ka-bob-sees—"

"Hungry?"

She shook her head. "I was admiring his speed."

"Auctioneer speed."

They walked on, the chains of syllables rippling through the air behind them.

They passed a woman six feet tall leading a Doberman. The Doberman had an orange rosette attached to its collar. They passed a stall selling tiny paper cups of orange liquid.

"Kool-Aid?"

"Orange gin. Let's get one. Let's get two." The paper cups were the size of the cups nurses give you in the hospital with one pill in them.

"To us," Stenner said. She met his eyes for a fraction of a second. They tossed back the gin.

"*Ja!*" said an old man next to them. "*Leve de Koningen!*"

Stenner smiled at him. They walked past a circle of onlookers watching a sidewalk artist as he knelt on the pavement, putting the finishing touches on a portrait of Princess Beatrix. Stenner stopped to take a look. Claire was surprised he wasn't in more of a hurry, but he seemed nonchalant, detached.

The artist put a sharp streak of brown chalk on the side of Beatrix' face and another near her nose. They watched him smudge the lines. The musculature of her face emerged.

A small group of punks formed part of the circle around the artist. Two of the boys had Mohawk haircuts, the center strip of hair splattered with orange paint. A girl in pink tiger-striped pants and with a butterfly tattooed on her cheek suddenly jumped onto the center of the portrait and ground her foot into Beatrix' nose. She tittered nervously, appealing to her friends for support. The artist took a step toward her. One of the Mohawks drew her back into the circle, raising his hands in a warding-off gesture.

"She din't mean nothing. You can fix it, cantcha?" He flipped a couple of guilder coins down on the ruined portrait.

One of the other girls, who was dressed entirely in black, wearing black leather gloves smeared orange and strange bulbous wraparound sunglasses, skittered away like the insect she resembled. The remaining crowd clucked their sympathy and tossed some more coins onto the pavement. Claire tossed some of her own, and then they moved on.

"It's such a weird juxtaposition," she said, "I mean these completely wholesome Dutch families, these kids in the paper crowns—and then all these punks."

"Halloween."

They came up to a barricade, manned by a policeman.

"We'll have to go around."

"I wish they wouldn't tattoo themselves. You can't get them *off*, can you?"

"You can, but it leaves a scar."

They passed another barricade which seemed to be protecting a couple of television trucks. Tangles of wire and cable spilled out from the trucks, like entrails.

They turned a corner, passing a long graffito on the wall. HEY HEY IT'S MAY. FUCKING OUTSIDE STARTS TODAY.

"Jumping the gun," Stenner said. "It isn't even May yet."

The blue-and-white sign read TELEFOON TELEGRAAF. They went inside.

The harassed long-haired clerk, who bore a startling resemblance to a portrait of Jesus that Claire remembered from Sunday school, was trying to explain something to a Hispanic couple.

"The call will come through in the boooooth," he said extremely slowly.

The Hispanic man wore a denim jacket. On the back, ELVIS SUPERSTAR was spelled out in metal studs. The woman wore white leather pants, skin-tight, with zippers up the sides of the legs. They spoke in unison, in Spanish. The man began pounding the desk. The clerk began to act out a pantomime, first pretending to fill out a form, then going over to sit on the bench, then looking at his watch, then going to booth Number 12, picking up the phone and talking.

"Okay?" he said to the man. *"Numero* twelve. Got it? You see?"

The Hispanic man rubbed thoughtfully at his sideburn and said something in Spanish, also very, very slowly.

"This isn't going to work," the clerk said. "I have no idea what he's so upset about. *Sit down,"* the clerk said, pretending to sit. "Sitto downo." He pointed to himself. "I will call you"— he jabbed his finger at them—"when your call comes through."

The Hispanic man shook his head sadly.

"Anybody here speak Spanish?" the clerk yelled. "Any linguists here?"

Stenner offered to give it a try. "I took it in college." He spoke to the man in halting Spanish, and the man's face lit up in a smile. He nodded his head violently, did a little pantomime of his own to show the clerk that he understood, spoke rapidly to the woman in the white pants and went over, still smiling, to sit down.

"Thank you, man," said the clerk, shaking his head. "I mean thank *you*. People come in here, it's always an emergency, they get uptight, you know. I speak English, French and German—but Español, you know, uh-uh."

Stenner filled out the proffered form and slid it back across the counter.

"Washington," said the clerk. "Piece of cake. Booth eleven, five minutes. I just called Singapore, Islamabad and Mallorca. Islamabad was easy; it was Mallorca that was tough." He scribbled something on the sheet of paper. "Okay, that's it."

Claire could hear oom-pah-pah music filtering in from outside. They sat at the end of a bench, most of it occupied by a reclining man. The man had one shoe off, revealing a pumpkin-colored sock. He snored heavily.

"This reminds me of the Department of Motor Vehicles back home," Stenner said. "Total Third World scene."

"You mean all the cabdrivers," Claire said.

"Right. I sat there waiting, and the clerk was shouting out these names with great difficulty." He imitated a Southern woman's voice. " 'Nee-you-gen the Duck. Ernesto Rodriguez da Silva Y Compostela' even though she's totally botched the pronunciations, they immediately know it's their name—you know, they—"

Stenner's number was called and he got up, producing a particularly volcanic snore from the orange-sock man. The snore nearly dislodged him from the thin bench. Claire watched Stenner fold himself into booth 11.

Sergeant Van der Heyden took two steps toward Maarten Stalpaert and offered him a cigarette. The cabdriver lit it and appeared to be engrossed in the patterns the smoke made. Sergeant Van der Heyden crossed his arms. "Let's stop this nonsense. You and I both know I can have your license suspended."

"I don't know why you won't believe me," Maarten said. "I don't think you want to believe me."

"You took a terrible chance—a *desperate* chance, I would say—when you went around that lorry and onto the shoulder."

"I've told you that I didn't see the oncoming car. Certainly it was dangerous. I can tell you I was shaking for several minutes after that." He looked intently at the ceiling. "A close call."

"An evasive tactic."

"You are dreaming, Sergeant. I picked up a fare at the Rijksmuseum. I drove them to the Frans Hals Museum. That's *all*."

"I know you are lying."

Maarten shrugged.

"I am going to see if you can be detained," Van der Heyden said angrily.

Maarten shrugged again.

Commissaris de Groot recognized Van der Heyden's characteristically resolute knock even before Van der Heyden's well-groomed head peeked through his doorway.

"Come in, Sergeant."

"Sir. It's the cabdriver, Maarten Stalpaert." De Groot probed the bowl of his pipe with his pipe tool, dislodging a satisfying amount of brown gunk along with the loose tobacco.

"Yes?" he prompted.

"I'd like your permission to detain him."

"Oh?"

"He's lying. I *know* that he's lying, sir. I can feel it."

De Groot tamped some fresh tobacco into his pipe. "We are under a great deal of pressure about this case, Sergeant," De Groot said peevishly. He was not in the mood for Van der Heyden today. He had been up half the night with Willi—a bad night, full of terrible suppressed coughs. She had spat up blood and tried to hide it with a pillow. "We cannot detain individuals merely because we 'feel' they are lying."

"But sir, I must insist—"

De Groot held up his hand. "Wait, Sergeant, let me finish. We *can* legally detain him for several hours more, and that we will do."

Van der Heyden looked pacified. It turned out that he had been right about the reporter, whom he had identified from press records as one John Stenner, an American. At least when Reisbergen had gone to the man's flat, neighbors had reported a disturbance. A bullet had broken the back window of a Volvo parked across the street. Ballistics was comparing bullets now. Reisbergen had also reported that there was some sort of surveillance team watching Stenner's flat. Reisbergen was now watching the watchers. If the man Stenner was not Dawson's assassin, at the very least, something strange was going on with him.

"Take Reisbergen with you the next time you interrogate this cabdriver. This evening, say, let him sit awhile. In the meantime, I would like you to canvass the hotels."

Van der Heyden's face went through an odd contortion and settled into a hurt expression.

"You don't find the hotel canvass an appealing prospect, Sergeant. But this is one of those cases where we must not let the proverbial stone remain unturned. We need to be thorough, by the book." De Groot lit his pipe and watched the swirls of smoke. "Take a supply of the artist sketches and the photographs, won't you? I'd like you to question the hotels about both our...suspects."

"It is possible he's with the woman, of course."

"What *woman?*"

"Didn't I say, sir? He ran from the museum with a woman. I'm quite sure I mentioned that. He got into the cab with her. A very pretty woman...er...blond."

"You *didn't* say before, Sergeant. You had better have a likeness drawn of her too. Well, go ahead then, carry on."

Van der Heyden stood rooted to the spot, despite the dismissal.

"And the other aspects of the investigation, sir? I mean Detective Reisbergen?"

"Reisbergen is organizing a team of sorts—God knows we can't spare anyone—to watch John Stenner's flat. And to watch the people watching John Stenner's flat. Then he is going to look into Mr. Stenner's background, associates. He should be free by tonight to help you with the cabdriver."

Van der Heyden went dejectedly toward the door.

"Sergeant?"

"Yes, sir?"

"Start with the large central hotels, and then move on to the small ones on the canals; then fan out as you wish."

"But this could take weeks!" Van der Heyden blurted.

"Yes, I know; and quite possibly, neither man has been to a hotel. Still, it must be done. In a day or two, we'll have some help. And maybe you'll get lucky."

"Sir."

Van der Heyden left without the normal bounce in his walk, and De Groot chastised himself. He could have thrown him a bone of some sort. Lately, he didn't much like himself. Willi's illness was peeling away from him successive layers of self-satisfaction, revealing his flabby inner self—an unappetizing mélange of selfishness, pettiness, envy, weakness.

The blood from Willi's mouth, the blood on the white sheet had made patterns like abstract flowers. And Willi's furtive movements when she tried to hide it, cover it up—he would never forget it. There was something animalistic about it; and her eyes, when he caught her out…like a dog's, ashamed. Trapped.

CHAPTER SEVENTEEN

STENNER'S CALL HAD NOT BEEN SUCCESSFUL. The frustration showed in his face, in the tightening of muscle around his jaw as he explained it to Claire.

"Zweifel hasn't come in yet, and his home number is unlisted. I have his number at my place, but..."

He held the door open for her. They made their way around to Dam Square. As they walked, Claire heard the band music reach a ragged crescendo. During the pause between numbers, she could hear the crowd, a rumbling, a kind of audible pressure. The band started up again, playing "Danny Boy." They rounded a corner and emerged onto the square.

The viewing stands, which were jammed with people, were surrounded by magnificent orange azaleas in huge tubs; the pavement in front of the palace was completely laid with sod. A line of policemen manned the barricades that separated the viewing stands from the rest of the square. They stared around, as Claire had watched

American Presidents' Secret Service men do—never focusing, really, never making eye contact, scanning. The crowd was too congested near the palace, and Stenner pulled her away toward the center of the square.

As they walked toward the War Memorial, Claire began to notice the policemen and -women scattered liberally through the crowd. There were Red Cross personnel, too, wearing khaki tunics and red berets. The crowd seemed volatile, skittish, ready to run.

There were people perched on anything high, to get a better view. A precarious crowd of four stood on top of a telephone booth; boys had shinnied up light poles. Claire watched a girl in green climb up onto one of the stone lions. A policeman tapped the lion with his nightstick. She got down, reluctantly, but with a sheepish grin. This scene was repeated, almost exactly, moments later, by another policeman and a boy in a leather jacket. The boy was not smiling.

"Is it almost time?"

"Five minutes, I'd say."

The number of uniformed police was astonishing. They prowled the crowd—policemen in jackboots, policewomen in sensible shoes. The bulk of their guns and billy clubs disturbed the cut of their jackets. A young man in an Aran sweater climbed up on top of the wall near the obelisk, and several policemen insisted he get down. He refused, and one policeman got a leg up from another and went after him. As the cop hoisted himself up, Claire caught a glimpse of the bared skin of his midriff. The young man came down; a policeman led him away.

The drums rolled.

Juliana and several other members of the royal family appeared on the balcony of the palace. Juliana was making a speech, and the crowd in the viewing stands burst into applause occasionally, but it was impossible for most of the crowd to hear her. A helicopter beat the air not far away, like a racing heart.

Claire could see policemen in Day-Glo flak jackets on the roof of the Nieuwe Kerk. In fact, they were all over the place, on all the rooftops, ringing the square. Juliana must have completed her speech, because a storm of shimmering confetti rained down from the balcony of Peek and Cloppenburg and hundreds of orange balloons were launched into the sky. The band began to play again, and the crowd, nearly drowned out by the helicopter, which had moved in closer, sang along.

" 'Orange Boven,' " Stenner said.

A smoke bomb went off near De Bijenkorf and the crowd surged away from it. Claire and Stenner had drifted over toward the Krasnapolsky. Claire watched an elegant hand with long red fingernails and a large emerald ring pull aside the curtains of the Krasnapolsky's coffee shop. She bumped into a man in a tweed jacket.

"Sorry."

Two policemen sprinted through the crowd; they grabbed and handcuffed a man in maroon corduroy pants. There was another smoke bomb near Peek and Cloppenburg. At each stimulus, the crowd surged; there was the implicit threat of stampede.

They made their way to the Rokin. The vendors were hastily packing up. They walked over the sidewalk portrait of Beatrix, now only smudged-up chalk. At the intersection of Spuistraat, they passed the statue of the street urchin, splattered with orange paint. A helicopter passed directly overhead; it beat in Claire's head.

When they reached the statue of Wilhelmina on horseback, a marching band in red-white-and-blue uniforms rounded the corner and began marching in place in front of the Vroom and Dreesman department store. Batons flew into the air and twirled end over end and were caught by girls with tassels on their boots. A man in a plumed hat, stepping high, started them off again, and they proceeded down the Rokin. Falling into step behind this wholesome marching band was another, ragtag, band dressed in street clothing, predominantly black. The second band was substantial—at least two hundred men and women. The first band reached Spui and the second was still pouring around the corner, shouting something in unison. It sounded to Claire as if they were saying, "M.A. Go A-Way." They had their own drummers beating out the rhythm, and they easily drowned out the first band.

"What are they saying?"

"M.A.—that's the mobile police, riot police. 'M.A. Go Away.' "

Several clusters of black balloons floated up from between some buildings across the street, looking like evil molecules. A woman tugging a child with each hand hurried past them. A man with an orange feather in the brim of his hat raised his fist toward the balloons and said, "Anarchists." Then he looked around, furtively, as if he hoped no one had noticed. A helicopter hovered into position overhead; it became impossible to hear the chanting. The threat of violence was palpable. Claire could read it on people's faces—wary eyes, jaws clenched tight; they all seemed on their toes, ready to run for it. She could feel it herself—a little twist of fear in her throat. A few yards ahead of them, some unseen disturbance sent the crowd rippling away. Claire spotted a small band of punks holding sticks and rocks. The man with the orange feather in his hat stumbled and fell. He said, "Oof." Stenner helped him up.

The crowd was so dense it was difficult to walk. Stenner cut for the openings deftly, and she followed him as if he were a blocker. They passed under the red awning of the de l'Europe to find the door locked. The concierge opened it and let them in.

"Getting bad out there?'

Stenner seesawed his hands. "Could go either way. The police—well, there are a *lot* of police."

"Yes," the concierge said apologetically. "They are fed up with this nonsense. You know we have a big trouble two months ago. People are getting tired of this—always broken windows. Still, no one likes police." He shrugged and gave Claire a big smile.

Claire went to the bar while Stenner checked with the desk about his phone call. The bar was crowded and raucous, and Claire couldn't find any place to sit down.

"I'm just going, my dear," said a gray-haired man with Ben Franklin glasses. She waited while he extricated himself slowly and arthritically from his chair. She was aware of several blatantly appraising glances directed at her. She sat down and stared intently at the only thing on the table that could legitimately serve as a focus—a small black-and-gold drink list. A man in a black pin-striped suit was approaching when Stenner came in and slid into the chair opposite her.

"Half-hour wait for my call. What do you want? Beer? Bloody Mary? Coffee?"

"Coffee."

While he tried to get the waiter's attention, conversation from the surrounding tables filled the air.

"I'm a fireman, really. I do these stories."

"Hey, hey, another bourbon on the rocks," said an Australian voice.

"Double on the double."

"Look at you, Jerry, suit and all. And a *tie*. You got a ticket to the church?"

"Get me to the church on time," sang the Australian voice.

"How did you manage? I couldn't get one."

"'Course not, you filthy scumbag. Where's that man with my bourbon? I'm not going to church bloody sober; that's totally out of the question."

"I don't see Twilley."

"Twilley didn't make it. I think Twilley stayed in London."

"Didn't want to ruffle his silver hair."

"No. There's a London story—did you hear?"

"There's a good man, thank you. Iranians holding hostages in the embassy."

Stenner gave up on the waiter and went to the bar. "Right back."

"—least it's *their* bloody embassy this time."

"—State Department guy getting drilled here. Europe's heating up, definitely heating up."

"Bunch of wankers you are, filthy bunch of wankers. You hear that? Have another?"

"—getting nasty out there, Jerry. How are you going to make it to the church?"

Stenner came back.

"What could they give me that I don't already have?" asked a petulant American voice from behind Stenner. "What could the *Post* offer that the *Times* doesn't already offer?"

"Do you feel that your career is at its pinnacle?" oozed a woman's voice.

"Well, I hope not, but it's hard to see where I can go from here, really."

Stenner leaned toward her and jerked his shoulder at the people behind him. "Do you believe this guy? Most of these journalists have a pretty bizarre life—parachuting in and out of crises. Firemen, like Jerry Nesbit said. Every once in a while you get a real self-satisfied asshole like this guy." Stenner said all this in a fairly loud voice; Claire was sure the man could hear.

"I'm off," said the Australian. "Wish me luck. I'm walking. I'm stumbling to church."

Bill Phillips strode in, nearly knocking the Australian down with one swaying camera bag.

"Jerry! So sorry. I thought you were in Teheran."

"Watch those cameras, Phillips. Bloody deadly weapons, they are. I'm not that steady a ship. You off to the church for the investiture?"

"No, I think there's more going on out here. I'm going to stick out here."

"This ship is sailing to church. Navigating the filthy streets of Amsterdam."

"Mind your step. It's heating up out there on the Rokin."

"This ship has sailed more treacherous waters than the bloody Rokin. See you, Bill."

The Australian lurched out of the bar. Bill Phillips joined Claire and Stenner at their table, settling all his camera equipment in a heap on the floor. He dusted off his hands and sank into the chair.

"I'm putting in for a burro. My shoulders are killing me." He hunched his shoulders up and down a few times and rotated his neck. "Either that or go the streamlined method—one camera, one fifty-millimeter lens. So—how are you? I'm wretched, absolutely wretched. Where's the waiter? I require a Bloody Mary. I think I may have overdone last night. I need to calm the reflexes."

He turned around and looked for a waiter.

"What do you think?" Stenner asked. "Have you ever seen so many cops? In Amsterdam?"

"Wait! There he is." He beckoned the waiter over. "Would you be good enough to bring us three Bloody Marys. Spicy ones."

"No, Bill, I'll have another beer."

"Three Bloody Marys and a beer." Claire and Stenner started to protest, but Phillips waved them down. "Don't listen to them. You'll just get confused."

"I've never known the police to maintain such high visibility here," Stenner said. "I've never seen one-tenth this many cops."

"Quite," Phillips said, rubbing his bald head. "We're going to have a big bang-up."

"After the last big bang-up, some higher-up decided they weren't going to take it lying down this time, I guess. Only from my experience, high police visibility tends to provoke what it pretends to prevent."

"Hear, hear. Well said, Mr. Stenner. May I quote you on that? Oh, I forgot. I don't quote. May *you* quote you on that? Thank God, here come the Bloody Marys. Waiter knows a desperate man when he sees one." He distributed them around the table. "The only bad thing about Bloody Marys is that they're just a *touch* too much like food, don't you think? As you know, I don't like drinking alone, but I *deplore* eating alone, so I beg you to join me. Actually, they're the ideal breakfast."

"It's lunchtime."

"The ideal lunch as well. I did want a herring too— but by the time I got back up the Rokin the vendors had all packed up and gone. There's something about salty fish and hangovers—is that well known, do you think?"

"I don't know. Did you get some good shots?"

"The best are yet to come—I'm quite sure of that. Tear gas. We're definitely in for some tear gas. Tear gas makes lovely smoke, dense, but thinning out nicely so you can shoot through it. Bit hard on the eyes, of course, but that's why the Japanese made telephoto lenses." He swallowed half his Bloody Mary in one gulp.

"I've got a call coming through," Stenner said. "I'll be back in a few minutes."

"Why don't I take Claire upstairs with me, then? The Dutch TV boys have a room up there, one of the rooms they're renovating. Right on the corner, perfect vantage point. We'll just have a look—all right, Claire?"

Claire nodded.

"Off you go, John," Phillips said with a wave of his hand. "I'll settle up here, and you find us up there when you've finished." Stenner went off, but not before he caught Claire's eye. He put a finger to his lips and gave a barely perceptible shake of his head.

"So, *Claire.* You're very quiet, my dear. Or is it just that I'm very noisy?"

"I'm observing, I guess."

"I hope I wasn't too much the bad influence the other night?"

He took her hand. She found his large hand reassuring.

"Oh, no. I think I knew what I was doing."

He looked her straight in the eyes. "Don't you worry, my dear. Whatever is bothering you, I can tell you're fundamentally a sound and stable person."

Claire laughed. "You can?"

"Don't make fun of me. I have an eye for these things. I'm *paid* for my eye, you know."

"I see."

"Now my paid eyes must go upstairs to see what they can see."

He flagged the waiter down. "Put this table's drinks on my bill, will you? Room One Forty-two." He held out his arm for Claire. "Shall we?"

A television crew manned one of the windows. Phillips approached a man in a Hawaiian shirt.

"Johan, what's going on out there?"

"Ah, Bill. Hello." He gestured Phillips over to the window. "The battle lines are forming." Claire saw him point in the direction of Dam Square.

"But they're too far. I can't get a shot from here."

"Well, they are not going to stay there, are they? Besides, the rioters' line is forming right out here."

"Oh, yes."

Phillips called Claire over to an adjacent window.

"You see, down there by the Spui is where the police are making a line."

Claire could make out a phalanx of policemen, white shields held in front of them, white helmets gleaming.

"Look," Phillips said. "The canal boats are taking off. Can't say I blame them—all that glass."

Claire watched the canal boats backing out of the tour-boat terminal, just below them and to the right. The streets were jammed with people, and she could hear the chanting quite clearly: "M.A. Go A-Way. M.A. Go A-Way. M.A. Go A-Way." One of the canal boats tooted its horn in rhythm to the chant, as the convoy passed along the canal past the hotel. A strange collection of smaller craft approached the riot zone from the other direction. Kayaks, rowboats, canoes. There was a raft with a giant Heineken keg as a superstructure. One rowboat had a large hand-painted banner suspended between two poles fastened fore and aft. The banner read: AMSTERDAMMERS NEED HOMES NOT PALACES.

"Look," Phillips said. "Here comes the first rush."

The line of helmets and shields bobbed weirdly as the police advanced, like a segmented creature. The faint pops of tear-gas canisters were audible. The Dutch TV crew had been lounging around, drinking coffee, smoking; suddenly they were all business. The cameras whirred into action; they shouted directions to each other; they leaned perilously out the window.

The tear gas could be seen now, vertical columns of smoke rising from the street. The police looked menacing, android, in their helmets and shields and gas masks. They reached a point about three blocks from the hotel, just past the statue of Wilhelmina, and the crowd charged them, hurling cobblestones   and sticks. The police retaliated with an escalated tear-gas attack. The rioters, heroic in their own way, picked up the tear-gas canisters and tossed them into the canal or back at the police. Claire was surprised to see that the water didn't extinguish the canisters; they smoked away, bobbing on the surface of the canal. She wondered if it was special tear gas—Amsterdam tear gas, Venice tear gas, flotation tear gas.

The rioters began to build a barricade, using some construction sawhorses as a base and piling on anything handy—sticks, street signs. Before it got very sizable, a tanklike vehicle rumbled around the corner.

"Water cannon," Phillips said. He levered himself half out the window.

The water cannon fired a jet of water, bone-cracking in its impact. Briefly, the rioters disappeared behind their corner. The police stayed put two blocks away. The water cannon retreated.

"I'm going to see how John is doing," Claire said.

Phillips folded himself back inside. His eyes were red and teary. "I'll see you later, then, maybe downstairs. I thought I might go out, but they've laid down an awful lot of tear gas. I think I'll have to wait. They're going to start trashing the stores any second."

Claire knocked on the door, and when he opened it, Stenner seemed surprised to see her.

"Oh, it's you," he said, and gave her a hug. She stood stiffly, accepting the hug, as if he were an uncle or an acquaintance of her parents'.

"Well," she said nervously, "did your call go through?"

Stenner lit a cigarette. "I talked to Zweifel."

"And?"

"And he told me to catch the next flight to Anchorage. No, no, I'm kidding." He shook his head. "This thing keeps getting weirder. First he acted like I was his long-lost son, he was so happy to hear from me. Then he asks me where I am. Amsterdam, I say, as he knows. Then he starts talking in this strangled voice, his conspiratorial voice—I know it well. 'But are you at home?' No, I'm not at home. We dance around for a while and then he tells me he needs to know where I am right now and what my phone number is and that I'm to stay put and someone will get in touch. I wasn't sure it was you—you know, when you knocked on the door. So, I guess some guy is going to show up or someone's going to call me...Shit. I wish I knew what the fuck was going on here."

The chanting from outside went on: "M.A. Go A-

Way." The carillon began chiming out its half-hourly tune. A loud crash from across the street drew them to the balcony windows. The rioters had attacked the show windows of Vroom and Dreesman. They were dragging out furniture and props and big, jagged pieces of glass and heaping them onto the barricade. Two of them extracted a mannequin, held it triumphantly aloft and installed it on the top of the barricade. The mannequin, clad in lavender pegged pants and an oversized sweater, stood sentinel.

Suddenly the whoop of sirens started up, and from around the corner at the rioters' backs came a convoy of white police vehicles at fairly high speed. They were led by a van, followed by two small police cars, then five policemen on Vespas. The density of the crowd they were trying to drive through inhibited their speed, and they were heavily bombarded with rocks. One of the Vespa drivers was struck in the head and fell off. One of the other Vespa drivers managed to stop and haul the fallen policemen awkwardly onto his own machine. The van drove up onto the sidewalk to go around the barricade, and the rest of the vehicles followed.

"Are they out of their minds? I mean to drive into that mess on Vespas? They're lucky they didn't all get killed."

A helicopter thudded overhead. Claire could see only its shadow, hovering over the rioters. A few of them hurled rocks straight up toward it. These rocks fell down again, of course, and one of them injured a girl. Two men carried her off around the corner.

"Jesus."

Despite the helicopter, the chanting was still audible. A man wearing camouflage pants was beating out the rhythm on a metal plate in the road with what looked like a crowbar. The helicopter swung away. The captured

Vespa was being driven around in circles, its horn augmenting the chant.

"I'm glad the helicopter went away. I don't like them."

"I find them reassuring. In Vietnam, you'd be stuck somewhere and you'd hear a helicopter and that meant someone was coming to get you out."

"How did you know it wasn't an enemy helicopter?"

"They didn't have helicopters. It was an amazing advantage—not that it did any good."

"They're so...prehistoric; they look like giant insects."

"Didn't do much good in Iran the other day, either."

For a while, the riot settled into a pattern. The police would advance firing tear gas; the rioters would toss the canisters into the canal or, occasionally, lob them back toward the police. Then they would counter-attack with rocks. Everyone seemed content with a two-block standoff. The canal looked unearthly, Dantesque, plumes of smoke spiraling up from it as far as Claire could see.

A group of six or so managed to scale Vroom and Dreesman and reach the first-floor overhang. A great cheer went up from the crowd as this group ripped down one of the long red-white-and-blue banners. They tossed it down, and the people on the ground held it aloft like a canopy and marched around. The Vroom and Dreesman group also managed to detach one of the large gold-colored crowns that served to anchor the streamer. It appeared to be quite heavy, but they succeeded in lowering it to the street.

The police advanced a little closer and fired a concerted barrage of tear gas. One of the rioters set the barricade on fire, and for a while the whole scene was obscured by smoke.

"How did he light that fire so easily? When I was a kid, it took me an entire Sunday *Times* and about half an hour."

"Gasoline."

"I'm beginning to feel like a voyeur or something, you know?"

"They're not performing for us. Maybe for the TV guys upstairs. Think how much stranger it would be if you were doing something else instead of watching it. I mean, suppose you were sitting here reading *Remembrance of Things Past* or something. Or having a spot of tea and doing the crossword. Now, that would be—" He stopped suddenly when the phone rang, but he seemed immobilized, and Claire went to answer it. It was for him.

It was Richard Scott.

"Hey, Richard! I've probably called you twenty-five times in the last twenty-four hours..." Stenner's voice trailed off as he realized that he'd never actually reached him.

"It just occurred to you that I don't know where you are."

"It crossed my mind."

"This is the call you've been waiting for. I mean, you called Zweifel and Zweifel called...my...boss, and my boss called me." Scott laughed nervously. "And I called you."

"There's one question that presents itself."

"Who's my boss."

"Hey, that's the one."

Scott paused. "Alexander Carley."

Stenner held the phone away from his ear. "Oh, shit."

"Look, just stay right there. I'll be right over. I'll explain everything. Just *trust* me."

"Alexander Carley," Stenner said in a neutral voice. "Okay, Richard. I'll meet you in the bar." Stenner hung up.

"Alexander Carley," Claire said, "Isn't he—"

"CIA," Stenner said. "Ex-CIA. Well well well."

"I remember him," Claire started, thinking of the Watergate hearings.

"Scott is a writer," Stenner said in an insistent voice. "The guy turns out more stuff than I do—I mean the guy's *prolific.*" He lit a cigarette. "And he's a fucking spook." He rubbed her shoulder in a distracted way and shook his head. "Well, it certainly explains a few things."

CHAPTER EIGHTEEN

DOWNSTAIRS IN THE BAR, the tear gas was intense. Stenner ordered two beers, and the bartender nodded.

"Are you staying in the house? It's a bit messy."

"It's worse down here than it is in the rooms."

"It comes in from the canal. One of our windows got broken."

They carried their drinks into the Restaurant Excelsior, which was closed, and watched the riot through the Excelsior's bank of street-level windows. A girl had removed her shirt, and using a section of the banner as a boa, she danced down the street toward the massed policemen. The police had gained about half a block's territory since the barricade had been set on fire. Rioters were busy rebuilding it. Claire watched two of them hoist the mannequin, now soot-streaked and naked, up to the top again.

The water cannon made another foray, but as soon as it left, the rioters poured back into position. The police tried a charge, but as they moved within range of the rocks thrown by the rioters, they were so heavily bombarded they retreated.

"Mr. Stenner?" the bartender called.

The telephone call was from Scott.

"You didn't tell me there was a war going on there at the Munt. Listen, the de l'Europe is temporarily not letting anyone in unless he is a guest of the hotel. Can you meet me at the Café Rembrandt? It's unbelievable. The Rembrandtsplein is having a big party and the Munt is having a war."

"You are wanting to go *out?*" the concierge asked, a sad look crossing his face. "But this is surely foolish. You see what it is out there."

"We have an appointment," Stenner said regretfully.

"You see in this room here, we have already many refugees." They followed him to the door of the sitting room. "They are afraid to go out." He lifted his hands out to the sides. "And who can blame them?"

Claire glanced into the sitting room. It was crowded with people, mostly elderly people, sitting stiffly composed, as if they were in church. One bridge game was in progress on a coffee table.

"I would be willing to try it," a man with a thick mustache said, "but Marie absolutely refuses."

A very old woman wearing a pink hat with a veil that extended all the way over her substantial nose said, to no one in particular, "I've lost my handkerchief. It's embroidered with daffodils. Hasn't anyone seen it?"

"We really must go," Stenner said to the concierge. "I'm sorry."

"It was a gift from my granddaughter, you see..."

The concierge unlocked the door. "Please do be careful." He gave Claire one of his huge, winning smiles.

The sky was a blank, neutral color, near dusk. Tear

gas pricked at Claire's eyes and nose—exactly the same sensation as being about to sneeze.

Stenner pulled on her arm and stopped walking. "Do you want to go back? I didn't even think. You don't have to come."

"No, it feels good to be out. As soon as I saw the door was locked, I started feeling trapped."

"He said it was calm over there—a big party."

And it was. The whole square was engaged in having a party. The cafés were crowded, and people spilled out into the streets. A rock band was set up in the center of the square, and Stenner could see the jerky bobbing forms of people dancing. Two old women holding plastic champagne glasses passed them. *"Leve de Koningen!"* one of them saluted.

"Sure," Stenner said.

"Ja! Leve de Koningen!"

As soon as they went through the door of the Café Rembrandt, Scott jumped up and approached them.

"Hey, you made it."

Scott's physical appearance was a mass of contradictions. He was dark-skinned, but had a spray of freckles across the bridge of his nose. He had boyish, almost baby-faced features, and his hair had receded nearly to the crown of his head, giving him a high, domed forehead. His long legs and short, heavily muscled upper body made him look top-heavy.

Stenner introduced Claire, and then Scott pulled him aside, toward the bar, to get some drinks.

"I expected you to be alone, Sten. I mean, do you want her to hear all this? It's not such a good idea."

"I'm not sure I give a fuck," Stenner said, but he drifted back to the table while Scott waited for the drinks.

Claire's hand was surprisingly cold. "It might conceivably be safer for you if you don't take part in this conversation. Do you want me to take you back?"

"No. I'll just wait for you. Is that okay?"

He went to get her drink from Scott.

"What's this you're drinking?" he asked her.

"Scotch and water."

"Scotch and water? You don't like Scotch. Remember? Remember our liquors-of-the-world discussion?"

"That's why I'm having it—it's a gesture toward moderation. I could have had ginger ale, but I thought that would be going too far."

"Way too far."

Stenner left her and sat down across from Scott. He lit a cigarette. "So. Sooooo..." He shook his head. "You're a spook."

"Part-time. *Very* part-time. Mostly, I *am* a free-lance writer. You know that I couldn't turn out all the stuff I've written in my spare time. This is just a little sideline."

"Just a little sideline, shit." He took a long swallow of beer. "It's been quite a day or two for me. I'm feeling jerked around like a fucking trout or something."

"You sure you want to talk here? We could go to your hotel. Or my place."

"I'm sure I don't want to go to some little room with you. I'm damn sure about that."

"Okay, okay. I'll lay it out for you. Okay?"

"I'm listening."

"Okay. First of all"—Scott leaned forward—"Alan Dawson was one of Carley's singletons, recruited way back, right at the end of the war." He leaned back in his chair. "Do you remember that piece you wrote for *Analysis,* about the moles in the Agency?"

Stenner nodded.

"Well, that was right on. It blew Carley's mind, how you pieced it out. Anyway, when Carley left the Agency, he kept on working on that, accumulating evidence. And one absolutely vital piece of evidence is the property of Maurice LeClerc, who is Director General of Internal Services at French Intelligence."

"SDECE."

"Yeah. And LeClerc is on the Circle Group Steering Committee, just like Dawson. Carley knew that Firelli was going to propose the assassination of the Shah, and he asked Dawson to tape it. And..." He stopped abruptly. "Dawson got the tape to you? He made the tape?"

Stenner nodded.

"You heard it? It's okay?" Scott asked anxiously. "The tape's okay?"

Stenner nodded again.

"Well, Carley was going to use that tape to blackmail LeClerc into turning over his phone-trap records for a couple of days in 1975."

"Phone trap—what's that? A trace?"

"It's a device that traces and records incoming calls to a particular phone. And LeClerc has these records, and we know that they are the *goods,* but he won't turn them over. He's...he'll only go through *official* channels. He just won't cooperate. Anyway, if you'll remember, December sixteenth, 1975, was the day Zverkov was murdered in Senlis. And there was a phone call to LeClerc that day that said, in essence, that there was a double-agent operation going on in Senlis, involving Zverkov, on the sixteenth, and that *no surveillance was necessary* or desired. LeClerc passed this on to his Counterintelligence man, Frédéric des Lauriers. Des Lauriers clued in the KGB and the KGB got Zverkov. Sisyphus knew something of the sort had happened, of course, but he had no access to the Agency. He pestered LeClerc but LeClerc wouldn't say boo. You see, the KGB knew, from the phone call, that there would be no watchers. No CIA—because the mole was directing the operation—and no SDECE either, so, zip—bye-bye Zverkov. Of course, even LeClerc knew what was what a couple of years later, when Des Lauriers defected. But LeClerc is such an officious son-of-a-bitch that he still wouldn't give up the phone-trap records. And those records are *proof*. Whoever made that phone call—that's one mole for goddamned sure. We only know about the phone call because des Lauriers has turned into something of a lush and mouthed off to one of our people in Moscow."

"One of *whose* people? You mean Carley is still running a network?"

Scott stopped and took a drink. He rubbed his forehead. "That would be pure speculation on your part, John. I can't get into that. I can't comment on that." He squinted his eyes, like a headache sufferer in a TV ad.

Stenner laughed. "You sound like some fucking hack for the Department of Transportation. You can't *comment on that*. You know that? You sound like some government hack." Stenner drank the rest of his beer and lit another cigarette. "I need another beer."

When he came back with the beer, Scott massaged his forehead and then cleared his throat in a formal way.

"Look, John, I know you're feeling...betrayed. And I'm sorry. This sounds corny, but I hope it won't interfere with our friendship." He looked down at the table and ran his finger around the rim of his glass.

"I'm afraid that hope is going to be short-lived, you

know. I mean, you're kidding. Betrayed? Is that how I'm feeling? Betrayed is the least of my problems. Getting shot at is just a bit more troubling; standing next to a guy who gets blown away; walking into some kind of trap in my apartment. I can already see what my role in this little number was; I was the cut-out, right? I was the cut-out, and I came this fucking close"—he held his thumb and forefinger a sliver of air apart—"to getting cut out for good."

"I know you're pissed—"

"Stop telling me you *know* what..." Stenner's peripheral vision informed him that heads were turning in their direction, and he lowered his voice. "Go on."

"You're right: you were the cut-out, to protect Dawson. Dawson was too important to burn, even for this. If Dawson couldn't hook up with you, I was the fallback. Once the transfer was made, Dawson was supposed to call Sisyphus and tell him. And we figured you'd call Zweifel."

"You figured I'd call Zweifel."

"You *did,* didn't you? I mean, here we are."

"And how does Zweifel fit into all this? Another part-time spook?"

"Hardly. He just owed Sisyphus a favor, a big one. So, that was the drill. As soon as Dawson called in to say the transfer had been made, Sisyphus alerts Zweifel. If, for some reason, you didn't call Zweifel within a couple of hours of the transfer, I was to clue you in. Zweifel would have instructed you to call LeClerc, get his comments on the assassination story. To LeClerc, it looks like *legitimate* pressure, a press leak. Dawson might have been suspected, but his connection with Sisyphus isn't known, and anyone could have been the source. You call LeClerc, get his comments, get his side of the story. Then you call Firelli, you call all of them. Zweifel is swearing he's ready to go to press any minute, and that's when Sisyphus parachutes in to save the day. Zweifel owes him a favor; he can get the story killed. But LeClerc has to do something for him. All kinds of pressure from the other people on the Steering Committee comes down on LeClerc, and—well, you get the drill." Scott tried a smile.

"I get the drill. I'm the point man and I'm walking blind. And then what was *supposed* to happen? To me, I mean? Sisyphus gets his favor; I've been working my ass off on this story. What then? I say, 'Oh, well, I guess they don't like the story.' "

"That was when you got wised up. You would get the mole-in-the-CIA story."

Stenner looked at the ceiling. "You fuckers."

"You still get that."

Stenner shook his head.

"We would have wised you up in the first place, but Sisyphus wasn't sure you'd play."

"I might have had a reservation or two. I love this. I really do. Circle Group is ready to take out the Shah, the well-protected Shah, the Shah who is always photographed surrounded by Dobermans, and then there's me. Of course, my bodyguards are…"

Stenner's attention was diverted by several excited shouts from outside and a large mob of people running at high speed past the front of the café. A man and a woman with bandanas covering their noses stumbled inside. People in the room began standing up. A waiter came in, set down his tray of drinks and locked the front door. A new clutch of people ran past, followed by police wearing gas masks.

The waiter said something in Dutch. Then he said, "Go inside."

When the first tear-gas canisters popped, half the

outer-room crowd was already inside. Canisters exploded in rapid succession, like firecrackers. Stenner looked around for Claire and spotted her sitting at the bar. Everyone had now reached the relative sanctuary of the inner room, and the waiter locked the inside door and turned off the lights in the outer room. Tear-gas canisters could still be heard, but more faintly—thwup thwup thwup.

The room was almost silent until the accordion player, whom Stenner hadn't noticed, broke into a rendition of "Silent Night." The tension dissolved into laughter and conversation. The bartender began dispensing wet towels and slices of lemon. He set several pails of ice water on the bar, stacked up napkins, bar towels, and invited people to help themselves. From outside came the sound of breaking glass, a lot of yelling and shouting. The accordion player led the crowd in a short version of the Hallelujah Chorus.

"The war moved," Scott said.

"But the party goes on."

Stenner threaded his way through the densely packed crowd toward the bar. The tear gas was thick enough to make everyone's eyes stream with tears. He put his hand on Claire's shoulder. "You all right?"

She dabbed at her eyes with a red-and-white bar towel. "Yes. Never a dull moment."

"Actually, she's been quite brave," said a large man with a beard who was sitting next to her.

Claire frowned, feeling patronized, and took a sip of her drink. She waved her hand and made a perfunctory introduction. "John, this is Keis. Keis...John." They nodded back and forth, a bit warily.

"I won't be much longer," Stenner said. "Want another drink?"

Claire shook her head.

"I won't be long."

"No one's going anywhere for a while," Keis bellowed. When Stenner was gone, he asked, "Is that your boyfriend?"

It seemed simplest to say "Yes."

Claire could just make out the sinister shape of the water cannon on the street. Water thudded against the windows with such force she was surprised the glass didn't break. She remembered seeing news film from some demonstration—fire hoses turned on the demonstrators, bodies flying backward.

"What?" Keis was saying something.

"I was saying what do you think of your President, Mr. Carter?" he asked.

Claire seesawed her hands in the air.

"*We* think he is a disaster. You know, we count on your America, but not anymore. The Russians invade Afghanistan and your Mr. Carter boycotts the Olympics. Does he think this is foreign policy? Oho!"

"I'm not going to defend him."

"Did you vote for him?"

Claire sipped her Scotch. Scotch had always tasted medicinal to her. The taste of the Scotch, the body heat radiated by the dense crowd, the smoke, the tear gas—she felt feverish.

A fever dream: I am in an Amsterdam bar, trapped by a riot, talking to a nice stranger about Jimmy Carter. She felt she must have missed a transition somewhere.

The accordionist was playing "My Old Kentucky Home."

"Ah, I am glad you didn't vote for him."

"But I did vote for him."

"Ahhhh. But why?"

"There was a prevalent feeling that a peanut farmer

from Georgia might make for an interesting change of pace."

"I will never understand."

"I can't drink this anymore. I need a beer."

"Maybe it makes no difference. Here we have a saying: 'No matter who you vote for, the government always gets in.' "

Water thudded against the windows. Keis signaled the bartender for two beers. "Anyway," he went on, "I'm not sure government makes foreign policy anymore. These elitist groups—you know, the Bilderbergers, Circle Group—they seem to make more and more agreements totally without anyone knowing it. Gentlemen's agreements, only I'm not so sure they are gentlemen. Do you know Circle Group had a meeting here this week? Nothing in the press...no publicity. I only know this because I have a friend who works in the Amstel Hotel—this is where they have their meeting."

Claire was breathing shallowly. *Circle Group.* Suddenly Keis seemed less amiable; he seemed to be looking at her with grave concentration. Was he deliberately leading the conversation?

"What do you think Circle Group was here talking about?" he demanded.

She shrugged. "The monetary system. Something like that."

Her beer arrived. "That's just it," Keis said. "We don't find out. They keep it all secret."

Claire wanted to angle the conversation back to Jimmy Carter. "I should have known better than to vote for Carter," she said. She tried for a chagrined look. "I should have known from his smile. He speaks a little while and then..." She did an imitation. "You know. The Soviets have invaded Afghanistan..."

❖ ❖ ❖

Stenner was finishing up his account of what had happened to him during the last two days. "So, would you care to give me the benefit of your expertise and make an educated guess on the identity of Dawson's killer? The identity *group*—let's put it that way. The identity of the group that is making my life so fucking exciting."

"It's the Agency, we think. It *could* be Circle, but we don't think so. Sisyphus thinks the Agency picked up his meet with Dawson. They *sense* that Sisyphus is closing in on them; they've stepped up surveillance measures. Still, it's pretty rotten-quality work—I mean, all this shooting. That's unnecessary; that tends to raise eyebrows."

"Raise eyebrows—uh-huh."

"And then they struck out twice on you."

"Let's call Quality Control immediately."

"I didn't—"

"Do you have a little map with pins too? Where's John? Not at home? Oh darn, here he is in the canal. How did he get there?"

"I know it must seem—"

"I mean, you're pretty fucking cerebral here. 'Pretty rotten-quality work.' " Stenner drummed his fingers against the wall. "So now what?"

"Now we go get the tape and drive to Düsseldorf and give it to Sisyphus. No need to go through this newspaper number anymore."

"God, it's hot in here." Stenner took off his jacket. "Supposing I don't want to go to Düsseldorf?"

"You ought to get out of here for a while. Until the deal goes through. They might—"

"Have another go at me?" Stenner cut in, affecting a

British accent. "Couldn't blame the chaps, really. Bit of a loose end, I am, me and my tape. Have to tidy that up, don't we?"

"We can protect you. Once—"

"*Protect* me. Thanks. I appreciate that. I'm deeply grateful."

"The car and driver are ready."

Stenner glanced over toward the bar. "What about Claire? She's been with me. She's been seen. Is she in—"

"She could be in some danger. It's possible. Remote, but possible." Scott rubbed his forehead. "I could arrange...I think I could arrange for her to come along."

"Düsseldorf?" Stenner shook his head. "You fuckers." He stood up. "I'll tell you one thing: I don't want your fucking *story*. Get another patsy. It's gothic romances for me from now on."

"That's the way you feel now, but—"

"Cereal-box copy, greeting cards..."

"There seems to be a lull out there," Scott said. "I think we should go."

It was the sixth beer Keis had consumed since he'd first sat down with her outside, before the tear gas had driven them in to the bar. Claire didn't know why she was keeping track. The cumulative effect seemed to be that he was even more earnest than before, and that his grasp of the English language was slowly loosening. He was talking about the meaning of punk.

"Just take the—what do you say—unisexual [which he pronounced oo-ni-sexual] aspects. With the hippies, the men were looking more like women, you know. With the punks, is the opposite. The women are looking more like mens, more tough, more *macho*, you agree?" He held up his empty glass to the bartender. "*Twee bier.*"

"No, not for me."

"I drink it, then. With the punks, is just the same as the Hare Krishnas, you know? The way they dress—it's a uniform. They all look alike, in a way. It supposed to be an expression of...what you say...individual, the individual. But I don't think this is true. What do you think happens if a punk does a bank robbery? It's a great disguise, see? Who would remember what kind of nose, what kind of ear? Some people might remember what they wear—you know, their *costume*. But what they look like? I don't think. Think of the police description: we are looking for someone with pink hair and safety pins in their ears. This could be *any*body."

Claire saw Stenner making his way toward her.

"This will happen," Keis said, nodding his head. "Yes, this kind of crimes will happen."

"I think I have to go now," she said. Stenner had a strange, dazed expression on his face.

"But we are just *starting*," Keis protested.

"We're going to make a dash for it," Stenner said. "It seems relatively quiet out there."

"Maybe I see you again," Keis said. "I come here again."

"Nice meeting you," Claire said like a sixth-grader.

"I look for you here."

When they were outside, Claire noticed she was still carrying the bar towel. She clutched it over her nose and mouth.

"How long does it take this stuff to die down?"

"Spice of life," Stenner said in a manic voice. "It takes a couple of hours. But we hardly have to worry. How would you like to go to Düsseldorf?"

"Düsseldorf," she said noncommittally.

"Not up there on your Places to Visit list? Hey, they have great beer! Pork, too. Wonderful pork. Swineflesh, they call it there. So straightforward, those Germans, you know? So direct. At least linguistically. So we'll spin on up to Düsseldorf, have some beer and swineflesh and sour cabbage—umm *ummm,* you're going to love it, baby, don't worry."

"John," Scott started, but just then they emerged from the diagonal street leading from the Rembrandtsplein to the Munt and were confronted by a line of police. Their white helmets gleamed in the moonlight; gas masks dangled against their chests. One of them said something in Dutch.

"We don't speak Dutch."

"You can't pass here."

"But we're staying at the de l'Europe. How are we supposed to get there?"

"One moment," said the policeman grimly. He looked around, confusion clouding his young tired face. "Remain just here," he warned, pointing at their feet.

"Well, I guess they advanced," Stenner said. "I guess they pushed them back. Push 'em back, push 'em back, waaaaaay back."

"They'll think you're drunk," Scott said.

A skeletal phone booth glittered across the street—all its glass panes knocked out, sparkling in heaps on the pavement.

"I wish I were drunk."

The policeman came back. "I will escort you to the hotel." The concierge peered out at them and unlocked the door.

"Are these guests of the hotel?" asked the policeman.

"I am glad you are safe," said the concierge without a

trace of a smile. "These two are staying here." He pointed to Claire and Stenner. "But this other gentleman—I am sorry. You see," he said, looking directly at Claire, "we are now *really* filled with people too frightened to return to their homes and hotels. I am sorry, but the other gentleman cannot come in now. The police—they have promised to escort all these people home, but not yet."

"Okay," Stenner said. "We will meet you back at the café. No, wait a minute." He turned to the concierge. "Is it possible to get a taxi now?"

"Oh, yes; that is how we are getting the people out, some of them. It depends on where you are going—Dam Square is sealed off, and the Waterlooplein."

"No, he lives on Roomervischerstraat."

"That is possible."

"We'll meet you at your place," Stenner said.

"Can't I just wait down here for them?" Scott asked.

"No. I am so sorry. It is not possible."

"Let's go," said the policeman.

"It will only be a few minutes," Scott appealed.

"I said let's go," the policeman repeated, putting his hand on Scott's arm. "There is a taxi rank operating now in Leidseplein."

The concierge went behind the counter himself to get Claire's key, but instead of handing it to her, as he began to do, he dropped it suddenly on the counter, as if it were hot and had burned his fingers.

"Good evening to you," he said formally, without looking at Claire. She wondered if he was just angry with them for going out.

Stenner was standing at the entrance to the bar, leaning over so that a man she didn't recognize could speak to him. The bar was full, as was the Restaurant Excelsior. The piano player was halfway through "Smoke Gets in

Your Eyes." The irony was not lost on the red-eyed crowd, and several of them sang along. All of them faltered, eventually, forgetting the words, except for one surprisingly true soprano, finishing the song to a round of applause. Stenner disengaged from the man he was speaking to and turned toward her.

"What's all this Düsseldorf stuff?" she asked. "I can't tell if you're kidding or—"

He put his arm around her. "C'mon upstairs."

She had trouble with the lock, and Stenner took the key from her and opened the door. He took two steps forward and stopped so suddenly she bumped into his back. Then she saw the two men in the room.

"John Stenner," said the younger of the two men in a breathless voice. He had a gun, and it was pointed directly at them. "Please do not move," he added in a slightly embarrassed tone.

This admonition was totally unnecessary, in Claire's case. She felt fixed firmly in open space by an invisible line drawn from the gun barrel to her chest; pinned, like a butterfly to a display board.

"Put your arms slowly to the side, up, like wings," said the man. "Just so. Now, take three steps forward."

Claire stumbled forward.

"Not you first, miss. First Mr. Stenner."

For a giddy moment, Claire remembered playing Mother May I? in the schoolyard. The older man slipped behind her and shut the door. He said something in Dutch that made the man with the gun blush. Then she was summoned forward and they were frisked—a friendly word for a humiliating procedure.

"We require you to come with us to answer some questions concerning the murder of Alan Dawson," the younger man said.

"You might let them know we are the police," said the older man in a sarcastic voice.

The younger man shot an angry glance at him. "I am Sergeant Van der Heyden of the Amsterdam Police and this is Detective Reisbergen."

"You tried to shoot me," Stenner said.

"No, sir, I did not," said Van der Heyden, blushing.

"I would like to see some identification."

"We *are* from the Amsterdam police," said the older man, flipping his wallet open close to Stenner's face, "and we simply have some questions to put to you."

"Should you call the Embassy?" Claire squeaked.

The older man's hands flew out to the side. "You can do this of course, but you know what they are. They will not be of help at this stage. Look"—he slapped his hands together—"we believe, Mr. Stenner, that you were an eye-witness to a murder." Van der Heyden started to interrupt, but Reisbergen stopped him with a chop of his hand in the air. "We need to take your statement concerning this. You will have legal advice. Then we will release you. The young lady is free to stay here."

"I must advise her not to leave Amsterdam," Van der Heyden said earnestly.

"You are advised not to leave Amsterdam," Reisbergen echoed in falsetto. "Will you come along now, Mr. Stenner?"

Stenner shrugged and shuffled toward the door. Claire trailed them into the hall.

"Put your gun away, Frans, for God's sake," Reisbergen castigated. "You like to give some heart attacks to those old people downstairs."

"Where are you taking him?" Claire demanded in her mother's imperious voice.

"Here is my card, miss," said Van der Heyden. "I must

also point out that we have taken your particulars from the concierge, so do not try something foolish, please."

Claire followed them down to the lobby. The concierge cast her a sorrowful look as he went to unlock the door. A woman with her hair in icy silver waves came out of the sitting room to peer outside. "You'd think they'd keep a little better order," she said to Claire, "with all those tourists in town. Wouldn't you?"

Claire stood there clutching the bar towel. The piano player from the Excelsior was playing "Tennessee Waltz."

CHAPTER NINETEEN

WHEN CLAIRE RETURNED TO HER ROOM, she felt too visible, as if there were still people in there—policemen, men with guns—watching for an errant move. She walked stiffly to the balcony doors and looked outside. Workmen across the street were hammering sheets of plywood over the exposed display windows of Vroom and Dreesman. She closed the curtains and put the sergeant's white card in the exact center of the white table. Her body felt so dense and heavy, it seemed her skeleton could barely support her.

She walked to the telephone in a detached, somnambulant way and called the desk. They put her through to the American Embassy.

An impatient woman's voice asked what she wanted.

"I'd like to report an incident," Claire said in a newscaster tone. "An incident involving an American citizen named John Stenner." The words snapped efficiently out of her mouth. "That's S-T-E-N-N-E-R. He was arrested this evening..." She paused. "He may not have been arrested. He was taken from his hotel at gunpoint by the Amsterdam police. For questioning."

"What was this in connection with?"

"I don't know."

"I don't know what you expect us to do," the voice said peevishly.

"I expect you to check into it. I expect you to protect his rights."

"What is *your* name?" the voice demanded.

"I am a concerned citizen," Claire said, and hung up. This conversation did nothing to restore a sense of reality, and on an impulse, while she still had the phone in her hand, she placed a call to Jeff. It would be half an hour, the desk clerk said; he would ring her back when the call went through.

Jeff would be worried about her. Jeff would be relieved to hear from her. Jeff would urge her to do... something, this or that...not nothing. The phone call to Jeff was a string to attach her to the actual, the tangible. She was Claire to Jeff, not "the girl," not "Miss," or "Madam," not the blond woman, not the concerned citizen, not John Stenner's "friend." She was just Claire to Jeff, the Claire who liked black olives, the Claire who left the top off the toothpaste, the Claire...

She went into the bathroom to draw a bath. "I don't know what I'm doing," she said aloud to the towels. The sound of her voice startled her. "I'm talking to myself," she said quietly, watching the bathwater creep up the sides of the tub. There seemed to be nothing to propel her into the future except the gradual progress of the bathwater.

When the phone rang, Claire's mind was on Stenner. She could imagine him slumped warily in a chair. The room would be dingy, utilitarian...

She stood dripping by the phone, moving the receiver from one ear to the other as she clumsily put on the terry-cloth robe.

"Your call to New York."

"Yes."

The phone began ringing in New York. She could picture the room exactly. The blue-and-white bedspread, the white dust ruffle, the bookcase, the pre-Columbian statue on top of the bookcase, the worn spot in the Oriental rug, the shades with their scalloped edges and slightly yellowed fringe—they would be pulled down, the tassels drooping over the windowsills. The dresser, the David Hockney print. Somehow she could not imagine Jeff.

The phone rang on. Maybe she couldn't imagine him because he wasn't there; maybe it worked that way. Maybe she couldn't imagine him because she rarely saw him sleeping. He always got up first. Maybe he was staying at *her* place—the other woman's place. Maybe the woman would answer the phone. The line cracked with static.

"Hello," Jeff said. And then when she said nothing, *"Hello."* Suddenly, she could imagine him perfectly. His hair sticking up at the crown, a crease on his cheek from the pillow. She squeezed her eyes shut.

"Goddammit! Bad connection. Hello! Is that you, Claire? Is that you?"

She hung up.

She climbed back into the bathtub and lay there a long time, hardly moving. After a while, she seemed to lose the sense of where her body stopped and the water began. Motionless, dissolving.

She must have fallen asleep, because she woke up with a jerk, her heart pounding. She jumped out, slopping water on the floor. The water was cold; her fingers were shriveled, deeply gouged. She toweled herself off and put on a nightgown. She had a nasty, dry feeling in her throat. She wanted to call Room Service for some ginger ale, but she was afraid. She was afraid...she didn't know what she was afraid of...

She placed a phone call to her parents and chain-smoked cigarettes until it went through. Outside, the workmen had finished boarding up Vroom and Dreesman. A pair of policemen lounged under the sole un-smashed streetlamp.

The phone rang in Nyack.

"Who is it?" her mother asked sleepily. "Is it the middle of the night? Who is calling, please?"

The sound of her mother's voice restored her equilibrium, as she had guessed it would. She resented it a little, the depth of the relief her mother's voice provided.

"Claire! It's you! How are you? Are you all right? Jonathan! Wake up, Jonathan! It's Claire!"

"I didn't mean to wake you up."

"Oh, I'm so relieved to hear your voice. I couldn't care less. Tell me how you're doing. Are you coming back at all soon? We've been worried."

"Worried?" her father's voice broke in. "Your mother's been goddamned frantic, Claire. Someday, if you're ever a parent, you might understand that..." He went on for a while, berating her, and then extracted the name of the hotel, its phone number, her room number. His voice softened. "Look, I don't mean to be so grouchy. I know you're having a rough time. And I know, I know you're old enough, I know you're able to take care of yourself. But you go off half-deranged, you know. Look, just take care of yourself," he ordered.

"Claire," said her mother in a tentative voice, "I'm not sure whether to tell you this or not, but...well, Jeff has been calling two or three times a day to see if we've heard anything from you. He says he feels an utter fool. He's desperate to know where you are, to talk to you. Claire"— her mother paused and took a deep, excited breath—"*he wants you back.*"

"Please don't tell him where I am. I tried, I even tried to call him, but when he answered the phone, I just couldn't speak to him. Not yet. Tell him I'm all right."

"You're sure..."

"I'm sorry I didn't call before. I mean, I'm sorry you were worried. I've got to go now. I'm very sleepy."

"We love you, Claire."

"Love you too."

Stenner sat alone in a room much like the room Claire had imagined, except that one wall was covered with a clumsily painted mural of a tree. Probably the result of some institutional beautification project, meant to cheer the prisoners. The tree had been foliated with yellow, brown and blue leaves. Many of the leaves bore the scratchy graffiti of prisoners denied any implement save their fingernails.

The room was furnished with a battered khaki desk, all its drawers locked, and a large number of folding metal chairs. Stenner had lined up six chairs and was stretched out on the seats. As a bed, it was only marginally more comfortable than the floor.

During the interrogation, he had admitted to knowing Alan Dawson, explaining that Dawson was a source and also an old friend of his ex-wife's family. He had met Dawson at the restaurant, and they had intended to part company at the Rijksmuseum, where Stenner was meeting Claire Brooks and Dawson was intending to get a taxi. He had explained his flight from the shooting: he had thought Van der Heyden the assassin, had thought Van der Heyden was firing at him. He had described the flat-faced man and confirmed that the police sketch resembled the man he had seen. He had denied that the taxicab had taken "evasive action." He said that once in the Rijksmuseum, he had remembered seeing Van der Heyden at the police station when picking up his press credentials, and illogical as it sounded, it seemed to him at the time that the police had shot Dawson and were trying to shoot him. He denied knowing that the police were following the taxicab and said that the taxi driver had "scared him to death."

He stared at the ceiling. There was a crack running diagonally from one corner to the light fixture, a recessed fluorescent lamp.

After running through the same questions a number of times, Van der Heyden and Reisbergen had started arguing in Dutch. Another policeman had summoned them away.

The crack in the ceiling resembled a river. Several tributary cracks ran off the main one, and just before it reached the light fixture, it splintered into a kind of delta. Stenner closed his eyes. It seemed to him that the policemen had been gone a long time, although there was no reason to trust himself in this. They had taken his watch, placing it in a brown manila envelope along with his wallet and keys.

He would try to go to sleep. He concentrated on a tiny blue dot, in the center of his forehead. He invented a tiny blue dot and willed it to expand. Thoughts and images disrupted his concentration at first: What would Claire do? What would Scott do? Were those footsteps? The chair was pressing on his ribs. His neck hurt. All these thoughts, and the hundreds of others that flickered momentarily through his mind, were swallowed up by the expanding blue dot. Eventually, it became larger than he was, as large as the room. He fell asleep.

In the dream, Claire was brushing her teeth. The bristles of the toothbrush kept coming loose and she was spitting them into the sink.

When the phone rang, she woke up very quickly, but still felt as if there were foreign objects in her mouth.

"Is John Stenner there? Could I speak to him, please?"

"No. I mean no, he's not here."

"Claire? This is John's friend, Richard Scott. I've been trying to call; your phone has been tied up. Can you tell me—is he on his way over here?"

"No."

"Well, where is he? Can you tell me where he is?"

"When we came back to the room, there were two Amsterdam policemen here. They've taken him to the station for questioning."

"About what? The tape?"

"They said he was an eyewitness to a murder."

"Did they take the tape?"

Claire hesitated. Düsseldorf, Stenner had said. Scott is a spook. The less she knew about it, the better.

"What tape?" she asked. Her voice was too high.

"But we were coming back there so he could give me the tape. When they wouldn't let me in, both of you, or at least John—John was coming here to…give me the tape."

"I'm sorry. I—do you want the name of the policeman?"

"Okay, yes, give me that."

After she hung up, Claire went to check on the tape. It was still there, in the suitcase she'd reserved for dirty clothes, hidden in its sock. Stenner hadn't remembered to find a better hiding place. She left it there. Richard Scott called again.

"Look, I don't blame you for not trusting me, but all that Düsseldorf business—we were going to go to Düsseldorf with the tape."

"I'm sorry, I—"

"All right, look, if the tape is there and you know where it is, someone a lot less friendly than I am is going to come looking for it sooner or later. Put it somewhere—hide it until you see John again."

"But—"

"It's good advice," he said, and hung up.

Commissaris de Groot looked at his watch. Three A.M.

The riots had been far more severe than anticipated, and as the night wore on, his staff had dwindled to almost nothing. There had been two homicides during the night as well.

Even Van der Heyden and Reisbergen had been pulled away from interrogating Stenner in the Dawson case and dispatched to assist in the final mop-up. More than two hundred people had been injured, half of them police. Some fool threw a brick at a police horse and sent it trampling wildly through the crowd. Van der Heyden was unlucky enough to get a balloon filled with paint dumped on his head. "I like him this way," Reisbergen joked, "as a blonde—don't you?" When Van der Heyden looked like he might cry, De Groot sent him home.

Just after that, the puzzling phone call from Rob Davenport had come. Davenport was an old acquaintance from the OSS. Before Willi got so ill, they'd been rather friendly with the Davenports, seeing them socially several times. Of course, Davenport was not calling in the middle of the night to make a social engagement; he was also the CIA's Head of Station in Amsterdam.

And he wanted a favor. He understood that an American, John Stenner, was being detained for questioning in the Dawson case. Would De Groot mind if a couple of men came by and put a few questions to Stenner when they were done with him? De Groot was not sure about that; he would give it some thought and ring Davenport back.

Davenport must have been in more of a hurry than his slow, drawling voice had indicated. Less than ten minutes later, another phone call came. Apparently, De Groot's was not the only arm being twisted.

The Chief of Police sounded disgruntled on the phone, as well he might have been, given that his crowd-control tactics had gone so spectacularly awry. He ordered De Groot to cooperate with Davenport's request, and suggested that De Groot turn over the man Stenner to Davenport's men. And then the Chief had suggested that De Groot "not push too hard" on the case. De Groot had come right out and asked him,

"Does that mean I'm not supposed to solve the case?"
"It's really an American affair," the Chief had said, in an embarrassed tone. "You're to just go through the motions."

De Groot shuffled down the hallway, balancing two cups of coffee in one hand and a bottle of brandy in the other. He was surprised to find Stenner asleep. It was the rare detainee who was able to sleep in Room 23. He set the coffee cups down on the desk and poured some brandy into his own.

"I've brought you some coffee," De Groot said, gesturing at the second cup. Stenner rubbed his eyes. "Would you care for some brandy in it?"

Stenner rubbed his neck and stretched his arms. "Putting me at ease?"

De Groot pulled out his pipe and filled it carefully. He spent another minute getting it going. "It's late, Mr. Stenner, and I'm far less concerned with your ease than you might imagine."

"I'll take some brandy in my coffee."

"I have read your statement concerning Mr. Dawson's murder as told to Sergeant Van der Heyden and Detective Reisbergen. Have you anything to add to what you have already told them?"

"No."

De Groot pulled on his pipe and found that it had gone out. He lit it again.

"I think you are telling the truth, Mr. Stenner, but not the *entire* truth. As it happens, I am not interested in the entire truth. Indeed, I have been told rather directly that it need not concern me—you see? For instance, if your meeting with Mr. Dawson was such an innocent social occasion, why were two gentlemen carrying out surveillance on your flat the night after Dawson's murder? Why was the rear window of a car parked across the street from your flat destroyed by gunfire?"

De Groot finished off his coffee with a slight grimace.

"Frankly, I found these facts intriguing. Now I must dismiss them from my mind. Later on this morning, some—what shall we say, *colleagues* from the United States wish a few words with you. Once they arrive, the Amsterdam police will officially release you, although we may need your cooperation as a material witness if the man with the flat face is located. Actually"—De Groot looked at the ceiling—"I don't suppose even that will be necessary."

"Wait a minute," Stenner said. "Am I being held? Or what?"

De Groot gave all his attention to putting the cork back into the neck of the brandy bottle.

"I must be on my way," De Groot said. "Good day, Mr. Stenner."

"Wait a minute. What *colleagues*?"

De Groot left without replying. Stenner sat where he was for a while, then lay back down on his makeshift bed, staring at the crack in the ceiling.

He must have fallen asleep again, because when he woke up, two men were standing directly above him. Their faces were distorted by the angle, and for part of a second he thought they were hallucinations.

"Okay, buddy. Rise and shine," said one of them in a flat Midwestern accent.

Stenner sat up and rubbed his eyes. "I need some coffee."

The Midwestern voice belonged to a well-built man in his mid-forties. He had stylishly cut silver hair and coal-black eyebrows. The other man was smaller and younger, with gingery hair. The only memorable thing about him was his protuberant eyes.

"Does this look like the Hilton, you flaky fuck?" he said in a hostile growl.

The other memorable thing about him turned out to be surprising strength. He grabbed Stenner's forearms in a painfully tight grip. "Stand up."

Stenner stood up.

"Let's go someplace more comfortable," said the silver-haired man in a placating tone. "I'm sure we could *all* use a cup of coffee. I know I could."

"I'm not stepping out of this room with you until I know what it is you want," Stenner said.

"Oh, I see," said the bug-eyed man. "Well, what we *want* is the tape Alan Dawson gave you."

Stenner composed a puzzled look. "Tape? I'm not sure I understand."

The bug-eyed man tightened his painful grip on Stenner's arms and spoke in a voice hardly above a whisper. "I've spent the last twenty-four hours chasing your ass and I'm not in the mood for games."

"What he means," said the silver-haired man in a distracted, businesslike tone, "is that we had ascertained your location only fifteen minutes or so after the cops picked you up. And the way we did it was by tracking you through your reporter friend Frits Zonneveld. Why did you ask him to bring you a tape recorder yesterday morning if you didn't have a tape that you really wanted to hear?"

"Because I'm a reporter," Stenner started, "and I need tape recorders to do interviews. I didn't have time to get mine."

The silver-haired man straddled one of the chairs, sitting on it backward. He shook his head almost sadly.

"Mike, go ask De Groot if the boys who brought him in searched his hotel room."

"I want to see De Groot," Stenner said.

"Then ask De Groot to step in here for a moment, would you, Mike?"

The bug-eyed man left. The silver-haired man got up and walked around the room. He had an assured, athletic walk. He stopped near the mural of the tree and put his foot up on a chair. He rested his elbow on his thigh and rested his chin in his palm. He smiled at Stenner.

"Can I give you some advice."

It wasn't a question.

Stenner wondered if Scott had somehow got the tape from Claire.

"We've had a bad day, Mike and I, and if I were you, I'd just hand over the tape and say goodbye to us. I'm a nice enough person, but Mike will hurt you if he has an excuse."

"I don't believe this."

"I have a theory about guys like Mike. Being in intelligence, that's an acceptable way for crazy guys to be crazy. They get *paid* to be schizos. They *like* leading a weird life. They get off on it, you know; they're romantics. My theory's the same for war heroes. You get a lot of little schmucks that in the war turn out to be great soldiers. Brave as shit, you know. Show me somebody who's too brave and I'll show you someone not quite right upstairs. Same with Mike. He's too *zealous,* you know? Did you ever read about the Zealots? I was reading about them the other day. They were a Jewish sect, you know, resisted the Romans right up until the fall of Jerusalem." He stood up. "Goddamn, I'm rambling on. Anyway, the *advice.* If the tape's in your hotel room, we'll *find it,* you can count on it. But you can probably save yourself a few aches and pains, possibly some *agony,* if you just tell us where it is."

Stenner shrugged and looked at the floor.

"How'd you get into the writing business, anyway? I've always wanted to write a book, you know?" He smiled wistfully and stretched his arms up toward the ceiling. Stenner couldn't avoid noticing the gun stuck in his belt. "I'm going to retire soon. Four more years, get my pension, go into the private sector—some security firm, whatever. Maybe I'll do that part-time and write a little spy novel—who knows?" He laughed—a genial, friendly sound.

Stenner couldn't believe it. Any minute the guy was going to whip out his wallet and show him pictures of the kids. What he really reminded Stenner of was a magazine salesman, the kind of guy who spots a tennis racquet and says, "I see you play tennis? Me too." Or he spots a piano, and asks "Who's the musician in the family?" Anything for a hook, anything to get started. Stenner yawned.

"Tired, pal? Me too." Salesmen used those words too—pal, buddy, friend—hoping for some resonance. "And there's only one way both of us are going to get any rest soon." He jabbed his finger playfully toward Stenner. "You cooperate."

"Where are you guys from?"

"I'm from Chicago," the man said, and laughed. Stenner was sure that was the truth; his accent confirmed it. "Mike, he's from Georgia. My name is Ed, by the way."

"I mean who employs you?" Stenner corrected.

"Oh, I don't think we want to get into that area."

The door opened and Mike came in, trailed by a very tired-looking De Groot.

"Ed, they didn't search his room," Mike said.

"Don't they need a search warrant for that, or something?" Stenner appealed to De Groot. A few strands of De Groot's hair had escaped the trap of his hairdressing and hung down on his forehead. A gray stubble covered his chin. He looked like a derelict.

"Yes, they do, Mr. Stenner, but I'm afraid they've already been granted that document. If that's all, I'll go."

Stenner was furious. He looked up at the ceiling fixture, listing in his head all the people he was furious at: Scott, to begin with; Carley; De Groot; this neighborly Ed; this little shit Mike.

"I want you to arrest me," he said to De Groot.

"I'm sorry," De Groot said, and turned toward the door. He paused there and turned around, wagging his finger mournfully at Mike and Ed.

"I don't expect any harm to come to this man."

Stenner was grateful for the gesture, but it was just a gesture.

Ed said, "Okay, buddy, let's go."

CHAPTER TWENTY

CLAIRE WOKE UP WORRIED ABOUT STENNER. She called the policeman's number on the little white card and was put on hold. She waited, impatiently, for what seemed like a very long time. She was in audio limbo; she began to believe they'd forgotten her. She decided to hang up and call again. Just as she started to hang up, a voice came on the line.

"Sergeant Van der Heyden is not expected in for another hour or so."

"But what about John Stenner? Is he still there?"

"I have no information about a Mr. Stenner."

"But—"

"I should wait until Sergeant Van der Heyden arrives if I were you," the voice advised, and then broke the connection.

She got dressed in a hurry, a plan forming in her mind. She remembered Richard Scott's voice on the telephone, advising her to hide the tape. "It's good advice," he had said, just before hanging up. She put on her shoes. Just to be on the safe side, she would take the tape to Centraal Station and put it in a locker. The safe side? She went downstairs. Was there really a safe side?

She scribbled Stenner a note and left it at the desk. She asked where to get a tram to Centraal Station. She waited at the tram stop under a skeletal shelter. The plastic sheeting that had been there to protect people from the rain was gone, probably part of the barricade. She worried about what to do with the locker key: should she hide that somewhere too? She could put it into her coat pocket and then check her coat somewhere—a museum, maybe. But then she would have to do something with the coat check.

The tram was coming.

She was worried about Stenner, but she was also excited. She felt a little guilty about feeling excited. She had seen people on television, witnesses to some calamity, zestfully giving their accounts of the disaster. The tram stopped and she got on.

Mike drove the metallic-green Saab with the same hostile aggression he displayed in conversation. Stenner noticed his own fists clenched, his foot applying an imaginary brake. He sat in the back next to the silver-haired Ed and found these pathetic signs of vitality slightly cheering. He was surprised that his nervous system had enough energy left to squander on imaginary brakes.

Looking out the window, he saw a surprising number of windows boarded up with plywood. Obviously, the riot had been widespread—not confined to the Munt and Rembrandtsplein. All the plywood, replacing what had been glass, gave the streets a defensive, sullen look.

When they got to the desk at the de l'Europe, Ed flipped open his wallet to display some identification and spoke for about a minute in fluent Dutch. He was promptly handed the key. The desk clerk focused his attention on Stenner.

"The lady just left—you did not see her outside?"

Stenner shook his head.

"She asks me where to get a tram for Centraal Station. She left you a note."

Stenner extended his hand, but Ed took the note, which he read aloud in the elevator.

" 'Hope you're all right. I'll be back soon. Love, Claire.' I'm *sure* you're going to be all right, John. Right? Maybe you can even get that cup of coffee."

As soon as they were in the room, all the geniality evaporated from his voice. "All right, let's not waste time, where is it?"

Mike had already moved to the dresser, rummaging through the drawers. Stenner watched him for a moment—he was tossing Claire's underwear onto the bed—mesmerized by his efficiency.

Ed tapped him on the shoulder. "Hey, I said where is it?"

Stenner could see it was pointless to stand there and watch them find it, but he didn't move or say anything. It was clear to him that this was stupid, an imitation of cinematic defiance encouraged by the hundreds of cowboy movies he'd seen as a kid. The stupidity of it was emphasized seconds later when Mike picked up a pair of Claire's underpants and ripped them in half to provide a visual distraction, while Ed wrenched Stenner's right arm up behind his back in a surprisingly quick and economical motion. A soft, almost feminine sound came out of Stenner's mouth.

"We can tear up everything in the room," Ed said in an entirely reasonable voice, "and I can dislocate your other shoulder, or you can tell us where it is."

At the most, Stenner thought it would take them ten minutes to find the tape; probably less. "Okay," he heard himself say, "it's in that blue suitcase, wrapped up in a sock."

Mike moved to the blue suitcase and dumped the contents onto the floor. It was a small pile, and it didn't take long before Mike announced that the tape was not there.

Ed yanked up hard on Stenner's arm. There was a certain crystalline quality to the pain that ensued, and Stenner heard himself scream. The scream seemed distant and then stopped abruptly when something was put into his mouth. When he could focus again, he tried to create a sincere look in his eyes, to convince them he wasn't lying. He watched Mike pick up Claire's passport from the top of the dresser.

"Hey, Ed, what if the girl took it?"

Ed relinquished his grip on Stenner's arm. "Maybe," he said in a tentative voice. Stenner's arm swung down to his side with a whoosh of pain. "Let me see that passport." Ed flipped open the passport to Claire's picture. *"Not bad,"* he said in an appraising voice. Stenner tried to say something through the fabric in his mouth. "Give me the car keys, Mike," Ed said. "I'll go after the girl, just in case, and you sit tight and check out the rest of the room." Stenner wanted to try to stop him, but he took two steps forward and Mike thrust a hand toward his chest while Ed slipped out the door.

Claire was wasting time looking for a locker with a lucky number. Multiples of three were lucky. She was disappointed that locker 27 was taken. That was the luckiest number—three times three times three. Number 9 was taken too, but 81 was free, and she put the tape in there, inserted the guilder coin and turned the key. She tapped the locker door three times and put the key into her wallet.

She retraced her steps back toward the tram stop, frowning. Superstition and magical thinking were not good signs. There had been times in her life, mainly during her adolescence, when superstition had dominated her behavior. She made continual deals with fate. If I hold my breath all the way across this bridge, then my parents will never die in a car crash. If I drink this entire glass of water without taking a breath, then my father's physical will be okay. Her mind had been continually on the prowl for bad portents, bad portents that had to be counteracted by complicated rituals. Good signs she seized on with medieval fervor. Fallen eyelashes, wishbones, four-leaf clovers.

Even now, she noticed she was walking funny, automatically avoiding cracks. She stepped on a couple of cracks deliberately, to loosen the grasp of this nonsense, then began stepping on every crack—an old trick that undid the danger of stepping on one or two. She forced herself to look ahead, not at the floor.

Should she go to the Rijksmuseum now, check the locker key in her coat? It was too early—it was only seven thirty; it wouldn't be open yet. Besides, she hadn't figured out what to do with the claim check.

A silver-haired man with jet eyebrows stood near the door, staring at her. She altered her course slightly and veered to the left toward a different door, so she wouldn't have to pass too close to him, but he strode rapidly toward her and put his hand on her arm.

"Claire Brooks?"

A rush of air came out of her mouth, as if someone had punched her in the stomach. She was absolutely certain she'd never seen this man before. There was no benevolent way he could know her name. He tightened his grip on her arm, and she leaned back away from him, flailing ineffectually at his hand. Before she knew she was going to do it, she screamed.

"Shut up," said the man, panicking. "Let me talk to you."

A solid-looking man wearing a faded Ohio State sweatshirt stepped forward from the small group of passersby that had paused when she screamed.

"What is the problem?" he asked pleasantly. He had a Dutch accent. The man loosened his grip on her arm.

"No problem," he said, and lifted his hand in a placating gesture. Claire lunged away from him and pushed out the door.

The next thing she knew, she was on a tram, pushing rudely through the first crowded car. People were trying to make room for her frantic progress, deferring to the demented sounds that were coming from her. She was panting for breath; it sounded as if she were growling. She reached the back of the first car and stopped for a moment, squeezing her eyes shut, willing the tram to shut its doors and move.

When she opened her eyes again, she saw the head of the silver-haired man bobbing up the steps. She started through the second car. The tram lurched into motion.

She and the silver-haired man were having a slow-motion race through the crowd. At least he wasn't gaining on her. But when she got to the last car—and there was only one more— what would she do?

She would be trapped. The only thought that came to her mind was that she had to go to the bathroom. She stood next to the rear accordion door, bracing herself against the sway of the tram. She put her finger on the button that opened the door.

"Rokin," announced the driver's amplified voice, and her finger pressed the button. But the tram had not stopped, and it seemed to take a long time before it did. The door wheezed open in slow motion, and she stumbled down the steps.

The first thing she came to was a bank. She pulled against the brass handle futilely four or five times. Locked. The next door was a tour-bus office, and as soon as she got inside, she saw that it was one of those efficient, stripped-down places with no possible concealing space. Fluttery clusters of tourists stood around fingering tickets and brochures.

"Those who have not boarded the bus for the Keukenhof Garden Tour, please do so at this time," said a man behind the counter.

"Oh that's us, Clara, isn't it?" said a woman in a fire-engine-red coat and matching pillbox hat.

Claire bought a ticket. "It's the first bus, right outside," the clerk said in a bored voice.

Claire joined a group heading for the door, but at the door she paused and peered out, looking both ways, feeling like a comic-strip character. The silver-haired man was not in sight. The phrase "The coast is clear" drifted through her head. She felt like Nancy Drew.

The bus was crowded. She found a seat next to a gray-haired woman with a large nose. When the driver loped athletically up the stairs and pulled the door shut, she realized she'd been holding her breath. She sank back into the seat.

"You only just made it, didn't you?"

"Yes, I was lucky." Claire's voice was surprisingly normal. "I overslept."

"Well, it was well worth the effort. It's a splendid day for it. We couldn't have more perfect weather."

Claire looked out the window. "Yes, you're right. It is. I was in such a rush I didn't really notice."

"I'm Florence Highgate," the woman said, extending her hand, "from Connecticut."

Claire's hand automatically grasped the woman's. "Claire Brooks, from New York."

"My dear, your hand is so cold. Well, we're neighbors—isn't that nice? I hope you're enjoying your visit. That was certainly quite a ruckus last night."

Claire was aware that some sort of response was required.

"I..." she started. "I'm so cold," she managed.

"Why, you poor thing, you are. You're shivering." Florence Highgate bent over and then produced a surprising magenta all-weather coat. "Please take my coat. I only brought it along in case the weather should turn. Are you sure you're all right?" She spread the coat over Claire like a blanket. "Perhaps you should have a little nap. I'll wake you when we start passing the tulip fields, if you like."

"Thank you so much," Claire murmured, and closed her eyes. She wanted to put her head on Florence Highgate's capable-looking shoulder. She wanted to be Florence Highgate's daughter, fatigued by jet lag but seizing an ideal day to go on a sight-seeing tour of the Keukenhof Gardens.

She tried to think. She barely had enough energy to stay conscious. Thinking about what to do seemed a cumbersome effort, as if she'd recently suffered a stroke and rehabilitation were not yet complete.

Once they got to the Keukenhof Gardens, she would call Stenner.

Who knew how far away it was?

A geographically inclined section of her brain reminded her that Holland was not a large country.

And if Stenner was not there, then what?

She definitely lacked the energy for contingency plans. And she still had to go to the bathroom.

"Ladies and gentlemen," said an amplified voice. "Welcome to Holland Sky Tours Motorcoach Excursion to the Bulb Fields and Keukenhof Gardens. Before I begin repeating everything in four languages..." The microphone emitted a high-pitched whine.

Claire opened her eyes.

"Excuse me," the guide went on. "The electronic language is one I don't speak; I'm sorry." The people on the bus laughed, as most captive audiences do at the slightest excuse. "As I was saying, let us establish what languages we need. How many speak English?"

Nearly all the hands on the bus reached up. It was almost like going to camp.

"*Deutsch?*" No one spoke German.

"*¿Español?*" No one spoke Spanish.

"This makes it so much easier. *Français?*"

A family of four near the front of the bus timidly raised their hands.

"Very well."

Florence Highgate closed up the book she was reading, Barbara Pym's *The Sweet Dove Died,* marking her place with what looked like a Popsicle stick. She removed her reading glasses and let them dangle on her chest, suspended by a pearl chain.

Jeff had given Claire *The Sweet Dove Died* for

Valentine's Day. It was on the second shelf of the bookcase in their bedroom, toward the right side.

"Before we arrive at the bulb area, which runs more or less from Haarlem to Leiden, let me tell you a bit about the history of bulb cultivation in Holland and the incredible 'Tulipmania' of the eighteenth century, when single bulbs sold for fabulous sums..."

Apart from occasional minutiae, like the precise location of *The Sweet Dove Died*, like the guava-paste label Scotch Taped to the kitchen cabinet, Claire's life with Jeff was fading, losing clarity. It was the opposite of myth: the bold strokes were missing; only the details were convincing.

"*...les narcisses, jacinthes et tulipes étalent à perte de vue leurs tapis multicolores,*" said the guide.

She wondered why she'd tried to call Jeff. For reassurance, she supposed. But the moment she heard his voice, she'd known there was no reassurance to be had from Jeff. Florence Highgate's magenta coat was more reassuring.

"At the Keukenhof, millions of bulbs are planted, more than six million at last count..."

And now Jeff was having Second Thoughts—at least, according to her mother. That should have gratified her, but it only made her feel more dislocated.

The guide informed them that the bulb fields were coming up now, and he would just let them feast with their eyes.

"Feeling better?" Florence Highgate asked.

"Oh, yes, much better." She tried for a convincing tone.

"Are you sure?" Florence Highgate's eyebrows furled with concern.

"Look." Claire gestured toward the window. The bus had crested a small hill to reveal a field of blue flowers that seemed to stretch on forever.

"Hyacinths!" Florence Highgate enthused. "Do you smell them? Heavenly."

The sweet, spicy smell of hyacinths swept through the bus, encouraging a gushy chorus of oohs and ahhhs.

They passed fields and fields of flowers. Claire wanted to see them from the air. They passed one field of fully blooming yellow tulips, one red tulip in almost its exact center. Several people on the bus simultaneously pointed out the red tulip. "Look at that red one! Look, there's *one* red one right in the middle."

By the time the bus pulled into the parking lot at the Keukenhof, the camaraderie, the forced gaiety had begun to grate on her nerves. Even the sensible Florence Highgate was chortling at the practiced jokes of the tour guide. All along, she'd half-expected the florid bald man across the aisle to lead the group in "Ninety-nine Bottles of Beer on the Wall."

CHAPTER TWENTY-ONE

BEFORE THEY PASSED THROUGH THE GATE, the guide told them that they were free to wander on their own or accompany him on the guided tour. They were to rendezvous back at the bus at one o'clock.

Claire detached herself from the group, not without enduring a twinge of guilt at Florence Highgate's concerned look. She hitched up her shoulders in what she hoped was a self-reliant way and strode off toward a blaze of daffodils.

Did she really seem that needy? Or was Florence Highgate one of those people with extra, free-floating concern, ready to fix on any handy person or cause?

She followed the signs for something called the Juliana Stand, hoping for a rest room, hoping for a phone. The gardens were spectacular, and as she walked—by the streams, by the rock gardens, by the ponds, the swans, the dazzling flowers—she began to feel better. Maybe she'd been mistaken about the man with the silver hair.

It was crowded inside the Juliana Stand, and it took her a while to find the rest room. There were huge floral arrangements inside the building, each one flanked by a large photograph of a member of the royal family. People clustered around these mammoth bouquets and posed. Flashbulbs exploded. She passed a slide show which was packed with viewers. She couldn't figure out why people would be inside, in the dark, looking at slides of flowers when there were millions of flowers outside.

After she went to the bathroom, she looked for the telephones. There was a line. While she waited, she realized she didn't have any change. She decided to have a cup of coffee in the restaurant. She carried it out to the *Warmeterrace,* where heat lamps took the chill out of the air. Yes. Maybe she'd been mistaken about the silver-haired man. Maybe he was someone she'd met, a friend of Jeff's, a friend of her parents—just someone surprised to see a familiar face. Maybe he hadn't been chasing her on the tram. Maybe he'd just been moving toward the back.

The more she thought about it, the cozier this notion seemed. Had she met the man with the silver hair at the party her parents gave for Irene? She could almost conjure up the memory.

Stenner was probably back in the hotel by now, wondering where in the hell she was, worrying about the tape.

She took the last sip of her coffee and went to stand in the cashier's line. She had forgotten to get change— she'd probably need quite a bit to call Amsterdam from here.

The man in front of her disagreed with the cashier about the amount owed, and they ran through the items on his tray, one by one.

The path that approached the restaurant wound

through a stand of birch trees and finished in a flight of broad, shallow steps. Claire watched an old man wearing a beret make a slow, painful ascent. The ground under the birch trees was planted with daffodils, and they stirred in the breeze, nodding their heads.

The man in front of her finally reached an agreement with the cashier and counted out his money with slow precision, smoothing out each bill and extracting the exact change from a see-through plastic change purse.

She was extending a five-guilder note toward the cashier when she saw the silver-haired man come up the steps. He did not look like a friend of her parents'.

The cashier was smiling and asking her something in Dutch. She ran out of the line, still holding the five-guilder note in front of her and went inside. It was crowded and disorienting, flashbulbs pulsing like strobe lights. She ruined one family's photograph, stepping between them and their photographer just as the flashbulb burst in a ferocious blast of light. She could feel her heart thrashing in her chest. She saw the family's eager, aggressive smiles slowly dissolve and angry, puzzled expressions begin to form. Next to them, the large photograph of Beatrix smiled on steadily like a beauty queen. The five-guilder note fluttered in front of her. She held it thrust forward like a flashlight. Yellow blotches pulsed through her vision.

She scanned for an exit and found one: UITGANG.

The silver-haired man stood outside, lounging against a bench. She was transfixed. He smiled a lazy, satisfied smile. He levered himself into a standing position and began to move toward her. She reversed directions and went back inside. INGANG.

She pushed her way through the throng. A man in

a red blazer asked her something in Dutch. The room throbbed with people. Blood hummed in her ears. She stood in a throng near a gigantic bouquet of orange flowers. A photograph of Juliana loomed over them, beaming.

Don't panic, she commanded. What does he *want?*

Recollections cascaded: the plunge into the canal, the bullet shattering the back window of the car, the voices on the tape reluctantly opting for assassination. She fumbled the locker key out of her purse and held it in her fist. The man had followed her to Centraal Station, followed her here. He couldn't possibly want anything but the tape. Her hand was already sweating. A flashbulb popped, and briefly, she couldn't see. When her vision came back, everything looked bleached. She saw the man's silver head bobbing toward her and moved toward the blue-and-white UITGANG sign near the slide show.

How many exits were there? She looked behind her and glimpsed the man's head. She reached the exit and the door swooshed open with an electronic jerk. She blinked, afraid she would see the man outside, lounging, smiling; afraid that she was caught in a nightmare, that the man would be replicated at each exit.

She began to run along the path that rimmed a large circular planting of orange tulips. She looked back over her shoulder and collided with a woman pushing a baby stroller. The baby's mother looked at her angrily and said something harsh in French.

"I'm sorry. I'm sorry." Claire knelt down to straighten the umbrella, rigged to the stroller to shade the baby, which had been knocked askew in the collision. "I'm so sorry."

She looked back and spotted the man.

She leaned over and pushed the key under the bark

mulch covering the dirt of the tulip bed. A small wood-
en sign poked out of the ground. ORANGE BOVEN, the
sign read. She estimated the distance between the sign
and the edge of the bed so she would be able to find the
key again.

She was still crouched down; she doubted the man
could see her. She waited until she saw him take the left
fork where the path split to go around the circle of orange
tulips and began to run back toward the building. In her
peripheral vision, she saw the man stop and turn to follow her.

She pushed through the crowd toward a door that
showed the silhouette of a woman. DAMES.

As soon as she was inside, she realized it was a mistake, a trap. The man had seen her go in; he would just
wait until she came out. There was no window, no emergency exit.

A woman in a flowered dress stood at the sink washing her hands. The ruffle on her hem rose and fell slightly with this motion and Claire stared at it, mesmerized. A
woman in a pink pant suit was changing her baby's diaper. The baby lay on the cold tile floor, placid and unmov-
ing. A pacifier bobbed in her mouth. The mother
crouched on the floor, her pantsuit gaping at the back to
reveal a patch of skin nearly the same pink as the cloth.
She had a large brown mole on her spine.

Claire's attention shifted to her own hands, which
were holding each other. Bits of brown mulch clung to
them, and she moved hypnotically toward the sink. One
faucet had a disk of red in the center of its handle, the
other, a disk of blue. Claire was impressed at this sensible
system.

She soaped her hands with the care of a surgeon and
let the water run over them for a long time. The paper-

towel dispenser was stainless steel. Her distorted reflection confronted her.

It seemed to her that people were staring, although she saw no reason to trust her perceptions. She felt conspicuous.

She walked toward the toilet stalls and went into one, bolting it shut. Scrawled in felt-tip on the inside of the door was one huge graffito: FUK OFF.

At first Claire listened intently to sounds—the gush of water, the crinkle of paper towels, the gurgle of toilets, the voices, mostly Dutch, that she couldn't understand. Twice some British people came in, and once, some Americans.

Whenever the door was opened, there was a rush of sound from the crowds outside. She listened carefully for sounds of alarm, afraid the silver-haired man might burst in. She stared at the tiles.

Her legs started shaking, and she watched her feet in a detached and slightly embarrassed way, the way you might take notice of someone with a deformity. The tassels on her loafers bounced. She pressed her hands down on her thighs and let her head droop toward her knees. She shook her head, feeling her hair slide slowly from side to side, and began to cry. She made absolutely no noise except for small, controlled intakes of breath.

She felt hopeless, helpless, profoundly fatigued. Her feet, which had started moving on their own, stopped shaking. She could almost feel her blood crawling through her veins, just enough to maintain body heat. She took deep, even breaths, as if undergoing anesthesia.

She waited peacefully for a revelation; she waited for a plan to emerge from some resourceful inner core.

The truth was that she was trapped in a metal cubicle and the only discernible future was that a malevolent man with silver hair was waiting for her to come out.

As a child, she'd been an avid fan of survivor stories. She'd loved pioneer books, *Robinson Crusoe,* survival manuals, the Boy Scout Handbook. She'd imagined a life fraught with emergencies: only a person who knew how to live by her wits, only a person who had mastered the clove hitch would stand a real chance. Her father encouraged it. Once the two of them walked a stretch of the Appalachian Trail, living off peanut butter sandwiches and tepid metallic water from their canteens.

She sat up slowly.

The large letters on the inside of the stall door once again advised her to FUK OFF.

All at once, she felt silly. She'd been reduced to near catatonia by this man and all he'd ever done was put his hand on her arm and speak her name. It was ridiculous to suppose that he could accost her in this very public place. She could scream. She could throw a fit. Someone would help her. Some person of authority would come.

Her hands were icy cold. She left the cubicle and went to the sink, letting warm water flow over her hands. Two punk girls came in. Claire washed her face. One of the punks, a girl with pink hair wearing a black leather jacket, went into a stall, while the other, a blonde with her hair chopped off short except for one plume of hair that hung down over her face, repaired her makeup in the mirror.

"It was a crazy idea, coming here," the blonde said in

a Cockney accent. "Now that he's got himself busted, what are *we* supposed to do?"

"We can sleep in the caravan until he gets out," said the voice from the stall.

Claire absorbed their story while she dried her face. The blond girl, Minnie, didn't want to stay with her apparently arrested boyfriend, Turk. In fact, she wanted to go back to Liverpool and get her old job at the chemist's back. Turk was crazy; not just crazy crazy—he gave her the creeps. But she couldn't call her mum and dad for money—Dad was still redundant; they hadn't *got* any money.

The other girl came out of the stall. The back of her leather jacket read DEATH IN CAMBODIA. Minnie began to cry, and the other girl comforted her—a vision unsettling enough to make two Dutch matrons nearly apoplectic with contained shock.

Maybe it was when Minnie began to cry that Claire got the idea.

She remembered the people weeping from tear gas in the Café Rembrandt. She remembered the man at the bar, Keis, earnestly talking about punk. About punk as a disguise.

"What am I goin' to do, Carmen?" Minnie wailed. "What am I goin' to do?"

"Well, I guess you could come with me to Munich. Only my brother's not all that crazy about *me* coming. You know, he's got all those little kids. Look, love, you can always go to the Embassy. They'll send you home—they've got to, haven't they?'

Claire must have been staring, because Carmen turned to her, eyes glaring through heavy black rims.

"Take a bloody good look! Don'tcha know it's rude to stare?"

"I'm sorry," Claire said. "I thought maybe you could help me and I could help you."

"Get off."

It took Claire a while to convince them that she was serious, that there was a man following her, that she had to get away from him, that she'd give them money for Minnie's clothes.

Claire described the man. Carmen went out for a minute and came back in. "Yeah, well, there's a man like that out there." She looked at Claire with a suspicious, scrutinizing look. "You're not daft, are you?"

The money had convinced them, or at least persuaded them. Claire came up with about a hundred and fifty dollars in cash—some of it in guilders, some in dollars. Carmen counted it up with a cashier's efficiency.

Now Claire was wearing Minnie's clothes: pink-and-black tiger-striped tights with holes in them and a strange black tunic, ripped and pinned in various places, its ragged hem stopping well above her knees.

Minnie and Carmen were giggling as Carmen cut Claire's hair with fingernail scissors.

"You can't have the plume in front; it just won't go that way," Carmen apologized. "Minnie had hers done by a professional."

Claire stared at her feet. Blond clumps of hair on the floor. Minnie's pointed leather boots hadn't fitted, and Claire was stuck with her incongruous preppy loafers. Tassels and fringe.

"I feel like I'm playing dress-up," Minnie giggled. She modeled Claire's slacks, silk shirt and blazer.

Claire was relieved that Carmen hadn't been able to

manage the plume in front. Minnie's hairdo reminded her of some fish—the angler fish?—the one that has a growth arching forward from its back fin to dangle in front of its mouth like bait.

Carmen dusted hair from Claire's shoulders. "There. Now, can you manage your eyes?"

Her efforts were too fainthearted to meet with Carmen's approval.

A few minutes later, Carmen stood back to admire her efforts. Two black oblongs surrounded Claire's eyes. She looked like a raccoon.

"Hey, you look smashing! I swear no one would recognize you."

Claire didn't recognize herself.

"We'll walk right by the bloke. Are you ready? Min will have to stay in here a few ticks. I'll walk out with you."

"I'm not ready. Let me smoke a cigarette first."

"You're better off just doing it. I know; I've been in a tight spot myself once or twice."

"All right."

Claire never thought she would be accepting advice from somebody with pink hair. From somebody with DEATH IN CAMBODIA on her jacket.

"Good luck," Minnie said cheerfully.

Claire and Carmen walked right past the man with the silver hair. They walked down the steps and through the grove of birch trees.

"You'll have to get used to people staring. They either stare or they won't look at you at all."

They said goodbye near a duck pond. A few families were picnicking. Children tossed breadcrumbs toward the ducks and swans. Parents cast apprehensive glances at Claire and Carmen.

After Carmen left to go back to Minnie, Claire felt
conspicuous. Deformed. She missed Carmen; she didn't
like being the only one, the solitary freak.

It was twelve o'clock. In an hour she would be back
on the bus. She had to call Stenner; she had to go back
and dig up the key.

Under no circumstances would Florence Highgate
offer her magenta coat to someone who looked like a
raccoon.

CHAPTER TWENTY-TWO

ALTHOUGH HE WAS DOZING, the telephone did not startle Sisyphus. He slipped effortlessly from sleep to waking and answered the phone on its second ring.

"Carley."

He had reached that deep state of fatigue where a transcendent alertness replaced the ordinary tics and wobbles of a tired mind.

"There's been no change," Scott said in a ragged voice. "Stenner is still in the de l'Europe and one man is still with him. The other man has not returned."

"We must suppose that is good news. Have you managed to find out who is in charge of the Dawson investigation?"

"Yes. De Groot. Commissaris Hendrik de Groot. In the absence of any terrorist claims, they are treating it as a straightforward homicide."

"De Groot," Sisyphus said slowly, as if savoring the syllables. "That, Richard, is a bit of luck. It's about time we had a bit of luck."

"I see," Scott said in a dead monotone.

"No, I doubt very much that you do see." Sisyphus hung up.

He leaned back in his chair, stretching his arms overhead; a smile played on his lips, directed at the acoustic tile on the ceiling. He was in a state of elation. Before he made the phone call, he wanted to calm down.

He had been frustrated and confused all night long by Scott's phone calls. That Scott should have been outside Stenner's hotel, ready to leave for Düsseldorf with Stenner *and* the tape, only to be thwarted by a *riot,* was a frustration almost too great to tolerate. Sisyphus had begun to wonder if this was one of those operations doomed to hit every conceivable snag, doomed to fail.

Then, when Scott had reported Stenner returning to the hotel with two men, Sisyphus had thought it was all over. He had nearly gone home. When one of the men who'd gone into the hotel with Stenner came out, leaving Stenner inside with the other man, Sisyphus had berated himself for an hour for not getting more men to help Scott with the surveillance. That would have left a man free to follow the one who had left the de l'Europe. As it was, they had to stick tight there.

As the hours crept by, however, Sisyphus had been encouraged. If the other man had come out, Sisyphus would have expected to find Stenner dead in his room. But the other man had not come out, and the first man had still not returned.

So, the opposition had encountered a snag too. Stenner didn't have the tape and it was not in the hotel room.

Sisyphus sat up straight. A paper cut on his knuckle gave him a twinge. He curled the hand into a fist and the cut gaped open slightly, like a smile.

He unlocked his lower right-hand desk drawer and

extracted his personal address book. It was nearly forty years old. The indexing tabs had long since worn away; the paper was as soft and flexible as cloth.

Unlike those in his professional address and phone-number files, rigidly coded and cross-indexed, updated monthly, names in his personal book were written down according to how he thought of the people. He found Wilhelmina de Groot's number in the back, with the W's, under *Willi*. There were several crossed-out addresses and numbers, nearly a whole page, comprising a short geographic history of Willi de Groot, née Koningsberger. He looked at the dim scrawl. *Willi*. He could remember writing that; he could remember meeting Willi Koningsberger and writing her name in this book.

In fact, he had been in love with Willi—a fact he doubted she had ever guessed. He had always been adept at concealing his emotions.

Still, he had extended himself for her, in small and large ways, the largest by far being the escape via the underground he had engineered for her parents—the escape from occupied Amsterdam in the winter of 1944.

They called it Hongerwinter, the winter of 1944 – 45, when twenty thousand Dutch people died. Died of famine, died of cold. Tulip bulbs were a major component of the diet. There was no coal, no electricity, no gas, nothing but scavenged wood to burn for fuel.

Sisyphus had devoted himself to arranging the escape of these two people, squandering resources he had no right to squander, risking agents and escape routes, merely for the pleasure of looking at Willi's face when he told her they were safe in England, and later, safe in Canada.

Indeed, it was his wholly unprofessional conduct that drove the wedge between them. Once her parents were safe, he was haunted by guilt over the energy spent to save them, over the risks he had caused other people to take on their behalf...really, on his behalf.

After several ponderous nights, he came to view his love for Willi as a profound weakness, his passion a flaw in the dispassionate composure he needed to carry on his work. He had always taken his role in the world very seriously. Even then, he could see what was coming: the inevitable conflict with the Soviet Union, the expanded role of Intelligence.

He had arranged to have Willi reposted elsewhere; he saw to it that they became "just friends."

Still, he had suffered a terrible despondency when she got married. She had given him a glimpse—she had opened the door to that apparition, the Normal Life. When she married, he saw her more often for a while, safe from himself.

At times he was so profoundly lonely, so burdened by responsibility, his life made so arid by the necessity of denying himself trust in any human being, he had enshrined Willi in a little corner of his mind. Willi, yes—Willi was the one person he could have trusted. The problem had been that trusting Willi, he could not trust himself.

The last time he'd spoken to her, a few months ago, she'd been ill. He began to dial the number, hoping she was well again. It was a measure of how thoroughly he had conquered the flaw of his love for her that this hope had more to do with his need for a favor that her husband was in a unique position to grant than with his abiding affection for her.

She answered the phone herself, speaking Dutch. He could detect the quaver undermining her strong voice.

"Willi, it's Alex Carley."

"Aaaalex." The way she drew out his name, it seemed to have four or five syllables. "What a happy surprise. I am so pleased to hear your voice."

"Willi..." he began.

"Yes, Alex," she encouraged.

The thready quality of her voice alarmed him. "Willi, I..." he began again, but his voice trailed off. He looked at his hand, on the desk, clutching his address book. His hand looked ancient, cadaverous, dead white save the liver spots, patches of pigment gone unreliable with age.

"You want something, don't you, Alex? I can hear it in your voice. You always thought you were so clever at disguising your feelings, but to me, your voice has always been transparent." She cleared her throat—a strange, fluttery sound. "So, what could you possibly want from an old Dutch lady? I am intrigued."

"A favor, Willi. I am almost too embarrassed to ask, but it is extremely important, vital. It's a favor I need from Hendrik. You see—"

"Don't tell me anything, Alex," she interrupted. "Not if it's that important. I am very ill—dying, although no one says that."

"No!" The word burst from him. For a moment, his old feeling for her flared in him, and the thought of her dying filled him with despair. His cry had startled them both.

"I'm sorry. Alex, I'm sorry to be so...blatant. I have begun to abandon my manners. I just thought I should tell you because often I am given powerful drugs and I might babble."

"My God, Willi, you—"

"You know, I am really glad you called. I have been trying to get my courage up to call you." She paused. Sisyphus could hear her breathing. "When you know you are going to die, you like to sort things out. And...and I am sorry for many things in my life, Alexander, but the saddest thing, I think, was the way I...the way I...used up your love for me when you saved my parents." Her voice had lost nearly all its volume. "I am sure you thought I didn't know how much you cared…Why do I not like to say it? You loved me then, even though you never said it, and I…I loved you too. But I was not able to bear thinking about my parents starving to death. They were old; they were so helpless. I couldn't stand to think of them dying like trapped rats. But even while you were setting it up to get them out, I knew it would be the end of us, the end of you and me. I was making you to act against yourself. I was using love for power." She sighed—a sad, but satisfied sound. "I never regretted, exactly—how can you regret that your parents should live? But I want you to know that I did regret the consequence. I don't wish you to misunderstand me. Things change, of course. I love Hendrik very much. And I have been happy; I have been very happy. But there is always the sad allure to something that might have been."

He didn't say anything for a moment.

"Alex, are you still there?"

"Is there anything I can do, Willi?"

"Thank God. I would really feel a dunce saying all that to a broken connection."

"Willi?"

"Yes, Alex, you can come and see me. I should like to see you. In the meantime, Hendrik should be home in a short time, for tea. Call back in an hour or so."

This time, Willi hung up on him.

Willi set out the tea things on a tray, then went to have a rest. She dozed off and woke to hear Hendrik clattering in the kitchen. She could tell by the volume of the cabinet door banging shut that his long night had not been followed by a good day. She went into the bathroom and adjusted the scarf over her hair. It was growing back in now, an odd brown fuzz all over her skull, like a baby's first hair. She put on a dab of lipstick.

"Hendrik," she called from the living room. "I'm up."

No doubt he was sneaking a genever in the kitchen. She heard the tap go on. He was rinsing out the glass. He didn't go so far as to dry the glass and put it away, however, so his small genever glasses collected in the dish drainer. Perhaps he supposed she thought he was consuming lots of tiny glasses of milk. She smiled; Hendrik was not a devious man.

He emerged proudly through the doorway, bearing the tray. He had bought a bunch of freesias, which he'd stuffed into an undersized vase.

"Ah, very pretty. Thank you."

He poured the tea and handed her a cup. "So, how was your day, Willi?"

"Not so bad. Quite pleasant, really. I even managed lunch out with Madeleine."

"How is Madeleine?"

"Exactly the same. She spent the first ten minutes being terribly oversolicitous—I had to make fun of her. Then she spent the rest of the time showing me little squares of color. She's trying to decide what color to redo her dining room. She'd get up and stand by the window and hold up a tiny square—*really* tiny, about the size of a postage stamp—and ask me earnestly what I thought. I'd sort of squint at each one and say something noncommittal. Do you know what she decided?"

Hendrik screwed up his eyes. "Hot pink? No. Fuchsia."

Willi started to laugh. "No, no. She decided on *white.*"

"It's white *now,* isn't it?"

"Of course. Possibly you don't know how many *shades* of white exist. Madeleine does, however, and she lined all these little squares up on the table, poring over them like a gemologist. Ivory white, oyster-shell white, Dover white—at least a dozen. Then she jumped up and said she had to go to her karate lesson." Hendrik was munching a tea biscuit, looking distracted. "You look so tired. How is the case going?"

"Disgusting." He stood up and shook his head. "Do you want to hear?"

Willi nodded her head and began rearranging the freesias.

"Well, you know, first there is this pressure from above about this case, like a—like a cloud sitting on my shoulders. I must cooperate with the Americans. Nothing explained, mind you. They also *suggest*—well, they *tell* me, really—not to work too hard on it. Then today, we find the suspect— you know, the man with the pushed-in face—I told you?"

Willi nodded. Hendrik's face was flushed with anger.

"He was found in a canal, dead. Overdose of heroin appears to be the cause of death. No other needle marks, though, and two broken wrists. The disgusting thing is that two children found him. Children! Six years old and nine years old! So..." He rubbed his hands ferociously together. "So, now I have my murder nicely solved. Reisbergen has made a positive identification. Of course, now I have a *new* murder." He grimaced. "I just wish they had the decency to dispose of people where children do not find them. They tell me this is not really our affair, this is not our concern...Well, when they are leaving bodies in *my* canals..." He sat back down in his chair. "Ach!"

Willi pinched off the stem of a freesia and added it to those already in the vase.

"You probably won't be pleased to hear that Alexander Carley called a little while ago and he wants you to do something for him. He wants a favor."

Hendrik abandoned his tea and went to the kitchen

to pour himself a genever. He took a sip and sat down, holding his chin in his hand.

"What does he want?"

"I asked him not to tell me." She finished with the freesias and sat back for a moment to study the effect. She coaxed the rubble of discarded stems and leaves into a neat square pile with the edge of her hand. Hendrik said nothing, waiting.

"When I was talking to him today, I was remembering when he helped me, when he saved my parents." She looked directly at Hendrik now. "I used his affection for me to make him...to make him act against himself. I don't like to make the same mistake twice."

"Oh, Willi—"

"No, let me finish. So if what he asks is too much for you to do, then, *please,* don't do it. If it is something you don't mind so much, then I wish you would do it." She swept her hand through the air, as if she were wielding a blackboard eraser. "It would make me feel more...balanced."

Hendrik came to sit next to her on the couch and took her hand. "Yes, all right, Willi. We will see. We will see what he wants." He squeezed her hand. "There's no need to worry until we know what he wants."

CHAPTER TWENTY-THREE

CLAIRE HAD DECIDED TO LOOK for another phone and not to risk using the phone at the Juliana Stand immediately. She'd walked by the silver-haired man once; there was no reason to press her luck. She had an hour before the bus left. After she called Stenner, she would go back to get the key.

On her way to the Juliana Stand she'd noticed a large gray windmill near the entrance to the park. There might be a phone there, and she headed for it. As Carmen had predicted, reactions to her appearance alternated between rude consternation (gaping eyes, elbow-tugging and pointing) and a kind of deliberate oblivion (as if she weren't there at all). As she walked she felt highly conspicuous and totally invisible by turns.

She climbed up the stairs inside the windmill. There didn't seem to be a phone. She stopped to look out the window at the fields of flowers. To the left was a sea of yellow tulips and behind them, fading into the distance, a hazy square of purple. Directly in front of the windmill was a field of green—tulip leaves and stems. The flowers had been cut off. An irrigation ditch ran at the edge of the field, and next to it lay a heap of red tulip blossoms, tattered and already fading to translucence.

She hurried back toward the Juliana Stand, worried about time. She had to get change, she had to call Stenner, she had to find the key. She worried about getting on the tour bus. She turned off on the small path that led to the Stand. She entered the small grove of birch trees, thinking that it might be best to pretend someone had given her the bus ticket; she couldn't possibly explain her bizarre transformation. She should have saved enough cash to take a taxi; she should have been thinking ahead.

The silver-haired man fell into step beside her and locked his arm through hers. "Before you scream," he said in a low, urgent tone, "think of John Stenner. Before you scream or do anything stupid, just think of the position he might be in right now."

Her breath went out of her, and she stopped so suddenly that the man lurched forward a couple of steps, nearly losing his balance. He pulled her toward a small bench off to the side of the path. They sat down.

"You can still come out of this with nothing worse than a bad haircut. An inspired try, Claire—may I call you Claire? But I speak Dutch, you see, and there were any number of Dutch ladies coming out of that john very distressed to see what you were doing to your hair."

Claire sat on the bench looking straight ahead. Even though she did her best to control herself, she began to cry.

"Look," said the man in what she was not deranged enough to accept as a kindly tone, "let's call John, shall we? Before you get any more upset, we'll call John and see what he advises you to do. Okay?'

Claire dabbed at her eyes with her knuckles. Her knuckles came away black with makeup.

As they approached the telephone, the man turned to her and offered a smile. "My name is Ed." His teeth were perfectly white and even.

It was awkward for both of them to fit into the phone booth. He kept his arm hooked through hers as he made the call, clumsily dropping coins into the slot and dialing the number with his one free hand.

"Mike," he said, and smiled over his shoulder toward the man in the Tyrolean hat who was waiting to use the phone. "Mike, I'm at the Keukenhof...I know, I know—I'll explain all that later. It wasn't there, was it?...No, I didn't think so. Listen, I caught up with the lady we were looking for and we'll be returning, so I want you to sit tight. Is John being cooperative?...Good. I want you to put him on...What?...Well, I thought I'd let her speak to him first just to save some commotion... Right. Let me speak to you again, right after...Right." He handed her the receiver. "All yours, sweetheart."

She heard voices mumbling, and then Stenner said, "Claire?"

"It's me."

"Are you all right?"

"Sort of. Are *you* all right?"

"Sort of covers it pretty well." He spoke to someone else—"Okay, okay"—and then back to her. "Listen, do you have it? The tape?"

"Should I say?"

"Look, the tape is not worth any heroic measures— or any *more* heroic measures. I mean, either you have it, or it's on its way...I mean, it would be *best* if you did have it; then I think they'd let us go."

"I sort of have it."

"This is a very qualified conversation."

She looked over her shoulder. The man with the Tyrolean hat glared at her impatiently through the glass. "I got worried when you weren't back in the morning. So I took it to Centraal Station and put it in a locker. But then, well, this man was following me. I'll tell you later. I buried the key in a tulip bed."

Ed grabbed the phone from her. "Put Mike on...Look, Mike..." He shot a glance at his watch. "Call Bicycle and tell him about an hour and a half. She just told Stenner she put the tape in a locker at the station and then buried the goddamned key in a tulip bed...Yeah, tell me about it—fucking amateurs...Hey, sit tight now. Don't worry about the backup man now—let's see what Bicycle says...Okay, okay, catch you later."

Ed smiled apologetically at the man in the Tyrolean hat as he and Claire left the phone booth. He applied slightly more pressure to her arm.

"Okay, darlin', let's get the key."

They headed for the bed of orange tulips. Unfortunately, there was more than one small brown sign identifying the tulips as ORANGE BOVEN. There were four spaced around the circle.

Claire tried to orient herself by reconstructing the moment when she'd hidden it.

"This is about where I bumped into the baby stroller."

"Hey, you wouldn't be lying about this, would you?" Ed asked with a smile. "You wouldn't be *delaying*?"

"No."

"Good. I *hate* deception. Okay, you think this is the right spot? Go ahead, find it."

Claire was beginning to wonder if she did have the right spot. She was swirling her hands through the mulch, but the key didn't seem to be there. She looked at the sign again, looked at the edge of the bed, trying to remember the angle.

A voice bellowed out something in Dutch. She turned around to find Ed in discussion with a man dressed in forest-green coveralls. Ed was speaking Dutch, getting out his wallet, but the man strode past him and tapped Claire on the shoulder. He said something in Dutch in a very angry voice.

"I don't speak Dutch. I'm sorry." She stood up.

"Another *English*," said the man. His eyebrows met in the middle, making a solid band across his forehead. "What are you doing?"

"I—I lost something here. A key."

"Out!" said the man.

Ed said something silky in Dutch and held out his wallet for the man's inspection, but the man furiously crisscrossed his hands in front of him and shook his head vehemently, refusing to look.

"Another one of her kind cuts down an *entire* big bed of tulips this morning. I don't care if you are Prime Minister, sir. Not to disturb the bulbs, you see! *This you must never do.* Leave the park at once, or I will have you arrested."

Ed spoke furiously in Dutch and the man finally agreed to look at his identification, but whatever he saw did not convince him.

"Fine," Ed said. "Great. We'll wait for the police." He jabbed his finger at the man. "I'll have *you* arrested then."

"Not to disturb the bulbs," the man said in a slightly less convinced tone. "You must come this way."

Ed looked at his watch. "This is going to take too long," he muttered. "Do you remember the number of the locker?"

"Eighty-one."

She didn't tell him it was a lucky number.

"You're *sure*. You're one-hundred-percent sure."

"I'm sure."

"I can get the Dutchman to spring the locker," he said. He tapped the guard on the shoulder. "I want your name."

He wrote the guard's name on a slip of paper.

"We'll go."

"Good. I will take you to the gate."

As the guard stood at the gate, making sure they left, he wagged his finger at Claire. "Don't try this things here. Don't come back."

Outside the gate, they stopped to make another phone call to the de l'Europe. "You better not be lying," Ed threatened before he dialed. "If that tape isn't there—Hey, *Mike*. The tape is in locker Eighty-one at Centraal Station. Call the Dutchman and get him to spring it. No, no, we couldn't get the key...Hey, I'll explain it later."

They got into Ed's car, a small car of light metallic green. It reminded Claire of an insect. She repeated the license number in her head: 43-RL-26, 43-RL-26.

"Buckle up."

"What?" 43-RL-26.

"Your seat belt." He leaned across her to push down the lock button on the door. 46-RL-26. Or was it 23?

"I probably should have waited for the cops," Ed said in his ingratiating voice. "I'm *trusting* you."

Claire was disturbed that she couldn't remember a license number for two minutes. So much for mental stamina. So much for visual recall.

"You"—he tossed her a winning smile—"have caused me a lot of trouble." Mr. Affable.

Claire didn't say anything.

"Got to hand it to you, though. If I didn't understand Dutch and hear those ladies talking about your haircut, I never would have recognized you when you walked out of that john. *Very* enterprising. You look totally—I mean *totally*—different."

Claire lit a cigarette.

"Hey, I'd appreciate it if you didn't smoke."

Claire pretended not to hear him.

"*Hey.* I asked you not to smoke. In a little enclosed area like this, if you smoke, I smoke too—it's what they call *passive smoking.*"

"Can't we just open the windows?"

He reached over and crushed her hand into the ashtray. The cigarette burned her, and a surprised, hurt sound came out of her mouth.

He went on, in exactly the same tone of voice, as if nothing had happened. "So, you're married, right? But not to this guy Stenner?"

Claire studied the mark on her finger where the cigarette had burned her skin.

"You want to know how I know you're married? Apart from your passport, which says you're married, you've got a ring on your finger that's settled into place like it's been there for a while."

Claire looked ahead to where there was a slight curve in the road and closed her eyes. She estimated that they would reach the curve when she'd counted to fifteen. She counted to fifteen and opened her eyes. Barely halfway there. So much for the accuracy of space/time perceptions.

"So, you don't want to talk. I'm not trying to *pry*, you know—I'm just shooting the breeze. I've got no *hostility* toward you; nothing's going to happen to you." His hand left the wheel and flicked toward her, open-palmed. "I just thought we'd pass the time."

Claire said nothing. She was frightened; the man seemed to have totally forgotten that quick brutal gesture of crushing her hand into the ashtray. Her hand went to push her nonexistent hair back over her shoulder—a gesture that was second nature to her. She'd always had long hair.

So much for long hair. So much for second nature.

"What do you think your friend Stenner's going to say when he sees you? He won't even recognize you, babe. I mean you were a very good-looking woman, but"—he gave a little chuckle—"you're not so appetizing now, you know?"

Claire played red car/blue car, a game she used to play while traveling to the mountains with her parents when she was a kid. She would pick out a color and hold her breath until she saw a car corresponding to the color.

"What are you doing?" Ed asked. "Some kind of yoga?"

Claire kept playing.

"You're not going to talk, are you? You're really not going to talk. Do you know how rare that is? Most people can't do it. Well, if you're not going to talk, you're going to have to listen to me sing."

He sang "Some Enchanted Evening" with bogus emotion and a ludicrous accent. He sang "Yesterday," and "Summertime," and "Just in Time."

There was a lot of traffic. Still, a yellow car didn't show up for a long, long time. Claire gasped for breath.

So much for aerobic capacity.

Ed sang "I Get a Kick out of You." He sang all the way to Amsterdam.

❀ ❀ ❀

The concierge intercepted them in the lobby as they walked toward the elevator.

"Can I help you?" he asked, eyeing Claire suspiciously.

"We're going up to her room," Ed said.

"Ah, yes. I remember you...you're the...I remember you from this morning. But this lady does not have a room here."

"It's me," Claire said in a raspy voice. She cleared her throat. "Excuse me. Claire Brooks. Room One Fourteen."

"Oh, no! But...oh...no, no, no. Your hair, madam..." He wagged his head sadly. She could see him crossing her off. Unreliable. Undesirable.

So much for hearts of gold. So much for the value of first impressions. So much for the kindness of strangers.

"I was..." she started. "It..." The concierge continued to wag his head. Claire ran her hand through her short, bristly hair. There was no way to explain.

She felt out of place in the elegant elevator. An impeccably groomed woman in a gray suit brushed a piece of lint from her lapel and shot Claire a frightened, hostile look. The elevator ascended sedately. Claire smiled at the woman. The woman looked appalled and even more frightened.

Claire understood: she resembled a person who would smash the elevator's mirror, scrawl an obscenity on the wall in lipstick, push the emergency button for fun, attack the woman in the gray suit.

She felt a tug of attraction from the emergency button, as if she should perform the expected outrage.

She hid behind Ed as he rapped on the door.

"It's Ed."

A man with gingery hair opened the door. She saw Stenner sprawled on the bed. He looked up from his newspaper.

"Holy shit, Ed! Who's this you dragged in?" Mike said.

"This is Rocky Raccoon. Naw," he said in an aw-shucks voice. "This is Claire. She had a make-over. Did you get the Dutchman? He ought to have the tape by now."

"Claire!" Stenner said, rising from the bed. "What happened? I mean, how..." His arm was in a sling made out of a bath towel.

"It's a long story," she said. "I—"

"Will you shut up?" Ed snapped. "What are you telling me, Mike? What are you saying?"

"You heard me," He clapped his hands together. "Operation terminated."

"What the fuck?"

"Op-er-a-tion Ter-mi-na-ted."

"But this was priority," Ed accused. "This was going to get me a promotion! Talk about spinning your wheels! Fucking shit! Are you *sure*? Let me call." He started for the phone, but Mike laid a restraining hand on his arm.

"No, I'm not *sure*. I'm just making this up to get a rise out of you. Of course I'm *sure*. I called De Groot to give him the locker number, just like you said. He said thank you very much for the information and that I should call Daven...that I should call Bicycle. Bicycle said the operation was terminated, that I was to wait for you, we should come in and he'd explain. He wasn't too thrilled either."

"I worked my ass off," Ed groused. "I'm living on nerves. I haven't slept for forty-eight hours."

"There's a reason," Mike said patiently. "There's a logical reason, and the sooner we get going, the sooner we'll find out what it is." He herded Ed toward the door.

Ed seemed to recover his composure. At the door, he stopped and raised his arm in a gesture of farewell. "Sorry about the arm, man. I threw mine out once wrestling. Two weeks, I was fine. Ice," he advised in parting.

When the door closed, they fell into a wordless embrace. Claire's eyes were squeezed shut; she could feel her warm breath against his chest. They stood motionless, for a minute or two, locked together as if by magnetic force. Claire started to pull away, but Stenner squeezed her harder with his one arm. "I thought..." he mumbled. "I was worried."

When they stepped back from each other, they both spoke at once: "What happened"

"What happened to your arm?"

"I think I dislocated my shoulder. But Jesus...what happened to *you*?"

She drifted away from him, toward the bathroom.

"I need to take a bath and change my clothes. I'll tell you..." She stopped at the door and shook her head. She held her face in one hand and started laughing—a semi-hysterical giggle. "It's a long story," she managed.

"You can't. I mean, De Groot is sending a car for us. It should be here any minute."

"I'm going to wash my face. At least that. Who's De Groot? Who *are* all these people? What's going on?" She looked in the mirror. "Oh, God."

She washed her face once, but that didn't get all the stuff off her eyes. She heard the phone ring. She washed her face again. Even so, the towel came away with smudges of black.

"The car is here."

"I'm coming." She rubbed at her eyes. It seemed to be necessary to remove a layer of skin to get the makeup off. Her eyes were puffy and red.

She looked like a patient ineptly prepared for brain surgery. Or a P.O.W. Or a collaborator. Didn't angry villagers take women collaborators and chop their hair off? Didn't she remember some movie? *Ryan's Hope?* Sarah Miles?

"Let's go," Stenner said.

A bored patrolman waited at the door to drive them to the station.

"So?" Stenner said, gesturing at her clothes. "So come *on*. What happened?"

"Well," Claire began, "your friend Scott called when—I mean after they took you away, but you seemed so pissed off at him, I didn't know...and then he called back and gave me some advice—to hide the tape. And then when you didn't come back..."

Despite this incoherent beginning, she told the rest of the story in straightforward narrative fashion. When she finished, Stenner sank back into the seat.

"So you were saved by some guy—'Not to disturb the bulbs!' " He started laughing. "It's a *great* story. You're going to love this story someday. It's a *great* fucking story."

But she was crying.

"Hey, hey, I'm sorry."

"I don't know *why* I thought...Now look at me...my hair..."

"You were *heroic.*"

"But I wasn't; it wasn't for anything. I just turned myself into a freak. The only thing that helped was this...whoever...terminated their operation."

"Come on, it's not so bad. Your hair's not so bad. When you're that pretty, it doesn't really matter. I think short haircuts can be very appealing." It was a gesture; he didn't sound convincing even to himself.

"Mm-hmm. Sure."

"Okay, we're talking...I'll give you some examples."

There was a long pause.

"I guess it's a short list," she said, and rubbed at her eyes.

"Okay, we're talking Jean Seberg, hmm? Jean Seberg in *Breathless.*"

"That's one."

"Mia Farrow. Mia Farrow in *Rosemary's Baby.* Hmm? Hmmm?"

"Great. One of them gives birth to Satan or something; the other one..."

The driver pulled up to the curb. "Here we are. Ask inside for Commissaris De Groot's office."

"I'm not talking *life-styles,* Claire; I can't be responsible for that. I'm talking *hair.*"

He held open the door for her. "You're going to like this one: *Audrey Hepburn.* The *gamine* Audrey Hepburn—okay?"

Finally, she laughed.

CHAPTER TWENTY-FOUR

ANOTHER BORED PATROLMAN escorted them to De Groot's office and after ducking his head inside, said, "You may go in now."

De Groot was standing with his back to them, watering plants on the windowsill.

"Please sit down." He turned and gave them a tired smile. "Once I start watering them, I realize I can't remember the last time I did it, so if you don't mind, I'll finish."

The plants, in fact, looked luxuriantly healthy, their foliage an almost iridescent green. A fluorescent tube in the ceiling fixture flickered annoyingly, accompanied by a staccato crackle.

"They look healthy, don't they?" De Groot put his large orange watering can on top of a file cabinet. "These are the survivors; I have long since killed off all the faint-hearted specimens."

He sat down behind his desk, humming to himself.

He opened a drawer and produced a cassette, which he let drop; it landed on the desk top with a sound like a slap.

"Well, there it is. They brought it to me from the station only five minutes ago. Ach, what a life." He leaned back in his chair and stared at the ceiling. "Two men are dead—one probably good man, one probably bad man. I am doing favors for both sides of some American fight I don't understand. Two boys sailing sticks in the canal have the bad luck to run them aground on a corpse. Amsterdam is half plywood; I see you, Mr. Stenner, have your arm hurt. Twisted—isn't that a cliché in English: 'twist your arm'? Did they twist your arm?" De Groot chuckled; it was a surprisingly jolly sound.

Stenner wondered if De Groot was drunk.

"Exactly," Stenner said. "They twisted my arm."

The fluorescent tube fluttered and emitted a prolonged electric fart.

De Groot pushed his hair back from his forehead. "It is possible that this light is going to drive me insane. Let's go across the street and get a drink. I will buy you a drink—several drinks, perhaps." He lurched up from his chair. "Oh, the tape. Almost. Almost I forget the tape." He picked it up from the desk top and slipped it into the pocket of his jacket.

Once they were seated at the small battered table and had their drinks, De Groot raised his glass to them, then took a long swallow.

"I must apologize to you, Mr. Stenner, for turning you over to the 'colleagues.' I was not really given a choice; but then, it seems there always is a choice, really." His long white fingers played with one of the coasters on the table, thick cardboard coasters commemorating the advent of Beatrix' rule. "Yes, I would say there always is a choice."

"Can I ask you..." Stenner started. "I mean, what made you change your mind?"

"My wife." De Groot nodded his head. "Yes, my wife, Willi." He drained his glass and gestured to the bartender for another. "My wife, who is dying; my wife, who is dying *bravely*." He shrugged. "At first, I have no reason not to cooperate, not to do the favor. In fact, I am told...But then my wife asks me to take it back and she has a good reason, and I do it—that's all." He shrugged again. "At first they can't believe it; I threaten to have them up on murder charges—not that I would get anywhere, but it would wreck their—what do they say?—their *deniability*. It would...it would make a mess. These kinds of people, they like to stay in shadow." De Groot chuckled. "Of course, this will make a mess, too—quite soon. But still, you see, they can't get rid of me *instantly*. I would still be around long enough to make a mess. Do you know what?" He looked up at them and his face lit up. "I am glad to be going. I am *relieved*."

Claire and Stenner exchanged bewildered looks.

"This came as quite a shock to me—I thought I *liked* my work; I thought it meant so much to me. It was like when I was a boy. I couldn't see at all well." He hooked his fingers around the stems of his glasses and shook them slightly. "Of course, I didn't know that—I thought everyone was seeing the way I was seeing. Then we are taking a family trip in my uncle's car. We are all very excited, because *we* do not have a car. And my father gets lost. I am supposed to help him reading signs. And he is getting very angry at me, because I can read the signs only if we are right next to them. For the first time, they realize that I can't *see*. So, after that, I get my first pair of eyeglasses, and boom! A new world. This is like what

I felt today when I threaten them—and I knew this would cost me my job. Boom! I don't like my job." He stopped abruptly. "I am sorry to go on and on like this."

Stenner and Claire protested.

"Another drink?" They nodded, and he gestured to the bartender, describing a quick circle around their table with his finger.

De Groot thanked them for hanging onto the tape long enough to let him "do this favor for Willi. Once they have the tape, there is nothing I can do. I would just be squawking."

"Claire is to thank for that," Stenner said.

De Groot shook his head sadly. "My manners have disappeared. I did not even introduce myself. Hendrik de Groot. And you are?"

"Claire Brooks." She took the offered hand.

"And I am to thank you?"

"Well, no, really, I think John—"

"Claire is being too modest," Stenner interrupted. "Really, it's a wonderful story..." He turned toward her. "Do you mind?"

Claire shook her head. Stenner had correctly perceived that having just told him the whole story, she didn't relish running through it again.

"When I didn't come back from the police station, Claire got worried, so..."

Listening to Stenner tell the story, Claire found it amusing, exciting. He spoke with a lot of gestures—now he was pretending to cut off his hair. De Groot and Stenner started laughing, and Claire found herself chuckling along with them. But at the same time, she wanted to break into Stenner's narrative and tell them that it hadn't been like that at all. From the moment Ed said her name in Centraal Station, everything she did was done out of an awful desperation.

She remembered sitting in the rest-room stall staring at the FUK OFF graffito on the door. She remembered the drab, gray feeling of being trapped. Whatever she'd done was the frantic scrambling of a cornered rat.

"And then, when she went to dig out the key, a security guard threw them out!" Stenner adopted a stern Dutch accent. "Not to disturb the bulbs!"

Claire thought Stenner told the story better than she did.

"Of course, Ed, he's got all this I.D., but he realized it would take too long, I suppose, and involve too many people, so he just called Mike and told him to call you."

De Groot took off his glasses and rubbed at his eyes. "Saved by the bulbs, once again. In the war, in the Occupation, people lived on tulip bulbs." He seemed to find this thought sobering and stared anxiously at Claire for a moment. "I am sure this was not really so amusing for you. I get a feeling about this Ed. He seems like such a friendly person—you would call him a 'nice man.' "

"Nice guy," Stenner corrected. "Everyone would say, Oh, Ed, he's a nice guy. Even as he was pulling my arm out of its socket, I felt like a wimp for complaining. I felt like I ought to be cracking jokes—you know, 'Well, if it means so much to you...' "

"I think he is probably a psychopath," De Groot said. "I always worry for people that smile too much. I think you"—he gestured at Stenner and then at Claire—"were both lucky not to have the tape with you when you encounter this nice guy. Once his task is accomplished, he would think of you as another loose end. Why not put you in the canal with the other loose end? He has no reason to think any harm will come to him from this. On the contrary."

Claire felt strange, as if there were some pressure differential between her body and the air around her—the same feeling you get in a rapidly ascending elevator. She swallowed rapidly. I'm at loose ends, she thought. I am a loose end.

De Groot was speaking to her.

"What?"

"I was saying that in the Great War, women sacrificed their hair for the war effort. I can't think what they used it for." He turned to Stenner with a questioning look, then back to Claire. "Insulation, maybe? I don't know. Anyway, you are a patriot." He pronounced patriot with a soft a.

Claire's heart seemed to be accelerating. The room was emitting a high-pitched whine. The air itself seemed to be taking on a new texture. Geometric patterns danced in front of her eyes. She looked at Stenner. He appeared to her through a kind of herringbone weave. She could feel the air going into her lungs faster and faster. She felt that if this accelerating pressure didn't stop, she would cross some barrier of tolerance and...

"Are you all right, Claire?" Stenner touched her arm.

"Yes." She pinched the edge of the table between her thumbs and forefingers. The feeling began to subside. *Anxiety attack,* commented an interior voice with her mother's accent. *Stress-related. Hyperventilation. Perfectly natural under the circumstances.*

De Groot was standing up. He patted his jacket pocket. "I'll keep this, if you don't mind. I've already rung

Mr. Carley, and he will be arriving tomorrow to collect it. In fact, he asked if you could come to dinner tomorrow night—I nearly forgot." He patted his pockets, searching for a piece of paper, gave up, and scrawled his address in pen on the back of the coaster. Claire watched the ink sink into the porous cardboard. Fine lines spread out from each stroke of his pen like capillaries from veins. "There," De Groot said. "Can you read that?"

Stenner nodded.

"I can't." De Groot smiled. "I'm a little drunk, I think." He inclined his head slightly to the left. "This is the first time in a long while I have been a little drunk out of celebrating instead of drunk out of despair. Perhaps God will spare me a big head in the morning." He laughed a little. "I talk too much; forgive me. I will see you, then…tomorrow at six? We must be eating early because he has to catch a plane, you see." He shook hands with each of them firmly and started toward the door, but stopped abruptly after three or four steps. He turned around and struck himself a mock blow on the forehead.

"I forgot to pay for the drinks. I almost left you with the bill." He settled up with the bartender and then stopped back at their table and sat down next to Claire. He put his arm around her shoulder.

"You look so sad. Do you mourn for your hair?"

"Oh…I don't know."

"Hair is very important to women. I know this because my wife, Willi, she lost all her hair. The chemotherapy, you know? And she is sadder for her hair than for anything. She is strong as steel about everything else, but her *hair*, this is the catastrophe; for her hair she is very hard to console. I say, 'Willi, Willi, hair is not so important. Hair will grow back.' Still, she was so sad, I went out and bought her three hundred guilders' worth of beautiful scarves. Three hundred guilders! Worth every bit. I will make Alexander Carley buy *you* three hundred guilders' worth of silk scarves." He looked directly into Claire's eyes. "Still, it will grow back."

"Thank you," Claire managed. "I know it will."

"Now I *really* must go," De Groot said. "See you tomorrow." He walked, a little unsteadily, out the door.

Claire followed him with her eyes. "What a kind man," she said. She felt tears coming into her eyes and stared up at the ceiling. "Oh, God, I'm going to cry. Say something."

Stenner looked at her. Without the distracting mass of her hair, her face looked, if anything, more beautiful. He reached over and put his thumb in the indentation under her cheekbone and drew it slowly along until his thumb reached her mouth She kissed his thumb, almost absently. He ruffled the hair on the back of her head.

"Was he right? Is it the hair? Is it the hair *per se?* Do you want to go out for scarves? Right now?"

"It's not the hair *per se*." She rubbed her knuckles into her eyes. "I don't know. The concierge at the hotel— he hates me now. He *liked* me, he liked me a lot, and now..." She tried to snap her fingers, but they were too moist and slipped against each other. "Look at that. Can't even snap." She dried her fingers off on the tunic and snapped them. "Like that, he hates me, he won't even look me in the eye. I see myself in the mirror and I don't even recognize me. But it's not that. I don't know, I don't know. Maybe I'm just tired."

"I had that experience," Stenner said, "not recognizing myself. When I was fifteen I was trying to incinerate my acne with a sunlamp. Two hours later—I mean, I wasn't under the sunlamp for two hours, I would have been dead. Anyway, a couple of hours after my session with the lamp, I looked like bread dough. Two little raisins for eyes. I thought my face would explode. The flesh kept expanding. My mother came home and looked at me and started moaning. I missed two weeks of school and had to keep my face coated with Vaseline a quarter of an inch thick. I remember writing a few poems about Vanity. I mean, I was after this pinkish surfer look and I got—I don't know—Hieronymous Bosch." He leaned back in his chair and lit a cigarette. "God, I'm tired."

"I want to take a bath." Her voice was feathery, breathless. It didn't even sound like her. "Haven't there been a lot of baths? Haven't a lot of baths been necessary?"

"Do you think we could draw a parallel about the frequency of baths and stress? Like full moons and crime? I want to take a bath too." He rubbed his face. "And I need a shave. And I want to change my clothes. Do you know these are the same clothes I had on when we went into the canal?"

She swept her hands along the ragged tunic. "Hey, if you think *you* want to change clothes…"

Stenner stood up. "We'll take baths, we'll change our clothes. I mean, let's just slow it down here. Then we'll go out to dinner at some nice, quiet place."

She stood up.

He put his good arm around her and kissed her neck.

"The neck is a plus. It was hard to get at the neck before."

"You're reaching. There *are* a few good points. It'll dry in a jiffy."

"There you go."

"I won't have to curl it. I won't even have to *comb* it. What about your arm?"

"Maybe I'll go to the hospital. They'll fix me up with

a better-looking sling."

"Do you want me to go with you?"

"Oh, no—I'm not getting between you and your bath."

There was a café across the street. A red-and-white banner read CHAMPAGNE DE CASTELLANE. Stenner stopped walking and leaned against the wall.

"Let's not walk. Let's get a cab."

There were twenty or thirty identical posters plastered to the wall. The posters read: TOURISTS! YOU CAME TO AMSTERDAM FOR SENSATION. ACCEPT JESUS.

"Taxiiiiii!" yelled Stenner in mock desperation. "Taxiiiii!"

To their amazement, a taxi made a U-turn and screeched up to the curb.

Stenner gave her a goofy, pop-eyed grin. "Hey, my timing's back!" He opened the door for her. "My timing's been off, way off. This is a good sign."

Stenner directed the driver to the de l'Europe; but Claire insisted he should go to the hospital first.

"Is there a hospital near here?" she asked the driver. "What's the closest hospital?"

"Binnengasthuis."

"Okay," Claire said. "Take us there first."

When they arrived at the hospital, Stenner kissed her on the mouth—a kiss that began as a gesture, but lasted much longer. All around her mouth, Claire's skin burned and tingled from the tiny abrasions caused by Stenner's beard. He got out of the cab and kissed her once more through the open window—this time a ritual kiss.

"I'll call you when I get back to my flat." He slapped the flank of the taxi, as if it were a horse, and sent it on its way.

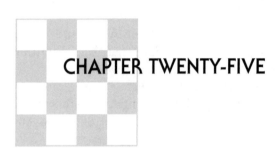

CHAPTER TWENTY-FIVE

CLAIRE WAS RELIEVED WHEN STENNER got out of the cab. She didn't feel like talking—or even listening.

The concierge approached her at the desk while she waited for her key. The expression on his face was that of a man who has just eaten a bad oyster.

"Madame will be checking out tomorrow? That is what we agreed when you came, yes? We will be needing your room."

"Of course," Claire mumbled. The key seemed heavy. She walked toward the elevator.

"Madame has a visitor?" the concierge asked, as if it were a question.

"No." She shook her head.

"Yes, Madame has a visitor in the sitting room." He pointed toward it, and she walked automatically in the direction indicated. If she'd stopped to think about it, she would have gone straight to her room and bolted the door. Stenner was at the hospital. Who else would be visiting her? Who else that she wanted to see?

There was only one person in the sitting room. Jeff. It was Jeff, sitting in one of the formal chairs with the yellow upholstery, reading Paul Theroux's *The Great Railway Bazaar.* He looked up briefly and then, when she didn't match his memory, went back to his reading. She stood there patiently, like a lamp, and waited. Something must have nagged at his mind, though, because he looked up again and then jumped out of his chair, dropping his book on the floor.

"Claire! Jesus Christ, is that you?"

"No, it's Olivia Newton-John," she heard herself say. For a second, she understood one of the reasons the punks did it: for the electric snap of shock from people.

She stood with her hands at her sides, enduring his scrutiny. She watched his face register a series of expressions; the dumb look of shock sharpened into distaste and then gave way to a patient, parental concern. He approached her gingerly and put his arms around her. They stood there patting each other, like elderly relatives at a funeral.

She walked toward the elevator without saying a word. She caught him staring at her clothes, as if the rips and tears in the tunic, as if the striped tights were emblems for faults in her psyche. His eyes were busy, summing up; he studied her industriously, like an engineer surveying storm damage.

They went into the room. She closed the door.

"They shouldn't have told you where I was. They promised."

"I'm profoundly glad that they did. My God, Claire! Look what you've done to yourself!" His hands shot out toward her so abruptly, she fell back a step. He drew his hands back and cradled his face in them. "It's my fault, but I never—"

"I'm going to take a bath."

He reacted to this pedestrian announcement as if

she'd slapped him in the face. She could read his mind: *I have driven her insane.*

"You're going to take a *bath*?"

"Look, Jeff." She spoke in a voice so low he bent toward her to hear. "Despite appearances, there is a logical explanation for this." Only when she slapped at her body with her hands did she realize how angry she was. "But before I explain *anything*, I'm going to take a bath." She turned toward the bathroom and opened the door. "Not that I owe you any explanation."

She locked the door. When she turned on the water, she realized this was a grotesque replica of the minutes after Jeff had said, "I'm leaving you." Jeff was out there, probably sitting on the bed; she was locked in the bathroom. Her face in the mirror, the ruthless haircut restored her temporal balance.

The longer she sat in the deep water, the better she felt. The water restored her vigor; she soaked up energy like a droopy plant. When she stepped out of the tub, she realized she'd forgotten to bring any other clothes in with her. She put on the terry-cloth robe.

When she walked into the room, Jeff's eyes fastened on her like magnets. There was a palpable pull of energy between her body and his eyes. Her body had an almost painful clarity, as if all her nerve endings had migrated to the surface of her skin. She could feel her body begin to tremble.

"Claire," Jeff said.

She could feel the minute resistance of the air as she turned her head.

"Let me get dressed. We can go out to dinner."

She picked out some underwear, a slate-gray skirt, her pink silk blouse. She got dressed in the bathroom. He'd seen her body a million times, but it was different now. This was the Jeff who had left her; this was the Jeff who had left her for "someone else."

When the phone rang, it was like a reprimand. She knew it was Stenner.

"Claire," Jeff yelled in a tight voice. "It's for you."

Of course it was for her. She took the receiver without looking at him.

"Hello," she said in a wispy voice. "That was—that was Jeff. He was here when I got back, waiting for me." She laughed nervously. "I called my mother the other night. She told him where I was." She felt as if the words were splitting in half. Half of them were explaining to Stenner; the other half were aimed at Jeff like darts.

"Well," Stenner said, "Wellll, I guess we're not on for dinner."

"I'll call you tomorrow."

"Okay. Take care."

"Wait! Don't hang up. How's your arm?" she asked lamely.

"Dislocated shoulder. It's all right, though. It'll be all right."

"I'll talk to you tomorrow."

Stenner hung up. She stood there with the receiver to her ear for a moment, feeling guilty. Feeling discovered. Why should she feel guilty? She put it back into its cradle, thoughtfully.

"Who was that?" Jeff asked, predictably.

"John Stenner."

"The reporter?"

It figured that Jeff would know who he was and she had not known. Jeff paid attention to by-lines, rock-and-roll composers, inventors; Jeff gave credit where credit was due.

"Yes."

"Did you sleep with him?"

"Why are you here? Why did you come?"

"Did you sleep with him?"

"I can't believe you're asking me that." She went to the top dresser drawer and took out her jewelry case. She poked around until she found the silver hoops; she slid the wires through the holes in her ears.

"Did you fuck him?" he asked softly. "I want to know."

The Munt Tower carillon began to chime. It sounded cheerful and banal.

"Yes," she said finally.

"Goddamn." He shook his head softly and looked at the floor. "Goddamn."

"You started it," she said, before she could stop herself. "Now you know what it feels like. I never would have done it, never *never*..." She broke off. "I'm sorry." She laced her fingers into her hair and drew them through. She ran out of hair before she expected to, and her hands met in thin air above her head.

"Did you enjoy it?" he asked in a whisper. He'd turned his back to her; he was standing at the balcony doors. She could see his shoulders vibrate.

Even though she'd heard what he said, she gave him the chance to let it go. She said, "What?"

"I said: *Did you enjoy it?*"

She made a show of putting on her trench coat. She buttoned all the buttons except the top one. She drew the belt through the belt loop, pulled it taut and tied the ends instead of buckling them.

"Let's go out."

She walked over to the bureau to pick up her purse and before she had any hint of it, Jeff whirled from the windows and threw her down on the bed. He crouched over her, pinning her arms under his knees.

"I said: Did you enjoy it?"

She wanted to close her eyes; she wanted to turn her head to the side, as animals do when they don't want to fight anymore. She wanted to offer her neck for the ritual killing bite. But the proprietary anger in his eyes kept hers pried open. When she spoke, only her mouth moved. A ventriloquist's dummy.

"Jeff. What are you going to ask next? How large was his penis? What positions did we do it in?" Her voice kept getting louder. "Did I come? Did we do it right here? In this bed? Did I suck—"

"*Shut up!*" He pressed his hand over her mouth, hard. She closed her eyes.

The bells from the Munt Tower stopped.

Jeff let her up. She heard a car horn blare from outside, then the screech of brakes. Another averted collision.

She stood at the side of the bed and brushed off her coat, as if she'd fallen down outside.

"I'm sorry," Jeff said. "I wasn't expecting...I came here to ask you to forgive me, to ask you to come back home." He gave a wry little smile. "Maybe it's better this way. We both have something to forgive." He nodded his head slightly, then more definitely. He seemed to be focusing on his shoelaces. "I can understand it—a Rebound Affair. I know how emotional you are. If I put myself in your shoes, I might well have done the same thing."

He was making excuses for her; she was not responsible. She couldn't think of anything to say. He nodded his head up and down a little harder, a sadder-but-wiser expression occupying his features.

She could hear her travel alarm ticking.

"You were right...what you said...I started it. Whatever happened—I'm really responsible; it's on me." He tapped himself on the chest. "I came here prepared to take a few days off—here, home, wherever you want; as long as it takes to work this thing out. The thing is, Claire, I realized—I don't want to lose you."

His eyes fastened on her with such earnest concentration, she felt she might evaporate; he might absorb her.

She shut her eyes. The look on his face was not a new look. It was a new situation, but it was the quintessential Jeff look. Intense, perfectly focused, the Capable Man Look. She opened her eyes.

She felt the lure of old patterns. She could feel herself beginning to revolve back into his orbit, the stray electron captured by the charged nucleus, the satellite by its planet, their lives meshing again like familiar gears: Jeff and Claire, Jeff and Claire, Jeff and Claire.

The Look relaxed slightly; he managed a smile. He took a step toward her. She backed up.

"Let's go out," she said in a brittle voice. "I really am hungry."

On the street, he said, "God, Claire, your hair. You had such beautiful hair. It's almost like…self-mutilation."

She strode ahead relentlessly; she was almost running. "Well, I'll tell you about it." She turned down a street. "I saw a place down here." Halfway down the block, she knew it was the wrong street and she turned around to get back to the Rokin.

"Do you know where you're going, Claire?"

Despite the fact that she was leading the way, he clasped her elbow, as if he were steering her.

"I saw a Norwegian place, or something, down one of these little streets."

They turned down the next street and she spotted it, relieved. The Restaurant Copenhagen.

"Well, it's a Danish place."

"Scandinavian, anyway."

They sat next to a large table of boisterous German businessmen just finishing their meal. For dessert, the Germans were drinking beer and aquavit. The aquavit bottle arrived encrusted in ice. They took turns telling jokes, and there were periodic volcanic explosions of laughter. Claire ordered a martini.

"Dutch courage," she mumbled.

"*What?*" Jeff leaned forward from the din of another German eruption. She shook her head that it was not important. "Maybe we should ask for another table," he suggested.

"No," she said. "They're almost done." The waiter brought their check in a small wooden shoe and placed it in front of a man in a pearl-gray suit.

"Why do you not bring separate bills, as I ask?" the man inquired sternly. Thick arabesques of smoke swirled from his cigar.

The waiter shrugged and thought about it. "Too much work."

"Too much work!" The man convulsed with laughter and then translated the joke for his friends. Ferocious blasts of laughter ensued, accompanied by knee-slapping and back-slapping.

Jeff said, "You could have picked a quieter place."

She shrugged. Jeff could not make her feel responsible for the Germans. "They're having a good time." She sipped her martini. "We're not in a hurry."

"I'm waiting for this 'logical explanation' for your barbaric haircut. Just tell me, did a *professional* accomplish this? Did you *buy* those awful clothes?"

The Germans were loudly discussing who owed how much. She was already planning to grab their own little wooden shoe with the bill in it when it came, before the waiter could set it on the table. Shoes on the table, according to Grandma Beebe, were bad luck. Everything was so precarious, it was important not to overlook any opportunity to influence chance. She searched Jeff's face for traces of Grandma Beebe, but what she saw was the Capable Man, leaning forward, impatient.

"A girl cut it with fingernail scissors." She fished the olive out of her drink and popped it into her mouth. He looked concerned, but understanding, like a parent who has just listened to his child incorrectly recite the alphabet. The Germans were making a noisy, high-spirited exit.

She leaned forward. "A girl cut it with fingernail scissors in the ladies' room at the Keukenhof Gardens because there was a man outside waiting for me and I thought if I disguised myself, I might get away from him."

The concern on his face deepened to worry, and he had such a dubious look, she wondered for a second if she were making it all up. His idea of order was disturbed. He caught his balance by deciding to humor her. A little mirthless smile curled his lips.

"I see. And did it work? Did you get away?"

"No." She shook her head. Actually, she knew she should have started at the beginning. She knew she was being unfair. "He never would have recognized me, but he speaks Dutch, and he heard other ladies coming out of the ladies' room talking about what I was doing to my hair."

She broke off when the waiter arrived to take their order. Jeff seemed grateful for the interruption.

"Well, it wasn't really me that he was after," she continued. "There was this tape, you see..."

She could see the patience leaking out of Jeff's face.

"Actually, I didn't have the tape, but he didn't know that. I had put it in a locker at the station and buried the key in a bed of tulips."

The look on his face made her laugh, and when she

began laughing, he laughed along with her, relieved. He stopped after thirty seconds, but she couldn't stop. She was out of control, shaking and wheezing—silent laughter except for little squeaking sounds that were squeezed from her throat. Tears rolled down her cheeks.

It was Jeff's facile assurance—she might as well have told him that little green men had come down in a spaceship and cut off her hair.

Eventually, her laughter succumbed to his stern, serious look. He looked at her carefully, as he had in the hotel. She could almost hear his mind tick over: original estimates had been too low. There was structural damage.

"Okay, Claire, let's be serious now. I came over here because I realized I made a mistake."

"Look, I know what I said sounded crazy, and I should have started at the beginning, but every single word I said was true…"

"Oh, come on, Claire." Annoyed. "You're hysterical. I can understand that. You're angry. I can understand that. But I want to talk about the real world here, you and me. Let me say what I came here to say." He leaned forward eagerly.

"Okay," she acquiesced.

"When you went away—I never expected you to do that, by the way. Anyway, when you went away, I worried about you. It was just like you said that day I came back to the apartment—I didn't want you to do anything *crazy*. I wanted you to be all right. I still felt responsible for you. I still cared for you very much." His voice was compelling, liturgical. She fell into its rhythm. "And then when you were actually gone—that was probably the best thing you could have done. It woke me up. I became obsessed with you—I talked about you and worried about you. Allison— that's the woman's name, the one I was involved with— got very irritated about it."

The waiter brought their appetizers and a basket of bread. Claire levered morsels of smoked trout off the bones. *Allison got irritated. Allison got irritated.* She cached the phrase in her head: a future weapon.

"I don't even know how this thing with Allison got started. It just kind of happened, you know? And then you sort of think, Why not? And it kept on going." He looked up at the ceiling. "I think it was the sex that confused me, really. It was so exciting, I confused it with being in love. But after you left, I started thinking about it. It's our puritan morals or something—clandestine sex has got to be more exciting. It stands to reason—it's new, it's forbidden. But after you left, and I was thinking about you all the time, I began to realize that it wouldn't always be like that. It wouldn't always be new; it wasn't even clandestine anymore. After a while, it would be like it was for us; it would just be part of things. And I realized that that's the way it should be, just part of things, and that I didn't love Allison at all. That my life was with you. We'd built a life together and I was throwing it away for cheap thrills."

This was such a sweet, reasonable, well-thought-out speech, Claire didn't understand why she continued to feel distracted, aloof. She had a bone in her mouth. She located it with her tongue and as discreetly as possible removed it and put it on her plate. The skeleton of the trout lay revealed like a zoological specimen. A cuckoo clock loomed above her on the wall. The suspended weights resembled pinecones; they shifted perceptibly. Ichthyology, Claire thought. Ichthyology is the branch of zoology dealing with fish.

"I have to admit," Jeff went on, leaning back slightly, "I never thought you'd have *time* to get involved with someone else. I'll have to come to terms with that." He frowned and took a drink of his beer. "But you're obvi-

ously in some kind of emotional shock. I should have
known I was taking that risk."

"You and me," she mumbled. "You and me."

"What?"

"Let's get a bottle of wine. White wine."

He looked around for the waiter, and gestured. When
he turned back to her, he smiled. "As long as we're over
here, I thought we could go to Paris or Rome, or someplace...you know, take a vacation."

She was chewing on a piece of bread. There didn't
seem to be enough saliva to moisten it. She couldn't swallow it; it stuck to the roof of her mouth.

"I had to kind of twist your mother's arm to get her
to tell me where you were. Not too hard, of course—she
was worried about you. She knows what you're like."

She thought of Stenner's arm. She gulped down the
diluted remains of her martini; it was enough to get the
bread down her throat.

"What am I like?"

"You know what I mean."

"I *don't* know what you mean. What am I like?"

"You're sort of like your father. You're unpredictable;
you're emotional."

"I'm predictably unstable," she said evenly.

His smile was revealing. It arrived across the table
with the smug density of a cultist's grin. He saw a pattern
in everything, a logical progression, steps to be taken. She
remembered the bloody bark of agony when the car hit
Poppy; the way Jeff's eyes skidded away when he said "I'm
leaving you"; the back window of the orange Volvo
exploding into cracks.

The waiter brought their entrées. Her piece of veal
resembled the continent of Africa. She gulped wine and
severed South Africa from the mass.

"Suppose I came into the bathroom one morning and told you I was leaving you for another man? What would you have done?"

Jeff had given this some thought. He would not have left, as she had. He certainly wouldn't have refused any communication with her. The very opposite: he would have insisted on discussing it at length, finding out what was lacking in their relationship that she had to go outside it to fill a need. He probably would have suggested a marriage counselor.

She cut a tiny chunk from Africa's western bulge. Senegal? Guinea? Her geography was fuzzy. *Fill a need. Allison was irritated.* Her appetite evaporated; she abandoned her utensils to the tablecloth.

"...Paris," Jeff was saying.

"What?"

"I think I'd like to go to Paris, rather than Rome."

"No."

"Okay," he said in a disappointed tone. He spun a conciliatory gesture between his stretched hands. "Whatever you want."

"I mean...I mean...no, I don't want to go someplace with you, on vacation, and I don't want to go back home with you. I—"

"But we went through all that. If I can forgive you, you can forgive me." He leaned forward. "What *do* you want?" He had a pinning-down look.

She stared at her fingernails. "I don't know."

"I don't know," he mimicked in a quavery voice. "But I *do* know. I want you back. I want us back together."

She shut her eyes. "Just because you know...but I don't, I don't know."

"You realize you're not making sense."

"It makes sense to me," she said in a sullen voice. "It

makes more sense than pretending you can erase things...like pencil marks."

"I'm not talking about *erasing* anything. Shit, you think it's that easy for me." He invented an imaginary conversational partner with a tilt of his head. "Oh, Claire—well, at the first sign of trouble she took off and went to bed with the first guy she ran into." He tilted his head back to her. "I can *forgive* that because I can understand it, but I can't *forget* it." He drummed his fingers on the table. "I'm not erasing anything. I think it's worth some *effort,* that's all. I'm willing to *work* on it."

The waiter materialized at the side of the table and began to clear the plates.

"Madam did not like the veal?" he asked in a worried voice.

"I just wasn't hungry, I guess."

"You care for some dessert?"

They demurred. On second thought, Jeff ordered a cognac.

Jeff had the assessing look on his face. He took a sip of cognac and ran his finger across his lip.

"Why do you say things like 'I guess I wasn't hungry'? There's no guess about it. Either you're hungry or you're not."

"Stop it."

"I'm sorry. But I can't understand you—you don't want to go on vacation with me, you don't want to come back home with me...What *do* you want."

"I don't know. *I don't know.*"

"What are we choosing between—me and this guy you just met? Come on, Claire. Be serious."

"I need some time to think," she said in a melodramatic voice, a soap-opera voice.

"Are you seriously suggesting that I leave you here like this—to *think?*" Jeff had a little chuckle with himself. "Be serious, Claire. Look at you—you're freaked out. I can't leave you here like this. You should see yourself. You should *listen* to yourself. All I'm getting from you is 'I don't know' and some crazy story you made up about men being after you and cutting your hair." His hands shot up into the air. "You need some help." His hands floated down slowly, like sea gulls. "You need some help," he repeated. His hands settled on the table.

"Alan Dawson," she said in a low voice.

"What?"

"Alan Dawson. You see..." Alan Dawson would explain her hair. Alan Dawson would justify the black tunic and the pink-and-black tights. Alan Dawson's death was an event in the real world, canonized by *The New York Times*.

They walked back to the hotel. Jeff was apologetic about jumping to conclusions, and then excused himself in the next second. That her bizarre appearance was the result of an emotional tailspin was a "natural inference" to draw. He was sympathetic about her "ordeal." He congratulated her on attempting to get away by "dressing up"—a "very Claire move, *pure* Claire." His tone was affectionate, but it sounded to her like an accusation. He seemed to be implying there was a more mature way to do it, a more adult alternative. He brought up Paris again; he brought up Rome. He slid a chummy, everything's-okay arm around her shoulder. She drifted toward the statue of Wilhelmina on horseback and stopped walking. She stared down at the canal.

"I meant what I said about not going anywhere with you. I know it sounds...I know..." She couldn't look at Jeff; she looked at Wilhelmina's foot. "I have to think. I need a little time."

"So." He ran his hand along the leg of the horse. "You vant to be alone." He managed a sarcastic little laugh.

She stared into the canal.

"I just don't understand. I'm trying—I'm really trying. Here I am, practically on my knees. Do you want me on my knees?" He knelt down and stretched his arms up, supplicating. "There, now I *am* on my knees."

"Don't. Get up."

"I made a mistake." He cupped his hands around his mouth and yelled. "I made a goddamned mistake." A passing couple stopped for a moment to look at them and then moved on. "I'm begging your forgiveness here. As soon as I could find out where you were, I came. Right away. What else do you want? What else do I have to do?"

"I don't know, I don't know...it's not your fault."

He got up and stared morosely at her, his hands dangling at his sides. "You don't know. Now how can I deal with that? You don't know." He cupped his hands around his mouth again and yelled. "She doesn't *know*! She just doesn't know! You see? I'm even willing to make a fool of myself—you know how hard that is for me, don't you, Claire? You know that my repressed little Midwestern heart doesn't take to making scenes. But for you? Anything. Whatever you want, if you ever figure it out."

The moon came through the clouds and lit up the canal, and then disappeared again.

"I'm not sure I can explain," she began slowly. Jeff was still too furious to listen.

"Oh, no? Can you do better than 'I don't know'? 'I don't know' doesn't give me a hell of a lot to work with."

"It was...an article of faith." It sounded ludicrous when she said it, but she went on. "You and me, you and me, Claire and Jeff, Claire and Jeff. Then I find out it's Claire and Jeff and *Allison.*" The name "Allison" came from her lips in a hiss, without her intending it.

"An article of faith? How long did it take you to violate the article of faith? An article of faith? Fucking shit, you sound like my *mother.* I can't believe this. You and me and Allison and *John Stenner.* Isn't that about the size of it? Isn't it?"

"That was dif—"

"It's not *different.*" He took a step toward her and she actually stepped back, behind the horse's head. "I mean if it was an *article of faith,* shouldn't there have been a period of...*mourning*? Or did you just decide to make a clean break of it? I'm sorry. I'm sorry I said that."

She looked up at the sky. She could see the moon flying across the sky underneath the clouds. She reminded herself that it was the clouds moving, not the moon. It took a few seconds to adjust her point of view, to see the clouds in motion, to see the moon as stationary.

"It's...it's not your fault. I'm not blaming you. It's—I don't know—I had the idea in my head, Jeff and Claire, Jeff and Claire, and now I don't have that idea there anymore."

"That's great, honey. That's real clarity."

They passed the bar on the corner across from the de l'Europe. Neon letters spelled AMSTEL BIER. Claire could hear muffled music, muffled laughter.

Across the street, under the streetlight, a man stood leaning against the bridge railing, smoking a cigarette. For some reason, Claire was convinced it was Stenner. When the man tossed his cigarette into the canal, the motion was awkward. As it might be for a man with an arm in a sling. It was too dark to be sure; he was too far away to be sure.

The piano player was having a good time finishing up "Ebb Tide." Claire hesitated at the bar.

"I don't want a drink; do you?" Jeff said. "Let's go upstairs."

She stood still. "I do. I do want a drink."

He returned from the bar with a glass of wine for her and a glass of water for himself.

"You hardly ate a thing, and you drank most of the wine..." He left the implication in the air. He swallowed a yawn and leaned forward earnestly.

"Why is everything fine now?" she said before he got a chance to start. "You said it yourself—if *I'd* had an affair, you would have found out the reason, you would have tried to find out what was lacking. That's what I mean; something was—"

"Because it was *me* that everything wasn't fine with. I was into...risk taking there for a while. You know, investing in commodities, even those poker games with Lennie—high enough stakes to make your heart jump around. I was exhilarated by risk. I think Allison was just part of that; that's all it was."

"I—"

"But that's not what I want." He placed his hands on the table, palms down. Let's-get-down-to-business hands. "That's not what I want at all. Maybe it was just a kind of last-minute fling before I make the commitment I think I'm ready to make. I want to start a family, Claire. I want us to have a baby."

The word "baby" hung in the air, suspended. Her hands lifted off the table and began to make a gesture. They didn't seem to know the required moves and jerked around in the air for a while. Her right hand reached out for the wineglass and brought it to her lips. The word "baby" came out of her mouth. It made ripples on the surface of the wine.

"We should have talked about this years ago," Jeff went on. "We're not exactly kids anymore."

She hated him for saying the word *"baby"* like that. How many times, over the last eight years, had she said "baby"? How many times had she said the word "baby" in a shy, suggesting way? But when she said it, it was ethereal, a concept; the word was shelved, tabled—Not yet, the time wasn't right. But when *he* said it, now, it had the punch of reality; the decision had been made; Jeff had spoken; the plan was set in motion.

"I want to go up to my room now."

"Fine. I think you've had enough wine. I think that's a good idea."

"You can't stay in my room. You have to get your own room."

"Great." He tossed some bills onto the table. "That's just great."

Claire could feel her temperature rising. She could feel the blood speeding up, rushing through her veins, sparking into her capillaries. She started to walk toward the elevator. She watched her feet. Her feet were reassuring. Her feet seemed to know what they were doing.

Jeff sighed. "I can understand that you need to think things over."

She nodded her head up and down, gulping air. It seemed to her that her feet were beginning to melt. She could imagine herself melting from the feet up like the witch in *The Wizard of Oz*.

"Can I come up to get my suitcase?" He was holding the elevator door open. Although it was a rhetorical question, she nodded some more, and he stepped in. Her image shimmered in the mirror. Heat distortion.

He called the desk from the room. As always, he was charming on the phone. "Hiiiii. This is Mr. Brooks. This is a bit awkward, but I wonder if it's possible you have a room free for the evening? Just for the one night, I think." He glanced at her. "Wonderful. I'll be right down."

She wanted to take off her clothes. She wanted to take a cold shower. She'd read about curious cases of people bursting into flames. *National Enquirer* stories. Charles Fort. Unexplained phenomena. Spontaneous combustion.

"I'm all set," Jeff said. "I think you're absolutely right to insist on some more time. We don't have to straighten everything out in one night."

"I'll see you in the morning," she managed, in a surprisingly normal voice.

He squeezed her hand. She thought it might melt into his palm. "You know, you feel a little warm. Are you sure you're not sick?" He put his hand on her forehead. "Are you sure you're all right?"

She nodded. She smiled. After he left, she stood there awhile staring at the door. She took off all her clothes and lay down on top of the covers. She was asleep.

CHAPTER TWENTY-SIX

CLAIRE WAS HAVING ANOTHER BABY DREAM. This time, the baby was an infant, several months younger than the chortling dream baby of the sailboat. The baby squalled and shrieked in his wicker bassinet and Claire picked him up. She rocked him in her arms. She crooned: "What's the matter? What's the matter? It's all right, baby." Even though the baby was far too young to talk, he stopped crying, looked directly at Claire and said distinctly, "I want some milk, and my diaper needs to be changed." In the dream, Claire screamed.

She woke up.

She lay in bed for a long time without moving, watching the long white curtains that hung over the French doors to the balcony. From time to time the material would shudder, twitch, puff out slightly when the wind pressed through the cracks.

She tried a Jeff-like exercise. She posed the question: What do I want?

356

What do I want?

What *do* I want?

What do *I* want?

What do I *want*?

What do I want?

Only teasing replies surfaced.

I want a nice cup of coffee.

I want a nice cup of coffee and a cigarette.

I want a nice cup of coffee and a cigarette and the *Herald Tribune*.

So she tried saying it aloud: "What do I want?" Her voice sounded tinny and shallow.

She tried it louder. "What do I want?"

A cup of coffee, replied her mind, *a cigarette...*

It was pointless; she couldn't do it. She called Room Service.

What she didn't want was to go somewhere with Jeff. She got dressed. She poked around at her hair with a huge Mason Pearson brush designed to conquer long-hair snarls. What she didn't want right now was Jeff. She abandoned the brush for her fingers.

She began to pack up her clothes, carefully, neatly. The de l'Europe was expecting her out of this room at noon. She consulted her guidebooks and began to call hotels. She found a room in the Hotel Ambassade, on the Herengracht.

Jeff helped her move to the Hotel Ambassade. It was an old canal house, and he carried her suitcases up three narrow twisty flights of stairs. He approved the small, slant-ceilinged room, the view of the canal, the side view of the rooftops, the chintz bedspread. She felt like a sister being settled in collegiate rooms.

They were polite and helpful to each other all morning. They evaded each other in confined physical spaces. They avoided accidental bodily contact.

She insisted on riding with him to the airport. They discussed her need for some time to "think things through." She heard herself agreeing that there must be a deadline. The deadline was set for two weeks. Two weeks to consider. And in the meantime—no Allison and no Stenner.

Jeff's smile proclaimed how generous these terms were; the tilt of his shoulders revealed his cheer at this newfound flexibility. The Adaptable Man.

Claire sat in a plastic chair in the Café-Buffet at Schiphol Airport while Jeff went through the cafeteria line to get some coffee and rolls. Across from her, Jeff's attaché case, a gift from her parents, perched on another plastic chair, saving his space.

He came back with croissants and coffee. He took small, efficient bites, as if consciously eating solely for nourishment. She excused herself to go to the ladies' room.

When she came back, he was fiddling with his briefcase, hastily putting away his Day-At-a-Glance. He smiled at her in a distracted way. In his head, he was rescheduling conferences. He was penciling her in in two weeks. Paris and Rome were Xed out. She would occupy the top of a page. He was penciling in a squash game with Ben. He was penciling in a discreet explanatory phone call to Allison. His Day-At-a-Glance was methodically filled with notations, day by day, week by week—a network of appointments and activities.

Eventually, his flight was called. He was penciling in the Chinese laundry, one of "her" chores: pick up *shirts*. He pretended to be listening to her, to be talking to her, but she could see that his mind was thrust forward, patrolling the future. Actually, she admired his firm grasp on the future, his recorded lock on the past.

When they walked to the gate together, he threw a comradely arm around her shoulder and smiled warmly, a man who had done the Right Thing.

When they reached the gate, he surprised her by lingering, despite repeated warnings over the PA system that it was time to board the flight. He tightened his arm around her and looked her directly in the eyes. This time, there was nothing perfunctory or detached about his smile. "I love you, Claire," he said. "I'll be waiting. When you left...I found that I need you. You understand." He shook her shoulder a little. "I'm afraid I blew it." He gave a sad laugh. "I need you...and now you don't need me."

Despite the intensity and appeal of this confession, her feelings didn't rise to meet his. It made her feel isolated, bereft, the way her heart stayed stiff against him.

She penciled in a hug.

But when she was in his embrace, in his familiar arms, she felt like staying there. It was safe, comfortable. Even though she was making him leave, she had a left-behind feeling, an abandoned feeling. She wasn't sure she could do without him, do without his grasp on her future. It would be so easy to stop him now, ask him to stay, abandon herself to his plans, his schedules, the industrious life of his Day-At-a-Glance.

For herself, she couldn't think beyond the trip back to her hotel on the blue airport bus. His flight was called again.

What she said was "You'd better go."

"I'll be waiting," he promised.

She watched him disappear through the gate. He turned around to smile at her, a man behaving admirably. He held up two fingers, gave her a bright look.

It seemed important, for some reason, to watch his plane take off, but when she found an observation point, she realized there was no way to pick out his KLM 747 from the others. She watched an Air Ghana plane trundle out toward the runway. It had a homemade look, as if it had been hand-painted by vocational-rehabilitation students.

The blue airport bus retraced her original route into Amsterdam, past the turnoff for The Hague, Utrecht, past the long buildings with lace curtains in every window, except the one with bamboo shades.

A week ago, she'd been riding along here dislocated and crazy because Jeff had left her. The best case she could imagine then was that Jeff would change his mind, want her back, beg her forgiveness. Now that that had happened, she couldn't understand why she was feeling...

She looked out the window. She saw a VW bug with what looked like a replica of the Liberty Bell bolted to the top. The side was roughly painted to read: CHRIST IS BACK. LUKE 24:13.

Chapter and verse. Chapter and verse.

She didn't want to think about her feelings. The next thing she knew she'd be reading some airport book, some touchy-feely book. Getting in Touch with Your Feelings. Touching Your Innermost Thoughts. The Revived Marriage Diet. Chapter and Verse.

Family family family, *baby.*

Twelve Days to Firmer Feelings. The Allergic Garden. Pulling Your Own Teeth.

She couldn't shake the left-behind feeling. If this doesn't work out with Claire...Jeff would be thinking. She was a contingency now.

The Contingent Marriage. Successful Investment Techniques for Vegetarians. The Weekender's Guide to Childbirth.

Jeff wanted to start a family now. If things didn't work out with her…Claire squeezed her eyes shut. Jeff's plans had a frightening power, an implicit reality. If her feelings hadn't softened toward him, it was because even at his most sincere, even at his most convincing, he failed to dissuade her from the way she felt now—like a component.

Jeff was in the air by now. Jeff was up above the power lines. Jeff was reading a book about railway journeys while his plane nosed toward the polar route.

She asked for her key.

"You have your passport now, perhaps?" the desk clerk suggested. He had wispy blond hair and dimples.

The Hotel Ambassade had wanted her passport, of course, when she'd checked in. She didn't have it because, according to Stenner, Ed had taken it when he went to follow her. And Ed hadn't remembered to give it back.

She said she would call again to see if it had been turned in. "If not, I guess I'll have to go to the Embassy. Is there an embassy here?"

"It is in The Hague, but there is a consulate here."

"Do you want my driver's license or something?"

"Your driving license?" This struck the clerk as amusing, and he chuckled to himself. "No, no, I don't think so. We will wait."

She called De Groot about her passport. He promised to call the "colleagues" and see if he could track it down. Would she be there tonight for dinner? She took down his address. Six o'clock? She would try.

She looked out the side window at the roofscape: a small forest of round chimneys among sharply angled eaves, one perfect equilateral triangle of blue sky. She stared at the triangle of sky for quite a while before she realized she was making deals with the future again. *If a cloud or a bird crosses the triangle of sky, I will not go to dinner.*

She lay down on the bed. It was ridiculous, waiting for signs to appear from the sky. Did she expect a sky-written message to appear? Advice from the universe?

The bedspread was shiny, smooth, covered with tiny rosebuds. She squeezed one eye shut and then the other, watching the rosebuds shift in her perspective. She did this in rapid succession and the rosebuds seemed to lift off the fabric and hover in space. She rolled over on her back.

Stenner would be there at dinner. Otherwise, he didn't know where she was; she could easily disappear; she could easily never see him again. So the question was: Did she want to see Stenner?

Did she *want* to see Stenner?

Yes.

She pushed off her shoes with her toes and heard them thump to the floor. As soon as she thought the word "yes," an advisory committee formed in her head to offer a dissenting opinion. It advised her to be careful; it reminded her of her promise to Jeff. *No Allison and No Stenner.* Surely she owed Stenner an explanation; certainly *No Stenner* meant no *sleeping* with Stenner. The committee suggested she steer clear of entanglements.

She wore a sky-blue knit suit and overtipped the cab-driver. She'd had her hair cut during the day; it was even shorter, but looked sleek, styled, deliberate. De Groot came to the door and kissed her on both cheeks, and then held her at arm's length to study her hair. He nodded his approval.

"You have lost that raggedy look. Yes, I like it. It looks good."

She looked past him for Stenner; Stenner met her eyes and smiled. De Groot introduced her to Alexander Carley, who insisted on levering himself into a standing position with his cane to shake her hand. He had a fragile look, as if he were made of porcelain.

"I understand you're the inadvertent heroine of our...operation. I'd like to thank you."

She was embarrassed and shook her head. "Oh, I don't think so. I'm not the heroic type."

He raised his eyebrows and fixed her with his china-blue eyes momentarily. She felt released when he glanced aside. "Of course you know Richard Scott and John Stenner."

She sat down, a little uneasily, on a Barcelona chair near Stenner. De Groot asked what she wanted to drink and she couldn't make up her mind. Eventually he suggested a glass of white wine, and she nodded with relief.

Alexander Carley was talking to Richard Scott—rather quietly, so she couldn't understand what he was saying. Stenner leaned toward her.

She felt her body change as Stenner leaned toward her. She felt it putting out frills, allurements. She felt the tightening here and there of certain muscles. She inclined her head at the optimum angle to display the curve of her jaw, the plane of her cheekbone, the tilt of her eyes—an angle learned years ago as a teenager, posing in front of mirrors. She saw her hand smooth out a rumple in her skirt; her hand stroked the fabric that covered her thigh—a suggestion disguised as a grooming gesture.

"I was afraid you'd gone back to New York," Stenner said. "You checked out of the de l'Europe."

"They...they needed my room."

He lit a cigarette. Punctuation. "What I mean is that I'm glad..." He broke off and smiled—a slow, lazy smile.

"How's your arm?"

He leaned closer to her and half-whispered. "You know, I followed you yesterday. You ate dinner at the Restaurant Copenhagen. He went back to the hotel with you. I waited for him to come out. When he didn't come out..." He shrugged. "I probably shouldn't tell you this."

She was thrilled by his confession. She smiled at him, took a sip of wine and made her own confession: "He got his own room." As soon as she'd said it, she was sorry. It seemed a breach of etiquette. Stenner squeezed her shoulder.

She was shocked by the physical effect he had on her. Her lips felt swollen; a flush spread over her face; her limbs felt heavy, languorous, each intake and exhalation of breath seemed charged with an erotic current. Close to Stenner, close enough so she could detect...She leaned back abruptly in her chair.

De Groot summoned them to dinner. He cleared away the place set for his wife, Willi. "She's not quite up to it, I'm afraid. But she will see you, of course, Alex, after we've eaten."

A bottle of Graves made its way around the table. De Groot ladled out fish soup over pieces of toasted French bread spread with garlicky mayonnaise. Alexander Carley waited until everyone had started on the soup.

"I'd like to propose a toast," he said in his reedy but compelling voice, "to everyone here. Everyone here has risked something to get this tape." He raised his left hand from beneath the table and held the cassette aloft. "Some of us have risked life and limb"—he inclined his head toward Stenner and Claire—"and our livelihoods"—he inclined his head toward De Groot. "To our success."

They sipped and waited for him to proceed, as it was clear he would. "This tape is the lever which will finally allow me to pry the last link of evidence free. It will enable me to rid our country of a traitor who has been damaging us badly for years. When I see Maurice LeClerc tonight, and he at last relinquishes the evidence he has, I will have Lawrence Prager in my grasp at last."

"Prager?" Stenner said in a loud voice. "The DOP?"

"Prager the DOP," Carley said. "Prager the Mole."

Claire tried to catch Stenner's eye, but his attention was totally fixed on Carley. What did this have to do with the tape? What did this have to do with the Shah?

"How can you be sure the phone-trap records will prove anything? He could have called from anywhere. A pay phone."

"The phone-trap records are the legendary smoking gun I have lacked for so long. I know, from other sources and other occurrences, when he called Paris, to the half-hour. I know where he was. *He was at his house.* I have a star-studded list of witnesses. The Pragers were giving a dinner party that night. The Director was there. Even moles have to obey the same social rules we all do—he could not tunnel to another phone."

"Even if the trap shows it was Prager's phone, if it was a Company party, it could have been anyone there," Stenner said. "The Director himself."

Carley shook his head. "There is the rest of the evidence, you see. Only Larry Prager knew..." He made a fussy gesture in the air. "Suffice it to say I have enough *warm* guns to arm a company, maybe even a battalion."

De Groot leaned toward Claire. "You look puzzled; if

you're not understanding all this, you are not alone. Could you help me clear off the soup?"

She got up and began removing soup bowls; she followed De Groot to the kitchen. Carley had barely touched his soup.

"Everyone is ignoring your wonderful food," she said. "It was delicious soup."

"Willi's sister Frederika gave me the recipe. Here, we just put the bowls in the sink—I'll wash up later."

"Is it bouillabaisse?"

"That was my mistake as well. I asked Frederika for her bouillabaisse recipe and she sort of rolled back on her heels and said, 'Bouillabaisse? You must mean my *soupe de poisson méditerranée.*' She barely trusted me with it after that."

"Did you listen to the tape?"

"No. So if you did, you know more than I do about this."

"It wasn't…it was—"

"Shhh." He put his finger over her mouth. "I'd rather not know."

"What's a DOP?"

"This I do know. The Director of Plans."

"For the CIA?"

"Yes, I'm afraid so. You know, I am so relieved to give that tape to Alex. He barely gets in the door before I press it into his palm." De Groot tasted a carrot and nodded his head. "Because once he has it, I know it is on its way out of here."

"And are you still happy to be leaving…your job?"

"Of course, there may be a letdown," De Groot said from the stove where he was deglazing a pan, "but yes, I am still feeling the same way. I can look after Willi, I can cook *soupe de poisson méditerranée,* I can go to sleep at night without sifting evidence in my dreams.

Would you take out this red wine? And clear off the white-wine glasses?"

No one seemed to notice her as she moved around the table, clearing the glasses and setting down the Bordeaux. She caught some phrases of their conversation.

"...he lost credibility fast."

"Philby was credibility. Burgess and MacLean were credibility."

"...trapdoor get pulled on Dawson?"

"My end, I'm afraid. We couldn't meet at Mountain. Prager's no fool...intensified surveillance. No one knew Dawson was my asset."

Claire went back to the kitchen to help De Groot. He was putting the finishing touches on the veal, scattering bits of parsley on the platter, spreading out a sliced-up lemon like a hand of cards.

"There. We are ready." She helped him carry the serving plates out to the table.

De Groot had just finished seeing that everyone was served when he excused himself to answer the telephone. The call was for Carley.

"As the cook, I don't believe we should wait for him," De Groot said. "Willi tells me he used to live on air. Claire, could you pass the salt?"

When Carley came back to the table, he looked different. It was as if his face had lost all its muscle tone; he had the slack look of a stroke victim. He gulped down his glass of wine and patted his lips with his napkin. De Groot refilled his wineglass.

"Bad news, Alex?"

"Yes," Carley said, almost inaudibly. "LeClerc is dead."

Stenner had a carrot on his fork and the fork was halfway to his mouth. "Dead?" he heard himself say. He put the bite of carrot into his mouth and chewed it. He set the fork back down with a clatter. It seemed very loud. "So, it was all for nothing?"

"No, not entirely," Carley said.

Stenner was remembering Alan Dawson falling backward, Alan Dawson's ruined face. Alan Dawson's surprised eye. He should have stayed at Dawson's side long enough to close his eye. He knew why they closed the eyes of the dead. When you looked into them there was nothing; there was your future. In the jungle, rain fell on the open eyes of the dead; birds ate them. In the jungle you could smell death before you could see it. You could hear death before you could see it...the flies. And when you got close enough to see it, you tried not to look.

"I had LeClerc under surveillance, of course," Carley said in his raspy voice. The voice grated on Stenner like chalk on a blackboard. It made his neck muscles contract involuntarily. "The men responsible were sloppy—another rush job. They were apprehended. It ought to serve." He gulped some wine. The color of the wine seemed immediately transfused into his face. "It will put me a few steps backward, but it will serve."

Stenner knew what Maurice LeClerc looked like; he had photographs in his transnational file. He imagined Maurice LeClerc dead, LeClerc with dead eyes.

"You knew it might happen," Stenner said in an accusing voice. "I'll bet you didn't warn him."

Carley was cutting up his veal into tiny pieces, all at once, as a mother would cut up meat for a small child.

"Before you get carried away with your distaste for me, Mr. Stenner, I wouldn't want you to...misplace your scorn. You think it's disgusting if I can turn death to my advantage. Keep in mind that *I* didn't kill LeClerc, or Alan Dawson, or even the man who *did* kill Alan Dawson. They all died to thwart me. They all died to protect Prager's position. *I* foresee that something might befall LeClerc and I have a contingency plan set up—that is a bit too rational, I suppose; that grates on your nerves."

"I didn't—"

"Let me finish. I don't often make speeches, but your delicacy is provocative. At any time over the past year, LeClerc could have given me the evidence, but he refused. And so, I had to *force* him. Someone once said that secrets are like guns—if you have one, it can be used against you."

"What makes you so sure the records are still there? How do you know LeClerc didn't destroy them?"

"Oh, they are still there. LeClerc was a meticulous man, a believer in history. He believed history is the custodian of the future. He would have been quite careful to preserve the facts in multiple notations. He surely had his own plans, you see. His successor is likely to be Bergier, and Bergier is a *much* more reasonable sort of man. In the meantime, the two assassins, who would have ended up dead, just like De Groot's man in the canal, will provide some interesting data, I am sure."

Stenner shook his head in an unconvinced way. De Groot refilled Carley's wineglass. "I understand what John is feeling, Alex," De Groot said. "You are like a spider in your net...excuse me...web. You are spinning, spinning, you are catching us up. You are talking about operations; you are talking about men as assets, as if you can spend their lives like you are buying a pair of shoes. We are not doubting—I am not doubting, anyway—that what you are doing is important, but..." De Groot furrowed his eyebrows. "...you are like this thing the astronomers talk about, the black hole, which can be detected only by its influence on the heavenly bodies around it. We are finding our orbits"—he gestured at himself, Claire and Stenner—"getting eccentric. It is this…no, it is your *attitude* that bothers us, this *tactical* attitude, which I suppose generals must have. The Chief of Police—he has it." De Groot spun his hand around in circles. "Do you see?"

"I've been compared to a spider before, but never a black hole."

There was a ragged cascade of laughter.

"But you and Claire here are different. It's Mr. Stenner—I can't let him get away with this knee-jerk reaction." Carley fixed Stenner with his eyes. "You suspect, or so your journalistic endeavors suggest, that our intelligence services are subverted by our enemies. And I, I *know* that they are *infested* with enemies. Not a popular word, I grant you, 'enemy'—these days, we are more likely to hear something like 'negative interface.' " He grimaced and chewed a tiny piece of veal. Stenner watched the muscles in his jaw work. "Believe me, they are enemies; they do not have our best interests at heart.

"You don't find it pleasant to have me so…calculating. I don't find it pleasant to watch us losing ground all over the world—Iran, Afghanistan, Vietnam. You were in Vietnam, weren't you Mr. Stenner?"

"Oh, yes," Stenner said. He lit a cigarette, cupping the match in his hand as if he were outside.

"Vietnam was the ultimate intelligence debacle. That was before the service was entirely ruined, but still…Essentially all the intelligence presented to the military and the various Administrations advised *against* anything but a very limited presence in Vietnam, and still, *still*, one or two people in the wrong places managed to subvert this essentially correct intelligence. One or two people did unimaginable harm. The squalor of so much death is unbelievable, so much *useless* death, so much *avoidable* death. That is what is heartless. Thinking ahead is not what is heartless. Where are you from, Mr. Stenner?"

"You mean where did I grow up?"

"Exactly."

"Stamford, Connecticut."

"I see," said Carley, nodding to himself, as if that explained everything. Stenner realized that Carley was, if not drunk, at least half-drunk. Carley teetered forward, seesawing his fork between his fingers.

"You think me cold; you think that is a flaw. Tell me, do you know what you get if you do something particularly heroic in the field of intelligence? And I don't mean the managers; I mean the soldiers, the field men. Do you know?"

Stenner shook his head.

"You get a secret medal. You get a *secret* medal. Most often, you have to die to get a secret medal, and meanwhile your name may be publicly besmirched to throw up a cloud of dust, as it were, for the enemy." He put down his knife and fork and then readjusted them to form a cross. He turned to Claire. "You look worried, my dear. Is it the fate of the West that's bothering you? Or...?"

"I had to explain to...my husband," Claire said. "I told him about...about the tape, about Alan Daw—"

Carley laughed—a strange automaton's chortle.

"Don't worry," he said. "Don't worry about *talking*. I think you'll find that no one will pay the slightest attention. Defectors, plots, conspiracies—this just produces a dull glaze on the listener in the absence of proof. Mr. Stenner can attest to that, I'm quite sure. People will merely think you—or your husband if he's foolish enough to repeat your story—they will think you've joined the lunatic fringe." He glanced at his watch. "It's precisely the *proof* that I'm after. And I must save some time here for Willi, before it is time to leave." He stood up and swayed back and forth, then steadied himself with his cane. He turned to go, but then hesitated and turned back toward them. "One more thing, though. I will tell you also, if it will make you feel better, that LeClerc's information was not the only thing at stake. It may seem fanciful to think that Circle Group would have succeeded in the attempt on the Shah. My own opinion is that Firelli would not have proposed it without some viable plan in mind. The minute I found out the tape was in safe hands, I set the wheels in motion. They won't dare now..." He seemed distracted for a moment. "As I told Alan Dawson, the Shah provides the only cohesion the Iranians have for the moment—they are united by their hatred. He must remain alive, at least for a while. The Khomeini regime—it is hard to think of Khomeini as an ally, but in this roundabout way, he is—the Khomeini regime must have a while to establish some kind of order. Then Iran will not be so vulnerable to attack." He frowned.

"Who is going to attack Iran?" Stenner asked. "Iraq?"

"Iraq, yes, Iraq. Also, just today I had reports of Soviet troop movements in Afghanistan toward the Iranian border."

He looked at his watch. "I apologize for the harangue. And I apologize to everyone, excepting Richard, for your forced participation in this...I really must go see Willi now."

"You will take her a piece of cherry tart?" De Groot asked. "And one for yourself? Also, coffee is ready."

Carley nodded. "Richard, you will tell the driver we will leave in fifteen minutes."

It was cold and humid outside; the streetlights had haloes in the mist.

"Where to?" Stenner asked Claire.

"Let's walk for a while. I think I ate too much."

A bicycle bell jingled behind them, and Stenner steered her off to the side. "What did you think? Of Carley?"

"He's one of those people who are too intense...I kept wondering if he was crazy. Is he crazy? He kind of gave me the creeps."

"He gives most people the creeps. He liked *you*. He admired you. When you were helping De Groot in the kitchen, he told us—Scott and me—that you put us to shame. He admired your *gumption*."

"My gumption. Is that what it was?"

They passed a movie theater. The features were *Histoire d'O* and *Donald Duck*.

They were walking through the red-light district. Prostitutes sat in plate-glass windows. Some of them were knitting; some were reading. They looked up occasionally to return the point-blank stares of passersby.

"You know, I still have no idea what's going on," Claire said. "It didn't seem to have anything to do with Circle Group. Or the Shah."

"You want to know?" He slid his arm around her shoulder. His arm soothed her. She nodded. "You want the ten-minute rap or the two-minute rap?"

"The two-minute rap."

They passed a window where the chair in the window, a rocking chair, was vacant. The chair was still rocking.

"Well, a long time ago..." Stenner began in a deliberately pompous tone. "No, seriously, it all started about twenty years ago when a KGB major defected. His name was Zverkov. What Zverkov said was that there were Soviet moles in most of the Western intelligence agencies. With Zverkov pointing the way, most of the services cleaned house. Big uproar. Some of the moles were flushed out, defected to Russia. We—I mean the CIA—didn't do much. Zverkov decided it might be unhealthy for him to stay in the U.S. and he was what they call "resettled" under an assumed name in France,

"Then a couple of other defectors arrived. They said Zverkov was full of shit, there were no moles in the CIA—at least, none in a position to do much damage. The CIA kind of split along this issue—those who believed Zverkov, those who believed the other two. Carley and the Director at the time, Keller, believed Zverkov. After I got into it a little, so did I. If Zverkov was right about the Brits, the Swedes and the French, why would he be wrong about us? What was in it for him? Anyway, when Watergate came along, Keller, who was the Director, was fired. A *thousand* other CIA employees were fired. Carley was maneuvered into a position where he had to retire. The Carley/Keller faction was no longer in control of the Agency—the other side was. Some people think that Watergate was actually an operation, a kind of coup within the CIA. And those people think the moles took over.

"Anyway, to get to the point. The day after Carley left, Zverkov was murdered in France. All this time, Zverkov had been living under protective surveillance—a job shared by the CIA and SDECE, French Intelligence. The French got a phone call the day Carley retired. They were told Zverkov was having a meet with a KGB major the next day, that this major was considering turning..."

"Turning?"

"Defecting. Anyway, the French were told by the CIA to lift surveillance for twenty-four hours. They didn't want the defector spooked—the CIA would handle it solo. The French did as they were told, and Zverkov was murdered."

"So that was the phone call Carley kept talking about."

"That was it. This happened five or six years ago and he's been trying to track that phone call ever since. Carley had been responsible, you see, all along for monitoring Zverkov's protection. The CIA denied making the phone call, they said the French had just fucked up. Then there was a kind of half-assed probe, an investigation, because all the codes were correct, but it didn't go anywhere. The CIA just let it be known that after twelve years, the French had let their attention wander, they'd assumed nothing would ever happen to Zverkov. *Carley* was even accused of burning Zverkov, which was nonsense, because Zverkov was fine, you know, for twelve years and then the day Carley leaves, or the day after, zap—he's murdered. It looked a lot like an object lesson. And LeClerc had these phone records, but he wouldn't give them to Carley because Carley wasn't with the Agency anymore. *Catch-22.* He gave the records to the Agency, for their investigation."

Claire shivered. "You're saying LeClerc gave them to the people who might have done it. And do you mean Carley is doing this now, on his own?"

"Well, there are two lines of thought about that. Maybe his retirement was a cover and he's still really part of the Agency, and conducting a secret investigation. I mean, there have been some other things, other guys who have disappeared. I don't think Prager is the only guy he went after." Stenner thought of the CIA officer who supposedly died of exposure in Rock Creek Park; he thought of the skilled yachtsman who disappeared while sailing on Chesapeake Bay. There were incongruous details in both cases. "And then, maybe he *is* doing it on his own."

They were in the heart of the red-light district now. In a single block, there were four or five porn theaters, ten sex shops, a number of arcades with X-rated peep shows.

"A couple of Carley's people have met bizarre ends,

too. There was a guy...actually, I don't think you want to know about this. I think the two minutes are up. I think the ten minutes are up."

"I'm glad it's over," Claire said. "I mean from our point of view—it's over."

"I'm wondering what will happen," Stenner said. "If Carley nails it down on Prager—Jesus *Christ,* you can't imagine what that will do. We'll have such a shitstorm, Watergate will seem like a Punch and Judy show."

They passed an incongruous group of middle-aged tourists being herded into one of the theaters by a blond guide in white pants. A hawker stood outside the theater shouting, "Real fucking live show!" Claire noticed the Mastercard and Visa decals on the box-office window. A woman in a red pants suit detached herself from the line, but was pursued by another woman in tweed.

"I don't think I can do it. I don't think I can go in," said the first woman.

"Come on, Donna. It's an *experience.*"

"Real fucking live show!" shouted the hawker.

"It's a big business here," Claire said. "You can put these shows on your Visa card. Even tour groups..."

"It's a big business everywhere," Stenner said. "In Washington, the porn district is six blocks from the White House."

They walked for a while without speaking. Claire was intent on motion. She was trying to remember the Seven Deadly Sins. Avarice, Pride, Greed. She corrected herself. Avarice and Greed were the same thing, the same sin. Avarice, Pride, Sloth. What else? Sleepy, Dopey, Doc...Envy. They came around the corner and passed the de l'Europe. She looked up at her old room. The light was on.

"Is Lust one of the Seven Deadly Sins?"

They passed the statue of Wilhelmina on horseback.

She rode on, in the mist-diffused glow of the streetlight. Light glinted off the bronze folds of her long skirt.

"Let's see," Stenner said. "Avarice, Sloth, Envy, Greed—"

"No," Claire interrupted with a laugh. "I just made the same mistake. Avarice and Greed are the same sin."

"Right. Lust, huh? Yeah, I think Lust must have been in there. We're talking *Pilgrim's Progress.* We're talking *Puritans.*"

"It must go back further than that. Isn't that from the Bible?"

"Possibly. My religious education was extremely shoddy."

"Mine too. All I can remember is how to sing 'Jesus Loves Me.' Let's see: Avarice, Pride, Sloth, Envy, Gluttony, Lust…"

"Very good. That's six." He squeezed her shoulder, but she stiffened and pulled away. "Wait a minute," Stenner said. "You're *worried* about lust."

It started to rain—a light, soft rain. "Well, you know, the red-light district. And—" She was going to tell him about Jeff, about her promise to Jeff.

"It's the man with the pitchfork," Stenner interrupted. "It's him again." Rain clung to the surface of Stenner's hair and sparkled in the light.

"It could be. It just could be him again."

"He's a persistent son-of-a-bitch. His high school graduating class voted him 'Most Industrious.' Not 'Most Likely to Succeed,' because there was a certain uncompromising quality. The cutline read: 'Beautiful dark hair [He had hair then], Chess Club, Future Farmers of America, middle name a dark secret."

"What was his middle name?"

"Agamemnon. His mom was into the classics."

They arrived at Dam Square. Unexpectedly, it was crowded with people. Crowds were queued up in front of the National Palace and the Nieuwe Kerk. Wreaths of flowers lay heaped around the War Memorial. They joined the queue waiting to go into the National Palace.

The interior of the palace was beautiful in a chaste way: handsome old chandeliers, and marble maps of the world and the heavens set into the floor.

The palace was open because there was an exhibition called "The Hidden Camera," a display of photographs and other reminders of Amsterdam during the years of Nazi occupation. There were photographs of the people Amsterdam hid during the Occupation: people living in attics, in cellars, in hidden alcoves. *Onderduikers,* they were called. It means "underwater." Underwater, in Amsterdam, instead of underground. People emerging from trapdoors next to toilets. People rooting through derelict buildings for wood. Groups of haggard people with six-pointed stars stitched to their clothing. The famous haunted face of Anne Frank. There were pictures of people boarding trains, trains with no windows. There was a glass case with an old coat inside, an old brown coat. Stitched to the coat was a six-pointed star. Stitched to the coat was the word JOOD.

Neither one of them seemed to know what to do when they emerged from the National Palace. They walked for a while in the soft rain. In one of the little streets off the Dam, Stenner stopped by a lamppost to light a cigarette.

"Do you want—" he began.

She put her index finger up against his mouth and pressed it against his lips very gently. "I promised Jeff I wouldn't see you," she said, speaking very rapidly. "Two weeks—that was the deal. But I don't want to be alone. I want to walk and walk until I'm very tired." Before she took her finger away, he touched it with his tongue. She pretended not to notice.

"Do you want to talk about it? Jeff?"

She shook her head.

They walked over a small footbridge. "I just wanted him to go away," she said in a small voice. "I felt...anesthetized. I didn't feel anything for him; I just didn't want him there. And that seemed...sad; that seemed wrong, after eight years..." Her voice trailed away.

They walked until the rain started coming down, and then came down harder. They took shelter in a bar called the Café de Trappist and ordered cognac. The bar had an excellent stereo system; it was blasting out Beatles tunes. The Beatles were singing "Let It Be." It was one of Jeff's favorite songs.

Stenner leaned over close to her, so she could hear him.

"I'm still trying to think of the seventh deadly sin. I know I'm going to wake up in the middle of the night and think of it." He smiled at her. He was trying to cheer her up.

"Wait a minute, I'll think of it." She volleyed him a smile. "I will." Claire closed her eyes. She could feel Stenner's breath on her cheek.

"Gluttony!" Stenner said triumphantly.

"Nooooo..." She wagged her head. "We got gluttony. I know, I know..." She squeezed her eyes shut. *"Anger."*

"Anger? Are you sure? Anger is a deadly sin? Anger seems more like a virtue lately—you know, people are into

expressing their anger. Someone actually said that to me not long ago: 'I'm angry with you, John.' I said, 'Quack, quack.'"

She could feel Stenner's knee against her leg. The Beatles were singing "We Can Work It Out."

"Hey, you can trust me on this. My father did a series—the Seven Deadly Sins. The *abstract* Seven Deadly Sins. Anger was a bunch of concentric circles, red in the middle. It looked kind of like a bull's-eye, except the juxtaposition of colors—they seemed to pulsate. It gave me a headache to look at it."

She took a sip of cognac. "My father is an artist," she explained.

"Anyone I know?'

"Byron Pemble."

"No kidding. Byron Pemble. I'm impressed." He lifted his cognac glass toward her. "What I mean by that is that I've heard of him."

"Let's go," Claire said nervously. "Let's get out of here." She did not want to talk about her father. She did not want to listen to music that reminded her of Jeff. She was not interested in small talk.

Outside, it was beautiful: the mist-diffused light, the soft indolent air against her skin, the shine of the wet streets, the way the headlights pooled on the wet pavement. The car tires hissing through the water sounded like sighs.

They walked for a long time. They talked as well, but Claire wasn't paying attention to that. She couldn't stop touching Stenner, leaning against him, putting her hand on his arm.

Eventually, she told him she was tired enough, she'd better go back to her hotel. She told him she was at the Hotel Ambassade. He remarked that it was quite near his place. His eyes left it all up to her. It seemed to require a lot of effort to walk now, like swimming against a current. They arrived at the door.

He touched her head, very lightly. Still she had the feeling her hair was rising from her scalp, as she'd felt it do once right before a lightning storm. She felt her hair was moving to touch his hand. He kissed her lips. Just that little kiss made her feel woozy in the pit of her stomach. Somehow, after promising she'd meet him for breakfast, she hurled herself through the door and made it up the stairs and into her room.

There was no solace in the room, not even the thin satisfaction she'd expected. The slanted ceiling seemed to pitch down at her. She paced; she kept bumping into things—the walls, the bedposts, the corners of tables. She tried lying down on the bed. Even the bedspread was stiff, unyielding. She couldn't lie still; she thrashed and tossed. The bedspread was bruising her. Finally she threw her clothes back on and flew out into the night air.

Even as she ran along the streets, even as the night air moved over her, she thought: I shouldn't be doing this, I shouldn't be doing this, I'm obsessed, I'm losing my mind.

When she got to his door, she was breathless. She watched her hand rap on the wood. "It's me," she said. "It's Claire."

He leaned her up against the wall just inside the door. "Oh, baby," he said in a strangled voice. She felt as bright as aluminum, as bright as mercury. She felt her skirt slide down her legs. She felt her panty hose being peeled off; a layer of her skin felt as if it were being peeled off too. Her legs burned. Her underpants slid off like water. She stepped out, one foot and then the other. His mouth cruised up her leg, leaving behind a ribbon of fever. He pinned her to the wall; she dissolved...

CHAPTER TWENTY-SEVEN

CLAIRE WOKE UP. SHE HEARD THE TEAKETTLE shrill from the kitchen, birds chirping, the insistent ringing of church bells.

"I'm up," she said, indistinctly.

"You're up?" Stenner called. "Stay there. I'll bring you some coffee."

"Sort of. I'm sort of up."

Sunlight ricocheted off the windowsill, off the white bookcase, off the metal parts of the stereo. It stabbed at her eyes. She sank back down in the bed and closed them again.

She had not intended this. She had intended to sleep in her prim room at the Ambassade, a Heidi kind of room; she had intended, she had intended...

"I see what you mean, sort of up."

"I feel stunned," she heard herself joke, "like the little bird..."

"Come on. Get up. Get dressed. It's Liberation Day. It's

the thirty-fifth anniversary of Liberation Day and there's a big parade right down the street. Parades are a wonderful way to start the day—it's the marching bands, I think."

She moaned. She scanned for her clothes. They were neatly folded and draped over a chair. At least she'd done something orderly, something...right. Or had Stenner folded her clothes? She couldn't remember.

In the bathroom, she made resolutions. She couldn't stay here in Amsterdam. With Stenner. She had no willpower. She would go to a travel agency; she would pick someplace to go. She would not drink too much. She would eat three square meals a day. She would write postcards. She would keep her promise: two weeks. She took a long time washing her face.

"Come on!" Stenner yelled. "It's time to go."

People were lined up along Raadhuistraat, cheering. World War II vehicles—armored personnel carriers, jeeps—rumbled along the street. Men stood on them, waving, men who had arrived in Amsterdam on May 5, 1945. Stenner told her they were following the historical route into the center of the city.

The people lining the parade route threw bouquets of tulips, bunches of daffodils onto the vehicles, and the old soldiers picked them up and waved at the crowd. The men on the vehicles were in their fifties and sixties—mostly Canadians, Stenner said: the Canadians had been the major liberating force. The men looked so happy, so proud. Many of them were dressed in kilts. "Royal Highlanders," Claire heard someone say. An occasional American vehicle passed, greeted by more subdued cheering. It made her sad.

The soldiers began to toss things into the road. Claire caught a package of cigarettes, a replica pack of Sweet Caporals. Stenner caught a chocolate bar.

Most of the people in the crowd were middle-aged, and as they heaved their bouquets toward the liberators, their eyes filled with tears. A woman in purple elbowed her way past Claire to the front of the crowd. A man in a kilt bent down to receive her bunch of flowers.

When the last vehicle passed, the crowd fell in behind it and followed to Dam Square.

The viewing stands were full of people again, but the feeling was entirely different from the mood on the day of Beatrix' investiture. There was a friendly, high-spirited, joyous feel to the crowd. The police were far less numerous and very relaxed. There were some speeches; there were some musical numbers.

Finally, a fanfare: a Canadian general was introduced by a Dutch dignitary. Claire strained to catch their names. The Canadian general was given a dove to hold in his hand; the hope was expressed that he would see fit to set it free, just as he had set Amsterdam free thirty-five years before. Claire stepped backward to make way for a woman pushing a stroller. There was a truck parked behind her; she thought it was strange that a truck should be just there. She noticed its odd, slatted sides.

General Higgins gave a short speech. He said that we must never forget what tyranny is; he said that he was very happy to be back in Amsterdam; he said that the liberation of Amsterdam was, of course, due to the efforts of *all* the Allied troops. Then he released the dove. Claire saw it spring from his hand.

At the moment he let it go, the slatted sides of the truck behind Claire were opened, and a cloud of doves whooshed free from their captivity and flew straight up into the air above Dam Square. They wheeled about, almost in formation, thousands of them. A huge cheer erupted from the crowd.

Claire thought she would never forget the sound the doves made as they rushed past her head—the beating wings, the rising cloud of birds. The band struck up "O Canada."

Stenner and Claire drifted off. They passed the War Memorial. Flowers and wreaths lay all around it on the pavement. People were being very careful not to step on them. They heard the band start on "The Star-Spangled Banner."

Claire slept alone that night in the Hotel Ambassade. There was no comfort in it, only a kind of grim satisfaction. She called Stenner in the middle of the night.

"It's me. I couldn't sleep."

"I couldn't sleep either."

"I have to go away."

"I knew you would. I knew when you didn't come home with me tonight, you'd go away."

"I promised. Two weeks. After eight years, I guess I owe him two weeks."

"Two weeks of contemplation—is that it?"

"I'm sorry."

"No. I think you should—I mean, otherwise you'll feel guilty. I can take two weeks."

"Still, it seems like a gesture...I don't know..."

"It's all right, Claire. It will be all right."

"It just seems like a gesture I have to make."

"Claire..." There was a long pause. "Sleep tight."

"I'm not good at being alone; I've never been any

good at being alone."

He laughed. "I was getting real good at it; I was getting to be a real champ."

"I'll see you tomorrow?"

"I'll see you tomorrow."

The night seemed empty, devoid of comfort or rest; it seemed to take forever. She was still awake when the sky began to brighten.

In the morning, she did errands and chores. She washed out her underwear and panty hose in the bathroom sink. She bought postcards and scrawled things on them. She bought stamps. She went to a travel agency. It took a long time to decide where to go. She decided on Crete. It was remote, but not too remote. It was a little tricky to get to, but not too tricky. She wanted airports, baggage transfers, currency exchanges. She remembered a dinner guest once, a woman named Samantha, talking about Crete. At the time, Samantha's stories had made her want to go there. She arranged the ticket: Amsterdam to Athens to Heraklion.

Round trip.

After she put the ticket into her purse, she wondered if she'd made a mistake. Was it Cyprus? Was it Cyprus Samantha had described so glowingly? She zipped her purse shut. It didn't matter.

She met Stenner at the Rijksmuseum for lunch; then they had their long-postponed look at the Vermeers. They took in the Rembrandts as well. *The Night Watch* had a room to itself; it occupied an entire wall and was protected by a sheet of glass. Most of the people looking at it appeared to be trying to detect where it had been slashed.

They went to the Stedelijk Museum and looked at the two paintings by her father that hung there.

Claire wanted to do something else ordinary.

"A stroll through the Vondelpark?" Stenner suggested. "A canal-boat ride? The zoo?"

"What if we rented a car? We could drive to the ocean. We could take a spin up to the Zuiderzee. Did I say that right?

"Yeah. Except they call it Ijsselmeer now. Do you drive?"

She looked at him. "Of course I drive."

"I don't."

She made an apologetic gesture.

"I ran over a dog. The very first time I got behind the wheel of a car, I ran over a dog. Not a little dog, either. A black Labrador. It looked so big, dead." He waved the memory away. "Anyway, after that, every time I hit a bump, I felt something dying under my wheels. It was a major distraction and had what they call an 'adverse' effect on my concentration. After I totaled the second car—look..." He lifted the hair from his forehead and she saw the diagonal scar. "The first time, I walked away; the second time, I went through the windshield. My parents bought me a very nice bicycle. And then I went away to school, and I didn't really need a car, and then, I don't know...I never learned."

They passed some shops. The signs said BOEKHANDEL, WIJNHANDEL. The license plates of the cars were more elongated than they were in the States. They passed an empty shop with a sign that said TE HUUR. It seemed important to Claire that she remember details.

"Well, there's lots of things *I* never learned," she said.

"I can swim, though—as you know. I'm what they call a 'strong swimmer.' That's one of those phrases usually added to a drowning obit, sadly. But those are the two things people are always shocked you don't do—swim and drive."

"Jeff can't swim."

Stenner didn't say anything.

"I don't even want to go," she said. "It seems like...it just seems like that's what I have to do."

He put his good arm around her shoulder.

"It's me," Stenner said, smiling. His smile alone was enough to make her heart beat harder. "It's my timing. Remember I told you my timing was off?" He looked at her morosely. "That's right. We're dealing with a crippled man here, a man handicapped by horrible timing."

They got tickets for the next boat ride. It would be a half-hour wait. They stopped for coffee in a tiny café full of '50s memorabilia.

"So," Stenner said. "Where are you going?"

"Crete."

"I knew you'd go to Crete."

She laughed. Elvis Presley was singing "Love Me Tender."

"Why are you going to Crete? I thought you told me you didn't like beaches."

"Does Crete have beaches? I didn't think it was a beach kind of place."

The waiter brought their coffee. The Platters started on "The Great Pretender."

"Lots of beaches. Famous for beaches."

"I thought of it as a kind of warm Maine. A warm Maine without trees."

"A warm Maine without trees. What kind of Maine is that?"

"Rocky."

"Rocky. I can go with that." He sang along with the Platters for a minute, stopping when the singer hit a high note. "Shit. I know I'm in trouble when the Platters sound like they're singing my song." Even though she sat stock-still and didn't say a word, he made a motion with his hand as if to fend her off. Then he shook his head. "No matter how I say this, it's going to sound...jive. What I mean is...you and I, you and I...we should be together, Claire." Only then did he look at her. "What I mean is, when you're *thinking*, think about that—okay?"

"Okay." She squeezed his hand. "I already am."

"Hey, guess who I called today."

She shrugged.

"Maarten. Remember Maarten the cabdriver? You know they held him for eight hours? Questioning him? Anyway, I told him I'd buy him dinner tonight. Will you come?"

"Sure."

On the canal boat, Claire listened attentively to the guide, who said everything four times—first in English, then French, then German and finally Dutch.

"...these houses are called the Twin Brothers."

"...notice this house with the double steps. Tax used to be charged according to the number of steps, and only the very wealthy could afford double steps."

Claire pointed out a man sitting three rows in front of them. "I'm sure that guy was at the Rijksmuseum. I thought I saw him at the Stedelijk, too."

Stenner sat up to look at him, then shrugged. "Probably just a coincidence—just another tourist." He leaned back again, looking up through the roof at the clouds.

"...this is a houseboat for stray cats. There are more than two hundred homeless cats on this boat."

A few minutes later, Stenner sat up straight and pointed toward the street. "There's my place."

There was a green houseboat tethered to the canalside. A woman wearing an apron was hanging out clothes. "There's the boat we swam behind," she said. "I wonder if they got their dinghy back."

"I don't see it."

"You know, I finally returned Willem Hofmans' blankets this morning."

"Did he give you some more hot chocolate?"

"He didn't recognize me at first. He didn't like my haircut."

"We should go by and look for the dinghy. I bet it's still tied up where we left it."

When they got off the canal boat, Claire asked if they were closer to the place where they'd tied up the dinghy or closer to the police station.

"The police station."

"De Groot said I could pick up my passport—he got it back."

Stenner squeezed her hand. "Shit. I don't want you to go. If you..."

She started to reply, but stopped herself. She looked up. A blue balloon, almost the same color as the sky, was caught in a tree. It bobbed and dipped in the breeze.

The graffiti on the walls of the police station were being worked on by a man wielding a wire brush. INFEXION, proclaimed the wall. EVER.

De Groot was cleaning out his desk drawers, putting

things into cardboard boxes. It took him a minute or two to find Claire's passport. He unearthed it from the chaos on his desk top. He was cheerful and effusive and wished them the best of luck.

"Have you heard anything from Carley?"

"Oh, no," De Groot said happily. "And I don't wish to. I am finished with intrigues. I am finished with all of that." He brushed his hand over a large asparagus fern. "Now I am wondering how to get these plants home without destroying them."

When they got outside, Claire flipped open her passport. She ran her finger over the imprint of the American eagle imposed on her photograph and looked at it closely. The eagle's wings stretched directly above her eyebrows. The clutch of spears in one talon decorated one cheek, the laurel branch the other. Her picture smiled back at her with a banal, eager-to-please look. She tilted the picture toward Stenner and laughed. "I don't even look like this anymore, do I?"

"No," Stenner said. He put his arm around her shoulder. "No, you don't."

CHAPTER TWENTY-EIGHT

CLAIRE WENT BACK TO THE AMBASSADE to pack and change her clothes. The underwear she'd washed that morning, festooned on the shower rod, was dry, if a little stiff. She put her suitcase on the bed and began to pack.

When she finished, she thought she might as well take a shower. Stenner and Maarten wouldn't be there to pick her up for another forty-five minutes.

And, she reminded herself, her hair dried quickly now. Hair that's only half an inch long doesn't take long to dry. After she came out of the shower and toweled off, she rubbed the fog off the mirror and studied her face.

She thought she looked almost androgynous—a bit like David Bowie.

She smiled at herself. Except her teeth were smaller. Maybe if she got some big earrings—maybe some larger earrings…

"Don't kid yourself," said the voice with the flat

Midwestern accent. "Don't kid yourself, sweetheart. It looked much better before."

Claire froze.

That was how she thought of it, as if she were another person: Claire froze. Her heart congealed, shrank; she felt it move in her chest, as if it were burrowing into some secret, less vulnerable corner of flesh.

She knew who it was without turning around; she knew it was Ed even before he stepped into view in the mirror. She registered his mocking smile, the funny-looking gun in his hand. She didn't move. Her muscles locked firmly into position. Ice.

"The rest of you isn't bad, though," Ed said, smiling. "Not bad at all. Come on, babe." He gestured with the gun. "Let's go into the other room."

She was paralyzed. She remembered an experiment in chemistry, when the professor sprayed a flower with liquid oxygen or liquid air, something like that. And then he took the frozen flower and whacked it against the table and it shattered. She felt like that; she felt that if she moved, her body would crack.

"Hey, I'm not going to hurt you," Ed said pleasantly. "Not unless you make me."

When she still didn't move, he walked toward her and touched her arm. Her hands exploded upward, automatically, it seemed. Their motion was abruptly halted by the sharp beveled edge of the mirror above the sink, and they fell back down. It must have hurt, because three of her fingers began to bleed, just below the knuckles.

She experienced the pain as a red line.

"Now look what you've gone and done," Ed said. He handed her a washcloth. He led her into the other room.

Do something, her mind was commanding her. *Do something, do something.* But she couldn't think of anything to do except sit down on the bed as he directed. He removed the suitcase from the bed and put it on the floor.

Finally, her fingers began to hurt. The pain revived her. The pain and the fact that Ed was no longer pointing the gun at her. He sat in the chair, the gun cradled in his lap.

"May I get dressed?" she asked.

"No, I don't think so."

"Why not?"

"You'll have to get dressed later, but right now, I think being naked will keep you in the right mood—in the mood not to do anything stupid."

She yanked the chintz bedspread up and started to wrap herself in it.

"Don't do that," Ed said, raising the gun. The gun had a silencer attached to the barrel. At least, Claire thought it was a silencer.

"Just sit on the bed, like you were before." He wagged the gun at her. He looked at his watch. "We've got an hour to kill before Mike gets here—before Mike secures your *boyfriend* and comes by to get us."

She was relieved and upset at the same time. At least he wasn't just here after her. But there went any chance that Stenner was going to come and…what?…rescue her. And Stenner. Her heart beat harder. What did he mean, *secure her boyfriend*? What did he mean by *secure*?

"While we're waiting, there's no harm in a man enjoying the view," Ed said. "I mean, it doesn't cost you anything, does it?"

"De Groot will find out." Claire wanted to talk about anything except the "view." "De Groot will—"

"De Groot," Ed said. "That old fart—forget it." He smiled his lazy, charming smile. "Let's just say we had a little restart. Let's just say the game plan changed."

"Why? Why did the game plan change?"

"Put your legs down." She was hunched up, knees to her chest, arms locked around her knees. When she didn't move, he walked over to the bed and put the gun barrel against her ear.

It was like holding a shell to your ear, to hear the sea. It roared in her ear.

"I said put your legs down."

She did as she was told.

He pinched the skin around her waist, quite coolly, as if he were in the supermarket, testing a piece of fruit. "Look at that," he said, with an admiring shake of his head. "No flab." He sat back down in the chair. "Do you work out? I mean do Nautilus or something?"

"I..." Her voice cracked, and she cleared her throat. "I run sometimes."

"Oh, yeah? Me too. People around here think you're nuts; they're not runners over here. I try to get out three times a week or so—that's all I really have time for. You've got to work harder at it, you know, the older you get; just to stay in shape. Do you ever race?"

She shook her head.

"No? Me either. I mean, I don't see the point of it— if you know you're not going to *win,* what's the point? You know what I mean?"

She nodded.

"I stay in pretty good shape, though, for a man my age. I'm forty-seven—do you believe that? Most people think I'm forty, tops."

Claire tried to swallow. There didn't seem to be any liquid in her mouth.

"My wife never has been in shape, not since the first kid, you know? That happens to women. You have any kids?"

She shook her head.

"She's as big as a house. Don't get me wrong—I love her dearly—but she is *big*. Of course, I have to get a little on the side now and then, but she doesn't mind. She understands that men are different from women."

Claire didn't want to know this. She didn't want to know any more.

"Where's your husband?" he asked abruptly.

"He's in New York." She was relieved.

"Ran out on him, huh?"

"No. No. He left me; he's the one who left me."

"Yeah? How come?"

"Someone else," she managed. "He found someone else."

"No kidding? He just took off on you? I've thought of that, you know, lately. I never would have left my wife when the kids were little. I couldn't do that. But now they're all grown up and away from home...Sometimes when you get to be my age, you think, Where the hell am I going? And you just want a change. You want to quit your job, you want to leave your wife, you just want things to *change*. I read a book about it—*Passages*. It's a regular stage in your life, you know. It's normal."

"I heard it was a good book," she managed.

"But Jeez," he said wistfully. "Sometimes you really *do* want a change." He fastened his eyes on her. "Do you think a girl like you—well, a *woman* like you—could ever be attracted to a man like me, an older man?"

There didn't seem to be a right answer to this question, so she didn't say anything.

Suddenly, his voice was thick with anger: "*I asked you a question.*"

"Not under the circumstances."

"*What circumstances?* What do you mean?"

"Not when I'm scared."

"Oh, no? Plenty of women *like* to be scared. They like it when you rough them up a little. My wife...my wife likes to get slapped around. That's when she wants it. Being scared turns her on." His voice seemed to be losing clarity. Either that, or she was just having trouble, she was just...

"Not me," she said. Her voice seemed barely to have the velocity to break the sound barrier.

"Look at your nipples," he said. "They're hard. You like it; you just don't know you like it. You've probably never had a real man."

He approached the bed. He put the gun barrel between her breasts and moved it up and down. It was icy-cold. She felt herself shrink. She felt her arms reflexively cover her breasts, her legs draw up.

"Don't do that." He slapped her face. "I told you before, didn't I? I told you to sit normal." He sat back down in the chair and wagged his head sadly. "I think I could be, you know, gentle with somebody, but I don't know how. I think there's a part of me that's never been touched—you know, a vulnerable part. It will just take the right woman to find that chink in my armor. I thought maybe you..." he said wistfully, "I thought maybe you could see that."

She remained utterly still. A word, a gesture might provoke him. He stood up and smoothed his hair.

"I guess not," he said softly. "I guess not. Because you won't even *fucking talk to me.*"

He moved toward the bed so rapidly that she screamed before she could stop herself. He smashed his hand over her mouth. The force of it took her head back into the wall. Her field of vision went black, with pulsating silver dots. She felt the cold of the gun barrel against her neck.

"You wouldn't talk to me in the car the other day and you won't talk to me now. Now I'm going to take my hand away, and I'm going to take the gun away, and you're going to talk to me, okay? But you're not going to scream." She nodded her head up and down. "Or else I'm going to give you a shot. Not a shot with the gun." He laughed—a pleasant chuckle. "Some Thorazine, some heroin, some LSD. You won't even know what's happening to you. I've got quite a little pharmacy in my briefcase over there. Do you want that?" She shook her head no. "Good. Because I don't want to do that, I just want you to talk to me—okay?" She nodded. "I'm going to take my hand away now. Okay? I don't want to hurt you."

His hand went away, but he didn't move the gun. "Say something."

"Hello." It was all she could think of.

"Very good. Now say 'Hello, Ed.' "

"Hello, Ed."

"*Verrrrrry* good. Now I want you to say something special for me. I want you to say 'cock.' "

"Cock."

He twisted the gun; it dug into her neck. "Not like that, baby, not like that," he crooned. "Say it like you love saying it."

She thought if he touched her, if he really did anything to her, he would kill her. If she could just get him to put the gun down, maybe she could kick him in the balls. Her plans did not extend beyond that.

"I can't," she said. "I can't unless you take the gun away. You said you would..." She saw he was massaging himself through his pants with his free hand.

"I'm going to put the gun down. I don't need the gun, do I?"

She shook her head. She watched him put the gun on the table next to the bed.

"Say it."

"Cock." She lingered over the word.

"That's better, baby. That's much better. Say 'Ed's cock.' "

She was trying to calculate the distance to his balls. She began to draw her leg back, very slowly. He noticed she was staring at his crotch and began fiddling with his zipper. She squeezed her eyes shut.

"Ed's cock." The sound of her voice came to her from a far distance.

"You want it, don't you? I can tell. Ed can tell. Say 'Suck my pussy.' "

She was working her hands behind her, to give her a little more leverage. Her leg was halfway drawn up.

"Suck—"

There was a loud noise, a muted explosion.

At first Claire thought he'd caught her, he'd got the gun, she'd been shot.

She was surprised because there was no pain. Maybe it took a little while for the pain to set in, as with her fingers.

Everything was black, blackish red. Then she realized her eyes were closed.

When she opened them, she couldn't see Ed. She saw a man climbing in through the window.

It was Richard Scott.

Then another man stood up, a man she didn't recognize, dragging Ed up with him.

Ed was unconscious. "He won't be out for long," said the stranger. He propped Ed up, half on the bed, half off it. Richard Scott picked up the gun from the table. He looked at her without looking at her.

"I'm sorry we couldn't come in before," he said. "We couldn't come in until he put down the gun, you know. I was beginning to think he was never going to put it down."

The way he looked at her without looking at her made Claire realize she was naked. She pulled the chintz bedspread up to her chin.

The stranger was holding a syringe up to the light. He injected it into Ed's arm. Ed looked about ten years younger unconscious. His face looked peaceful, bland.

Another man she didn't know came in through her door, followed by Stenner and Maarten, the cabdriver. Her little room was crowded with men, all talking at once. Their voices combined into a chaotic roar; she couldn't make out what they were saying.

Stenner came over and sat next to her on the bed. Her teeth were chattering; all at once she was incredibly cold. He touched her shoulder. She put her hand over her mouth to try to stop her teeth from chattering.

The man who had given the shot to Ed pulled Stenner aside. They appeared to be talking about her—they kept looking over at her; she heard the words "she" and "her." Some of the men went out of the room.

She wanted to get up, wash her face, get dressed, go to the bathroom, but she could only stay there, pinned to the bed. Stenner went out. He seemed to be gone a long time. Nobody paid any attention to her.

Stenner came back with a glass of brandy. She had trouble holding the glass; it jumped around in her hands. The brandy helped. She concentrated on the burning feeling it left behind as it went down her throat.

While she drank, she watched the man give Ed another injection. This injection revived him, but although he was awake, he seemed to be under the impression he was somewhere else, maybe his house. She heard him say, "Honey, I'm thirsty. Get me a beer, would you?"

A little while later, they all left. Maarten was the last to go, making a graceful exit, joking about what would happen the next time they got together. Stenner said he still owed him a dinner. Stenner walked him out into the hall.

When he came back into the room, he flopped down on the bed and gave an exhausted sigh. They lay side by side, just looking at each other, absolutely still, for a while. "I'm so glad," Stenner said. "I'm so glad you're all right." He propped himself up on his elbow. "I want to know exactly what happened."

After she told him, he shook his head, but he didn't take his eyes away from hers. He had a way of looking at her—his eyes never had that analytic look, that distracted look, that wandering focus that most people's eyes had. She loved the way he looked at her.

"So what he wanted was for you to talk dirty while he jerked himself off. Jesus Christ."

"Well, I don't know. That was as far as he got."

"I'm sorry. I'm so sorry any of this happened to you."

"I'm all right. Really. I'm all right."

A man came up from downstairs to fix the broken window. Claire didn't want to stay in the room while the man worked. She didn't, in fact, want to stay in the room at all. They decided to go to Stenner's place. On the way, they stopped at the *broodjeswinkel*. When Claire couldn't decide what kind of sandwich she wanted, Stenner bought one of each kind.

They sat on Stenner's floor, eating *broodjes* and drinking beer.

"What are we looking at here?" Stenner said, lifting apart one *broodje* to study the interior. "A chicken croquette *broodje*. Want a bite?"

"It's all yours."

"Good. I hate it when people take bites. Marlena was always on a diet. She wouldn't order any food and then she'd eat half of mine."

Claire laughed. She heard some people walking by outside, laughing. An echo.

"Okay," Stenner said. "Now I'm going to attempt to explain to you what happened, how you ended up with that lunatic in your room. I stress *attempt,* because the whole time Scott was explaining it to me, I was going nuts worrying about you, so I'm not sure I've got it straight."

"Okay."

He pried the cap off another bottle of beer. "Okay. Carley was on his way to interrogate the two men who assassinated Maurice LeClerc. Well, Carley got there, and much to his surprise, the two men were *not* hired guns, like the guy who took out Alan Dawson, but *Agency* boys—two bang-and-boom boys. Carley knew them, and he also knew they were *still* working for the Agency. Upon this discovery, we find Alexander Carley grinning like the cat that ate the canary.

"He is grinning in this time-honored manner because now he doesn't just have a hook into the French—he has what amounts to a nuclear device. He has two career CIA officers—we're talking guys with GS ratings—who have just murdered the Director General of Internal Services at French Intelligence.

"Well, Carley gets in touch with the *acting* head of Internal Services, who is Jean Bergier. In the meantime, he's interrogated these two hit men pretty thoroughly. They don't give him a line back to Prager. They *do* give him a line back to Rob Davenport, Head of Station here in Amsterdam. Davenport will link back to Prager; there's no doubt about that. And that's when Carley got us some baby-sitters, when he pried Davenport's name out of those two guys. Remember that guy on the canal boat? Remember when you said you thought you'd seen that guy in the Rijksmuseum?"

"The man in the sunglasses and the polo shirt?"

"Yeah, him. He was one of them. He was your baby-sitter. You just didn't recognize him—he's the other guy who came in through the window with Scott. He fucked up, by the way—he was watching your hotel from outside. What he didn't know was that Ed checked in there, yesterday. He had the room next to yours. We found that out from Mike—actually, Mike almost *volunteered* that information."

He touched her cheek. "Do you want another beer?"

"No. I'm fine."

"Well, Carley knew that Davenport would be expecting these two hit men to check back. Davenport—"

"Who is Davenport again?"

"He's the Head of Station here in Amsterdam. And they're not checking back. So Carley knew that Davenport would be getting worried. Davenport must have known LeClerc was dead, the operation was a success in that way—but why weren't his guys getting back to him? Davenport knew all this Amsterdam business—taking out Alan Dawson, chasing after us, all that stuff—he knew that was all to keep Carley from getting his hands on the tape. So when he found out Carley was in *Paris,* he knew he was in deep shit. At that point, Davenport's not worried about anything but his own ass. So, in a pretty pathetic desperation move, he sweeps up all the people he knows with any connection to Carley—and that includes you, me, De Groot—"

"De Groot—is he all right?"

"You were the only close call, the only one who was ever in trouble. The sweep also included four people in The Hague, a couple of people in Antwerp—Davenport's idea was apparently to trade us all to Carley in return for the two guys who hit LeClerc. *Fat chance.* Carley would no more have traded us than...well, that's another of those things you don't want to think about. It's no fun to think about that. Besides, it would have been too late, although Davenport didn't know it. Carley had already had his chat with Bergier. The French were very contrite: yes, LeClerc was about as smart as an artichoke; yes, *Mr.* Carley could have the phone-trap records in exchange for LeClerc's assassins. Thank you very much, and yes, in future, they'd be a touch more careful in dealing with their *official* American cousins."

"So Carley saved us, in a way."

"Well, before you write him a thank-you note, I think protecting us was kind of a by-product. I think he wanted to get his hands on whoever went after us. If he just wanted to protect us, he was in a position to do it a simpler way."

"But what would he want with the people who came after us?"

"Oh, this and that. He might want them to...say, testify if anything happens to the assassins. Assassins don't always live long in captivity—they're like pandas, or white tigers. Probably not that, though. He might want to turn them, use them himself."

Claire grimaced.

"Then again, most likely, he might want to *trade* them for something else, some favor. Carley hoards favors.

Intelligence operates on a primitive economic base at times—you know, the barter system." Stenner stood up. "Jesus, my foot's asleep. Okay, so anyway, Davenport's in the hot seat now; there's no way out for him. The funny thing is, he probably doesn't know Prager is a mole. There's no reason why he would. You don't question the DOP. The DOP is like God—you do what he says or"—Stenner made a gesture like an umpire's—"you're outta there."

"Prager's in the hot seat too, isn't he?"

"Oh, he's burning. He's on fire. But if things go well, he doesn't know it yet. Carley's got to persuade some-one—the President? I don't know. He's got to persuade someone to come down on Prager before Prager hears the rustling of the wind and takes off."

"But where would he go?"

"Moscow." Stenner grinned. "Hero's welcome. A large apartment. A dacha in the country."

"Vacations on the Black Sea."

"You've got it. Shopping privileges at special stores." He put his arm around her. "Anyway, it's over. It's really over."

Claire yawned. "God, I'm so tired."

"It's that post-adrenaline blues. Once you're out of trouble, your body says [he spoke in a deep bass voice], 'Okay, let's slow it down here. Let's slow it *way* down.' How about a cup of tea?"

She yawned again. "Excuse me. Yes, tea."

He picked up the leftover *broodjes* and empty beer bottles and carried them into the kitchen. By the time he came back with the tea, she was asleep.

The next day, they had their first argument.

Stenner let her sleep until almost ten o'clock, and

she was annoyed because her plane left at twelve-thirty and now she would have to rush like mad to make it.

"You're not planning to leave *today,* are you? Shit. Don't you think you should—I don't know—recuperate? I thought—"

"I'm going," she said stubbornly. "I might as well get it over with."

"You've already made up your mind—isn't that right? You're just going to go."

"I promised. Two weeks. That's what I promised."

"I don't know, Claire. I'm going to be...I can't help thinking about how shaky you were the first night I met you. And that was *before,* that was before all this mayhem...I think you ought to take it easy for a few days. Anybody could understand that; anybody would give you that."

She wished they had more to fall back on—more than just a week.

"You don't understand. I always keep my promises."

"Always? No matter what? That's downright dumb, you know?"

"Not *always,* not always. I just broke one the other night." She looked away from him.

Almost always, she kept her promises.

In a way, it was one of the things she liked best about herself. In a weird way, she was totally dependable.

In another way, this dependability was one of the things she liked least about herself.

She knew it for what it was: an ornate form of superstition.

Once she made a promise—that was a fragile link into the future. If she broke the promise, she ran the risk that the future would turn on her, that the imagined future would cave in.

Look what had happened. She had promised Jeff: *No Stenner.* She'd broken that promise and what had happened was Ed.

On one level, she knew the events were not related. But they were; she also knew they were. She tried to explain all this to Stenner.

Actually, he understood.

"You always keep your promises—I understand that now; they have a guilty grip on your soul. God"—he stretched out his hands toward her like an avenging angel—"will punish you. So—will you promise *me* something?"

She inclined her head.

"Promise me you'll come back."

She nodded.

"You have to say it out loud—I'm not sure what counts here. A nod might not have the necessary soul-biting weight, or something."

"I promise."

"All right! I'm at peace now; I'm a man at peace. Just for backup, do you happen to have your itinerary?"

She laughed.

CHAPTER TWENTY-NINE

CRETE WAS EXACTLY AS SHE'D IMAGINED IT. It was so much the way she'd imagined it, it gave her an uneasy feeling. It was like an extended *déjà vu* experience. She didn't like that feeling, those jolts of recognition. They made her nervous.

She'd tried to explain it once to Jeff. *Déjà vu* made her worry about the nature of time. It made her think time was not a continuum but a mass, that everything that was going to happen had already happened. And only the limitations of the human psyche made people experience the world in a sequential way. She didn't like that feeling, breaking the link in the sequence. Jeff had laughed at these notions—*déjà vu* was just a joke your mind played on you, a false memory, a trick.

The longer she was in Crete, the stronger the feeling got, as if she had always lived with a shadow Crete flourishing in her mind.

She tried to pay attention to surfaces.

408

There were things she liked. She liked the light, the buttery light of late afternoon. She liked the breakfasts of bread, butter and honey. She liked the way the honey pooled on the white plate. She liked the lemons in the white bowl in the hotel lobby. She liked the unintelligible alphabet. Without the easy guide of words, of symbols, the city lay before her revealed, visible— or perhaps she was just more attentive.

She kept to herself. Each day she walked for hours. She relied on motion. Each day she walked farther than the day before. She never got lost; her sense of direction was infallible. She never walked far enough to escape the feeling she'd been there before. She never walked fast enough to outdistance the shadow Crete of her mind.

She relied on patterns. Each morning she bought the *Herald Tribune* and saved it to read at night. She stayed in at night. She read the paper from front to back. She drank ouzo in her room and did the crossword puzzle, the Jumble. She read the classifieds: BUY DIAMONDS. ENGLISH MUM'S HELP. U.S. LAWYER ALL COURTS, ALL CASES, AGGRESSIVE. FATHER WITH THREE CHILDREN (AGES 10, 8 AND 4) REQUIRES IMMEDIATELY...She read the personals: URGENT: ANY INFORMATION ABOUT MARCOS VON ROMBERG PICOT. THIEDU, 7 RUE AUGEREAU PARIS...Shots in the dark. FRENCH GIRL 19, SEEKS AU PAIR 8 MONTHS. COLORADO, ARIZONA, MIDWEST. HAPPY BIRTHDAY GONZO, WHEREVER YOU ARE. Shots in the dark.

She drank the ouzo from tall glasses, with a lot of water. She never tired of mixing it up; it still intrigued her that two clear liquids, when combined, would turn opaque. She liked the opaque taste of it.

There were things she didn't like. The long, starry nights. The women in black, the black widows of Greece.

They hunched on the streets, cackling like crows, living off the crumbs of the past.

She preferred the bright polyester widows of the tour boats—the objects of so much derision. People thought them pathetic, but she thought them courageous—floating into the future, buoyed by their bright eyes, their bright clothes, their careful hair.

Each night, Stenner called. She sat next to the telephone, waiting for the satellite, the wire to deliver his voice. After his calls, she felt light, relaxed, able to sleep.

So it was that she learned from Stenner, before reading it in the *Herald Tribune,* that Lawrence Prager had defected to Russia. He was in Mexico; he was in Cuba; finally, he was in Moscow. The hero's welcome was on: the dacha, the Order of Lenin, the Black Sea vacations.

"Well, at least he's gone," one of them said.

Stenner told her he was going to Washington for two or three days, that he'd decided to do an article about Prager after all. He felt rejuvenated; he felt like his old self. Eager. He flattered her: she'd snapped him out of his malaise.

He was excited. It was a big story—a huge story. Carley was going to help him fill in the gaps—documents and so on. He was considering doing a book; his publisher was interested. But he would be back in Amsterdam when she got back. He could write the piece in Amsterdam—no problem.

And he would call her, he promised. He would still call her every night.

The next day, she didn't save the whole *Herald Tribune* for the night. She read the Prager story in the morning, digesting the details of Lawrence Prager's career, the shock waves rolling over the CIA, the trauma of his family. When he left, he left behind his wife of twenty years and his four children. Left them without a word. There were the usual interviews with childhood friends, parents, teachers, coaches, colleagues. They raked their memories for the stones they'd missed, the missed clues to his Soviet allegiance. Nearly everyone found something. "He was an all-American boy, that's how I thought of him. Of course, at times, he was *moody,* his *sportsmanship...*"

Claire worried about his wife, who was reported to be "under sedation." What would it be like to wake up one morning and find out your husband was "the traitor of the century," as he was being termed?

Claire knew a little bit about how Mrs. Lawrence Prager would be feeling. How gullible, how deceived, how humiliated. How stranded. Claire laughed at herself. Eight years was not twenty. And a woman named Allison was certainly not the Soviet Union.

She put the paper aside.

She was beginning to learn a few Greek words: *kalimera, kalispera, parakalo, efharisto.* They fell from her lips like coins, paying the debts of manners.

Walking so much was wearing out her shoes. She arranged to have some sandals made. A man drew the outline of her feet on brown paper with a grease pencil. She felt odd, leaving the outline of her feet behind in the man's shop. She said, "*Kalimera.*"

She thought about Jeff when she was walking. She thought about what to say to him.

She had already known, before she came, that there could be no going back to Jeff.

It was the way he'd said *"baby"* that night in Amsterdam. It wasn't his fault. It was the way she'd relinquished her life to him, day by day, over the eight years. She'd already given it to him. It was too late now. There was no way to get herself back, to redress the balance. Another year or two with him and she would just be a skeleton, fleshed out by Jeff's will.

She avoided thinking about how long it would "last" with Stenner. Maybe it would; maybe it wouldn't. She liked the way she was when she was with him. She liked the way he looked at her. She liked the way he smiled.

Since he wasn't there, she bought presents for him. She bought him a Greek sweater, a set of amber worry beads, several small blank notebooks from the stationery store, a bottle of Greek honey. The little heap of presents in her room assuaged her loneliness.

One night, he didn't call. The night before, he'd told her he might be flying back to Amsterdam, so she tried not to worry too much. He was in the air, she told herself. He was up above the power lines; he couldn't get to a phone.

In the morning, she felt good. She sat outside in the sun, eating her bread and butter and honey. There were only three days left before she returned to Amsterdam. For the first time, today, she felt free of the superstitious anxiety that had propelled her to Crete.

She could easily envision some kind of future with Stenner. In a way, they had known each other far longer than it seemed. They had been through a lot together; they had relied on each other. She didn't believe time could be measured out in equal chronological install-ments; she thought it expanded according to intensity.

As for herself, she had relied on herself, too. After all that had happened, she was still in one piece, still sane, still Claire.

She walked toward the kiosk to buy a *Herald Tribune* as usual, before they were all gone. She was wearing white pants and a red shirt with wide sleeves. She felt glossy, iri-descent, new.

As she was lifting the paper out of the rack, she saw the headline, just above the fold:

CAR CRASH CLAIMS CIA MAN

She fumbled for drachmas with one hand and flipped the paper over to read the story:

(Washington, D.C.)—Alexander Carley, 68, former Ex-ecutive Operations Officer of counterintelligence at the CIA, was pronounced dead on arrival at Sibley Hospital Tuesday morning, following an accident on the George Washington Parkway.

Also killed in the fiery crash was newspaper reporter John Stenner, the driver of the car.

Paramedics, using acetylene torches, required near-ly an hour to free the bodies from the twisted wreck-age at the foot of Spout Run Embankment.

In a tragic coincidence, the accident came only three days after Carley's identification of Lawrence Prager, until recently a top CIA official, as a Soviet agent. Prager is since reported to have defected to the Soviet Union.

There were no witnesses to the accident, which oc-curred in the early morning hours...

She stopped reading. A terrible feeling of need swept over her—for water, for food, for air, she didn't know—for something basic to human survival.

She deflected it with motion.

She squeezed her fist shut. The newspaper crumpled up to form a horrid, clumsy paper flower. She began to march around in a tiny, palsied circle, the newspaper held at arm's length, twitching in her hand. She would always remember the terrible noise that newspaper made, scratching the air.

All at once, she realized a crowd had gathered. She heard the babble of Greek voices. She heard someone say in English, "Do you think she's on drugs?"

She stopped moving.

She watched one of the polyester ladies detach herself from the gawking circle and come toward her. It seemed to take a long time for the woman to reach her. The woman put her hand on Claire's arm.

"Have you had too much sun, dear? Are you all right?"

"He was not the driver of the car," Claire heard herself say. "He was not the driver of the car."

"No, I'm sure not," soothed the woman. "Won't you come and sit down in the shade?"

"He ran over a dog," Claire said.

"I'm sure you're right, dear. Are you staying in one of the hotels near here?"

"It was not a coincidence."

"Can you just tell me where you are staying? Are you here alone?"

After a while, she remembered the name of her hotel.

"Hotel Olympia," she said fervently.

"Good," gushed one of the women. "Good."

Claire felt an absurd swell of pride.

"Are you all alone?" the woman asked again. "Are you staying alone?"

"Yes," she heard herself admit. "Alone." It sounded like a confession.

The women clucked.

They maneuvered her through the streets, one on each side, holding her hands. She lagged slightly behind them. They towed her forward like tugboats.

"...a doctor," one of the women was saying.

"...perhaps the hotel?" hoped the other.

Doctor, Claire thought. *Sibley Hospital.* One two three, she counted the steps her feet took. *Twisted wreckage.* Four five six seven. *Dead.* Eight nine. Ten. She stopped.

"Come on, dear—we're almost there."

While one of the women discussed doctors with the desk clerk, Claire remained tethered to the other one. Only the woman's hand on her arm, Claire felt, kept her anchored in space. She was studying the woman's hand— a capable hand, she thought—studying its wrinkles, its spots, its veins, when she saw, in her peripheral vision, Stenner walking toward her.

She backed away.

"What's wrong?" implored the woman. "Oh, my."

Claire squeezed her eyes shut. She concentrated on remaining absolutely still.

Ah, Claire thought, well, now I've really done it. Seeing ghosts. Gone over the edge, over the edge. She had a brief cartoon vision of a cartoon Claire, a Wile E. Coyote Claire, stepping off the edge of a cliff. The splayed body whirled around in free fall, gathering speed, diminishing in size. When it hit the ground, it flattened out like a pancake. It peeled itself *off* the ground and stood up. Pinwheels for eyes. Claire risked opening her eyes.

"Well," Stenner joked, "I expected you to be surprised, but..."

Claire sank down into a couch. It was not so much that she sat down, just that the force of gravity seemed unbelievably strong. The women hovered. She remembered her manners. "Thank you," she said. "Thank you so much for helping me. It was...it was a mistake."

"You're quite sure you're all right?" one of them asked, casting a suspicious look at Stenner.

"Fine. Yes, I'm fine now."

They moved off somewhat reluctantly, heads angled toward each other.

Stenner dropped into the couch next to her. "What's the matter? *What* was a mistake? Are you all right?"

"Well," she started. She took his hand and pressed it hard against her cheek. "Well..." Tears started dribbling out of her eyes.

"Claire," Stenner said.

She laid her head on his chest. She could feel his heart beating.

"I thought you were a ghost," she whispered. "I thought I'd finally lost my mind."

"Well," Stenner said. "I guess you don't like surprises. I'll remember that. No surprise parties, no..."

She sat up and leaned back to look at him. He had a tender smile for her, a fond smile. "No," she said. "I just read in the paper that you were dead."

"*What?* What paper? Where?"

Claire looked at her hand. Somehow she expected the crumpled-up newspaper still to be there; but of course, she must have dropped it to take one of the women's hands.

"The *Herald Tribune.* You and Alexander Carley killed in a car accident."

"Where can you get a paper? Do they have one here in the hotel?"

"No, they don't have today's yet."

He read the story over twice at the kiosk, and then they went to a café and he read it over several more times without looking up. Finally, he rubbed his hand over his eyes and looked up at her.

"Well, I'm feeling a little ragged, a little tired, certainly, but not dead." He frowned. "Someone is, though. Alexander Carley and someone else."

"Was it an accident? When it said you were the driver, I knew it wasn't. I thought—"

"Tragic coincidence," Stenner said. "I'm a suspicious man. I don't like 'tragic coincidences.' " He stood up and fumbled in his pockets for money to pay for their coffee. "Got any drachmas?"

On the way back to the hotel, she remembered to ask him how it was that he was there.

"Well," he said simply, "I missed you."

"I missed you too."

"I was flying back to Amsterdam—remember?—I told you on the phone." She nodded. "When I got off the plane, I was standing there waiting for my luggage, and...I don't know..." He shrugged. "I was afraid you'd change your mind, not come back; I was afraid you'd go some-where else and I wouldn't be able to find you. So I got on another plane, and another...and here I am." He squeezed her hand.

"Your timing is getting much better."

"You know what? This isn't like Maine at all, not even a warm Maine without trees."

When they got back to the hotel, Stenner stretched out on the bed. Claire sat down next to him.

"Do you think it was an accident?' she asked.

He put his finger over her lips. "Later," he said.

They made love in a slow, languorous way. Immediately afterward, Stenner fell asleep.

Claire propped up her head on her hand and elbow and stayed motionless for a long time, watching him sleep. She took a shower, she read for a while, she did the crossword. When he'd been asleep for four hours, she woke him up.

Over dinner, they discussed the possibilities.

"First of all," Stenner began, "either it was an accident or it wasn't. Carley's people at Mountain Security *plus* some of his friends from the various federal security agencies will be looking very carefully at his car, how the accident happened and all that. They'll keep the pressure on to make sure the inquiry is straightforward. They don't like 'tragic coincidences' either."

"But who was the driver?"

"Well, I think I know. Carley didn't drive anymore;

his leg bothered him. And when I got there, he knew I didn't drive. It was probably the guy who was driving us around all week."

"But it said John Stenner, the *reporter;* it was very specific."

"Well, I've been with him pretty much all week. It's probably just a mistake."

Claire wondered if it could have been some kind of warning.

Stenner took a bite of his dolmades. "I'm not dismissing that idea completely, but—despite all the things that have happened lately—I don't think so. I'd be worried if a lot of other people didn't know everything I know, or if Prager hadn't already jumped ship. Of course, Prager wasn't the only one; the investigations will flush out others. But the danger to them doesn't come from me, but from the CIA's Office of Security, and from that new oversight committee that's being formed. It's a little late, but the CIA is finally cleaning house. Now, if someone *did* knock off Carley—the KGB, say—it was an act of revenge pure and simple. He'd thrown all his energy into this Prager thing for the last two years. And revenge is not a normal motive in this business—it usually isn't worth the effort or the risk."

"So, what are you going to do now?"

"Stories. I've got a lot of stories to write." He refilled their glasses with retsina. "This stuff tastes better the more you drink."

"Want to try my octopus?"

"Are you kidding? I don't eat anything with more than four legs."

"I don't think they have legs. Arms."

"Absolutely nothing with more than two arms. I'm sorry—it's a religious constraint."

"Ah, it's kind of chewy anyway."

They walked back through the starry night.

"How would you feel about moving to Washington?"

"What?"

"I've been thinking—I'm not really enjoying working on this book. I've been...revived, I guess, by you, by everything that's happened. I want to get back to work."

Claire hesitated.

"It's a terrific city. It's got a great zoo, fabulous museums, the Kennedy Center, the *Library of Congress*—I mean, you don't get the Library of Congress with any other city."

"I don't know," Claire said. She pointed to the sky. "Look, a shooting star."

"What don't you know?" Stenner said in a worried tone.

"Well, I don't know," Claire said again. "No baseball team."